Many years ago Will Templeton worked briefly in the tax collectors' office, and, deciding that wasn't for him, he then tried his hand at such varied vocations as hairdresser, bricklayer and mechanic, before finally finding a place at Doncaster Register Office. He stayed there for over thirty years, working his way up from Receptionist to Superintendent Registrar, eventually throwing it all in to become a full-time scriptwriter. Over the years he has also written many plays which have been performed to glowing reviews. This is his first novel.

Also by Will Templeton

Plays, available for reading or performance

No Harm Done
Jenny's Friend
Another Bite
Sod's Law
Splish Splash

For permission to perform any of these plays please
contact: willtempleton@outlook.com

Births, Marriages and Death

Will Templeton

For Mum: I shouldn't have waited so long.

ACKNOWLEDGEMENTS

Many thanks must go to the people without whom this book would never have been completed. Looking over my shoulder every step of the way was Amanda Pope, who kept an expert eye on the procedural matters and also provided the amazing cover art; Detective Superintendent Una Jennings of South Yorkshire Police provided more invaluable information; Kath Middleton gave tons of useful advice to shape the final work and RGN Corrine Adamson assisted in medical matters.

The first time that the notion of murder crept lazily into being it was no more than a teasing prickle to the subconscious, dismissed casually, a ludicrous idea not worth the time it took to consider it. But as it returned and recurred with each instance of anger and humiliation that prompted its conception, it toyed playfully with the darker desires and passions usually kept buried under the heaps of bric-a-brac and "you never know when this might come in handys" disarrayed carelessly in the back bedroom of the imagination.

The rational mind resists the lure of the dark. Every time it raises its black snout to sniff the air it is cast back with a phobic shudder. When it became apparent that this thing had a life, was growing, feeding on the scraps it had been tossed in weaker, experimental moments, it was stifled mercilessly, suffocated out of all conscious existence.

But, once conceived, these things can never truly die.

Prologue

June

She was still breathing, at least. That was the first thing he noticed and it meant that now he could breathe, too. The girl stood back to let him further into the recovery room, then led the way to where she was lying. Through vision blurred by tears of relief he saw the shaved area with the large blue stitches pinching her wound closed, and thankfully noticed her eyes open briefly and her long, lolling tongue flick over her yellowy-white teeth. The wet shine of her black nose told him all he needed to know, so the veterinary assistant's words of comfort, explaining the process of the operation and the prognosis for recovery, washed over him like the warm breath which carried them.

She'd taken a nasty tumble the other day while she was chasing around like a damn fool pup after some dog half her age, and he felt sure he heard the crack of snapping bone all the way across the common. Too much weight for an animal her age, the vet had told him, but Arthur pointed out that she's always been a bit plump. Too much Labrador blood in amongst the Alsatian. What with that, and the over-long fur, she'd looked like a cuddly toy when they picked her out at the pet sanctuary over twelve years ago. Still did, when she turned those big, brown eyes up at him and the tip of her tongue jutted out between her teeth, like she was about to blow a raspberry. Her cheeky look, Arthur called it. But the healing process was much slower in an older dog. It would be a long time before the leg could support all that weight again. And with money being tight as it was... an operation like this didn't come cheap.

He knew what they were getting at. But she was all he

3

had, he couldn't just let her go because it might be inconvenient or expensive. So he had begged and pleaded, and finally broken down in tears right there in the vet's consulting room, before they eventually agreed to proceed. Terms of payment were arranged and a recovery plan worked out to ensure that Bexy would have the best chance of pulling through, and all their hard work and Arthur's money weren't being flushed down the pan. They assured him that *if you do all the right things, Mr Camm, there's no reason why your Bexy shouldn't be trotting around the field again – but these miracles don't happen overnight. If you try to rush things, push her too hard, she might never walk again.* He understood, he promised to take all the care in the world. There were other considerations: a general anaesthetic would have to be used, and that was another danger in a dog this age. But he'd heard there were milder forms of the drug available these days, so surely it wasn't as big a risk...?

He had countered all their arguments with reasoned logic or desperate pleading, they had acquiesced, and his reward was the rasping breath that huffed in time with the panting chest, and the laboured flick of the tail as she heard, smelled or sensed that he was there for her.

Arthur Camm looked up with a start as the girl spoke to him again. 'Eh? What?'

'I said, I'll get Mark to carry her out to your car,' she repeated with a tolerant smile. They were very nice here, the staff were; knew just how important a pet can be to an old feller on his own, like a member of the family. Closer than his own wife had been for the biggest part of their marriage, but that's by the by.

'Will you be all right at your end?'

She was judging him by his slight frame, worried he'd drop his precious bundle. No fear.

'I've lugged heavier than her about in my time, love, don't you fret,' he said. 'And I've never lost a patient yet.'

He bent and scooped up Bexy's limp form with

remarkable ease and tenderness, held her close, smiled at the pattering heartbeat against his cheek.

'Tell your young man not to bother 'imself. When he's hefted a dozen pregnant sheep from a snowbound field at midnight without losing a single lamb, then I might trust him with my Bexy.'

*

The girl gave a rueful smile as she watched Arthur lay Bexy gentle as a box of fine china on the back seat of his car and then hurl himself unceremoniously into the driver's seat. She had heard Arthur's arrival earlier as the unmuffled engine of his dilapidated old car had roared its presence, the tired brakes screeching to a halt. Now he twisted the key and the machine barked into life, juddering ominously. Leaving behind it a cloud of acrid black exhaust fumes the battered... *thing* crawled slowly away from the car park, the mild pace in deference to the delicacy of the passenger, she assessed. She imagined her father or boyfriend arriving to collect her in a car like that, and shuddered. What on earth was it? Nothing that had been in production during her lifetime, she felt sure.

But lifestyle aside, rough and gruff as old Arthur could be, she knew Bexy was in safe hands with him.

July

He never thought it would be so easy. He just asked them for it and they gave it to him.

Of course, there was the obligatory application form, but that was fairly simple - he knew the information they required by rote. And a hefty price tag, for receiving it the same day. But here it was, gripped firmly in sweating hands. So much damage for so little effort. Pass a few quid across the counter and they break your heart. Not that he let them see the devastating effect the birth certificate had on him. He smiled pleasantly as he pocketed his change, and even managed to thank them for their speed and efficiency.

He left the Register Office in a daze and sat in his car poring over the document again. She'd lied. Over and over again. He couldn't remember the number of occasions he asked for the truth and she swore on their son's life - *her* son's life, at least - that what she told him was nothing but the truth. But she'd lied. How could she? Knowing how important it was to him, how could she look him in the eye and with a hand on the boy's chest, squarely over his little heart, swear *on his life* that she was telling the truth?

To keep him quiescent, of course. A pledge like that would have to be accepted. It would take a stonyhearted man to question the veracity of an oath taken on the life of a child. So he had held his tongue. Kept the peace. Peace was what she wanted. But truth was his major desire, and the doubts were not to be dismissed, even on the face of such apparent frankness. This trip today he'd hoped would assuage his fears, eradicate the worries without involving her. Had the knowledge he gained confirmed her assertions she need never have known he came. But now, with the truth right here in black and white, and on a legal document to boot, she could deny it no longer.

But was he right to use it? It was a potentially lethal weapon and their marriage was in the firing line. Brandishing this certificate like a loaded gun could do no one any good. Except the divorce lawyers, and they had stung him already in the past. But what use was avoiding a confrontation if the resultant peace tottered precariously on spindle legs, this revelation waiting to knock them away at any moment?

He gunned the car's engine and sped away, the bitterness of his predicament burning in his gut like acid.

August

She closed her eyes and let sensation flow over her: the sizzling Spanish sunshine on her upturned face; the strong hand grasping her own, proprietorially firm, lovingly tender; her loose, light skirt brushing her knees as they walked, sandaled feet on dusty track. She couldn't remember such a mood of serenity and sheer happiness since the innocent joys of childhood.

Could he possibly feel the same? She took a sideways glance at him, squinting behind his dark glasses, lobster red and proud of it in a way that only the English can be. His confidence and charm had worn down her usual reluctance to mingle with the guests.

Father frowned on any association with foreigners: a large, scowling man, with strong Catholic views, he kept his daughters on a tight leash. If he suspected that Alicia was spending what free time he allowed her with, of all things, an *Englishman...* Oh, the fury! She remembered her sister, strapped till she bled, crying for weeks in the bedroom adjoining hers, after Father had discovered her dalliance with a holiday boy. *Holiday boys only want one thing*, was father's viewpoint. And to a large part Alicia agreed. Her sister's lover had never been heard from again. But this was a tourist area, and holidaymakers were a regular feature of their lives. Alicia saw more English, German or Dutch men than she did the local boys. Her one prior serious boyfriend, son of a tuna fisherman from the southern edge of the village, had forsworn her blushing modesty for the painted willingness and the regular availability of the summer swarm - girls who had left their men and their inhibitions far away at home. Foreign or local, *all* boys only want one thing.

But here was a *man*. He didn't treat a girl like a number

8

on a score-sheet, a trophy to be won and displayed like a medal, then forgotten as the next challenge came along. He didn't drink till he was sick, or paw at her as she flitted between the tables in the restaurant. He was quiet but confident; spoke to her as an equal - in her own tongue too, a feat that few of their visitors can manage. He ran a motor dealership in his own country, and was here chasing up franchise deals from several of the car manufacturers in the region. You need to have plenty of bluff and bravado in that business, she acknowledged, but there was more than smarm about his charm. There was a gentleness and respect when they were together that she had never known from another man since the days before her mother had died, and Father's softer side had died along with her.

She wasn't entirely inexperienced with the opposite sex – she hadn't pretended to be and he hadn't expected it. More than a few years older than her he had obviously seen his share of life, as he openly admitted, but, he told her, his work commitments meant he was never able to take the time to establish a lasting relationship with one woman before. But things were different now. The pressure was easing for him. Success in business allowed him to take on extra staff, delegate his workload and free up more time for himself. Time for a social life... time for romance.

Alicia didn't believe in fairy tales; never had, in all her twenty-two years. Even as a child she was level-headed and meditative, the quiet one to contrast her sister's wild-child persona. But something about the way this man spoke to her, how he was with her and, most especially, how she warmed in his presence, thrilled to his touch, made her feel that a powerful bond was growing between them. It was difficult to reconcile the short time she had known him with the strength of her feelings for him.

She felt the dampness below, the grittiness of the sand inside her clothes, and squeezed his hand tight at the memories they provoked. He turned his glistening smile to her and she just knew he must be thinking exactly the

9

same thoughts as her. By now they had reached the heart of the small town, wading through the cloying heat and intense sunlight lashing over them, bouncing from the whitewashed walls, and they split before her father's hotel loomed too close. They shared another brief kiss and promised to snatch some more precious time together after the evening meals had been cleared. Alicia felt as if all her happiness were being sucked from her body as his fingers left her hand and he turned away to climb the few steps to the ever-open doors. She watched him disappear inside and waited a moment before following, composing herself to face her father's discerning gaze.

September

The glare of the streetlights hurtled over the windscreen like fragile obstacles in the stolen vehicle's path. Alan's fingers fiercely gripped the seat in front of him, the single small diamond in his grandad's gold signet ring glinting at him disapprovingly. Kenny's movements had been so smooth and effortless – the metal strip down the window seal to pop the lock, wrenching off the steering column, tugging the wires from their housing, a quick baring and twisting, the engine growled encouragingly and they were off. Jake twisted round in the front passenger seat and showed Alan his bad-toothed grin, nodding mindlessly at the sensation of thrill that sparked through him with almost sexual intensity. Alan attempted to return the gestures, as was expected, but felt them to be a feeble reflection of Jake's eagerness. But Jake didn't seem to notice, waving a thumbs-up fist and turning back to peer ahead. Kenny was concentrating on the night-time road, watching for late pedestrians, waiting for his first 'buzz.'

Buzzing was the term used for the pursuit that Kenny had developed to add the extra rush of excitement to their nocturnal activities. At seventeen Kenny was already jaded to the dubious delights of Taking Without Consent and Reckless Driving and the many other crimes and misdemeanours at which he was adept. As the eldest, Kenny attempted to maintain the esteem of his younger associates by adding ever increasing degrees of danger into their deeds. Emulating an old film, they went through a phase when all their joyrides had to be accomplished at a speed in excess of fifty miles per hour, or else the driver faced a penalty - usually a good kicking from his mates.

Playing chicken with other cars had passed a few thrill-packed evenings. That, though, had stopped after Kenny himself failed a challenge when a bespectacled octogenarian breezed blithely by their hastily swerved vehicle as if there were no other car on the road.

Now Kenny had dreamed up the notion of buzzing pedestrians – a little like chicken except your opponent was not as scary. Not that Kenny would have admitted fear was a factor in choosing their latest target – it was just a new angle to the game. A game whose rules were still in the development stages.

*

When Betty Hoskins told the coach driver to drop her at the end of her street, instead of trying to turn the large vehicle in close quarters, she could not have realised that the thirty or so metres between there and her door were such treacherous territory. She certainly had no idea she was to become part of a trio of youths' dangerous game. Having enjoyed the WI day trip to Cleethorpes, as much for the company as the venue, she sighed in weary contentment as she waved off her friends on the withdrawing bus. Her legs were in much better condition than Marjorie Pearce's so the short walk didn't trouble her. Poor Marjorie, having to be carried on and off the coach like that – must be embarrassing for the old dear. Old? Betty kept forgetting that Marjorie was younger than she was. She smiled. They were all so friendly and welcoming – all very different people, some more friendly than others, but Betty never felt intrusive, even though she only recently joined their well-established group.

Alone now, the high euphoria of the day dwindled rapidly. Betty thought of the chill awaiting her behind her own front door. The central heating would have shut down some time earlier, but it was more than that. The house was the one she shared for so many years with her Larry, bless him. So loving, so loyal to the very end. Forgiving her her weaknesses and sins (*so stupid, best forgotten; put it behind us and move on*). The place was always cold these days... Not for the first time she pondered the merits of moving to another area, away from the memories, the loneliness, and her steps grew heavy as she climbed the slight incline towards the prim but sparse garden that fronted her home.

She heard the car roar past the end of the street behind her, then the screeching of brakes, followed by that distinctive whirring sound only made by a car travelling quickly in reverse. Some young fool driving too fast and missed his turn, Betty supposed, glancing back to see the car turning forward into her street. The headlights were high and bright, dazzling as it raced towards her, and she instinctively moved closer to the wall, even though she was already well back from the road. Then came another sound that only a car can produce – the dreadful whoomp of a tyre striking the kerb edge.

*

Jake squealed with excitement and Alan's head hit the roof as the car lurched with the impact. Kenny wrestled to keep control of the vehicle, eyes fixed on the frail form ahead, knuckles white where he gripped the wheel. Alan watched in stunned fascination as the car's front wing brushed the old woman's coat, the driver's mirror catching her arm a nasty whack. He spun in his seat to peer through the rear window, saw her clutch the injured arm, then her heaving chest, before slowly sliding down the wall, to be swallowed by darkness and distance as the car sped away.

Alan sat back in his seat and screwed his eyes tight shut, as if to squeeze out the sight of the crumpled figure in their wake. What the hell was he doing here? He was only a kid; he should be spending his days collecting conkers down the park, not spending his evenings chasing around in stolen cars.

It was late. There was still this car to dump – or torch –

before the night was over, so there would be no more attempts at car theft tonight. But with two or three buzzes each to their credit Kenny and Jake would be looking to him to have a turn soon, and despite his youth and inexperience Alan knew he couldn't put it off forever.

Screams of fear and anger as that old-type Fiesta sideswiped a bus stop the other night, showering those waiting there with shattered glass; the look of horror on the face of that fat bird in the supermarket car park, when Jake scooped a shopping trolley straight from her hands with the bumper of the silver Golf GTI; and now the old woman, slumping into a heap on the pavement behind them in a cloud of exhaust fumes. These images tore at his mind, jagged fingernails raked across his conscience. The gleam of amber streetlight on gold drew his eyes back to the ring on his finger. Alan recalled the last words his grandfather said to him, skeletal hands shaking as he pressed the ring into Alan's palm. *You will be a good boy, won't you lad?*

1

October

Thursday

The ambient sound levels in the Red Lion were generally considered conducive to conversation – on a Thursday, at least. Earlier in the week you would be okay, too. It was the weekends when things got loud. The average age of the pub's clientele dropped noticeably and the provided entertainment altered to suit. Disco music thundered out, two hundred harsh young voices rose to compensate.

But this was a Thursday and Edward Maxey relaxed at one of the many free tables, staring disdainfully at the meagre Halloween decorations dotted around the walls. All Hallows Eve was a week away but the fine line between acknowledging the occasion and just plain not bothering was being straddled with these sadly limp offerings.

Maxey contemplated the condensation trickling down the glass containing his beer. He'd opted for "Purple Monkey Dishwasher" this evening, a smooth, chocolate peanut butter flavoured porter which was sliding down nicely. Another one ticked off his list of hilariously named beers to try before he kicked the bucket. No music in here tonight, unless you wanted to pop a few coins in the jukebox; just thc low rumblc of murmuring from the couple of dozen visitors scattered around the spacious lounge room.

Maxey filled the time as he waited for his companion by discreetly peering at his fellow drinkers. A favourite pastime; people watching. By studying body language, mannerisms and expressions he believed he could determine their characters, get a feel for who they were, even at a distance. *Oh, come off it, Maxey, you're just nosy, aren't you?* The problem was that he rarely discovered whether any observations he made were correct or merely the deluded imaginings of an inquisitive mind. It was refreshing when one of those rare opportunities presented itself.

There were two of them; male, late-teens, swaggering up to the bar with the brashness that only youth mixed with ignorance can bring. The barman, a hefty item with receding hairline and expanding waistline, greeted them gruffly; their request for service meeting a blunt refusal. They persisted, pleading their case. He stood firm, arms folded: *don't mess with me.* They had eyes wide, arms spread, exuding innocence. His hand reached out to them, fingers beckoning – come on then, show me. What, money? Prove they can pay? No, ID. He wanted them to prove they were old enough to purchase alcohol. They fumbled in pockets, exchanging a smirk, ready to produce their secret weapon; they had come prepared.

Maxey rose and sauntered over to the bar. He had recognised the documents they had retrieved, grubby and dog-eared from being crammed into jeans pockets. Many years of familiarity allowed him to spot a birth certificate with ease, even from his table across the room. The barman, on the other hand, was examining the papers closely, long forehead crumpled with indecision, reluctant to accede the point.

'Problem?' asked Maxey, sidling alongside the youths, taking a nonchalant sip from his glass.

'Not *your* problem, mate!' one told him, insecurity worn as aggression.

'These two reckon they're eighteen,' the barman said, glad of an ally. 'These things look real enough, but I dunno...' He waved the papers helplessly.

Maxey took the proffered certificates from him, much to

the disgust of their supposed owners. The briefest glance at them; quality of the paper stock, colour and style of the print, the distinctive watermark, and he knew immediately. 'They're real, all right.' The boys smiled. Maxey continued. The boys stopped smiling. 'And there's a good chance that *one* of these lads is actually eighteen.'

'One?' asked the barman, turning his gaze back to the oh-so-innocent pair.

Maxey explained. Two birth certificates; one a standard certificate, A4 size, date and place of birth, parents' names; the other a short certificate, little square thing, much briefer details. Both for a child named John, both with the same date of birth. Coincidence? At first sight you might think they're for the same boy, until you come to the surname. That was different on each certificate. Different surname, different person. Obviously. Or so you would believe; as this barman was supposed to believe. The mother's maiden surname on the full size certificate matched the boy's surname on the smaller one. Another coincidence?

'We're cousins,' chipped in one of them, promptly.

'Good answer,' said Maxey. 'Quick, slick, well-rehearsed. So how do you explain the fact that they both have the same NHS number on them?'

'Dunno,' the lad shrugged. 'Typing mistake?'

Maxey's smile was a touch patronising.

'How do *you* explain it?' the other asked, adding 'you clever sod!' with an edge of venom.

'Like this,' Maxey said casually, unimpressed by the hostility. 'One of you, the real John, was born just a tad over eighteen years ago, shall we say... out of wedlock.'

They both remained silent, glowering at him.

'At that time, or approximately two weeks later, John's mother registered his birth, giving him her own surname, and was given this.' Maxey flapped the shorter certificate cockily before their faces. 'The date of issue tells us that. Then, no more than four years later, the aforementioned

17

mother married the previously absent father and they revisited the register office to register the birth again. This time giving the child the father's surname. This is shown by the date of registration on the second certificate, which also states that the birth was "re-registered on the authority of the Registrar General". That's the real giveaway. The full certificate supersedes the short one, which should have been destroyed way back then.'

'Destroyed?' asked the barman, eyeing the youths.

'Like this,' said Maxey, tearing both certificates into small pieces and dropping them carefully onto the bar.

'Oi!' one boy protested. 'You can't do that.'

'One of you was using a false identity to obtain goods by deception and the other was an accessory. That means you were both committing a criminal offence. I suggest that losing a couple of bits of paper is preferable to involving the police, don't you agree?'

'I was all for calling the police,' the barman told them, his large frame leaning menacingly over the bar. 'Now bugger off, the pair of you. You're both barred for life!'

They retreated unhappily, tossing back a few choice expletives as they went.

'Obliged mate,' grunted the barman, reaching another purple-labelled bottle out of the fridge. 'Refill on me?'

'Cheers,' Maxey smiled, delighted with himself. The chance to show off a little, and a free drink into the bargain; this was turning into rather a pleasant evening.

'This *re-registering* business, it happens a lot, does it?'

'Whenever a kid's parent's get married after the birth they should register it again,' Maxey said. 'A lot of people don't realise that. It should happen a lot more often than it does.'

'You must be a registrar then?' The question was accompanied by the rattle of the bottle cap into the bin.

'I have that dubious honour,' Maxey responded, with mock modesty.

'Must be an interesting job.' He carefully poured the new

drink onto the old.

'Must it?' Maxey pondered for a moment. 'It has its moments, I suppose. After all these years nothing much surprises me anymore.'

'I went to a Register Office wedding once.'

'Oh yes?' prompted Maxey, waiting for some exposition on the subject.

'Yeah,' said the barman, and wandered off to serve another customer.

'Well, that's interesting,' said Maxey to his glass, as he carried it back to the table. He sat meditatively for a moment and reflected on the previous interlude. It was good for the soul to give the ego a boost occasionally. He took immense satisfaction from the looks on the faces of the youths as they crumbled beneath the weight of his supreme omniscience. With a self-deprecating tut he chastised himself for his arrogance, but only half-heartedly.

He was still harbouring a secret smile when a shadow fell across him.

'That's a dirty look,' said the newcomer, joining him at the table. 'What have you been up to?'

Maxey's smile broadened, fuelled by his embarrassment at being caught out in his self-indulgence. 'Oh, nothing you'd approve of, Officer.'

Detective Sergeant Luke Preston bumped his glass down on the table, unaware of the slop of beer that spilled over the rim, and flopped wearily down on the chair opposite Maxey's. 'I am,' he said, pausing for dramatic effect, 'knackered!'

'Are they keeping you busy?'

'Damn right, they are!' Preston said. 'Unsolved burglaries are stacked up to the ceiling, I've got a mugging and an indecent assault come in this morning and I've been in court all afternoon waiting for a case that never even got called. Charges dropped 'cause the CPS got cold feet over the amount of evidence, or something. And to top it all off, Traffic are trying to foist these joyrides on to CID 'cause

19

they say it's murder.'

'Joyride murder?' frowned Maxey.

'Oh, apparently they're stealing cars and driving them at people,' Preston explained, wiping lager from his chin. 'Killed some old dear the other week.'

'Oh yes, that was on the news.'

'The car barely touched her but apparently she had a bit of a wobble in the ol' chest, according to the quacks. No leaking information to the press, by the way. That bit's been withheld.' Maxey attempted a Boy Scout salute to show his loyalty and trustworthiness. '"Further investigation required", so she won't be coming through your books any time soon,' Preston added.

Maxey smiled, despite the bluntness of the remark. He realised Preston was referring to the death registers he used in his line of work. Preston wasn't quite as callous as he appeared. This was just lads' talk. Two friends letting loose on a night out. Time enough for acting prim and proper during the day, each having public-facing jobs that required a certain standard of behaviour. They were both in their thirties, both were, or had been, married – responsible, respectable adults. But put them together down the pub, pour a couple of drinks into them, and they were just silly schoolboys again.

'And what do you think?' Maxey asked. Then, in response to Preston's puzzled frown, he added: 'Is it murder?'

'Nah,' Preston laughed, licking away a froth moustache. 'It's just a bunch of pillocks who've been getting their thrills by scaring people and went a bit too far. But we've promised to look into it and liaise with Uniform. Didn't have a lot of choice really, after the Super ordered us to.' He shrugged and went on hastily: 'Not that we weren't happy to oblige. All this cross-department rivalry is just a myth, you know. We're all one big happy family.'

'Do I detect a hint of irony in that last statement?' said Maxey.

Preston smirked. 'From me? I can't even spell irony.'

They each settled back with their drinks, washing away the day's fatigue like so much dust in the throat. Theirs was a long-term and comfortable friendship, easily able to withstand an occasional few moments' silence. It had survived a good deal worse than that, in its time. They'd been friends since they attended the same school, many years earlier, though Maxey was a couple of years ahead. Consequently their paths didn't cross until Maxey was in his final year, when Preston began dating his younger sister, Claire. Maxey and Preston hit it off immediately and developed a rock-steady bond, while Preston and Claire's relationship roller-coastered from high passion, romance and a hasty marriage to low hatred and belligerence, finally settling onto a plateau of indifference and apathy. It eventually came off the rails altogether in an unpleasant divorce, leaving behind nothing but acrimony, alimony and a sweet-faced angel named Kerry, now thirteen, feisty and independent.

Because her brother had maintained a close relationship with her ex-husband throughout those proceedings, and ever since, Claire had rarely spoken to Maxey for years. Remembering that he had never deliberately avoided speaking to her assuaged any remorse Maxey might feel over this, but it still left a vast sadness inside him like a cold, dark cave. But all that was history, and rarely mentioned between the two men now.

'So, how's work treating you?' Preston asked, feeling the quiet had drawn on long enough.

'Oh, you know,' mumbled Maxey, vaguely. He knew Preston harboured no deep desire to appreciate the workings of the Registration Service – this was his standard question for nudging a placid moment. For all their cosy amity Preston often expressed the opinion that companionable silences were for old married couples and if they ever went more than five minutes without speaking Maxey would be hearing from his solicitor.

Without voicing any further answer, Maxey contemplated Preston's question. The office was experiencing seasonal changes, he pondered. With a golden summer tailing off into a bronze autumn the numbers of marriages dwindled noticeably, whereas births, boosted by the previous winter's conceptions, as couples sought mutual warmth, were beginning to increase. As a Registrar of Births and Deaths *and* a Deputy Superintendent Registrar Maxey considered he had the best of both worlds. Confined to neither function he could one day be behind a desk, filling registers opposite bereaved relatives or joyful new parents, the next facing a heaving roomful of carnation-bedecked congregators or a jeans-clad couple and two strangers dragged off the street to bear witness for them. Though the list of duties expected of him was relatively restricted, even with the advent of such things as baby namings, reaffirmation of marriage vows and citizenship ceremonies, somehow every day still managed to bring its own surprises.

Today conformed to that pattern. Maxey recalled an incident from this morning he deemed worthy of mention, smiling at the anecdote even before he spoke.

Preston recognised Maxey's expression and mirrored the smile in anticipation. 'Come on then, what's tickling you?'

'I've just remembered this bloke who came in to the office today,' he began. 'I should have known there was something dodgy the way Roz – you remember Roz...?'

'Oh yeah,' said Preston with a lascivious leer. 'I remember Roz.'

Maxey laughed. Roz worked on reception and Maxey couldn't deny she was easy to remember. He himself remembered her far more often than was appropriate, considering he was a married man. 'Anyway, the way she called it through, with a giggle in her voice, should have put me on guard. But I just thought she'd been having a joke with the girls in the office and shrugged it off. Till he came in and sat down, handed me a collar with a little metal name tag on it, and asked if he could register the death of his dog.'

A pang of guilt soured Maxey's laughter as they shared the absurdity of the story. The old man was lax with his hygiene and dour in his manner, but he possessed a certain dignity when he spoke of his lost pet that managed to touch Maxey, even through his incredulity. He wasn't a stupid man, just a little unsophisticated; his lifestyle encompassed little outside the farming community in which he lived. 'He knew you could have pets buried or cremated,' Maxey told Preston. 'So why not registered, too?'

'Makes perfect sense to me,' smirked Preston.

'He was a nice old bloke, really,' Maxey said. 'He got quite embarrassed when I told him I couldn't help him. I did too, if I'm honest. This pooch was the nearest thing to family he had. I felt like doing the registration for him anyway.'

'I think you should have, you mean, old sod.'

'You're right! We should register everything. Dogs, cats, mice, whatever you like.'

'I trod on a spider on the way in,' Preston confided, behind his hand. 'Can I register that?'

'Sorry, mate. Not natural causes – you'll have to contact the police.'

Preston was still chuckling when he returned from the bar a few moments later, two more brimming glasses clutched before him.

'Are we going for a curry when we've finished these?' Maxey asked, accepting his drink.

'Do you think we should?' Preston said, vainly attempting to keep his face straight. 'We might end up eating your mate's dog.'

'You're a sick bugger, you are!' Maxey rebuked, but they both laughed again.

2

The landscape flashing past was harsh and unfamiliar. Jagged, rocky hillsides alternated with stark, barren fields, shorn of crop or sparse of pasture and the occasional bare, angular tree reaching grasping branches towards the train's steamy windows. Everything was brown and grim, compared to the bright golden glow of her homeland. And the cold...! Alicia was unprepared for the extent to which the climate could change so quickly.

But it wasn't so quick, really. The trip from southern Spain had been long and arduous, involving many train changes, long waits in lonely stations, overnight travel and cold and uncomfortable carriages. She looked at her watch – but of course, that was wrong now, out by one hour. Even so, she calculated the journey had taken just over four full days. It was strange to imagine that her letter would probably arrive before she did. Perhaps she should have just bundled herself up in a package and travelled as freight.

The heavy sky, which had been a dirty grey since morning, was beginning to turn a soiled navy, indifferent stars barely making the effort to peep between tattered clouds. Alicia was aching and exhausted, shifting her position on the hard seat for the millionth time. *Santa Maria!* what a horrendous sight, she thought, wiping clear the grime from a patch of window and squinting at the hazy reflection. Raking fingernails through unruly hair she sighed in frustration and slumped back, her critical self-image far worse than the perception of her fellow passengers, who saw only a beautiful young woman sharing their carriage. The ruffled black locks, combined with wide, dark eyes and pouting, naturally scarlet lips lent an air of innocent helplessness to her appearance, like a favourite doll, recently rediscovered and in need of love and attention. But the firm and lithe body beneath that pretty face belied such juvenile imagery. The many and frequent admiring glances cast her way by both male and female co-travellers alike were lost on her. Her only thoughts were of her journey's end, and the reception she would receive on arrival.

It was important that she should look forward, rather than consider what she had left behind. For Alicia López García was on the run.

*

To reach the Bombay Tandoori from the Red Lion, in Haleston, one has to leave Keel Road, walk south along Main Drive, crossing at the pelican, and then turn into Ellington Road about a hundred yards further down. The curry house is the second frontage on your right. If you happened instead to take the third turn after Ellington on the same side of the road you would find yourself in Dapron Street, home of the Earl Johnnie public house, named after a distinguished former resident of the town.

Now, the Earl is a different proposition to the Red Lion, being that little bit closer to the centre of town, and catering for a more "beer and skittles" type of patron, perhaps less distinguished than the establishment's namesake. It lacked the pretensions of grandeur displayed by its neighbours, with their chrome and neon splendour to dazzle the customers' eyes before they can read the bar tariff. Located close to the bus and train stations, and several taxi ranks, along with a MacDonald's, KFC and a number of other pubs, it tended to be rather more full than the Red Lion, even on a weekday evening.

Squeezing away from a crowded bar Jeff Rafferty made his way back to the table where his companion waited, the soles of his shoes rasping on the sticky floorboards as he walked. Adrian Lawson was drinking from a half full pint glass as Rafferty placed two more on the table.

'Steady on,' said Lawson, repositioning the glasses as Rafferty took the stool opposite him. 'I've only just got my car back from the police, I don't want to be banned from driving it.'

'You'll be all right with a couple,' Rafferty insisted. 'Gerrit down you.'

'Don't rush me,' Lawson said, running his hand through his thick, dark hair. 'It's not just driving that drink has an effect on, y'know. I don't want to disappoint the missus, do I?' He smirked, eyes glistening, and his face crinkled up in that way of his, which so many women found irresistible, and even men found disarming and charming. It was a look that caused and soothed more varieties of trouble than most men could manage in five lifetimes.

'Is it your wife you're worried about?' Rafferty asked, eyebrows raised in wonder. 'Or are you stopping off anywhere on the way home?'

For the briefest moment darkness clouded Lawson's deep blue eyes, as a grim suspicion passed behind them, but then that famous look returned. 'Whatever do you mean, Jeffrey?'

'It's the harem's night off, is it?' Rafferty pressed, a feeling that maybe he had touched a nerve bringing an impudent smile.

Lawson merely laughed and turned his attention to his drink.

Rafferty, recognising the moment had passed, changed the subject. 'You don't have to worry about being without a car, anyway. Not in your line of work.'

'It's not the car, it's the licence to drive it. That's one of the quirks of the motor trade, they expect you to have a valid driving licence for moving all those cars around.'

'You're not short of a bob or two, you could afford to employ someone to drive you around all day.'

'I'd rather not have to,' Lawson said, carefully replacing his glass on the table. 'Is this your way of touting for a job?

Is that what all the speed boozing is about? Unhappy at work?'

'No,' Rafferty groaned, reaching for his own glass once more. 'At home. It's Julie.'

'Bending your ear a bit, is she?'

'She says she feels "unsettled", or something,' Rafferty shrugged. 'Don't ask me to explain it, I never could understand women. I thought I'd try to pay her a bit more attention, y'know, be around a bit more. I might not even have come out tonight, except I had to deliver this.'

'What, another one already?' Lawson said, as Rafferty pulled a small, pink envelope from his pocket and slid it across the table. He didn't need to see the handwriting of the address on the front, or tear open the seal and read the contents, to know who sent the letter. Nor take in the unusual stamp and squint at the fuzzy, blurred postmark to know from where it originated. Lawson sighed and picked up the letter.

'She definitely seems keen,' Rafferty said, not even attempting to suppress his grin. 'Not opening it now?' he added, as Lawson slipped it into his jacket pocket.

'She'll wait,' Lawson told him. 'Besides, it might be a bit raunchy, I wouldn't want to put you off your beer.'

*

The train pulled in at Haleston station around thirty minutes after Alicia changed at Doncaster. Seeing the name of the town as the large sign swept into view, she finally peeled herself from the grimy window, stomach fluttering and head spinning. Her forehead felt cold and damp and she realised she had been peering out into the darkness for some time, hands shielding her eyes from the light within the carriage. She felt weary to the bone but the anticipation of the impending reunion buoyed her mood and gave strength to her failing muscles. Even so, she allowed herself a moment to catch her breath, as a queue of disembarking passengers filled the aisle, before stretching her aching legs and dragging her holdall from the overhead shelf.

The atmosphere in the station was chilly and damp as Alicia followed the crowds up the stairs and along the gantry, past all the advertising hoardings and stairwells to other platforms, towards the busy exit. She was not dressed for this climate, she soon realised, as the constant night breeze brought the soft, short hairs of her bare arms quickly erect. In fact she possessed no clothing that would be adequate for autumn in England. The small denim jacket she pulled from her bag gave scant protection, even added to the T-shirt and light canvas slacks she already wore. Her shoes were for wearing on the hot beaches of her home village, not for treading the wet concrete and rough tarmac of urban streets.

That Alicia was not prepared for what faced her was only to be expected, for she had left home in a desperate hurry.

*

Adrian Lawson's mind was in his pocket. The small, flimsy letter felt like a lead weight at his side. It constantly drew his attention away from the casual chatter that Jeff Rafferty tossed across the table at him.

'I might as well've stayed at home and faced the wife's moaning, at this rate,' Rafferty complained, flicking a beer mat in Lawson's direction.

'Sorry, Jeff,' Lawson said, reaching to pick the erstwhile weapon from the floor. 'I'm all over the place, tonight.'

'Mainly in a small village on the southern coast of Spain, am I right?' Rafferty wondered, cockily. The lack of response was answer enough. 'She's getting a bit carried away, don't you think? It's only a few days since the last one. If Julie gets to the post before me one of these days, there'll be hell to pay.'

'Yeah, I know. Sorry mate, I never meant to get you involved.'

'I can't understand why you gave her your real name in the first place, let alone *my* address!'

'I told you, her dad owned the hotel,' Lawson explained.

'Yeah, so...'

'So I had to hand over my passport at reception, didn't I? Lissy was working the reception when I arrived. She knew my real name already. When things got... *friendly* she asked for my address so she could write to me after I came home. She put me on the spot; it threw me, okay? I'm not daft enough to give her my own address and the first one that popped into my head was yours.'

'Thanks a bunch! You should have said straight out, it was just a fling. Thank you and goodbye.'

Lawson coughed out a horrified gasp. 'Are you kidding? If she didn't kill me herself, then her father definitely would have.' The image of the black haired, steel-eyed giant, sleeves pulled back from thick, hairy forearms, chef's hat limp from sweat and steam lolling on his head, thundered through his imagination, breathing fire. 'He was a huge great thing, and you never saw him without a nasty-looking kitchen knife sticking out of the strap of his apron.'

'Could be worse. She might've asked for your mobile number or email address or something. Electronic messages flooding in at all hours of the day and night.'

Lawson nodded, his face expressing his horror at the thought. 'Thank God her dad kept her in a medieval state of ignorance about such high-tech methods of communication.'

'Can't you write her back? Tell her you've moved?'

'I've not answered the last few she sent. I was hoping she'd take the hint from that.'

'But they never do, these young impressionable ones, do they? I thought you'd have learned by now: go for the more experienced women. Ones who've been round the track a time or two, and know the course rules.'

'That's the trouble, though,' said Lawson, all crinkle and twinkle. 'Young or old, experienced or pure as the driven snow, they all fall madly in love with me. No one can resist the old Adie charm.'

Rafferty shook his head in despair, but found he was grinning along with his friend all the same. It was true; when Adie switched on the charm offensive, no one was immune.

*

Two men drinking. It happens more on midweek nights, the weekends being more for groups, "the lads" out on the piss and the pull. Nothing wrong with letting your hair down and releasing the built up tensions once in a while. But if you want the chance for a bit of conversation or meditation at a more sedate pace, avoiding the desperate rush and the increased volume of the Saturday night crawl crowd, and without heading out of town, then opting for a midweek night seems the only choice.

While Adrian Lawson and Jeff Rafferty discussed the merits of diverse liaisons in the Earl Johnnie, three streets further up Main Drive the Bombay Tandoori played host to the wit and philosophy of Edward Maxey and Luke Preston.

'So, anyway,' Preston slurred, washing down a mouthful of rice with a draught of yeasty imported lager, 'I'm hanging about in reception when she comes in, right, and she's fit – *well* fit, y'know what I mean?'

Maxey grinned broadly and raised his glass – he knew what he meant.

'And the front desk bloke is busy doing... whatever he does, so I thought, why not, I thought. So I goes over to her, all "at your service, ma'am" sort of thing, and asks what's up, like.'

Maxey nodded eagerly, rapt in the story.

'And she says, "I want to see someone about sexual harassment," so I looked her up and down, said, "You've come to the right place" and pinched her arse.' Preston roared with laughter, highly impressed with his own humour.

Maxey sat stony-faced, blurry visions of lawsuits and complaints against the police force flashing through his alcohol-clouded mind. 'You didn't, did you?'

'Course not, you pillock,' laughed Preston, stunned at his friend's gullibility. 'It's a joke.'

'Oh, right.' Maxey chewed on a chunk of naan bread, hoping its stodginess would soak up some of the befuddlement swilling around his brain. It had been a long evening, incorporating much gratification of various appetites, and Maxey was beginning to feel that enough was quite probably enough. His throat refused to let the wad of dough slip past and the idea of taking another swig of his lager repulsed him. Coughing the bread into his serviette, Maxey pushed his plate away and flopped back in his chair with a sigh. He could see the waiters eyeing them up impatiently, all but one other table having long since been vacated.

Maxey found his eyes drawn to the occupants of that other table, a young couple deeply absorbed in one another's company. As their hands touched across the table, he noticed they both wore wedding rings. With the cynicism of one well familiar with the fleeting nature of modern marriages, Maxey found himself wondering if the spouse sitting opposite each of them was actually their own.

Back on Main Drive they waved down a black cab and bundled themselves clumsily into the rear. The driver was overweight and quite bald; his only evident hair growth was thick tufts in his ears and heavy stubble rolling over his jowls. He seemed weary and not inclined to conversation, or even politeness. He merely grunted in acknowledgement as they told him their respective destinations; Maxey and Preston exchanged a dismissive look and promptly forgot all about him until he drew in to the kerb a few minutes later.

'Thanks for this,' said Preston as he ducked out through the cab door. 'It's been a good night.'

'I've enjoyed it,' Maxey smiled. 'It makes a change to catch you when you're not working.'

'Most of my nights off lately – what few I get – have been spent slobbing in front of the telly. Last week I just sat there drinking vodka and watching re-runs of Friends on Comedy Central... Oh God, do you think I'm turning gay?'

'Did you stay on for Will & Grace?'

'No!' Preston told him emphatically.

'That's okay then,' Maxey reassured him. 'I think you're safe.'

They were both chuckling again as the cab drew them apart. As he travelled on in silence Maxey found his eyes growing heavy with the rocking of the vehicle and the drone of the engine, and was only brought back to awareness when they lurched to a halt and the driver turned in his seat and reached out a hand for payment.

Maxey barely had both feet on the ground before the surly driver pulled the cab around in a sharp arc and headed back to town for his next fare.

3

Grogan pulled forward to the front of the queue. It hadn't taken him long; there were only three or four other cabs ahead of him when he returned to the rank outside the railway station. Probably a lot of drivers were having the night off, to ready themselves for the weekend's heavy haul. He might have done the same himself tonight, as he often did on Thursdays, except that he had solemnly promised his wife that he would never raise a hand to her again, and the easiest means of keeping that promise was to stay out of the silly cow's way.

He stuck a podgy finger in his hairy ear and briefly examined the orangey-brown muck under his nail before casually wiping it on the leg of his jeans. He tapped a beat on the huge kettledrum of his stomach and hummed tunelessly in accompaniment as he watched for the next punter to approach. A train had disembarked its passengers a short while earlier but he had missed most of them when he picked up those two sniggering idiots outside the Indian. They were clean and smart and Grogan thought they probably had a bob or two, but if he expected a decent tip from them he'd been disappointed. Stingy bastards!

Maybe it was his own fault, Grogan mused. That daft bitch back home kept telling him he was too grumpy with folk, for which gem of information she'd usually been rewarded with a slap. But what if she had a point? The Pakis were constantly bragging about the tips they received from grateful passengers, and they were always grinning inanely and jabbering like monkeys on speed.

Grogan shifted in his seat – here came someone now. And it was someone he had no difficulty producing a smile for. Young, very attractive, dark hair and a nice tan. She looked a bit lost though, and evidently very cold, judging by the front of her clingy T-shirt: her denim jacket had swung open as she stooped to his window. He reluctantly tore his gaze from the girl's breasts and transformed his lecherous leer into an obsequious beam of greeting.

'Where do you want to go, my love?' he asked, his longest sentence all evening, hoping she would respond 'all the way'.

''Scuse,' the girl said, falteringly. 'But I have none of your money.'

'My money?' puzzled Grogan, wondering why she thought she ought to have any of his money. Then the girl's accent penetrated through to his consciousness and finally the peseta dropped. She was a foreign bird. 'Oh, you mean English money?'

'Yes,' she said apologetically, showing him a scattering of silver on her palm. 'And I have little of my euros left.'

'We don't take that crap here, girlie,' Grogan told her, and though the words were unfamiliar his tone obviously carried his message effectively enough.

She turned and stared around helplessly, speaking more to herself than to Grogan. 'Then how am I to get where I would be?'

The appeal in her voice touched a place beneath his grubby shirt but, a stronger influence than that, her firm, round buttocks were now directly outside his window and as he stared he discovered his hand was touching a place beneath his grubby jeans.

'Tell you what,' he said, 'as you're a visitor to our fair land, why don't I give you a ride for nowt?'

She turned back to him with a smile as he returned his sweaty hand to the steering wheel. 'You would take me for no payment?'

'Definitely,' Grogan said, smirking to himself as an alternative connotation of her words occurred to him. 'Jump in.' She was alone, frightened and vulnerable. Susceptible to and very grateful for the generosity of a stranger. A combination Grogan found completely

34

irresistible.

She showed him a crumpled piece of paper with a scrawled address in Merrington, a village just the other side of Clegganfield on the road that takes you to Sheffield. 'It is not far, yes?'

'That's right, love,' he assured her. 'We'll be there in no time.' And he pulled the cab out of Haleston Station car park, along the short stretch to the roundabout, then took the last exit onto the dual carriageway towards Doncaster.

Which is in entirely the opposite direction from Sheffield.

*

For all his affected nonchalance Adrian Lawson was desperately impatient to tear open that flimsy pink envelope and devour the contents. His breathing was fast and heavy as he pulled his shiny black Audi A8 into a lay-by about a mile beyond Merrington. A long, articulated lorry was already parked up there for the night, but there was ample room. Jeff Rafferty had managed another pint before they left the Earl, despite Lawson's repeated glances at his watch, and Jeff's own insistence that he didn't want to leave his Julie on her own for long. Leaving Rafferty staggering through his squeaky gate, slurring promises that Lawson's secret was safe with him, Lawson had sped away with a casual wave.

Now he plucked the letter from his pocket hungrily, but then hesitated before ripping open the flap. The ambiguity of his feelings disturbed him: at once dreading and eagerly awaiting each new communication. He told himself, as well as Rafferty, that the girl meant nothing to him but, in truth, she dominated his thoughts daily.

He assumed that when he boarded his plane home, after that business trip, what was it – nine? ten? weeks ago now, he was leaving more than the weather behind him. Why should this girl – this face, this body, this sex – mean more to him than any other of the many assignations he had known over the years? And maybe, given the chance to forget her, with the assistance of time and any *distractions* he could provide for himself, he might have been able to do just that. Forget her. But when her first letter arrived only a few days later, he was transported back thousands of miles to the sun-kissed shores of southern Spain, and the sun-bronzed arms of his little Lissy. Alicia – a musical name, he mused, then shook such foolishly romantic notions from his head. He had romance. Donna was for romance – the little woman back home. All the others were just for fun; a laugh, a distraction – something to make him appreciate his home and family all the more. Donna understood that, accepted his ways and turned a blind eye to what didn't concern her. For if all her needs and desires were catered for, why should she mind if his greater demands required external gratification?

Layna could never accept that. That's why they eventually divorced. She felt that she ought to have been enough for him – he'd married her and he should be satisfied and content. And, damn it, he'd tried. He went nearly two whole years after their nuptial night before seeking... more than could be found at home. Layna was a lovely girl, and if she'd been a little less selfish they could have made a go of things. As it was...

Lawson took a grip of himself, realising that he was merely delaying the moment. He switched on the overhead light and instantly cut off the world beyond the windows. All that existed were the multiple reflections of the pocket universe inside the car. Under such limitations his awareness of his immediate surroundings seemed more acute. The warmth of the seat beneath him, its curves gently embracing the base of his back. The clammy dampness of the steering wheel in his fist, and the traces of silvery grey powder still clinging to it from the fine brush of the police fingerprint man – woman? – *person*. Even the uncomfortable sense of detachment from his formerly favourite car, since some bastard had decided to swipe the thing, scatter his CDs in the footwell, leave footprints all over the back seats and then dump it up to its axels in mud on the allotments down the far end of Ockerby last Sunday night. Detachment resulting from a perception of violation, a spoiling of something precious. They only returned the car this morning, and Lawson had even been stuck with the bill for its recovery.

More delaying tactics. Lawson slowly turned the letter over and slid a finger under the flap, peeling the paper back, images of peeling away layers of flimsy feminine underwear flickering before his gaze. He hadn't kept any of her letters, of course. Far too dangerous. What if Donna found them? Just not worth the hassle. Was that a whiff of perfume? Something soft and flowery, a scent which mingled so well with the earthy musk of her hot skin. He'd have to wash his hands when he went in – mustn't forget. Did Jeff have the same problem, keeping the letters away from Julie? He experienced a fresh pang of guilt over what he'd done to Jeff. All the things he'd done. Jeff had been a good mate and to treat him like this...

God! Just read it, will you?!

So he did. As his eyes scanned down the page his chest became constricted and his throat was dry and tight. The words thunder-clapped from the paper like bullets shot straight into his brain. The heat seemed to drain from him, ever so slowly; first from his face and neck, then gradually down his whole body till his feet felt hot and swollen in his shoes.

But even as he crumpled the letter deliberately in his shaking fist he was wary of the two clumsy Xs drawn in lipstick below the elegant swirl of the signature. Wouldn't want to smudge that on his shirt, would he?

*

The rear view mirror showed Grogan a tiny, shivering creature gripping her holdall on her lap and appearing to be

37

a million worlds away. He briefly considered the best way to turn back onto the correct route without making her aware of his deception. But only briefly.

She licked her lips in what was probably genuine hunger, but which he saw only as a lascivious gesture, a come-on. Okay, her desires were undoubtedly aimed elsewhere than at himself, maybe even merely at a cheese toastie and a cup of tea, but in his imagination those damp lips were pouting at him.

He saw the lay-by up ahead. He'd used it before, when drunken birds preferred to pay for their journeys in kind, rather than cash; or they had practically passed out, too far gone to know what was happening to them; or if they were merely one of the Balham Estate prozzies he sometimes picked up for fun. But they were always rough birds, fat slappers who weren't worth looking at by daylight. This one was different. Slim, pretty, young and... clean. That would make a change.

Alicia felt the cab slowing. She could see nothing beyond the smeared and stained windows; they were far from any lights or houses. She began to feel the first pangs of doubt. This man, though brusque and unkempt, had appeared kind, generous, much as her own father could be with strangers back home – when he was in that frame of mind. But he had little else in common with Papa. His smell was unpleasant and his manners were crude. And his eyes were bulging and yellow and leered at her in an over familiar fashion.

And now he appeared to be stopping the cab, when they were obviously nowhere near their destination. The evening's chill was nothing to the icy sensation gripping her now. She couldn't believe how naïve she had been, getting into a strange man's car late at night. What would Papa say? Could his opinion of her be any lower than it was when she last saw him, hand raised, eyes and tongue blazing at her? Would she live to find out?

The growl of the engine coughed to a halt and Grogan

breathed noisily, scratched his stubbly chins and opened his door. Alicia sat frozen in the rear, eyes wide and starting to weep, staring at him in terror.

'Please do not touch me,' she pleaded, pressing back into her seat. '*Váyase! Déjeme en paz!*'

His bulk filled the rear door and his body stench invaded her senses. Alicia realised with dismay that his trousers were already missing. The stains on his shirt, the gleam of his bald pate, his stubby fingers clutching the door frame, the curve of his huge belly, swinging low to hide the threat he held for her – all these impressions flooded her mind in that moment.

'Don't fight, girlie,' Grogan rumbled, in a vain attempt to sound soothing. 'I don't want to hurt you. It'll be easier if you just relax.'

But none of his words, soothing or otherwise, could reach her terrified brain now. All awareness of her second language shuttered itself away and raw panic took charge. She pushed away from his lumbering approach, fingers scrabbling desperately at the opposite door catch. A sudden draught at her back surprised her and it was a second before she realised that she'd done it – she'd opened the door!

But then a huge, hot fist encircled her ankle and she was swept from the seat and landed with a thump on the filthy floor of the cab, her retained grip on the handle slamming the door shut behind her. She tried to reach it again but he had pulled her too far, her fingers scratched the interior panel ineffectually, just inches from the catch. Her breath exploded from her chest as his immense weight crashed down upon her. What little light the murky sky could cast was no match for the gloom within the confines of this tiny corner of hell.

Papa swore that the Lord's Judgement would fall upon her – was this her punishment for her sins? Surely no benign god would wish such suffering on any loyal soul. Her skin chafed where her clothes were being stretched and dragged in his rough grasp. His own bulk was impeding him, hindering his movements. The darkness was almost choking in its intensity; his fumbling actions were blind and clumsy. He was taking so long; Alicia felt her fear begin to subside and a cold rationality creep over her. She made herself small, curling tight beneath him so he had to lift his own lolling flesh aside to even reach her. He heaved himself upright, to adjust his leverage, and in the moment that his vastness was a vague silhouette against the open door behind him, and the dim moonlight glinted in the rheumy whites of his eyes, her hand flashed up to rake clawing fingernails across his face. He lurched backwards, found himself jammed in the doorway, arms flailing for balance. Alicia freed a leg and kicked out hard, once, twice, again, again, catching him over and over in the soft cushion of his stomach, hearing the wind forced from him, then a satisfying crack as she caught him with her heel across the jaw.

He disappeared from view, landing with a jarring whoomp on the hard ground. Alicia turned and opened the other door, scrambling through before he could react, raise himself up, give chase. Trees stretched ahead, promising the safety of cover, an enveloping darkness less terrifying than staying in the open. She raced in, branches and twigs catching at her clothes, undergrowth tugging at her shoes. Tripped and fell with a crash, cursing the noise she made. Froze where she lay, holding her breath, listening for sounds of pursuit. But all she heard was the growl of an engine and the rasp of tyres on gravel as a car sped away into the night.

4

Friday

Maxey knew, before he even went to bed last night, that he was going to suffer in the morning. On previous occasions drinking a pint of water before retiring had proved beneficial, but the thought of pouring any more liquid into his already bloated stomach had not appealed to him. Anyway, he'd not had that much, had he? It'd probably be all right. So he chose to forgo this simple but usually quite effective remedy and trust to luck.

Mistake.

The alarm clock plunged power drills viciously into his brain on each repetition of its shrill beep. He reached out a shaky hand and pressed several buttons – switching on the radio, altering the display colour, changing from British Summer Time to Greenwich Mean Time a couple of days early – before finally putting a stop to the painful din.

Nicola sat up suddenly beside him, immediately bright and alert, as always first thing in the morning. She shook her head and raked fingers through her long, lush dark hair.

'Steady on,' Maxey begged as the mattress rocked beneath them.

'God, you look dreadful!' Nicky greeted happily, swinging her legs from under the duvet. She strode naked across to the hooks on the back of the door, selecting her favourite bathrobe – worn smooth at the elbows and backside but still ever so comfy – and sliding into it.

She turned back to him while fastening the belt and he cast his bleary but appreciative gaze along the length of her. Now in her early thirties she still had naturally young-looking skin, taut and fresh, and a body kept lithe and slender through her regular squash games and running morning and night. A body that had never endured the rigours of childbirth, Maxey noted, with a mild pang of regret. 'There's no rush,' she always insisted, whenever that topic arose.

Tall and slim, but curvy enough to give the eyes somewhere to travel, her smooth torso disappeared, wrapped beneath towelling folds, and Maxey found he was smiling dumbly, despite his pounding skull.

'Are you still drunk?' Nicky asked in soft reproach.

'I hope not,' Maxey slurred, tongue still not quite awake. 'I've got to drive to work in an hour.'

'I don't know why you get yourself in that state when you have work the next day,' Nicky said, then teasingly: 'I'm just going to split a grapefruit and then I'm off for a quick sprint through the woods. Coming?'

'Out, woman!' Maxey ordered, waving a limp fist. 'Leave my sight!'

Maxey's lop-sided smile returned as he watched the door swing back to hide her laughing exit. Even pained as he was, Maxey was able to value the quality of the relationship they shared. Over ten years and still going strong. At a point some five or six years ago, when they might have grown complacent, indifferent or even bored, they watched Maxey's sister and Luke Preston tear themselves apart and found their own marriage invigorated from the shock of it. Tiptoeing through that battleground he and Nicola promised never to create such carnage of their own. Rules of communication, understanding and consideration were discussed, decided and strictly adhered to ever since, a policy that kept things warm and comfortable, but never dull. Common tact had stopped Maxey pointing out to Preston the gift his misery has bestowed, but he was tacitly grateful all the same.

Flipping aside the duvet Maxey staggered over to the dressing table. He tilted back the mirror and squinted at the hazy image wavering there. Leaning close his eyes appeared bloodshot and yellowy. Straightening his back and puffing out his chest he turned sideways and full on, considering his profile and physique. Not bad for thirty-bleurgh years old. No flab and noticeable curves at shoulder and upper arm, courtesy of the occasional stint at the local swimming baths. Casting his gaze lower he allowed a self-satisfied smirk to crease his strong, chiselled features. Difficult to detect the passage of time on this fine frame, biased though his viewpoint may be. He let out his breath in an explosive gasp and flopped back onto the bed, holding his head tenderly in his hands, careful not to let it fall off.

Staring at the ceiling wouldn't get him to work on time. He peeled himself from the bed and, grabbing a warm towel from the airing cupboard in the corner, he shuffled off to the bathroom.

*

'Are you getting up today, or not?' she called up the stairs, storming back into the kitchen and rattling the door in its frame behind her. It wasn't so much the thought of his playing around – after all, what's new there? – it was the fear that there may be more to it this time. Usually, if he strayed, he became more attentive at home, both helping around the house and in a personal way in the bedroom. Not guilty or furtive, more like he was happy with his lot again, returning with a renewed fervour. As if he was *inspired* somehow. Donna Lawson took it as a vindication of her loyalty, a justification of her decision to stick by her man, despite everything. If he played the field and returned to home pastures then she must be doing something right.

But he'd been distracted of late; something had upset the status quo, disrupted the happy home. She imagined she could trace it back to that last trip, the Spanish one. Yes, that was it, she was sure. When he arrived back he seemed effusive in his delight; to be home, to be with her again. As he always did. But somehow it felt less real than on other occasions – more forced than she had ever sensed before. And it hadn't lasted as long as it usually did.

He glided into the room, smooth and self-assured. That was the first thing she had ever noticed about him – he was certainly a good mover. Not five minutes from sleep and he was strutting around like a trained dancer. He'd got the physique for it, too – muscular and firm, lean and agile. Thirty-five, with the body of a twenty year old and the mind of a schoolboy. And the morals of an alley cat.

But he loved her, didn't he? Here he was, slinking into her kitchen, after God knows where he might have been last night. Just a couple with Jeff, he'd said, but who knew? She was his wife; this was his home. But even a cat will return to the place where its food dish is regularly filled, and it can get a scratch behind the ears just for purring the right way at the right time.

She felt herself stiffen as his arms swept around her and she suddenly realised – even if she wasn't losing him, he just might be losing her.

*

Herbert Osgood had neighbours. He lived in a quiet, suburban street, in the nice part of Merrington, so of course he had neighbours. Which made him a neighbour, too. Not a "nasty neighbour" of the type glamorised in the media – no loud music at all hours, no graffiti daubed on your doors or windows, no dog poo through your letterbox. But also not a "good neighbour" – no chit-chat over the hedge, no lending you his lawnmower, no picking you up if he passed you at the bus-stop on a rainy day. He kept to himself, head down, no bother. In an ideal world he'd have the whole street to himself, not have to share with another soul. Herbert knew though, only too well, that the world wasn't ideal, and other people inhabited the street too. But if he was conscientious enough to ensure he didn't encroach upon their lives, surely they could have similar consideration for him. That wasn't too much to ask, was it? And where that consideration was found lacking, it's only to be expected that he would do something about it. And there were methods of retaliation open to him. Nothing overt or confrontational, of course. Nothing that would add to his personal inconvenience. Just some subtle means of inconveniencing him, or her: the one who had perpetrated the supposed transgression against Herbert's peace and solitude.

So when that Lawson fellow from across the way persisted in parking his car on Herbert's side of the road - directly outside Herbert's front window, even though he had a perfectly good driveway of his own - Herbert decided he had to act.

He bided his time, waiting for the ideal moment. You couldn't rush these things, you know. It all had to be planned very carefully. Whatever he did he had to make certain it couldn't be traced back to him. He'd taken to keeping an eye on the vehicle at his gate, looking to see if he'd parked too close to the yellow lines over the ginnel entrance adjacent to Herbert's garden, watching how bald the tyres were getting. He even considered kicking out one of the rear lights, but his courage failed him at the last minute. What if Lawson was looking out of his window at the wrong moment...?

He couldn't believe his luck when he saw the evidence this morning. The news was full of it, all the time, so Herbert put two and two together immediately. He wasted no time in contacting the number they kept announcing. Called himself a "concerned citizen", tried not to give his name, but they'd pressed him, said they needed it if his claim was to be taken seriously. But he was a concerned citizen; it's just that his concerns were a little more personal than whether or not his neighbour was a killer. He just wanted payback. Maybe they would lock Lawson up for life. His wife would have to sell up, the shame would force her out. The house could be empty for some time.

Or someone might buy it straight away, fill it up with screaming children, and flood the front lawn with dismantled motorcycles and rusting washing machines. Herbert stared at the phone for long minutes after he replaced the receiver. Was it possible to retract the statement, nullify the call? Say he'd made a mistake? Would that get Herbert himself into trouble? He heaved a sigh at the unfairness of the world, then put the kettle on and pondered the bleakness of his future.

*

The night had been cold and terrifying. Alicia spent the first hours after Grogan drove away cowering in the wood, afraid he might return at any moment. She crouched against a tree, jacket pulled tight around her, attempting to ignore the scratching and rustling in the undergrowth, the shuffling and flapping in the branches overhead. Such sounds kept sleep well at bay, and eventually fear of the creeping things in the darkness, and the aching of her bent limbs made her rise and venture out of hiding.

She had no idea where she was. The hazy moonlight could barely penetrate the skeletal autumn canopy above, but by turning her back to the tree that had formed her shelter Alicia was able to retrace her steps and scramble gratefully from the dark woods. Finding the road she decided her most appropriate course was to turn back towards the town, and hope to find more reliable directions and assistance once there. Lawson's precious address was still in her pocket, but all her other possessions – the last of her money, her passport and ID, the chocolate bar she'd got from a vending machine in Calais – were still in her bag, which she last saw in the back of that monster's taxicab.

She pondered the idea of contacting the police. They ought to know of the dangerous man who attacked her, whom she had barely escaped. He might have killed her –

would certainly have raped her. He should not be allowed to remain at liberty. Also, the police might offer her food and shelter for the night, maybe even take her to her beloved's address in the morning – she checked her pocket for the hundredth time; yes, still there.

But they would want to know where she was from, why she was here, why she had left Spain in such a hurry. Might even send her back. Back to face her father's anger, back to atone for her sins. No! That was unthinkable.

As she walked along the unlit road she became aware of the sound of a car engine approaching from behind her, heading towards the town. Should she wave the car down, beg the driver to give her a lift? She was tired and hungry and in desperate need of help. But hadn't she already tried that once tonight? The memory of Grogan's slobbering weight pressing down on her flashed up horrifying images. What if it was him, scouring the country roads, looking for her? She quickly melted back into the trees before the car came too close.

It wasn't a taxicab, and the occupants appeared to be a middle-aged couple, from what little Alicia could discern in the darkness. She quietly chided herself for her apprehension, making her shy away from possible salvation. But it wasn't easy to shake off such dread and when another car drew near a while later, she found herself hiding again.

It wasn't until day was growing rapidly on the horizon behind her, chasing the night from the sky, that Alicia felt confident to remain in full view as any car approached. Houses were dotted along the roadside by now, with fresh-looking brickwork, small gardens, unfinished roads curling away between mirror-image, mock-Tudor facades – all hallmarks of a brand new housing estate, Haleston's suburban sprawl spreading cancerously across the rural landscape. Alicia ignored any car where she could see the drivers were men alone, waving hopefully at cars whose driver or any passenger was female. The first to stop was a dilapidated old Fiesta, containing a plump, dishevelled woman in her forties. Alicia saw she was wearing a shabby tunic with an official logo above the left breast, and her car, though dirty, smelled of furniture polish and bleach. Cynth, as the smiling woman introduced herself, seemed oblivious to Alicia's state of near-collapse and lengthily explained that she was out and about so early because she worked as a cleaner for the local authority, sprucing up the offices at the Town Hall in Haleston, for which she felt ludicrously underpaid, considering the unsocial hours and the state those animals left the toilets.

Alicia felt her eyelids becoming unbearably heavy as Cynth's pleasant but monotonous voice washed over her, and it wasn't until that tone rose in a note of query that she realised Cynth had asked her a question.

''Scuse,' she apologised, blinking wearily. Cynth asked again where Alicia wanted to be dropped off. Alicia was surprised to discover that Haleston town centre had loomed up on them while she sat trancelike in her seat, and a sense of panic caught her again as she contemplated being stranded once more in the middle of a strange place. She pulled the address from her pocket, the paper increasingly crumpled, and showed it to Cynth. Cynth glanced at her watch, nearly time to clock on, but the girl's distress was evident and the address was only a few miles out the other side of town. The roads should be quiet at this time. Decision made, she crunched the car into gear and headed out to Merrington.

The village was a small, post-war development spider-webbed around a single shopping and leisure area, grown from a simple rural community swamped by the housing boom. The street recorded on the rough scrap held in Alicia's sweaty, shaking hand swept ahead of her as she waved Cynth away a few minutes later. Cynth had shrugged off Alicia's effusive gratitude with the assurance that it had been no trouble and she was glad to help out.

The curious mix of joy and apprehension she

experienced walking along the pavement – *his* pavement, counting off the house numbers creeping ever closer to his door, was suddenly overshadowed as a painful cramp twisted her stomach and back. Dread crept through her at the thought that maybe the brute in the taxi had done more damage to her than she originally supposed. Maybe she was seriously hurt. Or worse – his insane, lumbering attack might have harmed the baby.

*

She wouldn't call it an argument, as such. He never let things go that far. If he couldn't sooth a prickly moment with soft words and warm arms, then he'd retreat to a safe distance, let tempers cool, and return later laden with gifts and flowers. A disarming tactic, she knew, but more often than not it worked. She didn't like tension between them any more than he did.

But Donna Lawson hadn't let her husband get around her with smiles and kisses, not this time. She pressed her assault, picking up on every little giveaway sign she had spotted since his return from Spain: the restlessness, distraction, avoiding her eye. He insisted that she was misreading him, getting it all wrong. He loved her. No one else could ever mean a fraction of what she meant to him, no one else could ever make him feel a fraction of what he felt for her. But even these words, so familiar and usually so trustable, so safe, were tinged with an insincerity she'd never heard before.

And now he'd gone. Retreated. Off to pick up Shane – a previously arranged appointment but nonetheless convenient for him. An excuse to disappear for a while. But she had to stay behind, the dutiful wife, and wait for him to return.

'That's stupid,' he'd persisted, whenever she brought up another objection. *That* is stupid, talking about the remark, not her. But the only interpretation of a comment like that was that he thought *she* was stupid. How dare he? On the other hand, surely he was right. What other woman would be stupid enough to allow her husband to treat her the way he did? His first wife hadn't. He messed around, she got rid of him. Simple as that. And they'd even had a kid to consider: Shane.

Shane. What a name! Who came up with that one? Wasn't that someone out of the Westerns? But with a mother called Layna, what could you expect? Poor little sod, he must get ragged something rotten at school. Still, that was their problem. If the boy felt strongly enough about it he could take it up with his father when he arrived to collect him – to spend some "quality father-son time" together. She bitterly considered the quality of the time she had shared with Adrian since Spain. He hadn't taken a day off work to be with *her* for a very long while.

She glanced about her at the stark, white kitchen, utilitarian not homely, and felt the empty loneliness of the bright, modern house beyond its tiled walls. It had never felt like a cold place to her before, but she shivered now. Who did she have to confide her misgivings in? No parents, no siblings; Adrian was everything to her. She hadn't even been allowed to provide him with a child, although she realised, even as she thought that last thought, that any child their marriage produced would have been for herself, not for him. He had his boy, his Shane. She had no one. Maybe not even Adrian any more.

Could she talk to Julie? They were supposed to be friends, weren't they? No, not really. Oh, they chatted amiably enough, even went on the odd shopping trip together, but Julie and Jeff had known Adrian when he was still married to Layna, and Donna suspected that Julie secretly blamed her for breaking them up. Julie must know that Layna had thrown Adrian out before Donna even met him, but there was definitely something that kept Julie that little bit on edge whenever she and Donna were in one another's company. Or was she imagining it? Maybe Julie just didn't like her, Donna thought. If truth were told, Donna wasn't that keen on Julie, either. The way she treated Jeff, little put-downs in public, sending him off like a skivvy to do odd jobs, put Donna off her a little, made her uncomfortable, embarrassed. But there was also a sense of condescension, like she thought she was superior, or knew something Donna didn't. Whatever it was, it didn't make Donna any more eager to share with the woman her feelings over her relationship.

So who *could* she talk to? How had it come to be that all the friendships that flourished since Donna and Adrian had married were the ones on his side, either people he had known previously, or new acquaintances that he had met? Where were all the friends she had known? Why did she never make new friends these days? Was she really so subjugated by him, his personality, his lifestyle, that she now had no real existence outside this bleak house?

There's no doubt that she hadn't the strength to change him, or to throw him out, so the question remained, if *she* left *him*, where would she go?

5

The autumn sunshine turned the morning's thin cloud cover into a fluorescent sheet of brilliant white, cheery and welcoming to most, but Edward Maxey squinted painfully behind dark glasses as he manoeuvred his aubergine 2.0i engine Mondeo through Haleston's circuitous one-way system. He'd seen the road he wanted, Garrison Street, just off to his right and scowled at the no entry sign facing him. Another four hundred yards or so along Roman Way to the roundabout, wrestling with the busy morning traffic trying to get to or from the railway station, bus station and the Centurion Shopping Centre all clustered nearby. Right onto Main Drive and then another right turn, across a crammed-tight line of oncoming cars, buses and lorries who might eventually and reluctantly let him through. Then it's back the four hundred yards along Centurion Road, the other side of the shops, to get back to Garrison just a few feet from where he was ten frustrating minutes before.

He turned into the spacious car park at the back of Haleston Town Hall, waving briefly to Bruce, the parking attendant. Best to keep on the good side of Bruce, who was as fierce and protective as a rottweiler when it came to unauthorised parking. If he caught someone slipping in to leave their car so they could nip back up the road to do a spot of shopping at the Centurion, the resultant bloodbath was not a pretty sight. And if he didn't catch them in time he'd clamp their car and rip the buggers apart when they came back. Marriage parties attending a wedding in the Town Hall's magnificent Victoria Suite were allowed to use the car park, but if they didn't arrive in a stretch limousine or a ribbon-bedecked Rolls Royce they had a struggle to get past Bruce. But Bruce recognised Maxey's Mondeo and waved him through, touching a respectful finger to the brim of his cap. You see, keep on his good side and you were fine.

The vast building loomed high above Maxey as he parked as close as he could to the back entrance. This rear aspect was less splendid than the pillar festooned frontage, as it had been rebuilt with less glamorous materials than the shining golden sandstone of the original construction, and a large, ugly redbrick annexe added, after sustaining damage during air raids in World War II. First built in the mid-1850s and opened by Prince Albert (without his wife Queen Victoria, a major disappointment to the local dignitaries of the day) the Hall was Haleston's admittedly less-ambitious response to the spate of grandiose municipal buildings appearing in towns nearby, such as Bradford's St George's Hall and the magnificent Town Hall appearing simultaneously in Leeds. The gleaming façade had been restored in the mid-1980s, behind a mask of scaffolding and tarpaulin that remained in place for months, removing 130 years' worth of caked-on grime. The mask came down amid cheers from visitors and townsfolk alike and was celebrated with an all-night street party that closed Roman Way.

Impressive though the Hall may be, it made little impression on Maxey this morning. Reluctantly he slipped off his sunglasses and dropped them into the glove box. He climbed out of his car and opened the back door, taking the jacket of his black pinstriped suit from the hanger just inside. As he buttoned up and patted down, nipping the knot of his tie tight and smoothing the Paisley-patterned lilac silk into place, he remembered with a smile his wife's staggered return from her run, just as he was readying to leave for work. Limited for time she always put more effort into these short runs, to gain full benefit from the exertion. Out the back door into the woods at the end of the lane, haring along the well-worn path like the hounds of hell were on her heels, then out onto the main road and back on the pavement to the front door. About a couple of miles, quarter of an hour at most, but she certainly gave herself a workout. She almost fell in through the door, face red and glistening, T-shirt and jogging bottoms plastered to her skin. She grinned mischievously at the sight of him standing in front of the mirror, sharp and immaculate, flattening an errant hair with a dampened fingertip. She lumbered towards him, blood pumping, lungs heaving and pores pouring.

'I love to see you all dressed up in your smart suit,' she gasped, reaching clammy arms out to him. 'Dead sexy! Come on, give us a cuddle.'

'Keep your sweaty body away from me, lusty wench!' Maxey warned, making the sign of a cross with both forefingers to ward her off.

They'd both laughed and then she had kissed him, gentle as a butterfly, damp arms held well clear behind her back, before clambering up the stairs for her shower.

Now, he checked the car was locked, took one last appraising look at his reflection in the driver's door window, then turned and entered the building using the staff entrance. He made his way up to the second floor via the back stairs, coming upon the rooms allocated to the registrar's department from the rear, avoiding the public area altogether. Off the stairwell, along a short corridor, was the private door to the staff common room, a small but cosy meeting area with comfortable chairs and a teakettle. From here other doors led to the registrar's offices, general office and the reception area. On the floor below, ideally situated at the head of the grand staircase leading up from the Town Hall's large foyer, was the Victoria Suite, three large, elegant, wood-panelled chambers – conference and function rooms most of the time, but also used for Register Office marriages. The central chamber, the largest and most elegant of all, was known affectionately as Big Vicky, and could be used when the guest list reached a hundred or more. Couples would have to pay more if they wished to take advantage of Big Vicky, because it had been classified as Approved Premises for the purposes of marriage. But at least that meant it was available for Saturday afternoons or even Sundays, which suited quite a number of prospective brides and grooms, not to mention the Registrars and Town Hall attendants and security staff who could apply for the overtime.

The staff room was unoccupied as Maxey entered, but the kettle was rumbling away to itself in the corner, sighing out a small cloud of steam. As he crossed to switch it off the connecting door to Reception opened and Rosalyn Peters entered.

'Morning, Roz,' Maxey smiled a greeting.

'Hi,' she responded with a flash of her own wide, open-faced smile. Did her gaze hold his for a second or two longer than was absolutely necessary, Maxey wondered, not for the first time. She stood a few tiny inches short of six feet tall, with wild brown hair tumbling to her shoulders and impressive curves at front and rear that could drag any man's mind away from whatever concerned him. Those curves were perhaps a little *too* impressive for Maxey's taste, he told himself unconvincingly, tearing his eyes away from Roz's thrusting chest and meeting that steadfast gaze again. He thought of Nicola's more subtle contours, disappearing into the comfort of her tired old robe a little more than an hour ago, and forced his eyes to consider the stack of chipped, stained tea mugs piled before him, and his mind to consider the promises he had made to his adored wife all those years ago. Their life and marriage had been happy on the strength of those promises and he was not about to risk all that, but the churning of emotions that this girl stirred within him was flattering, exciting and very, very scary.

As she stood by him, preparing two mugs, Maxey found himself straightening his back and stretching his neck, an unconscious and instinctive reaction. In her flat shoes he could barely edge his forehead above hers. In the fashionably large, clunky heels she chose to wear today her big, green eyes twinkled downwards into his as she breathed a query at him.

'Sorry?' he asked, blinking away the hypnotic effect of her gaze.

'Tea or coffee?' she repeated with some amusement evident in her voice.

He edged away from her, taking up position in one of the old, worn armchairs. 'Coffee, thanks.' He slumped back wearily, the previous evening's excesses catching him unawares once more. 'Black,' he added with a groan.

'Hard night, was it?' she asked, laughing at his slow, careful nod.

She made the drinks and brought them across, her long, loose skirt brushing against his legs as she passed. She sat in the chair by his and sighed deeply, sinking back into the welcoming upholstery. Her bright and shapely fingernails picked at a small hole in the chair's arm, plucking out tiny chunks of foam and then pushing them back in again. He guessed what was making her anxious and felt a little relief, the evidence of her lack of perfection loosening her hold on him.

'How long has it been?' he asked.

'Without a fag?' she guessed his meaning. 'About twenty minutes,' she admitted grimly, then grinned. 'I will give up, one day. But I enjoy it so much.' She closed her eyes and rested her head against the chair back. 'Could be worse,' she said mischievously, 'I could be an alcoholic.'

Whatever expletives Maxey might have offered in response were lost as Cynthia Jones bustled in from Reception, an upright Hoover, its cord wound tightly away, dragging along in her wake and a large, yellow duster exploding from the small pocket of her tunic.

'Just finished,' Cynth told them, snaking her plump form between their chairs on her way to the opposite door. 'I was a bit late this morning but I think I've done everything. People *will* keep on touching that reception window, don't they? There's fingerprints and greasy-forehead marks and splashes of spit and summat that looks like orange juice – some orangey liquid, anyway, I hope it's orange juice – all over it. It's a good job that glass is there 'cause it'd be all over you otherwise, wouldn't it love? And that ink still won't come out of Angela's carpet, no matter what I use on it. And I haven't dusted Eric's desk 'cause there's papers spread all over it – he didn't tidy up last night *again* – so I've left it, tell 'im. Oh, and there was summat on your floor,' this to Maxey. 'Customer's side, by the chair. I didn't know whether to throw it away or what to do with it, so I've put it on your desk and you can sort it out for yourself, 'cause it's nowt to do wi' me anyway. Anyway I can't stop to talk 'cause I've still got upstairs to do and I'm running behind 'cause I was late this morning, so I'll see you tomorrow, okay?'

The door clicked shut behind her and the trundling of the Hoover's wheels on the corridor floor slowly faded into the distance. Maxey and Roz looked at one another and laughed, Roz pretending to gasp desperately, as if short of breath. Maxey's eyes were drawn to where Roz's hand clutched at her heaving chest and he stood suddenly.

'Something on my desk, eh? Intriguing!' He crossed quickly to his door and slipped inside, re-emerging almost immediately with a strip of worn, brown leather dangling from his fingers, a small, silvery disk jingling against a buckle at the end.

'Bondage gear, is it?' Roz asked, one eyebrow raised. 'It doesn't go with the suit.'

'Dog collar.' Maxey said, examining the tag. 'That old bloke must've dropped it yesterday.'

'Oh, him?' Roz laughed. 'We've decided to award him "Nutter of the Week".'

'You've a cruel streak in you, Roz Peters,' Maxey mock-chided. 'He was just a harmless old—'

'Nutter?' Roz interjected, rising to peer at the inscription on the nameplate.

'Nutter,' Maxey conceded, conscious of her nearness, her

57

breast resting against his arm as she leant in close.

'What are you going to do with it?' she asked. 'Bin it, or send it back to him?'

'I think he'd want it back. He was very fond of the ol' pooch.' He sighed. 'Seems a bit impersonal just sticking it in an envelope, though.' He glanced at the address on the tag again. 'It's only a short detour from my way home, I could drop it off.'

'What, into the lair of the nutter?' Roz teased. 'On your own? With the dark nights coming in?'

'Or I could make a special journey tomorrow, couldn't I?' he pondered aloud. 'The weather's supposed to be fine for the weekend, it'll make a nice trip out.'

'Coward.'

'I just don't want to be late home tonight, that's all,' Maxey said, with an exaggerated shrug. 'Nicky's expecting me.'

'Yeah, right.'

'Well, you know the old saying: "Always put off till tomorrow what you don't fancy doing today".'

Roz laughed, then said, casually as can be: 'How is she, by the way?'

'Sorry?' Maxey frowned, puzzled by the tangential shift of the conversation. 'How's who?'

'Your wife,' she said slowly, as if to a child.

'Oh, she's fine,' Maxey said, and the image of Nicola's slender frame being swallowed up by the voluminous folds of her cosy robe flashed back to him again, bringing a warm wave pulsing through his body and a stupid smile to his face. 'Yes, she's great.'

'Well, that's good,' said Roz. Her voice was light and pleasant, her smile warm and sincere, so Maxey must have imagined the slight edge in her tone and the cool spark in her eye as she slipped through the door into Reception.

Maxey dismissed it as his own foolishness, exacerbated by his still-throbbing head, and felt this viewpoint vindicated when, within ten minutes, Roz was her usual cheerful, cheeky self as she buzzed through to him on his office phone.

'Hiya, Eddie-babe. Can you take this marriage enquiry on line three for me?'

''Course I can, Sweetheart,' Maxey said. Flirting seemed so much less dangerous over the phone.

'Ta, Petal.' She broke the connection and Maxey pressed the button to accept line three.

'Hello,' he greeted the caller. 'Can I help you?'

'I hope so,' came a wary female voice. 'I'm calling to find out what you need. You know, to get married.'

'Well, the first thing you'll need is a partner,' Maxey quipped. That black coffee seemed to have done the trick where his headache was concerned, and now he found himself in an unashamedly good mood. He had a beautiful wife, whom he loved and who loved him; a job which he found consistently engaging and interesting; and, even if she was only winding him up, an Amazonian goddess flirting with him on a daily basis. Life was grand!

'That might be a bit of a problem,' the woman went on.

'You'll have to bring your own, we don't supply them here,' Maxey told her. 'Most people arrange the partner before they arrange the marriage.'

'Aye, well. There's always summat to knock you back, isn't there?' She offered this pearl of wisdom with an ironic chuckle. 'No, it's just that he's still married, y'see. He's getting a divorce but it'll be a while before it comes through. I was wondering how soon we could make the arrangements for us to get married after he was finished with her.'

'Not until after the divorce is made absolute, I'm afraid. You have to be able to state truthfully that there are no legal impediments when you give your notice of intention to marry, and you can't do that until the proceedings are completed.'

'Oh, right.' She seemed to ponder this for a moment. 'Is that the same for me?'

'How do you mean?'

'Do I have to be divorced as well? I only want to book a date.'

Maxey smiled to himself, taking a deep breath. 'Er, yes madam, you do.'

'How long will that take?'

'I really can't answer that, madam,' Maxey said, straining to keep all trace of superciliousness from his voice. 'Hasn't your solicitor given you an idea of how long things might take?'

'Oh, I haven't seen one yet,' she said casually, oblivious of any inanity in her words.

Maxey stifled a laugh, disguising it with a throaty cough. Not in the office half an hour yet and already they've started. This woman certainly wouldn't be the last to make an unusual query today nor, he imagined, was hers likely to be the most outrageous. All part of the challenge of the job, he told himself. He wasn't going to let it spoil his day.

6

After cramming the clothes into the washer, shoving the vacuum back into the cupboard under the stairs and piling the breakfast pots into the sink, Layna Hewett peeped around the living room door to see how Terry was doing. He sat curled up on the sofa, giggling at some animated tripe on the kiddies' channel, looking far brighter than he'd appeared first thing this morning.

'All right, love?' she asked.

Realising she was watching Terry became quickly more subdued, a hangdog expression drawing down his features comically. Layna suppressed a smile. The little bugger, pulling a fast one. Skiving off school already, and he'd only moved up out of nursery a few weeks before. She always thought he enjoyed going, but this was twice in a matter of days that dubious, spontaneous illnesses had required he stayed home. Both times when his daddy went in to work early, she noted ruefully, so muggins here had to make the decision – play the heavy and send him off to school anyway, or fall for the doe-eyes and the "oh Mummy, it hurts" routine. Ron wasn't as soft as she was, as Terry had obviously cottoned on to already. Ron would've had him out the door with a figurative boot up the backside if Terry tried it on with *him*.

But why *was* he trying it on? He'd never complained before this term, was some new influence bothering him? Did they have bullies at that age? She determined to keep an extra vigilant eye on him from now on.

She could really do without the hassle today. She'd already had to phone the school to make excuses for Shane, when Adrian had insisted on having his day with him. Why he wouldn't just miss a week, Layna couldn't imagine. It's not like they were exactly joined at the hip – he didn't even phone him up at any other time. But he did insist on having his day. The Courts said so, so it had to be. And if she and Ron wanted to take him away on a Saturday, Adrian was doing them a favour by having him on Friday instead. Yeah, *big* favour. A bigger favour would be if he got his body here so she could get Shane out of the way and get on. But she'd still have Terry to drag around with her. At least she'd managed to get some clothes on him, but she couldn't drop him at her sister's 'cause she'd got the builders in this week, and Carole down the road would have him but she always goes to her mother's on a Friday. There was still the shopping to do, not to mention picking up the Euros at the travel agent's. Euro-sodding-Disney. Disneyland Paris. Whatever they called the bloody place these days. All very well if they were going for a week, but to try and see it all in two days is gonna be a nightmare. Still, too late to worry about that now. Ron had blithely gone ahead and booked it as a surprise. To make up for the fact that they didn't go away in the main school holidays, Layna suspected. He'd been a complete misery all summer, and was barely any more amenable now. Probably work problems, but he never spoke about it. He'd taken it out on the boys once or twice, so this was him making amends, she guessed.

The rasping roar of guns and bombs, the agonised cries of men and monsters tumbled down the stairs to her from an upper room.

'Will you switch that computer off and get your coat on?' Layna called huffily. Only the sixth or seventh time of asking. 'Your dad will be here in a minute.'

'You said that half an hour ago,' came the whining response.

'Well then, it must be nearer the truth by now, eh?' Hah! That shut him up. Maternal logic wins again. Layna was back in the kitchen, pouring hot water onto the bowlful of pots, when the doorbell rang. About bleedin' time!

'Where have you been?' she snapped as she opened to

door to her former husband.

'I'm not late,' Adrian Lawson protested, face wide with innocence before rumpling into a wicked grin. 'Much.'

Layna concentrated on her anger, fuelling it with her fury at the fact that the bastard nearly had her smiling. How did he manage to worm through her defences every time? 'Shane!' she bawled up the stairs, with a little more vehemence than she intended. 'Get down here now!'

'Tough morning?' he guessed, voice laden with sympathy.

'Like you care,' she sneered, despising how pathetic she sounded, wishing she could just be calm and civil when he came around.

'I do care.' A warm, firm hand caressed her shoulder. 'A little thing like a divorce can't change that.'

'Sorry,' she conceded, but shrugged his hand away all the same. 'I've got tons to do and no time to do it in.'

Shane appeared meekly at the top of the stairs. 'Hi, Dad.'

'Sorry for shouting, love,' Layna said, giving him a hug as he squeezed past her in the narrow hallway. She never made enough allowance for his situation, she acknowledged grimly. Only eight years old and two such vastly opposing father-figures to contend with. 'What have you got planned for the day?' she asked of Lawson as he ruffled his son's hair.

'Kickabout in the park this morning, McDonald's for lunch, then go see that film he's been going on about,' said Lawson proudly, a fine schedule for a father-son day.

'Oh, lovely,' she said, but the momentary hesitance in her voice put him on guard.

'I did consider a quick game of chess, luncheon in town followed by a trip round the local art gallery,' he said, 'But then I thought, sod that for a lark.'

'I wasn't being funny,' she said, repentantly. Her twinge of resentment at the shallow pleasures so appreciated by the boy were not directed so much at the free and easy manner in which Lawson showered them upon him, so much as at the jealousy she felt because she never had the time to do so herself.

'I know.' The smile was back in place and the caressing hand was curled around her upper arm, stroking comfortingly. 'I can see you're hassled. If there's anything I can do to help, you only have to ask. You know that, don't you?'

'Thanks,' she nodded, allowing the platitudes to flow over her. Then a sudden thought occurred as he edged back through the door. 'Do you mean that?'

'Of course,' he beamed smoothly, turning back to her. 'Anything you want.'

'Take Terry with you,' she said quickly, rushing on with: 'He's off school, nothing really wrong with him, and even if there is then the fresh air'll do him good and you'd really, really be doing me a big kindness and I'll pay you back somehow, sometime, I promise.'

'Terry?' said Lawson, clearly taken aback. He hadn't been expecting that, judging by the way his jaw dropped. She'd never asked him to take charge of her baby before; he'd be able to smell her desperation.

'Well...' His eyes took on a familiar twinkle as he replied. He always liked to help a damsel in distress, she knew, but hoped her mention of paying him back didn't give him any ideas.

'Mu-um!' Shane griped, hanging his head limply. Layna's face crumpled at the sight of her elder son's frustration. She didn't want to spoil the little time he could share with his father. She almost withdrew her request before Lawson interrupted.

'It'll be okay, son. We'll still have lots of fun,' he said with a smirk. 'He can be the football.'

Shane laughed and ran out to Lawson's waiting car. Layna smiled gratefully and lifted Terry's coat down from the pegs by the door.

Alicia had spent the last couple of hours in the park at the end of the road, hunched forward on a wooden bench, nursing her stomach and praying to the Virgin Mary for forgiveness and salvation. She didn't want to see Adrian until the pain had fully receded. She didn't want to have to explain to him the nature of her incapacity. Not until she had the chance to talk to him, see his reaction to her presence, gauge how he might feel about her news. The morning had grown bright and the sun tried its best to warm her. She saw it as an omen.

The many times she had played out the scene in her mind, during her long, exhausting journey, he always swept her up in his strong, warm arms, crushing her to his chest, his tears of delight dripping freely into her hair. But still shreds of doubt pierced her flesh with icy needles. Her empty stomach fought to heave and heavy feet dragged as she retraced her steps to her lover's door.

The gate groaned a complaint as she passed through, then startled her as it crashed back against its latch. The path was short but she felt she would never reach the end of it, to press the small plastic button in the jamb of the door, to face her destiny. Everything seemed to be happening in such interminable slow motion. A brief ding-dong echoed through the house, jarring with the thud-thud of the pulse pounding in her ears. A shadowy figure stirred beyond the patterned glass panel. The door handle rattled slightly as it twisted gradually downwards. The door swung away from her, darkened by the shadows of the house's interior. The man stepped forwards, into the daylight. Alicia, her face beaming, her body awash with renewed vitality, reached willing arms out to greet her lover, her man, the father of her unborn child and… oh!

Alicia stared in bewilderment at the stranger, his puzzlement reflecting back at her. She stepped back, embarrassed at the informality she had shown in the presence of a man unknown to her. She stammered an apology and scrabbled out the scrap of paper from her pocket, showing him the address. 'I'm looking for this house,' she said. 'For the man who lives there.'

'That's this house,' said the man carefully. 'I'm the only bloke who lives here.'

'There is a mistake, I think,' Alicia moaned, panic creeping through her on frozen feet.

'Sorry,' he shrugged. 'These things happen, y'know.' He made to move back into the concealment of the house, a hand already on the edge of the door, pulling it back into place.

'But wait!' she called. 'How am I to find my man?'

'I dunno,' he grunted dismissively. 'Put an ad in the paper?'

'I do not understand your words.' Her voice was taking on an edge of hysteria. 'I am from Cádiz.'

'I know—' he began, then his voice trailed away to an awkward splutter.

'What? How could you know?'

'Er, I just meant... that I could tell you were Spanish... from your accent.' The man's face had reddened and he glanced about shiftily, avoiding her gaze. 'Why don't you go on home, eh? There's nothing for you here.'

'Adrian Lawson,' she rattled the syllables at him like the chatter of a snare drum. 'I need to see him. He gave me this address.'

'That's not me,' he protested, snatching up a utility bill from the small table by the door and showing her the printing through the envelope's tiny window. 'See? "Mr J Rafferty." Same address. No Lawson. You've got it all wrong.' His voice suddenly softened dramatically. 'You really should go home, love. It's for the best, I promise you.'

'I cannot,' she insisted. 'I need to find him.' Fatigue, hunger and anxiety all crowded in on her, adding to the despair of her situation. All this way, all this time, for nothing? Tears streaked the days-old grime on her cheeks.

'Please help me.'

'Look, I...' His face crumpled with tortured indecision. He seemed on the verge of a revelation, mouth open to speak, hands gesturing ineffectually. Then his lips clamped shut and he turned away. 'I'm sorry,' he murmured guiltily as the door swung to, hiding him. 'I wish I could.'

Alicia screamed her anguish and hammered her fists on the door until it was snatched open again and Rafferty stood there, face now hard and cold and frightening. 'I said, go away!'

Startled by his change in demeanour Alicia turned and fled down the path, stumbling into a woman who had stopped by the gate, knocking a bottle of milk from the woman's hand. '*Lo siento!*' she spluttered hesitantly, looking from her to Rafferty to the spreading pool of milk seeping into the soles of her espadrilles. The shoes slapped wetly against the pavement as she ran from the place she had struggled so valiantly and for so long to find.

*

This time of year brought a kind of sadness to Adrian Lawson. Nothing too depressing, more a sense of heavy disappointment, but he never was one to feel things on too deep a level. It was seeing all the coats that did it. On the women. Especially the young, pretty women. Trench coats, jackets, anoraks; leather, wool, nylon, denim. It didn't matter, it was their mere presence that caused the mood. Because it meant the "fleshtime" was over – the warm summer days when outer garments were discarded and bare arms, legs and midriff were ever-present in the park, on the streets, everywhere you looked. What a shame, to have all those tight, lithe bodies hidden away for months on end until the sun deigned to show its face again. A young mum in the periphery of his vision bending to lift her toddler from a swing, stretch denim tight over buttocks and thighs, mollified him a little.

Lawson sat sprawled on a park bench, his carefree appearance markedly different to that of Alicia on another park bench in another park a short time earlier. His extended legs, crossed casually at the ankles, pointed towards the area where the two boys played, kicking their football to one another, laughing and shouting and running around with all the energy that can only be found in the very young. He squinted at them under heavy eyelids, half watching their antics while in the other half of his mind his thoughts tumbled haphazardly.

Women's clothing, or rather lack of, along with memories of summer, led to bikinis, to beaches, to Spain. To Alicia. So many trains of thought seemed to lead to Alicia these days. Her image danced before him constantly, relentlessly, allowing no respite. Dark, dazzling eyes; flowing hair; olive skin. Why this one, out of so many? He could no longer deny that it meant more to him than previous encounters, usually so easily forgotten.

The squeals of the boys penetrated his ruminations as Shane chased his brother across the grass. Children, so young. Alicia, so young. Too young? What's thirteen years, these days? Age is just a number. Maturity is what counts; attitude; how you act, think, feel.

Was all this merely a symptom of dissatisfaction with his lot? Donna was on at him more and more these days. He always thought he loved her. Felt sure he did. But now she was becoming tiresome with her fretting and questioning. She never used to bother him, even though he knew she suspected far more than she confronted him with. So was his love no more than the appreciation of her easy-going nature, her letting him get away with more than anyone else ever had? And now she was no longer doing that, was his love dwindling?

Love was supposed to mean one man and one woman, each other and no one else. That's what all the books and magazines said. But that was just so much crap. He was full of love, brimming over with the stuff. Plenty to share with all of them. Donna; passionate but submissive, there for him all the time, day or night. Layna; thoughtful, gentle of nature but so flustered when he saw her this morning, tempting him with promises of paying him back for his favour *somehow*. Alicia; so fresh and sweet and needy. All the others, past and present.

Would she do it? Alicia? Would she do what she threatened? Come here looking for him? She would try the address she had, the one she thought was his. He should warn Jeff, let him know what to expect. He'd been a great friend throughout this business, Jeff had, even if he could be a total arsehole about other things.

The football came from nowhere, striking him on the thigh, stinging like hell. He was startled from his reverie.

'What the f—' He caught himself just in time, remembering who he was with. The boys. Just kids. Just playing. He turned to look at them, saw Shane laughing and pointing at his younger brother.

Then he saw Terry. Tiny thing, petrified, wide eyed, frozen with fear. A damp patch slowly growing on the front of his jeans; tears already washing his cheeks. Stunned at this reaction Lawson rose and started towards him. Terry suddenly dropped to the ground, curling up tight, arms around his head. 'I'm sorry, I'm sorry,' he sobbed.

'It's all right,' Lawson promised, scooping the boy up in his arms, ignoring the urine stains, cuddling him close. 'I'm not angry, it's okay, shush now.'

Shane held on to Terry's hand as Lawson carried him back to the car, warm tears and hot piss wetting his shirt. He was a quiet lad but he'd seemed so happy up to that point. As their morning had progressed he had felt his aversion to the boy, simply because he wasn't his own, diminishing with every catch of the ball, every playground joke shyly recounted. He'd even entertained thoughts of acquiescing to Donna's hints about adding to the family. Briefly. Eventually he'd grudgingly had to admit that he'd come to quite like the kid.

Which only made seeing him in this state even worse. He felt gutted that a fraction of a second's flare of temper had caused such disproportionate distress. Getting Terry home was the priority now. He needed his mum. Oh dear, Layna. She wasn't going to like this. With a twinge of guilt and shame the notion went through his head that that "repayment" shag was probably now, well and truly, out of the question.

7

'You're a lying bastard, that's what I'm saying!' she hissed, face so close to his that he could feel the spittle strike his skin.

'I swear, I've never seen the girl before in my life,' Rafferty insisted, wiping his cheek with the back of his hand.

'So why would a complete stranger run away from you in floods of tears, eh? Answer me that!'

''Cause I told her we didn't want whatever she was selling, and to bugger off before I set the cops on her,' he asserted, his own indignation blazing to match his wife's. Why should he have to put up with all this? None of it was his fault. That bloody Lawson! Rafferty told him it would all blow up like this, one of these days.

'Yeah, right. And what was she supposed to be selling? She didn't even have a handbag. You must think I was born yesterday.'

'Well, what else then?'

'What else is she's your bit of stuff on the side, that's what else,' Julie Rafferty sneered, swiping a hand across the back of his head to emphasise the remark.

'Leave it out, you dozy bitch,' Rafferty laughed, though the sound was bitter and without humour. 'And you can keep your hands to yourself or I'll have to clock you one right back.'

'Oh yeah? When you're fuckin' big enough, hard man!' Julie shouted viciously, landing punches on his bicep and shoulder. 'She's some tart you've been screwin' who came round without telling you first, and you told her to piss off 'cause you knew I'd be home soon with the milk. You've been at it behind my back and now I've caught you out.'

Rafferty pushed her away with a firm hand at the pit of

her throat. Undeterred, she returned with a hard kick to his shins.

'Oh, for fuck's sake!' he snarled, rubbing his leg and collapsing back onto the sofa. 'I've told you, she's nothing to do with me, you stupid cow!'

Julie Rafferty stopped short at the unexpected inference in her husband's words. 'Oh? So who is she to do with?'

'Eh? What you on about, woman?'

Her voice was icy as she leaned over him. 'If she's nothing to do with you, then who is she to do with?'

'Nobody. Nothing. I don't know what you're talking about.' Rafferty was squirming beneath her gaze. He felt it and she saw it.

'Yes you do, and you're not getting off the hook until you've told me everything.'

'Why don't you just leave it, woman?' Rafferty snapped, lurching up from his seat and limping towards the kitchen.

She was after him in a flash, slapping at his back and shoulders. 'I won't leave it! Who is she? Come on, you bastard, tell me!'

'I've told you, it's not your problem,' he said.

'So you admit it's somebody's problem?'

'Stop trying to be clever.' He slammed the kitchen door between them. It shook in its frame with the impact of her kick. 'And you can fix the sodding door yourself if you put your foot through it.'

She followed him into the room, strode across to him where he stood by the sink. She took a breath, her voice a few decibels softer now, cajoling. 'If it doesn't affect me then why don't you just tell me who she is?'

'Because I promised... Oh shit!' He realised as the words escaped that he'd said too much.

'You promised? Who'd you promise? There's only one person you'd lie for like this,' Julie surmised. 'Adrian fucking Lawson! That bastard!'

'I thought you liked Adie,' Rafferty protested. 'Anyway, it's Donna's problem, not yours, so you can relax.'

'Relax? Knowing what that sod is doing?' Julie strutted round the kitchen, hands hovering near the heavy saucepans, then the knife rack. 'He wants his dick chopping off!'

'You said only the other week that Donna deserves all she gets, hitching herself up to someone like Adie,' he reasoned, puzzled by her continued anxiety.

'Yeah, well it's different when I know for a fact – when I've seen the slag with my own eyes.' The door crashed again as she stormed from the room. Her voice returned faintly from the other side. 'I'm going for some more milk.'

It was his turn to follow through a slammed door. He came upon his wife replacing the coat she had tossed aside moments ago, when she'd returned from her earlier trip to the shops.

'Where's my phone?' she asked, patting her coat pockets, retrieving her mobile.

'What do you need a phone for to buy a pint of bloody milk?' Rafferty snapped. 'What do you want to go sticking your oar in for? It's not our business. Let Adie and Donna sort themselves out.'

'How can she sort anything if she doesn't know what he's up to?'

'Why do you care? You've never been bothered about her feelings before.'

'Maybe it's time for us girls to stick together,' Julie said, turning away from him.

With that the front door slammed and Jeff Rafferty was left alone in the house. Alone but for his swirling thoughts.

*

The young woman opposite Edward Maxey looked weary to the bone. Her eyes were puffy and red, and darted about nervously as she slumped in one of the chairs at the other side of his desk. Her hair was dishevelled and her clothes rumpled and creased. When she first presented herself at reception Maxey thought her appearance was deliberate, after all, the just-fallen-out-of-bed look was *en vogue* at the moment, but Roz's concerned tone alerted him to her true condition. Closer inspection revealed the anxiety distressing her, the despair weighing her down. Roz's questions had flustered her, their attempts at understanding frustrated by the distractions of the busy reception, so Maxey offered to see her in the quiet privacy of his office. The piercing look with which Roz impaled him, as he led the troubled girl past the reception window, puzzled Maxey. What on Earth had he done now? She couldn't be thinking it inappropriate for him to be alone with a young woman; after all, it was a regular part of the job – new mothers registering births, brides-to-be inquiring about marriage procedures. Maybe she was mistrustful of his tact and gentleness, believing he might upset a vulnerable and frightened girl? Whatever it was would have to wait for another time, he had thought, closing the door on Roz's quizzical stare.

The main Town Hall receptionist in the foyer downstairs had sent up the frightened young foreigner, after she had initially called there, asking for Cynth the cleaner, and claiming to be a friend of hers. Cynth had finished work quite a while earlier and it was against policy to give out employees' addresses, so the receptionist expressed her deep regret that she couldn't help her. Such platitudes meant nothing to the visitor whose state of agitation became worse as her options evaporated around her. As her apprehension grew, so her command of the foreign language she relied on for communication diminished. The receptionist caught snippets that suggested that the unhappy girl had plans to marry and had lost the prospective groom. Latching onto this, and bearing in mind the Council's policy to pass all enquiries on to the relevant department as swiftly as possible to avoid cluttering up the Town Hall's elegant foyer, directions to the Registrar's offices were offered and the girl sent on her way.

Alicia, for such Maxey had managed to educe was the

girl's name, gradually calmed in the placid atmosphere of his office, as Maxey sat back and allowed her the time and space to relax. Slowly, piecemeal, she imparted to him the story of her harrowing journey from the peaceful village of her home to arriving here, both physically and emotionally battered and abused. He held his tongue as she spoke, knowing any strong expression of sympathy from him might crumble what little strength she had managed to scrape together as she related her experiences.

'So,' he said at last. 'What do you want from us here?' He fought hard to keep the sense of helplessness he felt so deeply from revealing itself through his voice. The register office held no current records of names or addresses, and had no way of discovering them. Other departments may be more successful, but he was disinclined to turn her away, considering her fragile state.

'The lady downstairs seemed to think you may have knowledge of where is my man,' Alicia said.

A tiny spark of hope rekindled in her eyes and Maxey dreaded throwing a damp blanket over that spark, extinguishing it forever. 'The electoral registration department is on the fourth floor,' he ventured, 'though I'm not sure how much help even they could be with just a name to go on.'

The spark flickered dangerously. 'Please don't send me away again. Is there no way you can help me?'

Maxey swallowed down the tightness constricting his throat. 'Tell you what,' he began, turning to his computer screen, 'Lawson's not an uncommon name, so let's see what we have on here. Who knows, we may pick something up...?'

'What is that you are looking at?' she asked.

Maxey frowned, puzzled. 'It's a computer,' he informed her, his ignorance of the state of foreign civilisation glaringly obvious.

Alicia laughed, and to Maxey the brightening of her features was like the sun breaking through after heavy rain.

'I know it is a computer,' she said. 'I meant what is the program you are looking at?'

Maxey felt the heat in his face and knew he must be shining his embarrassment around the room. But it was worth it to see her so cheered by his momentary foolishness. He smiled back at her, broad and toothy, and was startled to see her avert her gaze coyly, her skin flushing redder than his own. He cleared his throat and turned back to the screen.

'Erm, it's the births, deaths and marriage indexes. I thought that if we found some trace of him in here there may be an address, or something... I'll try marriages first.' His fingers busied themselves on the keyboard.

'You will not find him in there,' Alicia said. 'He told me he has never been married.'

'Well, no harm in trying,' Maxey replied, careful to keep the occupational cynicism from his voice. A guy in his thirties, good looking to hear Alicia talk, charming young women into bed while he's hundreds of miles from home, and not married? Yeah, right!

'Nothing in the last three years,' he said, scanning the results scrolling up his monitor screen. 'You're sure Adrian is his first name?'

'Yes, I saw his passport.'

'I'll try another few years, round it up to ten,' Maxey said, his face a grimacing mask of assurance. 'It'll only take a few seconds.' He input another request and soon more information appeared before him. Though the surname specified was not uncommon, in conjunction with the forename it threw up very few results. But not no results at all. 'Here we go,' he announced. 'We've got *two* matches.' Seeing the look appear on Alicia's face he attempted to temper the triumph in his tone. 'Of course, it's probably just a coincidence,' he murmured.

Because of the sheer volume of paperwork created at Haleston Town Hall it had long been the policy of the building to store all important legal documents in the capacious storm/earthquake/nuclear war-proof cellars, employing a team of staff with the monotonous task of copying everything held there to microfiche. With the advent of computerisation all new records were scanned and the older records had been transposed into a format recognised by PCs, with the result that within seconds Maxey was looking at a digital facsimile of one of the marriage entries called up by his recent search.

'Hmm, the age fits,' he said. He had been in his job too long to completely scorn the possibility of coincidence, even if his instincts suggested otherwise, so he scoured the information on his screen carefully for evidence of one thing or the other. A detail caught his attention. 'What did you say they called the man at the address you were given?'

Alicia scrunched up her face in an expression of concentration, which Maxey found endearing. 'Rafferty, I believe. Why?'

'Here, look.' Maxey turned the monitor to enable Alicia to see the screen. He tapped a finger against a pair of signatures towards the bottom of the image. 'The witnesses to the marriage, their handwriting's a bit scratchy, but does that look like "Rafferty" to you?'

Alicia's mouth sagged. 'What does this mean?'

'I think it means we've found your man.'

Maxey realised that Alicia was scrutinising the details of the marriage certificate intently, probably memorising the address at which Lawson and his fiancée were both living at the time of their marriage on the chance that they might still be living there now. Technically he should not allow her this liberty – the records were not freely accessible to the public, without the payment of the requisite fee – but he discovered he was not inclined to add to the frustrations she had faced already today.

Eventually he eased the monitor away from her, before swishing the mouse cursor across the screen and patting a few more keys. 'Now we've got a wife's name as well we can have a snoop in the birth records.'

Maxey was aware that Alicia had become very silent in the last few moments. For all the success of their investigations he knew Alicia was not hearing what she wanted to hear. When a couple of birth entries were added to the two marriages the feelings of anger and humiliation must have been immense. To travel all this way, abandon her former life, her family, to be with the man she had fallen in love with, had given herself to, bringing him the supposedly joyous news of his unborn child... only to face the fact that all he had told her, all she had believed, was lies. Maxey couldn't begin to imagine the extent to which all this must affect a good catholic girl from a restrictive background. Running away, losing everything, with nothing to look forward to.

'I wouldn't normally do this,' he said a short time later as she prepared to leave, 'but take this...' He found a compliment slip in his desk drawer and wrote his personal mobile phone number on it. 'If you need... Well, if there's anything I can do...' He shrugged helplessly. She smiled, a brave, proud gesture that clawed at his paternal instincts and he fought to stop his arms from scooping her up in a protective embrace.

He unrolled a twenty pound note from his pocket and slid it across the desk. 'At least let me give you this. It's not much. For bus fares. Get a sandwich. That sort of thing.'

She stared at the note for a long moment, horror and disgust playing across her pretty features, before snatching it up and cramming it into her pocket, glancing warily over her shoulder in case the saints were watching.

As he led her past reception to the main hallway he couldn't resist a brief squeeze of her shoulder before she walked away. She nodded, as if acknowledging an unspoken word of encouragement, then strode off, head held high.

Where to? Maxey wondered. Knowing this Lawson bloke had a wife and kids, would she still want to see him? Maybe she'd try to win him over, or confront him with what he'd done to her? Or would she go home and face the music, and her father? Perhaps she'd end up homeless and penniless, walking the streets...

Maxey swallowed hard, once again easing the dryness that had reclaimed his throat. He turned and was stopped in his tracks by the intent stare piercing the glass screen between himself and the pretty, young receptionist. He frowned, mouthed the question: 'What's up?'

Roz shrugged and returned to her work.

8

Herbert Osgood was becoming troubled. It was not that he felt any measure of concern regarding the welfare of his neighbours, more the fact that he liked things to follow a regular routine, and what he saw tonight did not fit in with what he expected to see.

Following a sunny morning, heavy clouds had gathered mid-afternoon, which, with the gloom creeping in so much earlier as autumn drifted towards winter, brought dusk descending abruptly upon Merrington village. That did not deter Herbert from claiming his regular seat in the comfy chair in the bay window. From here he could alternate his view from the large television screen, constantly on in the opposite corner, to the comings and goings on the street beyond the voiles hanging at the panes arced around him. A quite insubstantial barrier when it came to keeping the outside at bay, but all the more convenient for keeping an eye on events transpiring beyond. He held a cup of coffee in one hand, the other poised to part the lengths of flimsy material at the least sign of anything interesting occurring.

The television provided a lifeline to the world, however ephemeral or illusory that link may be. He watched the news programmes of course, just to keep things in perspective, but he loved his soaps and, more and more, the spate of "reality" shows that flooded the screen these days. Contrived situations designed to allow one to spy on the lives of others. Without the embarrassment of someone noticing the curtains twitching.

But still, he couldn't resist the lure of the lace – not an underwear fetish, but the temptation to peek through drapes of netting at the thinly veiled world outside. And it was something within this orderly world of neatly groomed gardens and litter-free pavements that caused Herbert's consternation this evening. An open door, no more than that. But a door that had no business being open. Not at this time of night. Not that door.

Now, the Powells at number 87, they often left the front door standing open, at all hours of the day, to give their horrible, shaggy mongrel free rein to come and go as it pleased. But not the Lawsons. Even in the height of summer they kept their front shut up tight, using the back garden for sunbathing and barbeques, and so on. The back was more enclosed, and angled such that Herbert couldn't see into it, unfortunately.

The door had been open for some time, and Herbert felt peeved that he hadn't noticed it *being* opened, or who had left it open, or why. He fidgeted with his cushions and played with the remote, unable to concentrate on the telly, his mind constantly returning to the open door opposite. It wasn't his business, he knew that, and if he were to go across there and enquire as to the reason for the open door, no doubt the occupants would be more than happy to *remind* him that it wasn't his business.

But it was niggling at him; he couldn't just ignore it. He'd been perched on the edge of his seat for long moments before he even realised he had moved forward from the sagging cushions that still bore the shape of his back. He paced to the door, then, yielding to his doubts, returned to the window, hesitantly back and forth, again and again, finally making it out to the street after the fourth effort. Decision made, he was quickly across the road and up the short, paved pathway dissecting the arc of immaculate lawn surrounding the Lawsons' house. At the door he stopped dead, hand outstretched, wavering between ringing the bell and pulling the door shut and running home, hoping he wouldn't be seen.

But that would just be silly. The act of a neurotic, compulsive personality. What would his wife – sorry, *ex*-wife – make of that? She'd found enough ammunition to fire at him when they were still together, complaining of his finicky nature, his fastidious ways. But what did she expect? *She* was the one who left the top off the toothpaste, and stored knives and forks in the kitchen drawer *in opposite directions!* And when he told her about it she either laughed outright, or got upset and called him irrational. Irrational? *Him?* They had four hooks by their front door, and four sets of keys to hang on them, so what was the point of putting two sets on one hook and leaving another hook bare? Rationalise that!

Breath racing, blood gushing round his system till his brain swirled in a dizzy vortex, Herbert leaned against the door jamb until his metabolism settled to somewhere near normal. How could she still wind him up like this, after all this time? It dawned on him that he must have been standing at the door for some time, and if anyone should be watching him from behind their curtains – *how dare they?!* – they would surely be wondering at his motivation. He slipped quickly into the gloom of the unlit hallway.

More than the hallway was swamped in gloom, Herbert realised. There appeared to be no lights on in the entire house. Not a problem in itself, if someone had been sitting watching their telly and not noticed the twilight settling in, but there was no sound of early evening programming rumbling out from any of the surrounding rooms. Should be the local news magazines at this time, or some imported American rubbish. But nothing, just total silence.

He shouldn't be in here, Herbert thought, glancing back over his shoulder at the door (*still open!*). What if the Lawsons were to return now, with him snooping around? He'd taken a couple of steps back down the hall before, with a deep, steadying breath, he regained a fragile grasp on his resolve. He was here now; just have a peep and get it over with. If there was no one about, nip off and pull the door behind him – this was a good neighbourhood, but you never knew when opportunists might be passing. Yes, that was a fair story; he almost convinced himself that his actions were altruistic. So if he met someone, just apologise and explain his concerns; they'd surely be grateful...?

The first internal door, just a few feet in on the right, opened into the dining area, as was evidenced by the large oval table dominating the room. The table was bare, its polished mahogany surface catching what little light still managed to creep in through the open curtains. Herbert knew Lawson was self-employed, working late on a regular basis; with no kids to worry about, he and his wife could have their tea whenever they liked. And maybe they preferred a tray in front of the telly (but that still didn't explain why it was all so quiet).

A few steps farther along the corridor, just before the point where the gaudily-carpeted stairs ascended into darkness, another door, this time on the left, led into what must be the living room. Or lounge, as Herbert preferred. That was it! *She'd* be in there, of course, *lounging.* Spark out on the sofa. His wife, that Donna. Pretty little thing; never spared Herbert a second glance though, snotty cow! She'd have come home, exhausted after a long day of doing bugger all, and needed a few moments' repose to recharge her batteries. So she'd kicked off her shoes and flaked out without a care, leaving the front door standing wide as an invitation to the whole bloody world! Dozy mare deserved to be burgled. Maybe he should pick up a couple of tasty trinkets on his way out, just to prove a point? No, now he was just being silly.

The lounge was even darker than anywhere else he had ventured so far, and very little was discernible for a moment. Someone must have been in at some point during the afternoon, for the curtains were pulled closed in here, though nowhere else in the house. As his eyes adjusted Herbert made out the vague shape of the telly and a bookcase against the pale wallpaper and the bulk of the sofa in the centre of the room. And a smell...! What was that awful stink?

What was he doing, squinting into the pitch black like a blind idiot? The time for worrying about being caught was long gone. He reached around the doorway, hand dropping by habit directly onto the light switch, this house being of such similar construction to his own. He immediately snatched his hand away in surprise; a slimy, tacky substance had met his touch, and was now daubed on his fingers. Unable to identify the unexpected, unpleasant matter he had encountered, Herbert risked the very tip of one finger to touch the switch again, stabbing at it hastily a couple of times until the rocker flicked and light flooded the room. He had to twist his head away as his eyes protested against the sudden glare of the high wattage bulb, but when he was finally able to turn his gaze into the room he found himself wishing he was still slumped before the large TV screen in the house across the road.

The stuff on his hand was darker and stickier than he would have imagined, but it was unmistakeably blood. It was smeared on the light switch, and drizzled up the wall, too. There was a large, impressive splash of it on the adjacent wall to Herbert's right, just this side of and a little above the carved pine fire surround, like the spectacular burst of a firework in the sky. Below this a trail of smudged blood drew Herbert's eyes down to where the crumpled figure of what he guessed must be Adrian Lawson lay. Guessed, because an excess of blood and brutality had permanently disguised the features of the body's shattered face. In his last moments the man had involuntarily evacuated his bladder and bowels, body fluids mingling with the draining blood, creating for himself a pool of filth in which to sit and die.

Oh God! thought Herbert, frantically rubbing his fingers against the leg of his trousers. They'll never get that stain out of the carpet!

9

He wasn't scared of the dark; never had been. On the contrary, he actually quite liked it. When it was dark – really dark – it was sort of comforting, like being snuggled tight in a huge, lumpy duvet, warm and secure and hidden from the world. After his parents had left for the evening, involved in their individual pursuits, Alan visited each room, turning out lights and closing curtains. He knew they'd be around sooner or later, and didn't want them to catch him home alone. Kenny and Jake, that is. They'd want him to go with them, tagging along on whatever loony game Kenny had come up with this time. And after what happened a couple of weeks ago (*the old bird had a heart attack; nowt to do wi' us, he desperately tried to convince himself*), and then again the other night, they had toned down their antics, but even so he wasn't keen to join in any more.

Never had been keen, if he admitted to the truth of the situation. They'd helped him out that time when he nearly got caught shoplifting, so they reckoned he owed them. Just happened to be there in the newsagent's, saw him do a runner with the X-rated glossy he'd snatched off the top shelf tucked under his coat, tripped the shop-keeper as he made to chase after him, then caught up with him themselves down the road and just sort of... *adopted* him. They approved of his methods and his choice of reading material, never realising that Alan had no real interest in the magazine, no real taste for the life of petty crime into which they had subsequently drawn him.

Thinking about it in the long, scary months since, Alan came to appreciate that his actions that day hadn't been about stealing, hadn't been about obtaining educational literature, and certainly hadn't been about becoming the latest member of a gang of moronic teenage reprobates. If he really wanted to escape with his purloined pornography he wouldn't have been quite so heavy-handed and obvious about it. Without actually waving at the bespectacled retailer as he slipped the magazine under his coat, by his attitude and demeanour he couldn't have made his intentions any more glaringly clear.

So he must have wanted to be caught, wanted the police to be brought in, wanted his parents finally to be shaken from their state of constant marital warfare long enough to notice the little piggy-in-the-middle. But it hadn't worked out that way. His "mates" made their fumbling rescue bid and, in the air of heady camaraderie that followed, this new relationship was born. It was just a pity that Kenny and Jake were too thick to comprehend that Alan simply did not want to spend time with them, to be their friend, to even know they existed, frankly. Especially when their escapades had resulted in deaths. The image of the old lady, clutching her chest as she slumped to the ground, which replayed over and over in his mind, had lately taken on the face of the grandmother he'd never known, but who smiled adoringly at his grandad in that photo on the mantelpiece. As he sat in the dark Alan twisted the gold signet ring on his finger viciously. The others might try to play things down, might not see what this was doing to him, but Alan couldn't dismiss the seriousness of their situation quite so easily.

Or maybe they *did* realise how troubled he felt, but weren't inclined to let him off the hook that easily. They'd dug their talons into him and now expected him to go along with them, whether he wanted to or not. That was a frightening thought, and one that kept him crouching here in the darkness as he heard the glass from that broken milk bottle on the pavement crunching under the tread of heavy boots, the squeak and rattle of the gate, then those same boots clumping up the short path. The familiar door chime sang out, followed immediately by an impatient rapping on the glass.

'Come on, Raff! You in there?' Kenny's voice, harsh and demanding, using their nickname for him, Raff, the diminutive of his surname, Rafferty. A blurry shadow drifted across the curtain as he tried to peer in through a gap, but Alan had been careful as he pulled the drapes across. He vaguely wondered if Kenny's clumsy tread would damage the flowerbeds below the window, but his parents probably wouldn't notice anyway; neither of them gave a toss about the garden. Alan himself was the only one who ever bothered to pull any weeds or mow the lawn, and then only as a chore to earn his pocket money. By the time Julie and Jeffery Rafferty staggered home, she from the bingo hall, he from the pub (or at least, that's where they told each other they were going), they would both be too drunk to know what state the garden was in.

'There's nob'dy in,' came Kenny's voice from beyond the window, then a muffled response from farther away. Jake hadn't come into the garden; he was probably doing his tightrope-walker impressions along their garden wall, or throwing himself into next door's hedge to see if it could take his weight. Kenny's footsteps receded down the path, then the gate clattered again. Alan was tempted to risk a peek through the curtains, to make sure they had definitely gone, but didn't dare in case they were hanging about wondering what to do next. They might even be spying on the house, suspecting he was hiding from them, trying to catch him out. He stayed where he was, on his knees behind the sofa. He knew he could outwait them, especially the hyperactive Jake, who couldn't go five minutes without either eating something, or kicking something. He curled up on the floor, head resting on his hands, smelling the dust and fluff of the carpet and listening for tell-tale sounds from outside.

*

As Maxey pushed the front door closed behind him he could sense the house was empty. He called his wife's name anyway, just in case, but the sounds, the smells, the very atmosphere that the presence of Nicky infused into a place were so obviously absent. He actually felt his mood slump with the realisation that she was out and marvelled at the effect she could have on him, even after all this time. A glimpse of something white caught his eye and he had to smile. She'd taped a note to the hall mirror, her usual spot: she often teased him that he couldn't pass a mirror without looking, so she knew he wouldn't miss it. Even with that thought in his mind he still ran a finger through his hair and contemplated his square jaw and deep blue eyes before ripping the note from its place.

Hmm, called in to work again. Extra shift to cover for illness. That hospital would fall apart if it weren't for Sister Maxey. Nicky had moved to Rotherham General Hospital from Haleston Hospital to take over the sister's post in paediatrics a short time ago and quickly established herself as a firm but approachable leader. It was important to her to keep her department running smoothly, hence her regularly working extra shifts at short notice.

Maxey slipped off his jacket, quickly rummaging through the pockets and retrieving his keys, wallet and phone. He pressed the buttons to turn the ringer back on for his mobile, as he usually kept it on silent while he was at work, and happened to notice the screen. One missed call. He called up the details but didn't recognise the number displayed. It didn't look like a cold-caller number. He dialled the number back, hanging up his jacket in the closet and dropping his wallet and keys into the drawer of the hall cabinet while he waited for an answer. He'd gone through to the kitchen and filled the kettle, all the while keeping the phone trapped between shoulder and ear, and was about to give up and ring off when the call was answered.

'Hello?' A puzzled, tentative voice. Male, probably young.

'Yeah, this is Edward Maxey,' he said. 'I'm returning the call you made to my mobile earlier.'

'Not me, mate. This is a phone box.'

'Really?' *Strange.* Maxey couldn't think of anyone who used a public phone these days; surely everyone had a mobile. 'Where are you?'

'I've told you, I'm in a phone box.'

Maxey sighed. 'Where's the phone box?'

'Just across from the Stag and Hounds, in Merrington.'

Maxey thanked the youth and rang off. The kettle started to whisper its gentle message that the element was warming up; Maxey prepared a coffee mug as he pondered the call.

He knew Merrington, sometimes went through it on his way to work in the morning, if the Doncaster road was busy, and had seen the Stag and Hounds as he passed. In fact, the more he thought about it, hadn't he and Nicky been there once with Luke and some girl he was seeing at the time, about four years ago? Quiet place, a bit horse-brassy, but somehow gloomy and unwelcoming – they'd not been tempted to go back. Who'd be calling him from there? Or, more precisely, from a phone box just outside?

With a shrug he spooned coffee from the jar and put the matter from his mind. If it was important, they'd call again.

*

Detective Sergeant Luke Preston leaned against his black Honda Civic Type R, elbows gently resting on the roof, careful not to let the zip of his padded over-jacket catch the gleaming paintwork of the door. The curving sweep of the metalwork before him showed the inverted reflection of the house opposite, and he glanced up to see the anonymous, white-suited CSI officers trailing in and out of the open front door, and the new DC Annette Lee, directing the PCSOs who were turning away any neighbours and sightseers who ventured too close. She was certainly keen;

Preston couldn't fault her there. Lee must be, what? Twenty three, twenty four? Preston briefly recalled the early days of his own career: young, dedicated, cocky as hell but with the sense to keep it in check at the right time. Having made it through the Police Cadet Scheme, eighteen months as a Special, joining up, a couple of weeks induction at Ecclesfield and then three or four months at the National Police Training Centre in Durham, Preston wasn't going to let his own exuberance muck up his chances when he finally got operational in Haleston.

God, he'd felt so good, striding out in his first uniform. His mother could barely stop hugging him, pride bursting the buttons of her garish, floral blouse, her lipstick staining his cheek like a bruise. His father couldn't give a shit, of course, but then, that feeling had been decidedly mutual. It was largely his childhood disappointment at his father's lacklustre lifestyle that had convinced the young Luke that he wanted to join the force, to do some good, to make a difference... maybe even get the old sod to notice him for once.

Moving into CID had been another boost to Luke's self-esteem, of course, but it meant losing the visual impact of the uniform. To compensate he'd got into the habit of flashing his badge at every opportunity, and even now, years later, always introduced himself to witnesses or suspects alike as *Detective Sergeant* Preston – none of this abbreviating it to DS like a lot of them did. He'd be even keener to drop his rank into conversation at every appropriate juncture if he could only get a bloody detective inspector's post. He'd passed the exams, he'd got the experience. His dilemma was he didn't want to leave the area, now his mother's health deteriorating and his daughter, Kerry, was finally beginning to escape her mother's clutches and spend time with him. He wasn't going to disappear now, when he had the chance to be a proper dad, not like his own. The prospects of promotion locally were pretty grim, and with recent budget cutbacks hitting the higher ranks, it was getting worse every year.

On the kerb edge the witness looked like a greyhound waiting for the trap gates to snap open as he gave his cursory answers to DC Lee's questions. Preston approached quietly, allowing her to continue. He marvelled at Lee's mask of patience. You'd almost believe she didn't want to grab Herbert Osgood by the front of his moth-eaten cardigan and shake the words out of him.

*

'And the light was definitely off when you entered the house?'

'I told you,' Osgood said, testily. 'I had to switch it on to see anything. That's how I got...' He looked down at his fingers, still stained red, and had to swallow down bile. He rubbed his hand against his leg again, making a mental note to put these trousers in to soak as soon as he could escape and make it back across the street. Huddled bodies rubber-necked just beyond the hastily erected tape barriers, which fluttered in the evening breeze where they stretched across the road in both directions. He cringed under their scrutiny, bloody nosy neighbours. When would this ordeal be over?

'You didn't see who left the door open?'

Herbert sighed. How many times would this girl make him tell her the same things, over and over? 'No. I don't spend every minute of the day glued to the window, you know.'

'But a fair few, though, yes?'

Herbert scowled at her. Was she taking a pop at him? Her expression remained blank, so he decided to let this one go. But he'd be watching her. 'My chair is in the bay, so I do see quite a lot of what goes on,' he admitted.

'We're trying to establish just when the incident might have occurred, Mr Osgood.' Annette Lee flashed him a smile of patient encouragement but Herbert could see it was

91

merely painted on. Why was everyone so fake? If she wasn't interested in what he had to say then why wouldn't she let him go home?

'Won't they be able to tell you that?' Herbert said, gesturing to where the white-suited crime scene workers still buzzed around the house, carrying metal cases in and plastic bags of evidence out.

'We try to gather as much information as possible, sir. Eye-witness corroboration of forensic findings can make a huge difference in closing a case. Anything you can tell us could be of vital importance.'

'Vital importance, you say?' Herbert's chest swelled and his voice took on a pompous tone. This was more like it. Finally she was recognising his worth. He glanced again at the onlookers, preening himself in their adoring gaze.

'So?' Preston said.

Herbert turned to him with a look of surprise, as if he hadn't noticed him standing there. He was shaken from his reverie by the impatient edge to the young man's voice. For a moment he'd been up on the stand in court, all eyes trained on him, the white-wigged judge shushing the gallery as they gasped in awe at Herbert's revelations and insights. 'Well, I'd have seen a lot more if your lot hadn't taken up so much of my day,' he snapped.

'Our lot?' Lee asked.

'Coppers.'

'Coppers? No, we're interested in what happened *before* you called us.'

'Not you,' Herbert said, in a tone reserved for teachers of particularly backward primary school children. 'The others.'

'You've spoken to other police officers already today?'

'Don't you talk to each other?'

Preston and Lee looked at one another with puzzled frowns. Clearly neither of them was aware of any other incidents involving him today. Herbert Osgood shook his head. Left hand doesn't know what's up its own sleeve.

'Uniformed fellow, this one was,' Herbert continued.

'Plonked himself down in my chair, stayed there best part of an hour, scribbling on his pad, drinking my tea. No wonder I didn't see anything going on outside.'

'When was this, exactly?'

'Couldn't say, *exactly*. But best I remember, it was between one and two this afternoon.'

'And why were the police here this afternoon, Mr Osgood?' Lee pressed.

''Cause I rang, this morning,' Herbert said. 'I suppose I ought to be grateful they came so quickly.'

'Why did you ring the police this morning?' Lee asked, her voice slightly distorted, Herbert noticed, filtered as it was through gritted teeth and a fixed smile.

He sighed, despairing at the state of modern policing. What hope for the nation if this was the standard? 'About the blood.'

'The blood?' Preston glanced over his shoulder at Lawson's house and the buzzing white-suits.

'Not that blood,' said Herbert, waving a dismissive hand at the current scene of crime. He turned and pointed across the street, to where Adrian Lawson's flashy car stood yet again at the kerb directly outside Herbert's front window. 'That blood.'

10

Now white-suited, gloved and wearing paper overshoes, Luke Preston looked as much of a snowman as the team of crime scene officers who still milled around, photographing blood splashes, picking tiny fibres from the carpet or logging every minute item in the vicinity. He stood on one of the small metal platforms that had been situated around the room so that the constant passage of feet through the scene would not disturb the gruesome evidence. On an adjacent platform, also all in white, stood Detective Inspector Andy Grieff, scowling at the horror around him.

'Are we even sure this is Adrian Lawson?' he grumbled. With the extent of the damage to the victim's face and head it was difficult to be certain by sight alone.

'We'll compare DNA on his toothbrush and comb,' said Dan Baxter, the Crime Scene Manager, as he rose from bending over the corpse. There was a note of hesitance in his voice, which the other men recognised. With the rise in familiarity with DNA methods, via television programmes and crime fiction novels, the probability of planting false specimens always had to be taken into account, casting doubt on the reliability of any moveable evidence. He tilted his head as he examined the corpse from different angles, giving him the appearance of a curious puppy. 'And what's left of the jaw against dental records.'

'His watch and medallion match that photo on the mantle,' said Preston, nodding towards the image of a grinning Adrian Lawson, shirtsleeves rolled up to expose hirsute, brawny forearms wrapped possessively around the petite but curvy frame of his pretty, auburn-haired wife.

'Get a decent shot of that watch,' Baxter told a nearby photographer.

'He wants it to look good when he posts it on eBay later,'

Grieff chipped in.

Baxter sighed and stepped back to allow the photographer to lean in.

'Good looking bloke,' said Baxter, earning himself a raised eyebrow from Preston. 'Shame.'

'Yeah,' nodded Grieff, straight-faced. 'If only it were just the ugly ones who got themselves murdered. It would be so much more comfortable for the rest of us.'

Preston and Baxter watched him, waiting for a smile or wink, which didn't appear.

'Not so pretty now, thanks to that.' Grieff pointed to the heavy brass poker lying on the carpet next to the body. The matching shovel and tongs were lying on the hearth where they had fallen when their stand had been knocked over. Shiny and clean they had clearly never been used for their intended purpose, positioned as they were by a fireplace whose contents were more decorative than combustible. Evenly cut logs that had seen no hint of a flame, surrounded by pine cones and a scattering of scented candles.

'Rustic,' said Baxter.

'Someone didn't have a lot of respect for Mrs Lawson's home décor,' Preston said, indicating the blood spatter on almost every surface in the room.

There was a low rumbling noise and, with a barely discernible grimace, Grieff pressed a hand to his stomach. Preston was readying a quip about approaching thunder but Grieff's sharp stare dissuaded him from uttering it.

'I don't suppose there's any doubt that the poker is what caused all the mess?' Grieff asked.

'There's always room for doubt before the pathologist's had chance to examine him properly,' said Baxter, maintaining his trademark caution. Facts were facts. Speculation was for academics and detectives. 'But it's a slim doubt. Impact marks certainly *suggest* a blunt instrument of the size and shape of the poker. Blood and tissue on the shaft *appear* to belong to this fellow down here.' He carefully lifted the poker from the floor and slipped it into a large, paper blood-evidence bag. 'If I were a betting man, I think I'd be putting my money on this as the murder weapon.'

'On the nose?' Grieff said, his eyes on the shattered face before him.

This time Preston thought he spotted a twitch at the corner of Grieff's mouth as he spoke.

'Has the pathologist given a time for the post mortem?' he went on.

'Not as yet,' Baxter said. 'She and your superintendent graced us with their presence briefly, to assure us of their seniority, then left us to it.'

Grieff grunted and gave a small nod.

Feet tip-tapped on metal plates as the two policemen approached the fireplace. Grieff picked up the photograph in gloved fingers. 'No sign of the wife?'

'Not yet,' said Preston. 'You thinking she might be hurt, too?'

'There's no trace of a second victim,' said Baxter from the doorway, as he passed the bag containing the poker to one of his colleagues. 'Not anywhere in the house, anyway.'

'Could a woman have done that much damage?' asked Grieff.

'Eventually,' Baxter told him.

'Eventually?'

'It took more than one strike from the blunt instrument to inflict this level of destruction.'

'I'd guessed that much.'

'The poker isn't a particularly heavy weapon to wield, so anyone could have swung it, and kept on swinging it, until you're left with...' Baxter waved a hand vaguely over the prone form.

'Porridge,' Grieff finished for him.

That shut them all up for a few moments.

Eventually Baxter managed to shake off the image. 'I don't know if this is significant or not.' He held up a small evidence bag, which showed a crumpled slip of paper through its clear sleeve. 'It was on the floor in the hall. Could have been dropped by anyone at any time, or by your killer as they fled the scene.'

'Apart from in here, the house is pretty pristine,' said Grieff. 'I can't see Mrs Lawson leaving dropped paper lying around. What is it?'

'Compliment slip issued by Haleston Register Office. Mobile phone number written on it by hand.'

'Register Office?' said Preston, stepping closer to peer at the paper.

'Is that relevant, Luke?' asked Grieff.

'Dunno,' Preston shrugged. 'It's just that I know someone who works there.'

'Okay, make a note of the number and follow up on that later,' said Grieff. 'Dan, can you check it for prints?'

'Of course,' said Baxter. 'It's been in and out of someone's pocket a few times by the look of it, but it was folded so there should be something preserved. I'll take it to the lab for chemical analysis.' He held the evidence bag up so Preston could snap it with his phone camera, before heading back out to the hallway.

Grieff held up the ornate, silver photo frame once more, felt the eyes of the smiling couple burning into him. 'Our next priority is finding the wife.'

*

The crowd of people standing in the middle of the street was what first alerted her to the trouble. It looked like the whole street was out in force. Plus a lot of faces she'd never seen before. And there, between the bobbing heads peering for a better view, was that a policeman? She could see the cap with the black and white chequered band around it.

Donna Lawson hurried up to the crowd, pushing her way through to the front, where the flimsy barrier held the people back, using the bulky shopping bags in her hands as weapons to beat a path. She lifted the tape and ran on, only to find herself blocked by a female PC at her own gate. Tall and slim, eyes firm and resolute against her tawny beige skin, the copper made an effective barrier.

'What's going on?' Donna demanded. 'Let me through.'

'Mrs Lawson?' asked the PC, a quiet urgency in her tone which chilled Donna.

'What's happened? This is my house. Let me in.'

'You *are* Mrs Lawson?' PC Jo Kershaw stressed, hands on Donna's shoulders.

Donna dropped her bags, shrugged off the grip. 'Yes, of course I am. Now, get out of my way.'

'You can't go in there,' Kershaw said, nodding to one of the PCSOs standing nearby, indicating he should go inside and let the detectives know that Donna had returned.

He re-emerged a moment later, followed by Grieff and Preston, hastily peeling off their crime-scene suits. Donna was quiet now, dread stealing her words.

'Mrs Lawson?' Grieff said, holding out a hand still clammy from the rubber glove that enclosed it seconds earlier.

She stared at it as if he were offering her a skinned cat, and she pulled her own hands out of his reach. 'Why won't anyone tell me what's going on?'

Preston gave his own and Grieff's suits to Kershaw, with a jerk of his head which said *get these out of sight*. She moved quickly, taking them to the nearest crime scene van.

'That's exactly what we intend to do, Mrs Lawson,' said Grieff. 'Is there somewhere we can go? Do you have a particular friend amongst your neighbours, perhaps?'

Donna glanced up and down the street, saw the greedy eyes of the hyenas all around, and shook her head with a scowl of distaste.

Moments later she sat in the back of one of the patrol cars, Grieff beside her, Preston in the front passenger seat, twisting to see them.

'What is it? Please tell me.'

So they did, as gently as possible, with as little detail as they could manage, but still she felt every bit of heat drain from her body within seconds.

Silence swelled in the close confines of the patrol car, crushing the breath from all three of them. Grieff cleared his throat, shattering the quiet. Donna looked at him, startled, having quite forgotten where she was.

'Were you expecting your husband to be at home today?' Preston asked.

Donna shook her head, rattling her thoughts into action. They waited for her. 'Yes. Well, no. I knew he wasn't at work, but he should have been out with his son.'

'*His* son?'

'Shane. To his first wife. He has him every Saturday.'

'It's Friday today, Mrs Lawson.'

'Is it?' She thought for a moment. 'They swapped. They're taking him away for the weekend, his other family, so Adie said he'd see him today instead.'

'Would he normally be home by now?' Grieff asked.

'I think he was going to the pictures. Depends what time the film finished. When he was with Shane I didn't have to worry about what time he came in.'

'Oh? Did you at other times? Worry about him? Where he was? When he'd be in?' Grieff's words were spoken gently but Donna flinched under the onslaught of questions.

'I didn't always know where he was,' she admitted. 'Or who he was with.'

'Affairs?'

She couldn't meet his gaze.

'And what about you, Mrs Lawson?'

'Me?' she said, indignantly. *What was he asking?*

'Today, I mean. Where were you?'

'Oh. I met a friend. Julie. Julie Rafferty. We met for coffee, about half twelve, one o'clock.'

'And then?'

'I went shopping. Shoes. Adie says I've got enough but

today I thought, sod him.'

'Why today, especially?'

But she wasn't listening. She was peering out of the car window, looking for her shopping bags. She remembered dropping them when... Ah, there they were. That black lady policeman had picked them up and put them safely by the front door of the house.

*

Grieff nodded to Preston and they both climbed out of the vehicle.

'I don't want to go at her too hard tonight,' Grieff said. 'Let's find her somewhere to stay and question her when she's had chance to get her head together.'

'Do you think this shock is genuine,' Preston wondered, making sure his back was to the car window, 'or do you think she's hiding something?'

'Bit of both, it seems to me,' Grieff said, glancing sideways at the newly widowed woman. 'Get the address of the son's other family and get round to them tonight. It's not right they hear about this off the news. Take a woman with you, to help soften the blow.' He glanced round the street. 'Where's Lee?'

'She went back to the station to chase up uniform for some info about blood on the victim's car.'

'Wait, what?' said Grieff, looking from the house to the street. 'His car? How could it have got on the car?'

'I don't know,' Preston shrugged. 'That's why we're following it up. Apparently the neighbour reported it first thing this morning, when we know the victim was still alive.'

A fine spray spattering on the car roof suggested that the heavy grey clouds were finally about to unload their burden, as the two detectives exchanged puzzled frowns.

*

The boys had been plonked in front of the telly, waiting until it was time to set off. Layna turned up the volume, told the boys not to worry, that their visitors just wanted to make sure everything was all set for their holiday, and joined the nice police people in the kitchen.

Ron put the kettle on and Preston and Kershaw perched on hard, wooden chairs at the small, round table. Layna's chair screeched across the tiles as she sat opposite the police woman and peered at her with a troubled expression. She noticed the glistening of moisture on the black corkscrew coils of hair emerging from beneath the copper's cap, testament to the worsening weather. She vaguely wondered about the driving conditions if this rain continued, but the tap of uniform buttons on the table as Kershaw leaned forward brought her back to the present.

'What is it?' Layna asked.

'Bit late for a social call,' Ron Hewett said, attempting levity. No one laughed.

'It's about your previous husband, Mrs Hewett,' Preston began. 'Adrian Lawson.'

Hewett's features hardened but Layna just looked confused.

'What about him?' Layna glanced at her husband, who turned to reach a selection of mugs down from the high cupboard. 'We've been divorced four years.'

'When did you last see him?' Preston asked.

'This morning, when he brought the boys back.'

'Boys? He had both of them with him? I thought he was only father to one of them.'

A teaspoon jangling on the worktop drew all their eyes.

'Sorry,' Hewett mumbled through gritted teeth. 'Dropped the spoon.'

Kershaw rose and moved across the kitchen to where he stood. 'Let me do that.' Hewett stepped aside without argument and took the fourth chair at the table. Preston felt Hewett's knees brush against his and shuffled on his chair awkwardly.

'Yes,' said Layna, placing a hand over her husband's. 'Terry is Ron's son. I didn't tell him I'd asked Adie to take him when he took Shane. He didn't know till I rang him later. He wasn't pleased.'

Hewett held his chin up in a dignified pose, but avoided Preston's eyes. 'He's not exactly the sort of influence I want my son exposed to,' he said. 'He treated Layna badly when they were married. If it wasn't for Shane then we'd have nothing to do with him.'

'I understand,' Preston said, nodding encouragingly.

Kershaw placed three mugs of tea on the table, then remained leaning against the worktop nursing her own drink.

'You said it was still morning when Mr Lawson returned with the boys.'

'That's right,' Layna said. 'I wasn't well pleased when he turned up so soon, I'll tell you.'

'He was supposed to have them all day?'

'Yeah, I had tons to do today, getting ready for our holiday.'

'Holiday?' said Kershaw. 'Going anywhere nice?'

'Booked Disneyland Paris for the weekend,' Hewett announced grandly.

'Very nice.'

'Driving down tonight, about four hours to Folkstone. There's a Shuttle just after two o'clock, get us into Calais before three. Then it's only about another three hours to Paris from there.'

'That's a lot of driving at that time of night,' Preston said, over the top of his mug.

'That's what I told him.' Layna cast a critical expression at her husband, but his stern return gaze made her drop her eyes.

'I'll be fine.'

'What reason did he give for bringing the boys back so early?'

Layna took a moment to get her thoughts back on track.

'Poor Terry got upset over something. He'd been poorly first thing, he said. That's why he was off school.'

'Skiving,' snapped Hewett, with a sneer at his wife. 'You're such a pushover, those boys walk all over you sometimes.'

'I think it may be bullying,' Layna continued. 'He seems so skittish all the time, these days.'

'He didn't say what had upset the boy?'

'He didn't really know. It came out of nowhere.'

'Strange.'

'Yeah, but Terry had wet himself, bless him, so Adie brought him home.'

'Shane, as well? Did he not want to spend the rest of the day with his own lad?' asked Kershaw.

'He'd got himself all dirty with Terry's wee, messed up his shirt and jeans. He said he'd have to go home and change first.'

'So you were expecting him back?' asked Preston.

'Yeah, but when he wasn't back by the afternoon I rang him and he said something had come up.'

'He didn't say what that was?'

'No, just "something".'

Hewett muttered under his breath. The words "typical" and "unreliable" could be discerned amongst the guttural grumblings.

'And what time would that be?'

'Which? When he dropped the kids off, or when I rang him up?'

'All of it, as best you can recall.'

'Well, he took them about half past ten, and he can't have been gone above an hour. I gave him a couple of hours to get back, so it must have been well after one o'clock this afternoon when I rang him and he said he couldn't come back. Shane was gutted.'

'I bet,' said Kershaw.

'You still haven't told us what all this is about,' Layna said. 'When you both turned up on the doorstep at this time of night, drenched in rain, I thought you were going to tell us someone had died.'

Preston glanced at Kershaw awkwardly, and braced himself. 'Well...' he began.

*

The Premier Inn on Barnsley Road, about six miles out of Haleston travelling north, was probably the cheapest and cleanest option for an impromptu overnight stay, when you are forced to leave your own home through tragic circumstances. Basic but functional, the room was warm, quiet and comfortable, a smart little *en suite* adjoining, with a powerful and very hot shower. That's what she had needed the most, once the police were gone and she'd finally been left on her own. But the harshest spray couldn't wash today away.

Donna Lawson sat on the large, firm and very inviting bed, wrapped in a towel, kindly supplied by the hotel. Drips from her wet hair mixed with the tears on her face and pattered heavily onto her bare thighs. She stared at the strange woman looking back at her from the large dresser mirror, vaguely wondering what she was doing in her room.

But it didn't really matter. Nothing mattered anymore. He was gone. Dead. Or so they told her. Believing them was her only option. She hadn't seen him. They wanted her to, it was expected, next of kin and all that, but they would have had to keep his head covered. Hide his face? His beautiful face? No. It was that cheeky smile, the twinkle in his eyes, which made him who he was. Would it even be Adie without that grin puckering his cheeks with the dimples he always insisted weren't there? She told them about particular features – a birth mark under his right nipple, a small tattoo of a winking devil on his left bum cheek he'd had done when he was seventeen – by which they could rule out any errors, but she didn't want to view him herself. She thought about that scene in all the TV programmes, the cop shows, where they wheel out the squeaky trolley with the lumpy shape under a white sheet. They peel back the cover and the wife gives out a trembling sob and buries her face in the detective's chest. Not wife – widow. That's what they were now. Like her. Because Adrian's dead. And in such a ruined state that they can't even do the peel-back-the-sheet bit that they always do on the telly. She wasn't going down to the bloody morgue so they could flash her the tattoo on his arse. Talk about undignified!

She picked up the mobile lying on the trim, dark wood dresser, her own bleary reflection the only thing showing on the black screen. Spending the whole day trawling the shops had worn down the battery and her charger wasn't among the few items the police had retrieved from the house for her. Holding the phone was merely a reflex action, anyway. Who would she call? She'd no family anymore, and her friends were few. Julie? Hah, if not for her then Donna wouldn't have been out, buying shoes she didn't want or need. *Just thought you ought to know, Donna love.* Why had she seemed to take such a bitter delight in imparting that devastating news? And why was it such a shock? Certainly not because she thought he was faithful. Was it the age thing? He'd strayed before, but, on those far too numerous occasions, he'd always come back. What if he thought she, Donna, was getting a bit old in the tooth. Could he be thinking it was time to bring his work practices home with him, and, like some rust-eaten thing crumbling in his dealership yard, trade her in for a newer model?

She came back to that barely stifled smile with which Julie had stuck in the knife, and suddenly it dawned on her. *The cunt was shagging him as well!* That had to be it. Everything slotted together. She'd never taken this amount of interest in their business before. And at the weekend, when his car had been nicked – he'd been cagey with her about where it was parked when it was taken, but she'd overheard him telling the coppers it was on Werrett Street, and that was just around the corner from Julie and Jeff's place. Jeff would be working, that lad of theirs was always out, so Julie would have been in on her own. But not on her own for long. Not once Adie arrived to ease her loneliness. That bastard! She'd kill him when she got her hands on…

Donna threw herself down on the neatly made bed, her body heaving with sobs.

11

Saturday

The autumn morning was unusually warm, though the sun had yet to dry out the roads after last night's downpour, so Edward Maxey cursed the mud which spattered up the sides of his pristine precious, only a couple of days since its last trip through the carwash. He took care on the narrow road, tarmacked but bumpy and pot-holed. Thick, unkempt hedges obscured his view around the many twisting bends, reaching their scratchy twigs and branches towards the shiny paintwork. Tires slid on the verge as he pulled in to avoid oncoming vehicles, and, during one particularly daunting encounter, he felt sure a tractor was going to shear off his front wing as it whizzed past.

A warning from the navigation app on his phone, clipped to the windscreen, informed him that his destination was close by. A break in the low hedgerow up ahead was marked by two worn posts which hadn't held a gate for some years. Easing the Mondeo through the space Maxey followed the bumpy lane down towards the farmhouse, its decrepit exterior suggesting the place had been long abandoned, rather than it being the current address of the person Maxey had come to visit. He pulled the car up on the rough yard in front of the house and checked the satnav and the tag on the dog collar once more, to ensure there had been no mistake. Nope, it all matched up – this was the place. He turned off the engine and picked up the collar.

Climbing out onto the slick ground Maxey was glad he'd worn his old trainers rather than any of his good shoes. If he had come here straight from work the previous evening, as originally planned, he would have regretted it the moment he stepped from the car. His knock caused more of the crumbling paintwork to flake off the ancient front door as he waited for an answer.

'Whatcha want?' came a gruff voice. Maxey turned to see Arthur Camm striding towards him across the yard. 'Oh, it's you.'

'Yes,' said Maxey. 'If you remember, you came to see me the other day.'

'I remember.' Camm held him with a hard stare, then turned his gaze onto Maxey's car. 'Got your nice, shiny motor all mucky.'

Maxey waved a dismissive hand. 'Oh, I'm not worried about that.'

'No?'

'Well, it'll wash off.' He showed the old farmer a feeble smile. 'Anyway, about the other day...'

'You was laughing at me.'

'No,' Maxey protested. 'Not at all.'

'Your girls was. When I came out o' your office I could see 'em. Thought I was a big joke, they did.'

'No,' he insisted. 'We were all touched by your loss, and your genuine affection for your dog.'

'Aye?'

'Aye. I mean, yes. That's why I'm here.'

Arthur grunted and raised an eyebrow. 'Best come in, then. I'm just putting the kettle on.'

Maxey was relieved to see that the inside of the house, though still somewhat dilapidated, was at least clean and tidy. The wooden chair he was offered showed signs of repair, but was sturdy under his weight. Arthur put the mug of tea down on the table next to the frayed, old dog collar that Maxey had returned to him. He ran a gnarled finger over the name engraved into the metal tag, and Maxey imagined he could see a tear waiting to roll down a wrinkled cheek.

'Are you here alone?' Maxey asked, looking out through

the kitchen window to where the fields swept up into the hills in the distance.

'Me an' about a hundred sheep,' Arthur said.

'Wow, that many? How do you handle that number without a dog?' Maxey grimaced at his own question. The matter must still be sore for the old man.

'Oh, I got a dog,' Arthur told him casually. 'Bexy was never no good at herdin'. House dog, she was. Different from a worker. T'other one's outside, in its kennel. Dun't come in 'ouse, that one.'

'Oh, right.' To Maxey a dog was a dog. The concept of pet versus working animal was slippery to grasp.

Arthur's eyes never left the rust-pitted name tag. 'Run a mile if a lamb so much as bleated in her direction.' A warm smile of recollection wrinkled his features.

'So just you, the sheep, and a dog with no name?' Maxey said.

'Oh, it's got a name,' Arthur said, straight-faced. 'I call it "Dog". Some pigs out back, an' all. Not many, but there's a few breeding pair. Healthy sows that churn out a couple of litters each, every year. Between the market and the table they just about earn their feed.'

'No family to help out?'

'Nah, Bexy's the only family I've had for a good few years.'

'How do you cope, on your own?'

'I just do,' Arthur shrugged. 'Y'ave to, don't you?' He felt as little inclined to enlighten this townie on the complexities of farm management as Maxey would have been to hear of them.

'I suppose so.' Maxey drank his tea, avoiding the chips and cracks in the edge of the mug.

Back outside Arthur walked with Maxey towards his car. The bright sunshine gave a golden sheen to the landscape, making the farm seem warm, welcoming and idyllic.

'What happens to this place when you...?' He stopped, and cast an awkward glance at Arthur. 'When you've gone?'

'Why should I worry? I won't be around to care.'

'Have you not made a will?'

'I've nobody to leave owt to,' Arthur said. 'Anyways, the bank owns more of this place than I do, it seems like.'

Maxey nodded sagely, as if possessing some knowledge of rural economics. He had enough trouble keeping track of his own mortgage. A waft of smoke drew his attention to the corner of the yard, where there stood an old, soot-blackened metal dustbin with holes punched in the sides. Flames licked up from the crackling contents, and Maxey saw the blue denim leg of a pair of jeans draped over the rim of the burner, curious stains marking the fabric.

'Is that blood?' he asked, only realising how rude his inquisitiveness might seem after the words had left him.

Arthur stared at the bin for a long, tense moment, before finding the words to speak. 'Bexy, when she... It was a mess.'

'Oh God, I'm so sorry!' Maxey felt his insides chill. He hadn't even asked how the poor creature had met her end. 'I assumed it was her age.'

'Some people treat that lane like a motorway, tear-arsing down past here at stupid speeds. I've no gate on there but it didn't matter, 'cause Bexy hardly ever left the yard, y'see. Just occasionally, y'know, if she saw a squirrel or summat. I don't know what took her out there that day, I just heard a screech of tires, and a thump, and this pitiful little yelp. Car didn't even stop, just raced off down the road. Some big, flash, black thing.' His face was hard and cold as granite. Maxey imagined he wasn't a man to get on the wrong side of.

Arthur strolled over to the bin and flipped the leg of the jeans into the fire. 'Some things you can't just wash off.'

*

'What's the matter wi' you?' Julie asked her husband sitting slumped in his battered leather armchair, as he clicked the

110

TV remote for the thousandth time. 'You've got a face like a smacked arse this morning.'

'Nowt's the matter wi' me,' Jeff grunted, avoiding her eyes, looking instead around the dull room with its faded wallpaper, tiled fireplace, old-fashioned three-bar electric fire on the hearth, family photos on the mantelpiece.

'Well, leave the friggin' telly alone then!' Julie reached over from her well-worn end of the non-matching settee and snatched the remote from him. He folded his arms and stared at the screen. She brought up the channel listings guide and scrolled through the available options, glancing over at him as he continued to sulk. 'Your face'll stay like that,' she warned him.

'Yeah? What's your excuse?' With her bleach-blonde hair tumbling wildly over her shoulders, heavy make-up and t-shirt stretched tight across an impressive pair of tits he could still see what had once attracted him to her, and might still draw the attention of others.

'Har bloody har.' She took a swing at him but he reacted quickly, leaning aside so her hand merely caught the chair cushion. 'Come on, what's up? You've been a right maungy sod since you got in from work last night.'

He sat forward aggressively, made sure he was in her sightline. 'Where'd you go yesterday?'

'When?' She shifted in her seat, kept her eyes on the TV screen as she worked the remote.

'Yesterday'

'When, yesterday?'

'When you went out.'

'Well, you've answered it yourself,' she said with a smirk. 'I went out.'

'Who'd you see?'

'What is this, a fucking interrogation?' She selected a channel at random and threw down the remote, turning to face him.

'Well?'

'You know who I saw.'

111

'Do I?'

'I went to see Donna, to tell her what your shit of a mate was getting up to behind her back.' She folded her arms and thrust out her chin, moral high-ground achieved.

'Is she the only person you saw?'

Julie's composure flickered for a moment. *What did he know?* 'Yes.'

'Nobody else?' He peered hard at her, daring her to lie to him.

So she did. 'No, nobody else.'

He sank back into the chair and looked away from her. 'Yeah, right.'

'What?' She made an open-armed gesture, all innocence. 'I told you I was going to tell her.'

Whatever retort he was going to make was lost as the sound of the front door slamming in its frame disturbed their stand-off. Julie jumped up and crossed to the window, lifting the net aside to see down the path. Alan slunk through the gate and away down the street.

'Where's he off to?'

'Away from you, I expect.'

'What's that supposed to mean?'

'Well, all he ever hears is your screeching voice.'

'Says you!' She stood before him, arms folded, sneering. 'You're worse than me. Checking up on me. "Where've you been? Who've you seen?" I could ask you a few questions of my own.'

He sat forward suddenly, shoved her aside with a rough hand on her hip.

'Oi!'

'Shut up, woman!' He peered past her at the TV set, still murmuring away, as it had throughout their altercation.

'Don't you shut me up!' Julie flared, hand raised to strike back.

'Shut the fuck up and look!' Rafferty roared. 'There, on the telly.'

The local news had started and the reporter, oblivious to

their dispute, was relating the main headline news of the day. 'Police have named the victim in last night's horrific murder in Merrington, near Haleston. The body of this man, Adrian Lawson, was discovered late yesterday afternoon at his home address.' The familiar smiling face beamed out at them from the screen, handsome and charming as he would never be again.

*

They're at it again! Constantly rowing and nagging at one another. Why don't they give it a rest?

Alan Rafferty shuffled along the cracked pavement, kicking at drifts of rusty-coloured leaves and tearing off handfuls of privet from his neighbours' hedges. The redbrick semis loomed either side of him, beyond tiny front gardens, as often paved or neglected as they were green and well-tended. Cars were parked nose-to-tail along either kerb, leaving little room for the occasional passing vehicle. Many a wing mirror had been sacrificed to dustbin collecting day. The scarlet-speckled elm outside number 57 dripped a miniature rainstorm onto him when he kicked the crumbly-barked trunk in passing. He had no idea where he was going but felt a sense of relief as he left the warzone far behind. There was such a sense of detachment in that house, these days. Like they weren't even his family, at all. Just a couple of strangers who'd moved into the room next to his. He wanted to bang on the wall and shout *keep it down!* when they set off on one of their sessions. When had it started to go wrong? There were holidays, first days of school, Christmases, many times when he had been the centre of attention, all they vowed to care about. His mother's arms around him, warm and snuggly; his father's large hand, engulfing his safely as they crossed the road, ruffling his hair as he buttoned up his coat. All long-gone, distant memories. Now they were so wrapped up in their conflict they barely noticed he was there. And probably didn't notice when he wasn't. There must be a best-before date for marriages. Some lasted longer than others. His parents' had long since expired.

The last properly happy memories Alan could recall were before his grandad took ill and suddenly couldn't go out for walks and trips to the park anymore. Before he turned into a walking skeleton and told Alan it was best not to visit him again. The poison had already set in at home, but at least getting out with grandad had been a chance to escape for a while. The old signet ring, worn thin and dull, tiny diamond looking lost and lonely, the initials barely legible, felt frail and ephemeral on his finger as he walked.

Lost in memories, he missed the hurriedly approaching footsteps until they were close behind him, turning and ducking just in time to avoid a bony elbow between his shoulders.

'Ah! Nearly got ya,' Jake yelled as his lunge carried him past his target.

'Jake,' Alan said simply, acknowledging his attacker's regular form of greeting. Even Jake's ugly mug, with his badly cut hair and his prominent overbite, was a welcome sight just now. Funny how, only last night, he had taken great efforts to avoid him and Kenny. But that was night time, when their antics were most unpleasant. At least in daylight they tended to behave a little less rowdily. Maybe he could pass a few harmless hours then find some excuse to leave them?

'Where've ya been, Raff?' Jake asked, panting from the chase. 'We've been looking for ya.'

'Nowhere,' Alan shrugged. 'At home. Nowhere.'

'We came knocking.'

'Did you?' Alan's expression suggested bafflement. 'Must've missed me.'

'Yeah,' Jake nodded. 'Must've.'

They lapsed into an awkward silence. Such lulls were usually filled with a joke or jibe from Kenny, followed by an ill-advised scheme or scam to pass their time. His absence was a physical obstacle between them. Alan cast a concerned glance up and down the empty street, as if expecting to see him emerge from behind a tree or parked car. 'Where's Kenny?' he asked, suddenly conscious that he had never before seen either of them without the other.

'Dunno,' Jake said.

He looked a bit lost, Alan thought. Kenny had always been the more active of the trio, urging them along, he and Jake following in his wake. Without his leadership they stumbled along the street aimlessly.

'Have you called for him?'

Jake nodded. 'His dad said he'd not come home last night,' he continued. 'Thought he was with me. Din't seem bothered when I said he wasn't.' His face scrunched into a distasteful sneer. 'He's a right twat.' He stopped and turned to Alan with a serious frown, what he needed to say clearly far too important to impart mid-perambulation. 'Kenny hates him.'

Alan nodded sagely and placed a hand on Jake's shoulder. 'Families are shit.'

Jake bobbed his head in a manner which somehow didn't commit to being a nod or a shake. 'Mine's not. My mum's ace. Gi'd me this.' He took a crumpled tenner from his pocket and waved it like a flag. 'Mars bar?'

Alan's grim expression smoothed itself into a smile, and they both ran off towards the shops.

*

Glad to be back on urban roads, with Depeche Mode grumbling about not being able to get enough over the CD speakers, Maxey manoeuvred through traffic and checked the time on the dash clock. He was pleased to see that his mission of mercy, to return the ill-fated Bexy's collar to its rightful owner, had not eaten up too much of his day. There was still plenty of time for him to get home, prepare a light brunch – lunch for himself and breakfast for Nicky, who

115

would be rising soon, having slept in after her late shift – then a quick change into his suit and out to the wedding at Ockerby Hall at three o'clock. Perhaps even time to nip to the hand carwash on Methen Road on the way. They always dried the car off nicely with a soft chamois and gave it a good wax finish, so he drove away shining.

Vague, non-specific memories drifted through his subconscious as he drove, the kind that float in unbidden on waves of music. The mate with the dyed hair and piercings (*"Don't you dare bring him into my house again!" "But, Mum…" "He's got fleas!"*) who had worked at the quirky old record shop on Stuckley Avenue (*since then a menswear retailer, then a fish and chip shop, something else…? and now a betting shop*) and introduced him to eighties' synth pop; the pretty girl at the thumpingly loud party held in a crumbling derelict house in Rotherham (*Gill? Val? Definitely something monosyllabic*) who had mouthed "just can't get enough" with that sultry and suggestive look in her eyes, then everyone scarpering when the police showed up to chase them off; his attempt to convey some of his enthusiasm for this particular music genre onto Nicky one drunken night soon after they met (*the first CD he bought her? Certainly one of the first*) and her disappointingly lukewarm response.

The images wafted away, like the smoke from the joint that Gill (*Val?*) shared with him that long-ago night, on the breeze through the glassless windows of the disintegrating slum, when his mobile, still held in its clamp attached to the windscreen, blared out the theme to the long-running TV show "The Bill", and Luke Preston's name appeared on the screen. Maxey smiled – that never grew old. He turned down the CD and swiped the phone screen.

'Hey, mate!' he called out, as he attempted to turn on the hands-free without taking his eyes off the road.

'Dude! You free for a quick word?'

'Yeah, what's up?'

'Best in person,' Preston said, a curious tone to his voice

that Maxey couldn't identify.

'I'm busy this afternoon,' Maxey said. 'Wedding.'

'Oh, right.' Preston sounded subdued, obviously something on his mind.

'How about tonight?' Maxey offered. 'Over a pint?'

'Yeah, can do,' Preston replied. 'Not town, though. Somewhere quiet.'

'Stag and Hounds in Merrington? That's usually quiet.'

'Okay. Not been to that one for a while. What made you think of there?'

Maxey frowned. 'Dunno, just popped into my head.'

'Fair enough. Half seven?'

'Super.'

'Duper.'

'Later.'

''Gator.'

With this familiar exchange the call ended and Maxey turned up the CD, just as the album returned to the beginning and the plunking synth notes of "New Life" kicked in. What did Luke want to ask him that he couldn't say over the phone? Was Claire giving him grief again? Their relationship was still pretty rocky, but he didn't like to involve Maxey in it, knowing it was unfair to expect him to take sides. Not likely to be anything to do with work, either. Luke rarely mentioned any of his cases when they went out socially. Then again, this didn't have the feel of a social thing.

Oh well, he'd find out later. Maxey concentrated on the road, as he squeezed between a row of cars waiting to turn right and some idiot who'd pulled up on double yellow lines to nip into the shops, and forgot all about it, allowing the music to carry him back into the past again.

12

''Gator?'

Luke Preston turned to the source of the query. Over a dozen desks were crammed into this one room, each manned and busy. Just his luck that there would be a lull in the general noise levels as he voiced his parting words to Maxey. At the desk closest to his Annette Lee smiled at him, an eyebrow raised.

'What?' he shrugged, tossing his mobile down onto the desk. 'He's a mate.'

'The one who works at the register office?' At Preston's nod, Lee continued: 'You think he'll be able to help with that phone number on the compliment slip?'

'I should think so,' Preston said, a troubled look scrunching his normally rugged features. 'I've just rung him on it.'

'It's *his* number?' Lee sounded incredulous. 'Does he often spend his afternoons brutally murdering people?'

Preston smiled. 'Not that he's told me about.'

'It is the sort of hobby you'd probably want to keep to yourself, though.'

'Guess so.' Preston scribbled *Max – 7.30 – Stag n Hounds* in his notebook, flipped the book shut and dropped it into the pocket of his jacket, hanging on the back of his chair. 'I'm meeting him later,' he said. 'Hopefully he'll remember who he gave the slip to.'

'I wouldn't imagine he gives his personal number to anyone who just walks into the office,' Lee said. 'Once we've got an idea of who had it we can start to work out how it got to the crime scene, see if it's significant or not.'

Preston's phone turned black as the screen lock kicked in and he pondered the call he'd just made. Why didn't he simply ask Ed there and then about the compliment slip?

What was this uneasy feeling that had niggled away at him since he'd first seen that piece of paper last night? He didn't believe for one second that Edward Maxey was mixed up in something unpleasant, but anything that brought his personal and work lives crashing together bothered him, and he felt it would be a more comfortable conversation if he wasn't within earshot of his colleagues when they talked.

He changed the subject. 'Did you manage to catch up with that plod about the blood on the vic's car?'

Lee gave a grumbling laugh which contained very little humour. 'Yeah, bloody nosy neighbour sent me on a wild goose chase.' Herbert Osgood's information regarding the red staining on the wing of Adrian Lawson's car had proven misleading. Annette Lee had found the PC who interviewed Osgood the previous afternoon, who in turn had been in search of information relating to the theft of Lawson's vehicle the previous weekend. When it was found the car had been examined, fingerprinted and the mysterious marks tested.

'Not blood?'

She stood, bringing a copy of a report to drop onto his desk. 'Oh, it's blood all right. Just not human.'

'Ooh,' he said, intrigued. He pulled the paperwork towards him and scanned the notes. 'Alien? Vampire?'

'Animal.'

'Boring.' He tossed the file back onto the desk. 'No need to send for Mulder and Scully, then.'

Lee took back the file. 'I shouldn't bother them for this.' She perched on the edge of Preston's desk and he tried not to notice how her trousers pulled tight over her thighs and buttocks. In a smart suit, no make-up and hair pulled severely back into a ponytail she was all business, but he remembered some photos on her phone, that she had once shown round the office, of a night out with friends. Dolled up she cut a completely different figure, an image that was difficult to shake, especially sitting so close. He cleared his throat and reminded himself of his rule about the mixing of

119

work and personal lives.

'I didn't think a baby like you would have heard of The X-Files,' he said.

'They covered it in history lessons at school, grandad,' she quipped back. 'What about the wife? Where was she when her old man was getting painted all over the living room?'

He glanced up at her, noting the blank expression behind the sardonic tone. She'd not taken long to assimilate the grim humour of the CID squad room. 'She came home weighed down with sack-loads of shopping, with till receipts and credit card slips covering the late afternoon.' The spouse of a murder victim was always the first person they looked at, though the incidence of male victims having been killed by a current or ex-partner was minimal, compared to how many females were murdered by the man they had taken as a partner. 'We still need to interview the friend who she says was with her earlier in the day, get confirmation of her alibi for that time.'

'So you don't fancy her for this?'

'It's too early to write her off completely, but after meeting her last night, my gut says no.'

'And the ex-wife? The one he'd been with in the morning?'

Preston remembered the tense atmosphere during the interview with Layna Hewett and her husband the previous evening. 'She'd been lumbered with two kids under nine years old,' Preston said, 'so unless she left them on their own, she's not likely to be our killer.'

'Maybe she asked a neighbour to watch them?'

Preston grinned, adopting an over-the-garden-wall housewife voice. '"Can you watch the little uns while I nip over to knock off my ex-husband?" "'Course I can, love, don't you worry."'

'All right, clever-arse.' Lee swiped his shoulder with the file she was holding. 'What about her current husband? He might have come home and looked after the kids while she popped out for a quick murder.'

He laughed, and made a note on his desk pad. 'We'll check when he left work yesterday, though I can't see him letting her go off on a killing spree when she should have been packing his undies for their trip to visit Mickey Mouse.'

'All right for some.'

He raised his eyebrows in her direction. 'Never been to the House of Mouse, Detective Constable?'

'Deprived childhood,' she said, sadly.

'Aww, bless!' Preston realised he knew nothing about her past, and pushed aside the notion that finding out more about her was an enticing proposition. 'So, we had surveillance on the victim's house for practically the whole day...'

'Surveillance?'

'The nosy neighbour, this Osgood fella.'

'Oh, yes.' She opened the file, glanced through the pages. 'Apart from pee breaks and making himself a cuppa he was there from about ten in the morning. Except, of course, there's the interval while PC Cawthorne interviewed him about the blood on the car. That took a little over half an hour, during which Osgood couldn't twitch his curtains.'

'So that's our window of opportunity, pun very much intended.'

'Possibly, but the door was closed when Cawthorne left.'

Preston frowned. 'What?'

Lee riffled through the file again. 'Both Osgood and Cawthorne have separately stated that they made a point of looking across the street at Lawson's house as the interview ended. The door was closed. It was a couple of hours before Osgood noticed it standing open and went across to investigate.'

'So why didn't Cawthorne go over and have a word with Lawson while he was so close? He'd just been told that the bloke was a suspect in a hit-and-run and there he was, just yards from his door.'

'He knew, although Herbert Osgood didn't, that the highly publicised incident was actually a miss-and-run, rather than a hit-and-run. That bit wasn't in the press release. So any blood we found couldn't belong to the old dear who died. He radioed it in anyway, and was told that the car had already been examined, so he figured he'd go and check out the report before taking any precipitous steps.'

Preston rolled his eyes. 'Oh, he did, did he?'

Lee sighed and closed the file, resting it against her leg. 'Also, he got the distinct impression that our Herbert was merely out to cause trouble for a neighbour he didn't get along with.'

Arms folded and eyes closed, Preston appeared deep in thought. Or half asleep. He blew a heavy breath, stirring papers on his desk. 'I hope it doesn't weigh too heavily on him that a simple knock on the door might have saved a man's life.'

'We don't know that,' she said.

There was a defensive note to her voice, and he wondered at her protective feelings towards the young PC. Would she act in a similar fashion over any colleague, or was this one special? He bit back the niggle of jealousy. 'No, you're right. We haven't narrowed down the time of death at all. If the killer left the door open, as seems likely, then he, or she, might have been nowhere near the area at that time, let alone inside the house swinging pokers around.' He slapped his palms down on the desktop and wheeled his chair back in a decisive movement. 'I need to get some fresh air.' Slipping his phone into his pocket, he took the file from her and dropped it on the desk. 'Let's get the wife's alibi sorted, then we can move on.' He scooped up his jacket and headed for the door.

He drove the Civic while she set his satnav to the address Donna Lawson had given for Julie Rafferty, her coffee companion of yesterday afternoon. They rang ahead on the way down to the car park, to ensure there would be someone in when they arrived, and the trip out to Merrington took under ten minutes in the Saturday afternoon traffic.

Lee was silent for most of the journey. Preston glanced across at her as he drove. She stared through the windscreen, her features a blank mask. It was an expression he'd seen on her earlier, when she returned from Adrian Lawson's post mortem examination. It was her first time – talk about being thrown in at the deep end. Considering the state Lawson was in Preston had offered to take her place, but she insisted she was ready. He asked how it went, she shrugged and they moved on to other things. He wondered if stoic dismissal was the ideal method of dealing with the trauma of seeing another human being treated like something on a butcher's slab, but once they got past it she seemed fine. Until now.

'Okay?' he asked.

The face she turned to him was casual and calm, her smile curious. 'Yeah, why?'

'You looked pensive.'

'Just wondering what it takes to drive someone to the point of taking another person's life. Especially in such a brutal way.'

She resumed her survey of the road ahead, and that hard mask returned.

Preston resolved to keep an eye on her.

The village of Merrington formed part of the north-western spread of Haleston's urban sprawl. With housing ranging from run-down to semi-affluent, the nicer properties tended to be found on the newer, farthest edges of the village. Preston and Lee didn't need to travel that far. The kerbside was busy with parked cars but he managed to find a slot just a few doors away from their target and they locked up the Civic and walked the rest of the way to the Rafferty residence.

At the gate Luke noticed a dried white stain on the pavement, streaked and diluted by last night's rain. He kicked shattered shards of glass into the base of the hedge, surprised that shops hereabouts still sold milk in glass bottles.

'Glass is making a comeback,' Lee told him, when he expressed his opinion aloud. 'Awareness of the impact of plastics on the environment has made dairies reconsider their packaging methods.'

'Oh,' he said, dumbly. She said no more on the subject, merely pushed open the squeaky gate and strode up the path, leaving him in her wake, wondering how the hell she knew that.

The door was opened by a tall, lean man in faded jeans and a black t-shirt emblazoned with the name and logo of a heavy metal band that Preston didn't know. He couldn't have been much older than Luke himself but his fair hair was thinning badly.

Preston had his ID ready. 'Detective Sergeant Luke Preston and DC Lee,' he said. 'We called a few moments ago.'

'Berrer come in,' Jeff Rafferty mumbled warily, retreating down the short hallway and leading them into the shabby living room. Julie Rafferty was waiting by the fireplace, ample breasts resting on her tightly folded arms, an expression which morphed between hostility and confusion playing across her cheaply attractive face.

Preston glanced around the room, the general atmosphere of drabness, wallpaper that had endured for far too long, furniture sagging from age as well as wear. Dust lined the photos on the mantelpiece. A couple of *Judge Dredd* comics were lying discarded on the floor. A large, widescreen television set, anachronistically modern amongst its dated surroundings, had been paused on a news report, a still image of a nearby street burning into the screen. The Raffertys gave the impression they were holding their breath, in anticipation of the interrogation to come. This far from the main road the street outside was silent; the rolling rumble of a washing machine in the next room was the only sound in the air.

Lee broke the hush. 'We imagine you've heard about your friend, Adrian Lawson, by now?'

'Yeah,' said Julie, her thick, starkly blonde hair rolling over her shoulders as she shook her head in appalled shock. 'Crazy.'

'Crazy,' her husband agreed.

'Crazy,' she reinforced. 'I were only talking to Donna yesterday. That's his wife, y'know. We met up for a coffee at that little place near the market.'

'Yes,' said Preston. 'That's what we wanted to talk to you about.' The tension in her stiff back seemed to intensify at this. He gestured towards the sofa. 'Do you mind if we...?'

She looked horrified at her rudeness. ''Course, love, sit yerselves down. Tea? Coffee? Jeff, get the kettle on.'

'Not for me,' said Lee.

'Coffee, thanks,' Preston said. 'Milk and one sugar.'

'Milk and one,' Rafferty repeated, nodding as he committed it to memory on his way to the kitchen.

Julie perched on the edge of the armchair. 'So, what about Donna? Do you think she killed him?'

Preston and Lee glanced at one another. 'Can you think of a reason why she might have wanted to?' he asked.

'Well, I don't want to speak badly of the dead, like, but he was, y'know, playing around.'

'Do you think she was aware of his infidelity?'

A grunt of bitter laughter emerged from the door to the kitchen. Julie cast a daggers look in that direction.

'Um, yes,' she admitted, squirming slightly. 'I told her myself.'

'Oh?' said Lee. Preston was impressed by how neutral it sounded – not accusatory at all.

'Yesterday,' Julie added.

'When you met for coffee?' Lee asked.

Julie nodded sheepishly.

Lee's raised eyebrow was subtle but conveyed much. The victim's wife found out that he had been unfaithful, hours before he was brutally murdered.

'But she knew what he was like,' Julie said quickly, though to Preston it sounded like she was defending her own actions in telling her, rather than denying Donna's possible retaliatory response. Then her voice took on a bitter edge as she glared at the faded carpet. 'He was a right dirty bastard!'

In the silence that followed she became aware of her husband standing by the kitchen door, steaming coffee mug in his hand, eyes boring into her like red-hot drill bits.

As Preston accepted the scalding drink, sipping carefully from it, Lee drew from Julie exactly what she had told Donna yesterday. And so they learned of the young Spanish girl who ran from the house, knocking the milk from Julie's hand, eyes streaming with tears of sadness, weariness and defeat. Of Lawson's trip to Cadiz on business, with a healthy dollop of pleasure mixed in. Rafferty stood, face glowing red as she disclosed his part in the sordid business, intercepting and passing on the scented love-letters and covering for his lecherous friend.

'What time did you and Mrs Lawson leave the café, Mrs Rafferty?' Preston asked.

'About quarter past one. Maybe a bit later.'

'Did she give you any idea of her plans for the rest of the day?'

'No, she'd sort of gone quiet. Just said she was going, and went.'

'And you?'

'Me?' said Julie, perplexed. 'What about me?'

'What did you do for the rest of the day?'

'What's that got to do with the price of biscuits?' She peered at them indignantly. 'You think I had summat to do with Adie getting killed?'

'It's just a routine question, Mrs Rafferty.'

She seemed to ponder this for a moment, before jutting out her chin proudly. 'Just went round the shops,' she said.

'The same ones that Mrs Lawson visited?'

'Dunno. I didn't see her again.'

'Do you have any receipts for any purchases? To establish a timeline.'

'I didn't buy owt. Just looked.' She spread her open, empty hands, adding a dismissive shrug.

'What about you, Mr Rafferty?'

Rafferty blinked vacantly, as if waking from a trance. 'Hmm?'

'What did you do yesterday?'

'Why?' If anything, he appeared even more affronted by the question than his wife.

'It's routine, dickhead,' she snapped. 'Tell 'em.'

'Well, after she set off to meet Donna, I went to work.' He frowned at the scratching of PC Lee's pencil in her notebook. She turned an enquiring smile to him, writing hand hovering patiently. 'Amazon warehouse in Donny,' he went on. 'I'm a shift manager in the despatch bay. I was on twelve 'til eight shift yesterday.'

'Doncaster,' Preston confirmed. 'That's the one on Balby Carr Bank.'

'That's right.'

'So you'd, what, drop down through Sempleby and Culvergate and get on the M18?'

'Yeah,' Rafferty nodded. 'It's shorter to go through Astbury and onto the A630 but that means you're going to hit a lot of the Doncaster town traffic, so M18's quicker. Twenty minutes. Half hour, tops.

'Out for about half past eleven, home by eight thirty?' Lee said, writing.

'No,' Rafferty corrected, flustered. 'I didn't get in 'til gone ten. I stopped off for a quick one at the Stag on the way home.'

'Hah!' Julie snorted. 'More than one.'

'How do you know what I did?' he snarled back at her. 'You were out yourself later than I was.'

''Cause you managed to get through more than forty quid. I checked your wallet this morning.'

'Nosy cow!' His arms weaved through the air, as if he was having trouble controlling them, fists clenching and flexing. 'I lost a bet on the boxing on the telly. Cost me thirty quid, if you must bloody know.'

'Yeah?' she sneered. 'Well, there's always summat to knock you back, isn't there?'

His face told them he'd heard that mocking phrase more than once or twice before. 'And where were you till after eleven?' he countered. 'Eh?'

'Only at bingo.' She was up and in his face. 'Rachael and Kelly will vouch for me. Ask 'em, go on.'

Preston raised a hand to placate them. 'We're not looking for alibis at this stage, Mrs Rafferty. Just a general sense of your whereabouts.'

He quickly finished his coffee and they made their escape. Moments later, back in the car, they sat and caught their breath.

'What a pair!' Lee gasped. 'I wouldn't want to be their kid.' They both had noticed the family photos, the comics, a boy's jumper thrown over the bannister rail, scuffed trainers by the front door. 'I wonder where he is.'

'As far away from that nightmare as he can get, I imagine,' Preston said, starting the car and pulling from the kerb. 'So, Julie Rafferty confirms that Donna Lawson was with her until one fifteen or later, then the shop receipts cover her 'til she gets home early evening.'

'Unless she lent somebody else her cards, sent them out shopping for her?'

'To provide an alibi?' Preston tapped the steering wheel in contemplation. 'Who'd do that for her?'

Lee pointed a thumb over her shoulder, in the direction they were coming from.

'Blondie?'

'Why not? She spent the whole afternoon round the shops and didn't buy anything for herself. And she calls herself a woman?' Lee smiled, so that Preston would appreciate the humour behind her gender stereotyping.

'They don't look like they're exactly loaded,' he said. 'Maybe she's a woman who exercises self-restraint.' He mirrored her previous smile. 'Rare, I know, but it can happen.'

'I'll set a uniform onto checking out those receipts,' she said. 'With a photo of Donna Lawson and Julie Rafferty for comparison. Hopefully the shop assistants will remember one or the other of them.'

'Okay,' said Preston. DC Lee was nothing if not thorough.

'What do you think *his* problem was?'

'Who, the husband?'

'Yeah,' she said. 'Don't you think he seemed a bit fidgety?'

'I reckon Mr Rafferty's biggest problem,' said Preston, throwing her a meaningful glance, 'is *Mrs* Rafferty.'

13

Jake's mum's much nicer than my mum, Alan thought glumly, snatching another cream cheese and ham sandwich from the stack in front of him and cramming it into his mouth. When he and Jake had arrived at the door she had welcomed them in with much cooing and hugging, glasses of cola in their hands before their muddy shoes landed on the hall mat. He and Jake sat either side of the tiny square table that took up so much of Mrs Harper's diminutive kitchen, while she fussed over them, peeling the outer wrapper from a packet of Penguin biscuits and tipping them onto a plate. There was no Mr Harper around to advocate caution over spoiling the boys, though Alan didn't know why. He was just a boy, after all. He'd never asked and Jake had never volunteered the information. Any who knew the details would dismiss it as the age-old story – he had stayed around while the bloom of his bride's youth and beauty still blossomed, but once the wilt had set in he had hopped over the fence to find greener grass. The fact that Jake's mum, even in full bloom, would never have appeared more than an uncultivated weed beside Alan's own mother held no interest to an adolescent youth looking for a maternal substitute. Blooming good looks took second place to thickly spread cream cheese, piled high with several slices of wafer thin processed ham surrounded by thick sliced white bread.

Parental issues were much on the boy's mind this afternoon. He had finally encountered Kenny's father, when he and Jake had grown bored of their own aimless pursuits and sought out their leader, the one with all the ideas. Wary as Alan was of what plans Kenny might propose, he was forced to admit that, without Kenny, they were merely wings without an engine. He made their plane take flight.

Without putting such fanciful analogies into words, they made the decision to call on Kenny once more.

Knowing Kenny's father of old, Jake held back and allowed Alan to take the lead up the short front path, past the wheelie bins, to the faded red door. The lumpy, hairless man who opened the door eyed his visitors with quiet menace and Alan was struck immediately with the image of a goblin from Lord of the Rings. As unobtrusively as possible Alan checked to see if he had pointed ears, and was mildly relieved to find that this man's ears more resembled trampled vegetables, rather than the auditory organs of cave-dwelling fantasy creatures.

On receiving no greeting from Kenny's father, Alan offered a meek 'Hello.'

'What?' came the grudging reply.

'Is Kenny in?'

'No.' He jerked a finger towards Jake, lingering by the gate. 'I told that lanky streak of piss earlier, he's fucked off.'

'Do you know when he'll be back?'

'Never, if he's got any sense.' He took a step back into the house, preparatory to slamming the door in Alan's face. 'Looks like he's finally taken the hint.'

With the crash of wood against frame still ringing in his ears, Alan rejoined Jake on the pavement. The eldest of their little gang, Kenny had been out of school for over a year already, leaving at the earliest opportunity. Unfortunately, he had found no source of employment since, much to his father's disgust, and his welcome in the family home had grown increasingly thin as time wore on. Encroaching adulthood and responsibility didn't impress anyone if you were forever leeching off your parents. His father had more than hinted that Kenny should begin paying his way soon, or look for alternative accommodation. That Kenny might have taken such a huge step without informing anyone of his plans clearly didn't concern his father. What his mother made of the situation wasn't known, but her opinions were rarely given, and even more

131

rarely sought, within that household.

While the prospect of escaping an overbearing father and an ineffectual mother were understandable to a refugee of the domestic battlefield such as himself, Alan was still puzzled by this sudden and unexplained disappearance. Jake seemed less troubled by it, shrugging it off with a 'Told ya' as he plodded along towards home, happy to have had his previous assessment of Kenny's father reinforced. Much as Jake was lost without him, Kenny could look after himself.

They were far enough from the main roads not to be concerned about the dangers of traffic, so the bronchial rattle of a maltreated car engine coughing into life farther down the street barely touched on their awareness.

'Come on,' Jake called over his shoulder, as he caught sight of Alan lagging behind, frowning back at Kenny's erstwhile home. 'It's nearly teatime. Mum's making sarnies.'

*

PC Jo Kershaw fixed her smile before she kicked open the door and re-entered the tiny interview room carrying two coffees in disposable cups. She placed them on the table, as far from the clunky, old computer as she could manage on the small surface, and grimaced apologetically.

'Not great, I'm afraid, but it's wet and warm.' As if to prove her point she blew on her hot fingertips and, with a quick, subconscious sweep of her hands over her already immaculate uniform white shirt and black trousers, she slid onto the plastic chair at her side of the table. She carefully arranged her legs around the cramped tangle of chair and table legs, easing as far back on her seat as she could, for fear of accidentally brushing knees with the revolting creature sitting opposite.

The neutral beige of the walls did nothing to dispel the claustrophobic effect of the windowless space, one of several such offices crammed onto this floor which doubled as taped interview rooms for suspects under caution. The thin walls afforded what privacy they could, but still the rumble of voices and shuffle of feet and chairs from neighbouring rooms filled the air like an invisible fog.

And then, to squeeze this overweight creature into such limited quarters merely caused further offence. Kershaw could tell that he had shifted the table to make room for his expansive gut while she was away fetching the drinks, as her chair was pressed against the small drawer unit in the corner of their miniature square.

She pulled the computer keyboard closer and, with an ostentatious flourish, she click-clacked in the password, looking at him expectantly, slim fingers hovering.

'Now,' she began, 'you're here to report a robbery?'

'Sort of,' said Grogan, unhelpfully.

'Oh?'

'More like, I wasn't paid what I should have been paid.'

'Ah, this is a fare for your taxi?' Kershaw had been informed of Grogan's name and occupation by the Civilian Enquiry Officer who had greeted him at the front counter, before he foisted the unpleasant specimen onto her to process the complaint.

'Aye, that's right. Thursday night, it were. Late on.'

'Thursday? Why didn't you report it yesterday?

'It happens, dunnit?' he shrugged. 'You pull up and they're out and away down the street before you can blink. Bastards! I wasn't goin' to say owt but the wife told me I've got to.'

'Your wife?' Kershaw almost smiled. He didn't seem the sort to be ordered around by the little woman back home. Had she witnessed the confrontation she might have been less amused.

'What's happened to you?' May Grogan had demanded of her husband when he came home that night. She was already in bed but had awoken when he lumbered into the bedroom. The bleeding had stopped but the scratches torn into his face were still livid and sore and his attempts to

133

laugh off the incident feeble and suspicious. Fare dodgers were common enough, but the fact that he had come close enough to sustain such injuries was more unusual. Three of them, he claimed, straight out of the pub and off their tits on booze and whatever else, and he'd clocked them in the mirror, whispering and plotting in the back, so he was ready to pounce when they tried to scarper. Grabbed one by the wrist but she'd turned and clawed him with her other hand, the bitch!

Lying there in the shadow of this mountain of flesh, May Grogan, petite and frail, looked as if she would be crushed like a fly had he rolled over in the night, but as he turned away from her and switched off his bedside lamp she glared doubtfully at the broad range of his hairy, wart-strewn back.

May had been the first up next morning, out to "clean" the cab, merely a pretext to cover having a good snoop round. Had she been pressed as to what she expected to find she couldn't have said, but the battered canvas holdall crammed under the seat wasn't it. Not the sort of thing a trio of drunken, female revellers spruced up for a night on the town would be carrying with them. And he hadn't mentioned that one of them was Spanish, as the passport tucked firmly into a buckled down pocket evidenced.

Maybe it had been left earlier, he reasoned weakly when she confronted him with it. He'd had so many passengers through the day, how was he expected to remember who was who?

It has to be handed in to the police, she'd insisted. If it belonged to his attacker then they had proof of who she was. They could get her nicked and maybe get the money for the fare returned as damages in court. If it wasn't hers then it had been mislaid and some poor lass could be wandering around in a right panic 'cause she'd lost all her stuff.

He mumbled a noncommittal response and went off to work, but she was waiting on his return and the badgering began all over again. Raised voices and raised hands hadn't dissuaded her, and he saw in her acid sneer that she knew, or at least strongly suspected, precisely what had transpired on that dark and secluded road so, short of admitting his guilt, his only option was to make this visit to the cop shop and repeat his tale of inebriated absconders.

Jo Kershaw was as dubious as Grogan's beleaguered wife, seeing the contents of the holdall spread before her on the small surface.

A few items of light clothing, nothing suitable for an English autumn. She noticed the loathsome man's eyes lingering on the simple, white underwear and she tucked it back into the bag out of sight.

There was a bar of confectionery with the word *chocolat* on the wrapper, same spelling as in that old Johnny Depp film that Netty had made her watch the other night. That was set in France, but the passport that she flicked through had definitely been issued in Spain. *España Pasaporte* and some elaborate coat of arms in gilt-work on the otherwise familiar red booklet's cover. Serious face on the photo inside, but Kershaw imagined the girl would be quite pretty when she smiled. Only a few months short of her own age, Kershaw noticed. None of this sat well with the story of a gang of girls trying to outwit a fat taxi driver.

'You hadn't noticed the bag in your cab earlier?' Kershaw asked him now. 'Before these girls got in.'

He shrugged, and Kershaw was glad she had removed the coffee cups prior to opening the holdall, as his whole body wobbled and his large belly jostled the table alarmingly. She imagined the dregs going everywhere.

'Didn't see it,' he said. 'But I don't check the cab between every fare. Could've been there ages.'

Kershaw saw Grogan out of the building a few minutes later, taking a breath of fresh October air, glad to be out of the confines of the cubicle. It had never seemed quite so constricting before, or the atmosphere so dense and noxious.

'Well, thanks again, Mr Grogan,' she said. He turned and, a couple of steps down from the smart, modern concrete and glass frontage of Haleston Police Station, his eyes were level with her chest. He didn't bother raising them to her face. 'We'll be in touch if we discover anything.' He continued to stare at her breasts. 'Or if we need more information from you.' That shook him from whatever fantasy was oozing through his mind. His eyes flicked up to hers, caught the intensity of her glare and, as quickly as his bulk would allow, he waddled off down the street.

*

'I now pronounce you... husband and wife!'

The two hundred assembled guests burst into applause and, without waiting for the traditional invitation from the registrar, the newly married couple enfolded one another in a tight and prolonged embrace, kissing passionately.

Several seconds passed.

'Okay, break!' Edward Maxey said, judging that the wrestling clinch had gone on long enough. This earned him an appreciative wave of laughter from those close enough to hear his quip over the engulfing music, which the hotel staff had put on as soon as the wedding had concluded. The bride and groom giggled in embarrassment and Rosalyn Peters called them aside to sign the register entry that she had been filling out while the ceremony took place.

There followed the customary blinding barrage of camera flashes as family and friends tried to outdo each other to take the most exceptional photograph of the occasion, one enthusiastic cousin climbing onto his chair for an aerial shot until the hotel's marriage co-ordinator rushed forward, muttering strong words about their health and safety policy.

Ties were loosened, waistcoats unbuttoned and fascinators removed as guests retired to the bar, one woman clutching her ivory, patent, stiletto-heeled shoes in one hand as she limped from the room. The atmosphere felt much airier and cooler without the mass of bodies consuming the oxygen, and the room far bigger now that Maxey and Roz were able to see to the far walls.

'I give 'em six months,' said Roz, screwing the top firmly onto her fountain pen.

'Cynic,' Maxey chided.

'It's too soon,' she explained. 'They've only known each other five minutes. They're still caught up in the "pash". Wait until she realises he clips his toenails in bed, or he finds out she leaves her shoes all over the house.'

'Don't all women do that?'

They watched as the hotel staff began stripping the row upon row of gaudily bedecked chairs of their stretchy covers and stacking them in high piles, preparatory to the quick change from wedding room into dining room.

'What a way to spend a Saturday afternoon.'

'Think of the overtime,' he said.

Roz stretched and flexed her shoulders as she slid the large, green marriage register into the black satchel, along with her certificates and pens. 'Hot bath when I get home, I think.'

'Is there anyone there to scrub your back?' Maxey said with a grin, slipping his long overcoat on top of his smart suit.

'Are you offering?' she asked, eyebrow raised.

'I don't think Nicky would approve.' He helped her on with her coat, giving her shoulders a firm squeeze as he straightened her collar. She writhed under his grip.

'Don't stop now, you tease,' she moaned, as he took his hands away.

He laughed, leading the way towards the exit. They responded to the friendly goodbyes and waves from the guests as they pushed through the crowd at the bar in the next room, emerging into the grand foyer of Ockerby Hall. The huge staircase of the recently renovated Victorian stately home swept away to their right as they approached the heavy main doors.

Maxey took his phone from his pocket, turning the

sound back on. He noticed the notifications for a missed call and voicemail on the screen and dialled up his messages.

'Aww, is she missing you?' Roz said, nudging him with her shoulder playfully.

'It's not Nicky,' he said. 'I don't know the number.' Though it did look vaguely familiar.

He lifted the phone to his ear and listened. She saw the curious expression crinkle his face.

'What's wrong?'

Glancing round at the public surroundings he jerked his head towards the main doors and led her outside. They stopped at the place where they had parked their respective cars on arrival earlier and he held out his phone in front of him to replay the message on speaker. Though the terrified voice was cracked and faltering, still the accent was unmistakeable.

'Hello? Please, hello? You must help me, I don't know what to do.'

Roughly snatching a packet of cigarettes from her coat pocket, Roz sighed and shook her head gravely. 'Oh, Eddie, what have you got yourself into?'

Racing through traffic towards Merrington moments later, Roz's words echoed in his mind. What, indeed, had he got himself into? He knew now who had called him the previous afternoon, and why the Stag and Hounds had popped into his mind during his call with Luke earlier. After the Spanish girl had left his office, despite his concern for her in the moment, she had barely entered his thoughts again. The fact that she would call him, a stranger, not merely once but now a second time, spoke of her desperation.

When he had shrugged helplessly and dialled back the number from which she had rung him, Roz tutted, blew a cloud of smoke towards him and walked away. The ring tone repeated for a long time before a breathless voice answered, and the relief when she recognised his voice was profound. Her words were garbled, half English, half Spanish, something about the man from the wrong house, and "my love", and lies, and blood. That was when her voice had finally broken into incoherency, when she mentioned the blood.

He ascertained exactly where she was in relation to the Stag, cut off the call and jumped into the car. He noticed Roz, still puffing urgently on her cigarette, leaning against her car watching him drive past. He offered a friendly wave, which was not returned.

Opposite the Stag and Hounds was the small park and play area where Alicia had waited yesterday, until she was ready to knock on the door of the address she had searched for so diligently. A few benches, swings, a slide and, at the other side of a large expanse of grass where children regularly ignored the 'no ball games' sign, was a dense patch of bushes. Alicia wasn't the first homeless person to take advantage of the growth, impenetrable to the eye, to spend a night huddled in its shelter.

As Maxey pulled up to the kerb near the gates he peered into the park, watching for signs of her presence. He felt sure she was looking back but couldn't see her, until he climbed out of the car and stood up to his full height, then she spotted him and broke cover of the bushes. He gaped in horror at the apparition rushing towards him, hair in disarray, face and clothing smeared in mud and grime. And blood. So much blood.

14

Edward Maxey sat in the quietest part of the Stag and Hounds, in the corner farthest from the door, at a table behind a wood-panelled partition. The froth on his pint of shandy was steadily dissipating as condensation pooled onto the table beneath the glass. He'd noticed an impressive display of craft ales on draught at the bar when he arrived, some with intriguing names, but as he slid his car keys into his pocket he knew he had to be sensible. Even though an extremely strong drink would be very welcome right now! He positioned himself so that he could see Luke Preston when he arrived and he waved as he watched him duck under the artificially low doorway and scan the interior.

Preston mimed waggling a drink in front of his face, in the universal sign language query of whether Maxey wanted a refill. Maxey shook his head and Preston headed to the bar.

Moments later he approached the table and slid onto the bench seat adjacent to where Maxey sat. 'Sup, dude?' he said.

'That's what we're here for,' Maxey responded, raising his glass to drink. It was another of their little rituals, developed over many years of easy camaraderie, though the secrets he concealed tonight gave the shandy a bitter tang. The taste of guilt?

He took in their surroundings, the dark veneer panels, fake beams, stone fireplace against a wall with no chimney, reproduction hunting scenes in gilt frames on every wall. Nothing as vulgar as a games machine or TV screen in sight, though the mock-aged look held a vulgarity of its own.

'It's ages since we came here,' Preston said, mirroring Maxey's appraisal of the room. 'I can see why.'

'At least it's quiet.' Barely half a dozen other customers were in the pub at this hour, even on a Saturday. Early, yet.

'What did they call that girl?' asked Preston, obviously referring to their previous visit.

Maxey laughed. 'If you can't remember, how do you expect me to? I can tell you who I went home with.'

'And how is the gorgeous Nicky?'

'Still gorgeous, thanks. She says 'Hi'.'

'Same to her, tell her,' Preston said. 'Heard anything from Claire?'

The question was lightly asked, but Maxey felt the weight behind it.

'Not for a while,' he said. 'You?'

'Only when I'm late taking Kerry back.'

'So, every week, then?'

Preston gave a wry smirk, then sighed.

'And you?' he said, in a change-of-subject tone. 'What have you been up to?'

Maxey tensed. It was the question he had been dreading. He took a drink of his shandy to hide his hesitation.

What the hell *had* he been up to?

The expression on Nicky's face when he had bundled his visitor through the front door that afternoon, swamped in his large overcoat, was one of horror.

'What the hell's this?' she demanded. Then the pain and terror that the girl exuded seemed to touch her sympathetic nature and she ushered her into the room. Nicky gasped when the coat was taken away and the horrendous state that Alicia was in was fully revealed.

'What happened?' She pushed Alicia's hair from her face and wiped at her smeared cheeks with her thumb. She held her still, tried to look into her wildly staring eyes.

'She's not spoken since I picked her up.' Maxey briefly related the details of his previous meeting with the young Spanish woman and her search for the errant lover who had taken advantage of her. And of what they had

141

discovered on the database about his true nature and situation.

'What was it...? Dawson? No, Lawson.'

At mention of the name both women turned to him suddenly. Recognition of the name drew Alicia out of her shocked stupor, and tears pricked her eyes again. But Nicky gaped at him, wide eyed.

'Not *Adrian* Lawson?'

'My Adrian,' Alicia murmured.

'That's him,' Maxey said, surprised. 'Do you know him?

'Haven't you heard?' Nicky hissed, pulling Maxey aside. 'He's all over the bloody news!'

'I've not heard the news. I always have CDs on in the car.'

'He's dead. Murdered. In a brutal and *bloody* way.'

Oh shit, Maxey thought. A tingly sensation crept up his spine and spread a chill through him. Had this tiny, pretty creature taken a man's life in an act of extreme violence? He realised that he kept thinking of her as a girl, but she was a mature woman, with adult emotions and sensibilities. He stared at her with new vision, and she gazed back with large, dark eyes full of misery. He took in the dishevelled appearance and all the blood turning a rusty brown on her clothes.

But Nicky sighed sadly. 'Oh, no.' The compassion in her tone shook Maxey, the heartbreak in her eyes. Then he saw it too. The blood was everywhere, hands, face, smeared on her t-shirt, but by far the greatest concentration of the stains was on the flimsy trousers she wore, across the front and down between her legs.

'It's *her* blood.'

*

'I did not kill Adrian.'

'Of course not,' Maxey said. 'We never thought so for a second!'

But they had. She saw it in their faces. Before they realised where the blood on her clothes had originated, they thought it was his. That she had taken his life, spilt his blood, bathed in it like an animal.

Since then they had repented their suspicion and shown her to the bathroom, given her a huge, soft dressing gown to drown in, and placed piping hot soup before her.

'He was not my Adrian,' she continued, bitterness creeping into her voice. 'This man full of lies.' The man who faced her yesterday.

So far removed from the sweet, loving man who had courted her back in the small tuna fishing village in the southern part of the Province of Cádiz. From the moment he stepped into the shade of the foyer of her father's hotel, out of the blinding afternoon sunshine, taking off his sunglasses and smiling warmly at her, she had recognised the gentle strength of the large Englishman. She'd checked him in, shown him to his room, lingered in his doorway to watch him throw his suitcase onto the crisp white sheets of the sturdy bed. He strode towards her, hand in pocket, thinking she was waiting for a tip. She blushed profusely, shook her head and ran back to the reception desk.

She often felt men's eyes upon her in the dining room, as she flitted between tables, delivering meals, clearing plates, like a bee in a patch of bougainvillea. But his scrutiny was kinder than the leer of the sun-reddened, soccer-shirted louts who called her "darlin'" and blew boozy kisses. Their type hadn't used to be a problem, but the growth of commerce and tourism in the nearby coastal towns had overflowed into the quiet villages, bringing a lot of welcome income but also a number of unwelcome visitors. The gallantry he displayed when he stepped in to warn off the unruly youths was unnecessary, for she had shrugged off the likes of them many times before this, but his kindness pleased and flattered her.

He was quiet and respectful, but radiated a natural charm that drew her like a moth, despite his apparent disinterest. Was the incident of his emerging from the bathroom without his towel while she was cleaning his room truly an accident? After all, she had knocked and called out. But then maybe, just maybe, she had heard the shower running when she entered, and stayed anyway. It gave them something to laugh about later, his laugh raucous and bold, hers shy, hidden behind a delicate hand, when she bumped into him on her return from church the next day. She enjoyed the clifftop walk while her father preferred to take the direct path back to the hotel, and her sister, still in disgrace and therefore not allowed such luxuries, scuttled along at his heels.

Not that Adrian's body was a laughing matter. Taut and muscular, broad shouldered and flat stomached, and sporting a thick mat of dark hair on forearms, calves and chest. And *there*. There, where her eyes lingered longest. It was only a second, but she shocked herself all the same. She was contrite during her confession in the morning, accepting the Hail Marys with appropriate grace, but couldn't deny the impure thoughts which sprang into her mind, even while performing her penance.

Gulls circled and cried above the clifftop and Adrian watched them keenly, seemingly oblivious to her approach until she spoke to him. They both apologised at once for the awkward moment the day before, then each dismissed the other's apology as unnecessary, then laughed at speaking over one another.

No one had shortened her name before, it wasn't considered polite in the village, but when he called her Lissy she smiled and blushed. After they located the rickety wooden steps and climbed down to the beach, he took her hand and opened his heart as they strolled along to a secluded cove. She believed him when he said he'd never met the "right woman" before. She believed him when he suggested that maybe he had now. When he laid her down on the soft sand and told her he loved her, she had believed his lies and treachery.

144

When he returned home she wasted no time in sending the first of her wistful and optimistic perfumed letters to the address she believed was his. She had sent several more before she began to wonder at the lack of response. But her faith was strong, and she persevered, filling the pages with hope and cheer and thoughts of the future.

Looking at herself in the mirror was something she had always considered vain and sinful, but now she stared at the curves and contours of her nakedness, and felt his eyes upon her. When her breasts became swollen and tender she imagined that they were pining for his touch, as she stroked and comforted them. She ignored the frequent abdominal cramps; her appetite was minimal since he left her behind, she was merely adjusting to her reduced diet. When her monthly curse was two weeks overdue, she began to fit the pieces of the puzzle together.

She couldn't accept that either the priest or the doctor would break their vows of confidentiality, yet she had told no one else, so how her father found out about her condition was a mystery. But, somehow, he did. He ranted and roared, and called down the Lord's Judgement, but surprisingly, for all that she cowered at his feet, the huge hands that flailed wildly in the air did not strike her, and the belt that still bore the stains of her sister's thrashings remained around his waist. But she couldn't trust that his reticence would hold for long, so she hastily packed a few meagre belongings, grabbed the passport that she had used only once before on a daytrip to Tangier, and ran from the only home, the only life, she had ever experienced. Ran into the unknown.

But the registrar man and his wife knew none of this. As they gently queried how she had found herself in her present predicament she commenced her story where he had left his earlier, with her leaving his office to seek out her lover.

A pretty young thing, in evident distress, can always rely on the generosity of strangers, so she was soon directed to the bus station and shown the correct route to the address she had memorised from Maxey's computer screen and hastily scribbled down on the reverse of the other, incorrect, address. She noticed with wry amusement that the streets passing outside the bus windows were the same she had travelled earlier, and recognised Rafferty's street only a few moments before the bus driver kindly informed her that she was at her stop.

Another random passer-by was pleased to point her towards the house she sought, but even before she reached it the screech of tyres startled her to a halt. The driver of the car which had pulled up so sharply to the kerb at her side sat staring at her in shock. Adrian. Her Adrian. Finally! Her bitterness and anxiety dissolved at the mere sight of him.

After a moment of frozen indecision he waved to the passenger side of his car, gesturing for her to get in. She joyfully raced to clamber into the vehicle, throwing her arms around him and kissing his face. He allowed this, but didn't reciprocate.

'She's just text me,' he said bluntly, without explaining who "she" was. 'She's gone out for coffee, but I don't know how long she'll be. We'll have to make it quick.'

She sank back into her seat and stared at him with incomprehension as he started up the car and pulled away, looking around far more cautiously than someone merely checking for oncoming traffic.

When he stopped the car again, only a matter of metres along the street, he peered at the window of the house in front of which he had parked.

'Good,' he said. 'The nosy twat isn't there. He must be in the loo or something. Let's get inside before he comes back.'

He jumped from the car and looked at her expectantly until she also got out. He crossed the street and raced up the path to the front door of the house opposite, letting himself in and jerking his thumb abruptly towards the interior.

'In. Quick.'

She hurried past him and he slammed the door closed behind her with a sigh of relief. With a firm hand on her arm he told her to wait there while he disappeared into a room to their left. When he called her in a moment later the curtains were closed and he had created a small crack with his fingers so he could peek out like a spy.

This furtive, nervous man no longer resembled the proud hero she thought she knew. He crossed back to her and took her by the shoulders, and the familiar spark in his eyes no longer whispered of love and adoration, it shouted out frustration and annoyance. She laughed at the redundancy of his words when he said 'You shouldn't have come.'

'Who are you?' she asked.

He frowned at her. 'What?'

'Was anything you told me true?'

He slumped onto the sofa.

She looked down at him. 'When you gave that smile to me and stroked at my skin and told me I was the most beautiful thing in the whole of Andalusia, brighter than the sun, more spectacular than the sparkling sea – see, I remember all you say – did you mean even a single word of that... that *disparates*? Or was it all just a show, to *mistificar* the stupid, ignorant village girl and have your pleasure with her?'

He stared at his feet.

'You can't even look me in the eye. I see before me now a weak man, cowed in shame and smelling of urine.'

That unexpected tangent seemed to jolt him into activity. He sniffed at his shirt, then stood and quickly unbuttoned it, heading for the hallway even as he peeled it off. When he reappeared moments later, fastening up a clean shirt, some of his resolve had been restored. When he looked at her now she sensed an intense sensation of disappointment, like she was somehow tarnished in his memory. The perfect image he had cherished since they

147

parted weeks ago was shattered with her reappearance; she had climbed down from her pedestal and become *ordinary.*

'You'll have to go,' he said, moving close, a gentle hand easing from her shoulder, up her neck, making a fist in her hair. Even now, after everything that had happened, she still felt a quiver at his touch, and hated herself for it. 'You're a beautiful, compassionate woman and I feel so honoured to have known you and spent a wonderful few days with you, but I have a whole other life here. One you're not a part of. And never could be.'

She swatted his hand away. 'So stupid, so stupid!' She slapped her own face, hard. 'You're not special. You're not different. What an idiot I have been.'

She struck herself again, and he grasped her wrists tightly.

'Stop that!'

Her resistance was brief and futile. She hung limply in his hands so he sat her on the sofa and knelt in front of her.

'You need to go home,' he told her, his tone soft and persuasive, the detestable words jarring in the voice she remembered so fondly. 'There's nothing for you here.'

She stared past him, at the mantelpiece, at the photo in its frame. Glistening filigree surrounding the smiling couple, sunlight glowing in their hair, twinkling in their eyes, teeth shining white. A happy scene.

'That's her, is it? She said through bared teeth. 'Donna?'

He glanced over his shoulder, following her gaze. 'Yes, that's—' He stopped, frowned. 'How do you know her name?'

'Oh, I know you, Mr Adrian Lawson.' She stood suddenly, forcing him back onto his haunches. 'I know all about you. Two wives! Two sons! You, the man who never found anyone to love.'

'What? Two sons? No, just one.'

'There's no need to lie to me anymore.' She pulled the slip of paper from her pocket, showed him the Register

Office seal printed there. 'They told me everything!'

His eyes showed genuine confusion, though she felt sure she had remembered it correctly. One child. Two. She saw his dismissive shrug. It was of little importance in the overall picture. He clearly just wanted to finish it. End this confrontation. Get the "hysterical girl" out of his way, out of his house, out of his life.

She securely crammed the compliment slip back into her pocket, confident that she'd made her point. 'I am shamed to have ruined my life for such as you.'

'Look, I'm sorry.'

'Your pity is worthless,' she spat. 'I cannot go home. I have no home. You have left me with nothing.' In that dark, desperate moment the tiny life curled deep within her tumbled through her mind and she decided that she would not tell him of the only thing he had left her with.

Pliant and yielding, too weary to object, she allowed him to bundle her out of the back door, over small, round paving stones sunk into a trim lawn to the gate in the rear fence. The ginnel would lead her out into the next street and she wouldn't be seen, he assured her, as if he were protecting her reputation rather than his own.

She made her way back to the park, a familiar landmark, somewhere she could sit and think, and try to make sense of the crumbling travesty her life had become. There was a phone box outside the park gates, just across the road from a mock-Tudor fronted public house. She still had a little of Maxey's money left, after the bus fares and buying herself some lunch earlier, so she gathered some change and squeezed into the glass box. That's when she tried his number the first time, she told them, but when his voicemail kicked in she panicked and hung up. He'd already done so much to help her, how could she impose further?

Her account skipped the rest of the day, jumping to her hiding in the bushes overnight, pulling leaves and twigs over herself for whatever comfort they might bring, eventually succumbing to exhaustion in the early hours, only to awaken in agony before the next morning had dawned. She prayed the moisture on her clothes was from the damp, dewy undergrowth, or perhaps she had wet herself unknowingly in her sleep. Rather that indignity than the alternative. But she knew. The cold, gnawing emptiness inside her, like something precious had been stolen. It was the Lord's Judgement, catching up with her at last.

She'd lain there for hours as strengthening daylight poked through the canopy of greenery about her, twitching with spasms, wishing for death to take her. Finally she resolved that she must take action of some sort, so dragged her pain-wracked body back to the phone box. Voicemail again, but this time she left her message, then collapsed onto the floor of the booth, lacking the power to even push open the door. If anyone saw her there, curled up in the dirt, they hadn't cared to offer assistance. When Maxey rang back a few minutes later she thought that maybe her luck was changing. Maybe the Lord thought she had been punished enough. Summoning the energy to return to her hiding place, she awaited her rescuer.

'What are you going to say to Luke?' Nicola Maxey said, dragging Alicia back to the daunting present. Her voice was heavy with worry and concern as she spoke to her husband.

Maxey looked at her blankly. 'Eh?'

'Tonight,' she went on, a little impatiently. 'When you see Luke tonight. What are you going to tell him?'

*

'Nothing,' Maxey said, with as much nonchalance as he could muster, sliding a beermat across the table to soak up the ring of moisture. 'The usual. Births, deaths, marriages. Same old same old.' He took another sip of his shandy. 'What about you? Anything interesting happen at work?'

'That's what I wanted to talk to you about, actually,'

150

Preston said, taking out his smartphone and calling up the photo gallery. 'You'll have heard about that murder last night? Just round the corner from here, as a matter of fact.'

'Was it?' Maxey said, affecting surprise.

'Yeah, someone made a right mess of a bloke in his own house.' He pulled a face. 'Nasty business.'

'I thought you'd take all the grisly stuff in your stride by now,' Maxey said. 'All the things you must've seen in your time.'

'Haleston is hardly the murder capital of the North,' Preston said. 'There've been one or two, but nothing as bad as this. His name was Adrian Lawson.'

'Yeah, Nicky mentioned it. She saw it on the news.'

'Hard to keep something like that quiet,' Preston grumbled. 'You didn't know him, then?'

'Me?' Maxey was genuinely thrown by this. 'No, why?'

Preston swung his phone round to face him and Maxey flinched.

'Bloody hell, I thought you were going to show me the body!'

Preston laughed. 'Don't worry, I wouldn't subject you to that horror show, mate.'

'What's that, then?' Maxey squinted at the photo on the screen. A little dark, taken in artificial light, and through some sort of clear film, he saw a piece of paper with numbers written on it. He felt the back of his neck and his scalp tingle and burn with the rush of hot blood, and hoped his face wasn't glowing bright red. 'Where'd you find that?'

'I'll ask the questions, punk,' Preston snarled, but his smile showed that he wasn't taking this interrogation too seriously. 'It's your number, isn't it?'

'Well, yeah.' There was no point in denying it.

'And your handwriting?'

Maxey reluctantly nodded.

'So whoever had this, you must have given it to them yourself.'

'I guess so,' Maxey mumbled, sounding as vague as

possible.

'You aren't likely to give out your private number to everybody that comes through the door,' Preston guessed. 'Do you remember who you gave this one to?'

'Umm...' So, this was the moment. He had to choose whether or not to lie to a policeman investigating a serious crime. Deadly serious. Worse still, from his perspective, lie to his best friend. 'Yeah, as a matter of fact, yeah, I do.'

'Oh?'

'There was a woman, barely more than a girl, pretty young thing.'

'Oh, yes?'

'Behave!'

'Like it doesn't make a difference when you're handing out your number.'

'Nothing like that.'

'Okay, go on.'

Maxey pondered, selecting his words with care. 'She was foreign. Her English wasn't great; it was difficult to understand her. She seemed quite distressed.'

'We've already got some information about a foreign girl. Spanish.'

'That'll be her, then,' Maxey said, wondering just how much his friend already knew.

'What did she want?' Preston asked.

'She was after personal information about someone.'

'Did you give it to her?'

'You know we aren't supposed to give out details like that.' Which was true, though not the answer to the question.

'But you gave her your number.'

'In case she became more coherent when she calmed down.'

'And did she ring it?'

'No.' *Shit, shit, shit!*

'Hmm. She's not likely to now, as this was on the floor in the dead man's house.'

'Oh my God!' Maxey felt the hole he was sinking into growing by the second.

'One last question, Mr Maxey,' Preston said, in a mock "serious copper" voice. 'Did you happen to pop out here to Merrington last night and bash the brains in of one Adrian Lawson, hereabouts residing?'

'Not that I remember.' He scratched his head and pulled a confused face.

Preston laughed. 'Fair enough.' He put his phone away and picked up his drink. 'We'll probably need you to pop in and give us your fingerprints, for elimination.'

'No worries.' Maxey's heart was still thumping. He was *fairly* confident that Alicia was not responsible for Lawson's murder, but there was still a chance she was lying. He was hindering an investigation at the very least, by not divulging pertinent information, and possibly harbouring a murderer in the process. He looked up as he realised Preston was talking.

'...and not getting anywhere. No witnesses and a bloody great gap in the timeline for the day of the murder.' He put on a high-pitched, broad accent. 'There's always summat to knock you back, isn't there?'

Maxey felt something stir in his memory. 'Why did you say that?'

'What?'

'That phrase, in that voice.'

'Just something one of Lawson's friends said today,' Preston said. 'Why?'

'I've heard it before.' He wracked his brains. 'Oh, I remember. It was somebody asking about arranging a marriage. A woman on the phone, yesterday.'

'Well, it's not that uncommon a phrase, is it?'

'Was this "friend of the deceased" on the market for a new husband?'

'Not that I'm aware of,' Preston said. 'Though the term "happily married" isn't the first label I'd pin on her.'

Maxey nodded. 'Probably just a coincidence.'

'Oh, and get this!' Preston said, smirking despite his frustration. 'We're only having to deal with crazy witnesses sending us on wild goose chases. Guy over the road points out there's blood on the victim's car, but it turns out it's animal's blood. The vic's blood is splashed around everywhere, and we're sniffing out animal blood.'

'How did you find that out so quickly?' Maxey asked. 'I thought it usually took a while to get samples checked.'

'It does, but luckily the car had been tested already after it was nicked the other day.'

'Nicked?'

'Yeah, those bloody joyriders I told you about. Swiped the soddin' thing, had their fun, then dumped it in the mud out near Ockerby. They must've hit somebody's dog while they were whizzing about in it.'

'A dog?' Maxey's mind was racing. 'What sort of car was it?'

'Big, flashy Audi, I think.'

'Black?'

'Yes.' Preston was intrigued. 'How did you know that?'

'Do you remember that old guy I told you about? The one who wanted to register the death of his dog?'

'Oh yes! Sad, old weirdo?'

'That's the one. Now, this may be nothing,' Maxey said, and part of him hoped it was, indeed, nothing. He felt sorry for Arthur Camm, having the only creature he held any affection for torn from him in so cruel a fashion. But another part wanted to draw attention away from Alicia, and assuage his guilt for the earlier deception. So he told Preston of his visit to Camm's farm and the nature of Bexy's demise, the bloody jeans in the brazier and the look in Arthur's eye when he spoke of that flashy, black car.

'So maybe,' Maxey supposed, 'he found out whose car it was and took his revenge!'

'But Lawson wasn't driving the car.'

'Well, Arthur might not have realised that.' Maxey was warming to the notion now. After all, if Arthur was the culprit then Alicia was off the hook. 'He somehow traces Lawson's address, confronts him over killing the dog, loses his temper and pow!'

'Pow?'

'Yeah, pow.'

'Over a bow-wow?' Preston's scepticism was obvious.

'You didn't see how pissed off he was.'

Luke Preston tipped back the last of his drink and looked at his friend over the top of his glass. 'Well, to be fair, there have been equally harrowing murders committed in the past for much flimsier motives than the loss of a loved pet. It's worth looking into, I suppose.'

'Brilliant!'

'I don't know what you're getting so excited about,' Preston said. 'There isn't a reward.' They both laughed.

'Hey, I've just thought,' Maxey said, his face suddenly serious. 'Should you even be on this case, what with me being involved and us being such good mates?'

'You think the force has got enough detectives that they can afford to leave their very best out of it when there's a juicy murder on the go? Anyway, you're not even a witness, let alone a suspect. Unless there's something you're not telling me?'

There was the briefest hesitation before Maxey's smile returned. He finished his drink and they said their goodbyes and "later/'gators" and made their way to the door. The pub was much busier now, a line of over-stuffed Barbour jackets leaning against the bar, probably attracted by the craft ales

Headlights danced across the metalwork of assorted four-by-fours, cast by Maxey navigating his vehicle through the now crowded car park towards the exit, and as the harsh, white beams flashed past the phone box on the opposite side of the road a niggling doubt wormed its way into his mind.

15

Jake was bored.

Autumn nights, with the change in hour bringing darkness much earlier, gave him longer to perform his mischief, but it wasn't the same on his own.

He'd already nicked a load of Hallowe'en decorations from outside a house, plastic skeletons, paper witches and real, carved pumpkins, and dumped them in neighbours' gardens all along the street. An abandoned beer bottle in the gutter had amused him for a few seconds, making a pleasing missile aimed at the nearest lamppost. That it missed its target and arced down, bouncing off the roof of a parked car, leaving an impressive dent, before shattering on the far pavement, didn't diminish the entertainment value in that brief moment. But it was all so transient. He needed constant stimulus, but lacked the imagination to come up with the necessary ideas to accommodate his boundless energy.

He hadn't wanted to show it in front of Alan Rafferty but he had to admit that he missed Kenny. He couldn't remember the last time he'd spent a whole twenty-four hours out of his company before. Not since that very first day, maybe a couple of years ago, when Kenny, then still a stranger, just one of the older boys at school, and some other lad he knocked around with at the time, had caught up with Jake on their bikes on his way home from school. Trying to intimidate him they had circled him, swearing and spitting, swerving closer and closer, until Jake swung his school bag into the face of the other lad, knocking him off balance so he came crashing to the concrete pavement with a grisly crunch. He launched a few good, hard kicks into the youth's face and groin, picked up the lad's bike and rode off at full speed, all before Kenny could even react.

Kenny chased after him, leaving his companion crumpled and crying, but instead of exacting revenge against Jake, he had expressed his admiration for the younger boy's "bottle" and recruited him as his new apprentice.

Apart from when Jake's mum had taken him to Scarborough for a week, or when Kenny's dad shut him up in his room one weekend after being brought home in a police car because he'd been caught moving traffic cones at some roadworks, the two boys had seen each other almost every day. Kenny clearly craved an audience for his escapades and Jake needed someone to follow. They hung around together at school at first, then, after Kenny left school, Jake would stop off at Kenny's instead of going straight home in the afternoon. Weekends found them mooching around causing whatever chaos Kenny conceived of to pass their days. So great was their mutual reliance it became rare to see one without the other.

So Jake had spent the whole of today waiting for Kenny to spring out of hiding, brimming with wild schemes. He ascribed Kenny's absence from home to an act of rebellion against his tyrannical father, getting some space, a little freedom. Kenny might leave home without a word, but surely he wouldn't leave Jake.

But he hadn't appeared.

Spending the day with Raff had afforded a little distraction, until the nesh bugger had gone home to get his coat. His thick jumper had been enough while they were running around in daylight, but as it got dark a fine drizzle had set in, leaving them damp and chilled. Jake wasn't bothered by it but Raff had started whinging, so they headed for his place. The second he opened the front door his mum had appeared, swiped him round the head and dragged him inside by the scruff of his neck.

'Where the hell have you been all day? We've been worried sick!'

Jake compared his own mother's reaction whenever she worried about his late return home; a hug and a kiss to the forehead, rather than a clip round the ear. But everyone was different, he supposed.

Finally giving in to the boredom, Jake decided to cut his losses and head for home. There might be something good on the telly, apart from all those bloody dancing and singing competitions, and he could get his mum to make him a hot chocolate and sit with him on the sofa till he warmed through. Nothing better than mummy-snuggles on a cold night. Jake could leave the shop-lifting and the joyrides and breaking windows and all the other acts of random disruption behind once he was home, his "dark side" slipped off like his damp hoodie on the hall stand. Indoors was another world, far removed from anything that Raff, or even Kenny, were aware of, and Jake liked to keep it that way.

He crammed his cold hands deep into his pockets, head hunched down in his shoulders. Curtains were drawn across windows on all sides and a shining mist floated round the streetlights as Jake increased his long-legged stride. He briefly considered taking one of the cars parked along the kerb, to speed his journey home, and he found himself glancing into their dark interiors as he passed, but without the others to share the thrill it wasn't the same, so he marched on. The night was quiet, just the bark of a dog from a house on his left, an overloud telly across the street, so he became aware of the rumbling roar from the car behind him, its tyres rasping on the wet road, long before the rusty old heap drew past him. The vehicle was distinct and easily recognisable, and Jake clearly recollected seeing it before, perhaps more than once. It drove by slowly, as if the occupant was looking for somewhere to park. It finally pulled in a little way ahead and the driver, a short, wiry old man, clambered out and moved to the rear of the vehicle, opening the boot with some tugging and jerking of the locking mechanism. Jake watched him bend over into the darkness of the boot space, rummaging around for some item or other, grumbling under his breath at its apparent absence.

At the moment that Jake came alongside the car the old man emerged from the boot and stood facing him. He expected him to speak, say goodnight, ask directions, something, but he remained eerily still. Jake had time to wonder why the old man was holding a rusty crowbar so tightly in his right hand. Then it struck him.

*

'Aww, isn't she cute?' cooed Mavis Camm, as the tiny bundle of fur peeped disproportionately large brown eyes out of the thick, woolly blanket it was huddled into. She tapped a stubby finger gently onto the wet, black nose and laughed as the puppy sneezed in response.

'Cute don't mean nuthin', does it?' Arthur said, fighting to resist the appeal of that tip of pink tongue jutting from under the dog's fuzzy moustache. 'What we need is a working dog. One who'll be able to tell one end of a sheep from the other.'

'She could learn.'

'They've got to have it in 'em by nature,' Arthur said. 'A Collie's what we want. Not some mongrel mutt.'

'We always get a Collie,' Mavis grumbled. 'And you always call them "Dog". Even the girls.'

'Well, I can 'ardly go round the fields shouting "Bitch" at the top of my lungs,' Arthur responded with a mean chuckle. 'People'd think I was calling for you.'

'Cheeky git,' she spat back. 'We're getting' this one. I want somethin' on that farm to show me a bit of affection every now an' then. 'Cause I sure as heck don't see any from you.'

The young pet sanctuary worker coughed awkwardly, to remind the couple of her presence. Arthur showed the girl a forced smile, inadequate for the purposes of persuading her that their exchange was all in good fun, but the best he could muster. At least he now knew why Mavis had insisted on coming here for a new dog, rather than pimping Dog out to old Anderson near the village, to mate with his beasts, like they usually did. That way they got the pick of the litter and ensured the pedigree was pure.

No worry, Dog still had a couple of good years in it yet. Let the daft woman have this one for now. Once it proved it was no good he'd wring its neck, chuck it in the pig feed and do the job of selecting the next Dog properly.

But that hadn't happened. "Bexy", as this creature soon came to be known, named after Mavis' Aunty Rebecca, *in a good way*, Mavis insisted, but Arthur knew it was because of the big, dopey eyes and moustache, had grown on them both soon after taking up residence on her blanket by the hearth. Arthur surprised himself and her by being as much a sucker for that lolloping run and lolling tongue as Mavis was. Of course, he was right about her aptitude for sheep herding, but by the time a new Dog came from Anderson's there was no question about Bexy becoming pig feed.

She joined them on their bed, a living bolster to reinforce a sexless regime that had endured for so many years that neither husband nor wife could remember who had chosen to abstain first. She enabled them to break the silence, gave them something to talk about before going to sleep. For a while bedtime was tolerable again. Eventually though almost all conversation, day or night, was conducted through the creature, by proxy, until they stopped talking to one another directly at all.

This situation suited Arthur just fine, but Mavis grew to feel that she deserved better than taking second place to the pet, and more than a husband she placed in a similar ranking.

The fact that Bexy spent more evenings curled up by Arthur's feet than hers only added to the resentment that Mavis nurtured. Once the decision had been made to clear out and leave the cantankerous old bastard on his own (*let's see how he manages without me*) Mavis knew that she could make the impact all the worse by taking Bexy with her.

Arthur was in the barn butchering a pig for the freezer on the day she packed her battered, leather suitcase. Bexy was in there with him, sniffing at the blood and wincing as the cleaver thudded into the carcase over and over again.

'Walkies!' Mavis shouted from the door. She waved Bexy's lead and the dog skipped over to her.

But she was wearing her best coat, Arthur noticed. She wouldn't put that on for a tramp across the fields. He followed them out, saw the open door of the old car, the suitcase jammed onto the back seat because she'd never got the hang of that tricky boot catch, and Mavis urging Bexy into the vehicle.

Mavis lifted her head in his direction as he came out of the barn, a cocktail of panic, desperation and sheer hatred stirring her features.

'Leave her,' were the first words that sprang from his lips. Not 'Where are you going?' or 'Why?' or 'Don't go.'

Sensing trouble Bexy slunk away from the car, turning her cowed head from one to the other of them.

'Come 'ere!' Mavis hissed, making a grab for the bush of soft fur on Bexy's chest.

'I said, leave 'er be!' Arthur shouted, starting forward angrily.

The fact he was still holding the large, bloody cleaver had completely slipped his mind, until her outstretched hand hit the dirt of the farmyard floor, still twitching, and they each wore the same dumb-struck expression as they watched the spurting gush of blood emerge from Mavis' coat sleeve and arc through the air. She stared at him, jaw slack, too shocked to scream.

Without being consciously aware he was doing it, Arthur weighed up the sheer bother of taking the woman to hospital, explaining matters to the authorities, then a future looking after a crippled wife, if he wasn't thrown into prison for grievous bodily harm, and decided it wasn't worth his while.

He swung the cleaver again.

And again.

Any guilt that bubbled up to the surface within Arthur's psyche was drenched by the wave of utter relief that flooded through him. Like the heavy yolk that the horses used to wear back in his father's day she had been a dragging plough, holding him back, making each day a burden. He had cast off an immense weight and felt light and free.

Bexy pined for her for a while, of course, and spent even more time at Arthur's heel than before, but was soon placated by the fact that there was now more room for her on his bed at night.

He burned her suitcase as it was, without even opening it. Whatever she had planned to take he knew he wouldn't miss.

Neighbours and friends, such as they had, were only too ready to believe that she had left him, and none amongst them, not even Aunty Rebecca, expected her to run to them for succour and support.

And the pigs fed well that week.

*

Bexy never felt jealous when Arthur went up the hill with Dog. She barely even remembered the time, many years past, when he had tried to tutor her in the ways of herding. Only that the attempt had failed dramatically. One sheep, she didn't mind. It could even be fun, jumping and barking, racing and playing. But when they swept across the field like a fluffy, white tidal wave, now that was terrifying!

So she was happy to leave Dog to all the chasing and rounding up and the "come-bye" and "away to me". She could mooch around the farmyard for a few hours, visit the pigs, chase a few birds, then Arthur would return and Dog would be straight back to the kennel.

But even Dog wasn't infallible. Bexy spotted the flash of white along the driveway to the road and clambered onto her four paws from where she had been slumbering in the yard in the last rays of the autumn sun. She knew that Arthur wouldn't be pleased if one of the lambs escaped, so she stretched and yawned and ran along to fetch it back. She took it steady, cautioned by the mishap of a few months ago that had resulted in that dreadful injury, but felt recovered enough to risk a light trot.

She cocked her head curiously at the white plastic carrier bag thrashing in the breeze where it had caught on the hedgerow across the road, feeling dejected at her foolish error. Not an errant lamb. Her act of heroism was wasted. There was no time for her simple, canine mind to register the large, black vehicle hurtling along the narrow road before it deliberately veered in its course to swerve towards her.

*

Alerted by the sound of the impact, and Bexy's mournful wail, abruptly cut-off, Arthur, midway through placing Dog's food bowl by the door of his kennel, dropped the dish and turned towards the lane gate. For all his age Arthur's eyes were as keen as they had ever been, and the image of that car roaring away down the hill to his left was sharp and precise. The smooth shape of the bodywork, the glint of the failing sunlight on the roof, the leering faces at the passenger and rear windows, laughing and rejoicing at their exploits. Those faces he would remember always.

The moments he took to convey Bexy's limp form to a safe place, start up the thundering monstrosity he called a car and charge off along the road in pursuit, he knew were far too prolonged for him to have any hope of catching the culprits, but he pressed his foot down on the accelerator anyway, the car's angry howl echoing his own.

A couple of miles down the road, just before the new road surface and the thirty-mile-an-hour road sign on the bend warning of the proximity of the village of Ockerby, the hedgerow around the entranceway to the patch of community allotments showed fresh damage, like something large and heavy had brushed clumsily past. Pulling as far off the road as the verge would allow, Arthur climbed from his car and peered over the hedge. The tracks of the vehicle he sought were clearly visible, ploughing across a number of the allotments, trellis and winter vegetables strewn in their wake. The car itself was sunk in the ground, spraying mud behind as it moved no more. Three doors opened and the laughing youths scrambled out, plodding through the torn up earth and clambering over the fence at the far side of the enclosure.

Arthur returned to his car and headed to where his local knowledge told him they would emerge. He found them laughing and joking and kicking mud from their shoes, on the road which bypassed the village and veered towards Merrington.

They paid little heed to the rusty old banger as it drove past them and parked some distance ahead. They didn't even notice the old man sitting in the car when they caught up with it a few minutes later. The man who watched as they passed. Who took in every detail of their faces and committed them to memory. He'd seen them all now; the two grinning idiots he observed already at the scene of the slaughter, but now also the third one, the youngest of the trio, the one who'd been driving the vehicle which claimed his poor Bexy's life.

Following them had been a slow and painstaking endeavour, but Arthur was nothing if not patient. Remaining as far back as he could without losing sight of them he crept along until the group had reached Merrington and split up, the eldest of the gang heading off alone along one street while the other two carried on further into the village. He parked up and left the car, following the lone youth the rest of the way to his door on foot.

With the knowledge of this boy's address firmly in his mind Arthur wondered what his next step should be. Back at the farm he sat in the dark and brooded on his options, nursing Bexy's body until she grew cold and stiff. He remembered his wife, and the cleaver, and the hungry pigs. But that was an accident, pure impulse. Such absolute retribution would have to be the last resort.

By the light of dawn Arthur had managed to convince himself that plans for revenge were futile and shameful. That the life of a pet, however beloved and loyal, was less than that of a person. Bexy's fur grew dry and rough, her eyes glassy and blank. Flies buzzed around the nasty gouges in her flesh where she had been pulled into the car's wheel arch. Arthur thought it was maybe time to take her from his bed and put her outside.

The next day, when he saw the damage inflicted by foxes or badgers during the night, he concluded that he ought to finally bury her. But the mound of turned soil in the top field looked bare and forlorn, unworthy of one who had brought so much warmth into his life. They laughed at the stone mason's yard when he enquired about a gravestone. They laughed at the register office when he asked about registering her death. In his dreams by night, and as he half-heartedly tended the sheep by day, his fevered mind showed him the faces of those young bastards in the car, Bexy lying in a bloodied heap behind them, and they laughed.

And they laughed!

The laughter echoed through his mind, growing louder and more pervasive with each passing day, hour, minute, taunting his every thought, his every deed. *Bexy's cold in the ground and they're laughing!*

He had to end it; he had to stop them laughing.

16

Sunday

Edward Maxey stared blindly at his bedroom ceiling, his mind awhirl. Nicola snuggled against him, slow breath on his neck, her body toasty-warm along his side. A lazy lie-in was a rare treat on a Sunday, so he remained still to avoid disturbing her, but he couldn't restrain the thoughts tumbling wildly in his head.

He'd lied to Luke. His best friend of almost twenty years. *And* a police detective working on a brutal murder case. Lied to his face. He felt like shit.

By the time Maxey returned from the pub the previous evening Alicia was asleep in the spare room, having succumbed to exhaustion not five minutes after he had gone out. Nicky had sympathised with him, understanding the awkward position he was in, not wishing any more than he did to subject the young Spanish woman to yet more ordeal after the past few days. But she then tempered that by suggesting maybe he should just have told the truth after all. If she was innocent then Luke would make every effort to prove that. If not, then having her under their roof could be placing themselves in danger. A person who kills once finds it easier to commit murder a second time – Luke had told them that.

He couldn't see the petite, pretty young thing having it in her to viciously slay another human being. But still, something about her story didn't ring true. How did she even know that Adrian Lawson was dead, if she had spent the night hiding in the bushes, as she told them? And if she had pocketed the compliment slip with his number on as she claimed, after flaunting it in front of Lawson, how had it been found at the scene of his murder? And Luke said they found the slip on Friday night, so how had Alicia phoned him again on the Saturday afternoon?

Nicky moaned in sleepy protest as he eased out from under her enfolding arm, and as her warm hand slid across his body he thought twice about leaving her, but these nagging thoughts were troubling and he needed to resolve them.

The dressing gown he pulled over his nakedness was not as cosy and welcoming as the bed behind him, but he cinched the belt tight and slipped through the door. He marched along the landing towards the door to the spare room, hand poised to knock, then paused momentarily as he considered the appropriateness of confronting their visitor in his robe first thing in the day. But his concerns were valid and important. And the voluminous robe covered more than most clothes did. And his wife was right there, just a few feet away.

But in that brief moment of hesitation the sound of unrestrained sobbing penetrated through the door upon which his knuckles waited to rap. He slowly lowered his hand. The horrors she had faced were beyond his comprehension, and he couldn't bring himself to inflict more torment upon her now. He stepped away, as quietly as he could, retreating to his own bedroom.

*

Luke Preston reached the door of the gents' toilets just as his boss, DI Andy Grieff, was coming out. Grieff stopped in the doorway, blocking his access.

'Weren't going in there, were you, lad?' asked Grieff.

Preston noted the slight breathlessness of his words, the minute beads of sweat up near his hairline, the unusual colour in his cheeks, and made a snap decision.

'No, sir.'

With a hand on his shoulder, Grieff steered Preston back

down the corridor. 'What do we know?'

Preston recognised the verbal shorthand. Grieff was asking for a hallway briefing on the cases he was working on.

'No more on the joyriders,' Preston began. 'Except there may be a possible link to the murder case.'

'Oh?' Grieff stopped by the water cooler and put a paper cup under the spout. 'And how does that work?'

'Rehydrating, sir?'

Grieff's expression was deadpan. 'Carry on, Luke.'

'A car which might just be the one stolen from the murder vic a few days before the killing,' Preston mumbled, aware how feeble the story sounded, 'might have been used to kill the dog of a local farmer.'

'You said "might" twice in that sentence,' Grieff said, sipping his water. 'That's not only poor sentence construction, but also suggests a lack of confidence in your own hypothesis.'

'I have it on good authority that this farmer is a potential nutjob, who might have taken his revenge on the car's owner, thinking he was driving it at the time.'

'Another "might"?'

'It's just a theory.'

'Hmm...' Grieff threw the paper cup into the bin and turned to carry on along the corridor, presenting Preston with the large, white square of his back. Preston noticed that the tail of his shirt was inching slightly from his belt and resisted the urge to tuck it in. Grieff entered the squad room and crossed towards his dinky office, partitioned off in one corner. Preston followed. 'Get someone to check it out, but don't spend too much time on it. It all sounds a bit tenuous, to me.'

Grieff gave a barely audible grunt as he lowered himself into his swivel chair, but there was no betrayal in his face of any discomfort he was feeling. Grieff's frequent visits to the bathroom were becoming a recurring joke around the station, and Preston was as guilty as anyone, but he wondered if there was more to it than just a weakness for curry.

As usual, Grieff read his mind. 'Not a word,' he warned, as he popped a Rennie from its bubble pack and chomped it.

'We do know the Spanish girl went to the register office looking for information about Adrian Lawson.'

'This friend of yours and the compliment slip?'

Preston nodded.

'Did he tell her where to find him?'

'He says not.'

'But...?'

Preston shrugged apologetically, embarrassed to be talking behind the back of his friend of so many years. 'He can be a bit of a pushover for a pretty face.'

'So she's still our main lead,' Grieff said, jabbing a finger towards the chair opposite him. He preferred people to sit when he was sitting. 'And the friend who was smuggling her letters to Lawson doesn't know anything about her?'

Preston pulled out the chair as far as the limited space would allow, lowering himself onto it at an angle to avoid banging his knees on the desk. 'She turned up out of the blue and he sent her packing. He says he never read any of the letters, and I suppose that must be true. Lawson would have been able to tell if the envelopes were tampered with. With physical mail you can't just click "mark as unread" and expect no one to be able to tell you've been snooping.'

'Why didn't he tell his good friend that his bit of holiday fun was in town?'

'His wife stuck her nose in and decided to grass Lawson up to his missus,' Preston said, a hint of scorn in his voice. 'So "good friend" Rafferty washed his hands of the whole thing.'

'Speaking of good friends,' Grieff began, leaning forward, elbows on his desk. 'This friend of yours, the registrar...'

'Ye-es...?' Preston wondered what was coming next. You never knew what to expect with DI Grieff, his expression

169

gave no clues.

'You're quite sure, being the pushover he is, that he didn't offer our little Spanish strumpet a lift over to Lawson's gaff and sit outside with the engine running while she nipped inside and pulped his skull?'

Preston pulled a face, not deigning to answer.

Grieff settled back in his chair. 'Who knew where Lawson would be?' He picked up a biro and tapped distractedly on the rim of a coffee mug. 'He was supposed to be out with his kid, but he had his mobile phone, so anyone could have called him and arranged to meet. Have the tech bods cracked his phone yet?'

'We're not likely to hear anything today.'

'Why not?'

'Sunday.'

'Is it?'

Preston knew Grieff well enough to know that he was quite aware of what day it was. This was his way of expressing his belief that the calendar should take a back seat to a murder investigation.

'There's probably only a skeleton staff on duty,' Preston said. 'They can't do everything.'

Preston wasn't certain if Grieff's scowl was prompted by the lack of technical support or the fact that the lid of his pen had become dislodged and dropped into the mug.

'Are we sure the wife is out of the frame?' said Grieff, fishing the pen lid out of the dregs of his coffee. 'I don't see her as the type to mess up her pretty little house like that, but confirmation would be nice.'

Preston watched Grieff flick drips of coffee from his fingers onto the carpet. 'Er, yes. Annette Lee sent PC Cawthorne round the shops, following Mrs Lawson's route according to her till receipts. Enough of the shop keepers recognised her from her photograph to be sure that she couldn't have been anywhere near home the whole afternoon.'

'Ah, the resourceful Netty Lee.'

'Netty?' said Preston, surprised at the familiarity. He'd never heard Grieff use the shortened version of her name before.

'Weekend name,' Grieff said. 'After all, it is Sunday,' he added sardonically, as he sucked coffee from his fingertips. 'Send Annette to see this farmer of yours, see if she can charm any information out of him. And you,' he said, pointing his lidless pen at Preston, 'find me this bloody Spaniard!'

Taking that as his dismissal, Preston eased himself off the cramped chair and slipped out into the CID squad room proper. He looked around for Lee but there was no sign of her amongst the bustle of bodies milling around the squad room. It was only half past nine on a Sunday morning, but he expected that she'd be in by now. He pulled out his mobile and scrolled through his contacts, but before he had time to tap the little green phone icon, Lee walked into the room, followed by another woman. On second glance he recognised the second woman as Jo Kershaw. Out of uniform and tight curls unrestrained by her cap, she looked quite different to when he had taken her with him to tell the Hewetts about Lawson's death on Friday night. She carried a battered holdall at her side.

'Undercover?' Preston said with a smirk, waving a hand towards her casual clothes.

'Day off,' Kershaw replied.

Preston ran his fingers through his hair and grinned. 'Wouldn't catch me here on my day off.' He cleared his throat self-consciously and sat at his desk. What the hell was he doing? In the presence of two attractive women and suddenly he's preening like a peacock.

Luckily the two attractive women seemed to neither notice nor care.

'I was talking to Jo last night about what we'd found out yesterday,' Lee said. 'When I mentioned the Spanish girl she told me about a sleazy taxi driver who brought in a lost holdall.'

Kershaw hoisted the holdall into view and dumped it on his desk. 'Sounds like she could be your girl.'

'Wait a minute,' Preston frowned. 'How do you two know each other, then?'

Lee looked at him like he'd just stumbled out of the TARDIS and asked her what year it was. 'We're married.'

'To each other?'

Kershaw laughed. Lee shook her head in despair.

Preston stood with his mouth open for what must have been no more than a second, but which felt like forever. 'Oh. Yeah. No. Right,' he stammered idiotically. 'That's great!'

They both smiled at his discomfiture.

'Yeah, it is actually,' Kershaw said.

'Spanish girl,' Lee said, digging a hand into the holdall and pulling out a passport. 'Remember?'

Preston nodded and took the small, red book from her, desperately trying to regain his composure. 'Right,' he said. 'Let's see who we have here.' He flipped open the passport, peered at the photo, and took his first look at Alicia López Garcia.

*

The living room curtains were open this time. When Alan Rafferty had approached the Harper home twenty minutes earlier all the curtains had been drawn tight. Not wanting to disturb the residents, and most especially not wanting to have the door opened to him by Jake's mother in her night-clothes, Alan had strolled on, shuffling along the cracked pavement, filling time until they arose. A couple of days ago Alan had hidden rather than spend time with Jake and Kenny, now he actively sought out their company. He pondered his own contradictory feelings. Dissatisfaction with his familial status made other, equally unsatisfactory connections more attractive. Whatever the case, weighing up his options, this seemed the lesser of a multitude of evils. Thankfully Margaret Harper was dressed as she greeted Alan on his return.

'Come in, love,' she said, backing up so he could enter. 'Do you fancy a bacon buttie?'

Alan smiled his shy response. He did indeed fancy one. He had woken early, chased from slumber by nightmare images of elderly women collapsing in the street, and he'd slipped out from home without having any breakfast and without waiting for his own parents to awake. They were unlikely to stir for another hour or so yet, but he intended to be well clear before they could start their bickering again. He'd been thoroughly embarrassed the previous night when his mother had dragged him indoors without even giving him chance to say 'tara' to Jake.

'Jake!' Mrs Harper called up the stairs. 'He's not up yet, the lazy bugger,' she told Alan. Her indulgent smile showed that she was far from cross at her son's indolence. She jerked a thumb towards the stairs. 'Why don't you pop up and wake him? Last door along the landing.'

She headed for the kitchen as Alan skipped up the stairs. At the end of the short corridor he pushed on the matt black door, confident he had the correct room as attached to the gloomy paintwork was a small sign which read "Jake's Den". As the door swung away from him Alan was aware that the interior of the bedroom was equally dismal, with wallpaper, shelves and curtains also black or dark grey.

He gently called his friend's name, not wanting to put on the light or swish open the curtains, in case it startled him. He knew that, were their positions reversed, Jake would take immense pleasure in leaping, knees first, onto the bed, while screaming Alan's name as loud as possible, and he mentally berated himself for his timidity.

'Jake?' he said again, slightly louder, shuffling closer to the shadowy bulk of the bed, kicking aside crumpled comics and discarded clothes. 'You awake, mate?'

His eyes growing accustomed to the darkness of the

room, Alan realised that the surface of the bed before him was smooth and flat. No occupant rumpled the quilt or dented the pillow. Alan flicked on the bedside lamp to confirm his findings, but he was already in no doubt. It was empty, and had been since Jake, or more likely his mother, pulled the quilt straight the day before.

*

'You needn't have come with me,' Annette Lee told her wife, and she drove through moderate Sunday morning traffic towards Arthur Camm's farm. 'I could've dropped you off home.'

'But then you would've had to find someone else to go with you,' Jo Kershaw said. 'And I was here already.'

'Off duty, though,' Lee grumbled. 'If this goes boobs skyward there could be trouble. You're probably not insured to be out with me, or summat.'

'I'll put in an overtime claim.'

'That'll go down well.'

'Anyway, what could go wrong? We're just going to ask some old fella what he was doing on Friday.'

Lee looked at her askance. 'An old fella who maybe just battered someone to death with their own fireside accessories.'

'Come on,' Kershaw said. 'Even Luke didn't think there was much likelihood that this was our man.'

'How long have you been calling him Luke?'

'Since he said I could on Friday night.'

'Well, *Detective Sergeant Preston* wouldn't have sent us out here on a wild goose chase, so stay alert.'

'Yes, Detective Constable Lee,' Kershaw said, adding, after a moment, 'darling.'

Lee shook her head, but couldn't fight back a smirk.

'Luke didn't say it was a shit-hole,' Kershaw said a few minutes later, as they rumbled down the bumpy drive, the dishevelled farmhouse looming ahead.

'He's not been,' Lee said. 'It was that friend of his who met the farmer before.'

'The registrar?'

'Yeah, he said that it was Lawson's car that killed this guy's dog, and he's been acting weird ever since.'

'I hate people who hurt animals.'

'Enough to kill them?'

'Shall we get a dog?'

'What?' Lee pulled the car to a halt in the unkempt yard and turned to Kershaw. 'What're you on about now?'

'A dog,' Kershaw said. 'Little pooch round the house.'

'It's a flat. I'm pretty sure there's a no-pets clause. And we're out all the time.'

'You're no fun.'

'That's not what you said last night,' Lee said, keeping a professional straight face as she climbed out of the car.

Kershaw took a moment longer before she emerged.

Lee was already mooching around the yard, peering into an old metal dustbin that had been converted into an incinerator. Empty, just a few traces of ash clinging to the sides.

'What you looking for?' came a gravelly voice from behind her.

Lee turned. A short, wiry old man stood there, gazing at her with hooded eyes, which gave him a dark and dangerous mien. He stood with hands crammed deep in his pockets, booted feet set apart. She could see why Luke's friend, Maxey, had thought he was strange. But who wouldn't be suspicious when two strangers pull up outside their house? She introduced them.

'Hello, I'm Detective Constable Lee and this is Constable Kershaw.'

He turned to find Kershaw, who had approached them from the car, standing at his shoulder. He looked her up and down.

'Just a constable?' he said, with a sneer. 'Shouldn't you be in uniform, then?'

'It's Sunday,' Kershaw said, hands on hips, a defiant glint in her eye.

He frowned but let it pass. 'What yer want?'

'Arthur Camm?' asked Lee lightly, trying to defuse the animosity.

'It's his farm, I'm the only one 'ere, so I guess I must be him.'

She smiled patiently. 'We'd like to ask you a couple of questions.'

'What about?'

'Your whereabouts on Friday.'

'Friday?'

'Specifically, Friday afternoon.'

'Why?' Camm appeared uncomfortable. 'What am I supposed to have done?

Lee and Kershaw glanced at one another, as Arthur squirmed between them. It wasn't unusual for the mere presence of the police to make someone prickly.

'Hopefully nothing,' Kershaw said, causing Arthur to turn with a jolt, as if he'd forgotten she was there. 'But we just need to be clear on where you were.'

'Well, I'd be 'ere, w'un't I?' he said with a forced shrug. 'I never go nowhere in the day.'

'Can anyone confirm that?' Lee asked.

'Only Dog,' said Camm, nodding towards the kennel in the corner of the yard, where a golden snout and black nose protruded from the shadows.

'Oh, you have another dog?' Kershaw asked, taking a few steps towards the kennel and bending to see inside.

'Another?'

'We heard you'd recently lost your dog,' Lee said gently.

'Did you?' Arthur frowned at her. 'Aye, I 'ad two dogs afore. One was killed. Run o'er in the road.' He thrust his hooked nose in the direction of the lane.

'That must have been very upsetting for you.'

'A dog's a dog,' Arthur said. 'Plenty more where she came from.' But Lee noticed he avoided her eye as he spoke.

176

'Hit and run, wasn't it?' she said, retaining that soft tone. 'Did you see the driver?'

'Nah, they were too far away.'

'They?'

'What?'

'You said they,' Lee said. 'Did you see more than just the driver in the car?'

'Dunno,' he shrugged. 'Like I said, too far away.'

Annette Lee gave him her trademarked patient smile and sighed, hands on her hips, her ponytail swaying in the breeze. She looked down at her feet and kicked mud from her shoes. 'I don't think we need to disturb you any longer.' She took out her car keys.

'What do you make of him, then,' she asked, after she had prised Kershaw away from the kennel and they were back in the car. She crunched the vehicle into the correct gear and headed back along the treacherous lane.

'Creepy, but I don't see him as a cold-blooded killer.'

'Cold-blooded? You saw the scene,' Lee said. 'That was definitely done in hot blood.'

'Even less likely then, I reckon.'

'Hmm...' Lee frowned as she navigated the car onto the narrow country road, turning back towards Haleston. 'He was vague about seeing the driver.'

'So?'

'If he did see the driver, he'd know that it wasn't our victim who killed his dog.'

'So no reason to pulp his skull.'

'Exactly.'

'And on the Friday afternoon he'd be pretty busy, running that place by himself, even if no one saw him.'

'Except Dog.'

Kershaw smiled. 'Yeah, except Dog.'

'I still think he's a weirdo,' Lee said, dropping a gear to power up the hill. 'But I don't think he killed Adrian Lawson.'

*

Arthur Camm watched the police women's car disappear up the road towards town and turned back to the barn, finally taking his red-stained hands from his pockets. He slipped inside, lifted down the long apron from the nail by the door, hooking the loop over his head, and picked up his discarded meat cleaver from the slab against the wall. A drop of fresh blood slid from the blade and hit the dusty concrete floor with a splat.

'Now then,' he said with a sneer. 'Where were we?'

Jake Harper, or what was left of him, blinked blood and sweat from his bleary eyes and whimpered feebly behind his gag.

The pigs snorted in anticipation.

17

'Talk to her'

'I will.'

Nicola Maxey gave her husband a dubious look, eyebrow raised, then climbed into her ten year old, lime green Vauxhall Corsa and settled into the warm familiarity of the seat. The position of every button, switch and knob was second nature to her by now. While ever it kept going she wouldn't consider changing it.

'I mean it,' she added, pulling the door closed.

'I will,' he mouthed through the window, and blew her a kiss.

With a sceptical shake of her head, she started the car, reversed quickly off the double-width driveway and raced off through the quiet suburban estate towards the main road.

The low-density housing estate known as Bracken Bank, in the picturesque village of Arkenbrough, was situated close to the Metropolitan District of Haleston's border with Sheffield Metropolitan Borough. This gave easy access to the M1 and M18, allowing Nicky to reach her job at Rotherham General Hospital in less than twenty minutes, quicker than when she worked at Haleston Hospital, even though that was physically closer as the crow flies. She could have taken the direct road to Rotherham but that would risk getting clogged up in the traffic through Brafthill, so she habitually took the motorway route.

In the dissipating cloud of exhaust fumes behind her Maxey shrugged off such geographical considerations and turned back towards the house, and their temporary visitor. He had left Alicia in the dining room, tidying the lunch things from the table. She had insisted on helping out, over Nicky's protestations that she was a guest and should leave it to Ed. He found her in the kitchen, washing their plates and mugs.

She made an even tinier figure than before, standing there in Nicky's borrowed clothes, jeans rolled up at the hem and even then still brushing the floor. Her own clothes were beyond rescue so Nicky had got rid of them, being careful to wrap them securely in black bin liners first.

When Maxey had spoken to Nicky after she awoke, revealing his concerns, explaining his reluctance to put pressure on Alicia, Nicky had insisted that he talk to her. But how did he broach the subject? Industriously wiping the crockery dry, this was the most animated he had seen her since their first meeting two days before. Emerging from their guest bedroom this morning she had shuffled her feet on the carpet, head sagging, eyes bleary and red. Her tribulations weighed on her like Marley's chains. There was still pain and residual bleeding, and Nicky had given her pills and pads and made sure she was as comfortable as possible. He'd left her to it – she was a nurse, she knew what she was doing.

Alicia laid down the tea towel and turned, giving a little gasp when she saw him standing in the doorway.

'Sorry.' He smiled, awkwardly. 'I didn't mean to startle you.'

'Were you watching me?' She seemed afraid. He was mortified.

'What? No! I was just waiting till you'd finished.' She stared at him and he felt moved to explain himself further. 'I'm concerned, that's all. You've been... poorly.'

'I lost my baby and the baby's father in one day,' she said. Her voice was dull and flat and he felt a chill in the pit of his stomach. What the hell was going on in this poor kid's mind?

He waved her through into the living room. 'I wanted to have a word with you.'

He lowered himself into the large armchair which dominated the room. She perched on the very edge of the adjacent sofa, alert and wary, like a little bird ready to fly away at any moment.

'What have I done?'

He deliberately controlled his voice, keeping it soft and calm. 'Nothing, don't worry.' Already he had mishandled this situation, lurking behind her while she was unaware of his presence, alarming her. 'How are you feeling?' *D'oh!* Stupid question.

She just frowned, looking miserable. 'Are you going to give me to the policemen?'

'No, no, please, just relax.'

She didn't relax.

He mulled over the questions which had been troubling him earlier. Which had been niggling away at him ever since Luke showed him the picture on his phone last night. That damned compliment slip! If only he hadn't given this girl his number. And there he went again, letting that young face and big eyes fool him. She wasn't a girl. By her age he had been at the register office for four years. Admittedly the first couple were spent answering the phones and issuing copies of birth certificates, but soon afterwards he had his own registers and stock and a position of authority and respect and he was letting his mind wander again... She looked so frail and vulnerable. Surely anyone who took advantage of such a delicate creature deserved all they got? Well, perhaps not the fate that Luke had described to him last night, which had been dished out to her erstwhile lover.

'I wanted to ask you a couple of questions about... about the other day.'

'Oh?'

'You remember the piece of paper I gave you? The one with my number on?'

Her hand went instinctively to her pocket. Except it wasn't her pocket. Not even her trousers. She shook her head, as if waking from a dream. 'I think I lost it.'

'Yes, I know.'

'You know?'

'The police have it.'

Her eyes were wide and frightened. 'They do?'

'You said you took it with you when you left Adrian Lawson's house.'

'Yes.'

'But the police found it at the house.'

'They did?'

Now she looked frightened *and* confused. He wanted to stop, tell her it didn't matter, make her a cup of tea.

Instead he pressed on. 'So you can't have taken it with you.'

'No.' She gave a helpless little shrug.

'So...?'

'So...?' Those big, dark eyes gazed at him expectantly.

'So, you must have dropped it?' What's going on? Maxey thought. I'm supposed to be asking her what happened, not telling her.

'Yes, I have dropped it,' she said, with a little nod of satisfaction. 'I am mistaking when I say I took it.'

Maxey sighed in frustration. This wasn't going as planned. He tried to gather his thoughts. He wouldn't make a great police interviewer. What else did he want to ask?

'The phone call,' he said suddenly, recollection striking.

'Phone call?'

'The second one, yesterday afternoon.'

'Yes?'

'How did you make it?'

'How?' His ambiguous interrogation had her bewildered. 'I still had coins...'

'No, no.' He was making himself flustered now. 'You didn't have my number by then. The police found the compliments slip on Friday night, there's no way you'd have memorised an unfamiliar number, so how could you have made the call?'

'Ah!' Her expression softened into a smile. 'I pressed redial.'

He stared dumbly at her. 'What?'

'Redial.'

'Redial?'

'I was very upset,' she said. 'In pain, dirty, confused. My clothes were... as you saw. I struggled even to get to the phone box. Then I reach in my pocket and the paper is gone! I am distraught!'

'Of course.'

'Then I remember,' she said, a note of pride in her voice. 'No one comes near the phone box all the day. I am looking out from the bushes. People go to the *taberna* across the road, people use the park. Many people pass by. And many are talking on the phone. But not the public phone. They all have their small *teléfonos móviles.*'

'Mobiles,' Maxey chipped in, captivated by her tale.

'Yes, mobiles. And so I realise no one is using the phone box since I use it the day before. I see a button, next to the numbers. It has a word on it'

'Redial?'

'Redial.'

'And it worked?'

She nodded happily.

Of course it worked, she'd called him. He grinned and shook his head. It was as simple as that. She had no number, so she pressed redial. Most people had mobiles these days, public call boxes were largely superfluous on modern streets, so it was a safe bet that she would be the last person to dial out from that one.

So no big mystery, after all. Maxey had a vague feeling that there was something else he'd wanted to ask, but seeing a smile on those pretty red lips at last superseded all other concerns. 'Well, that's that, then.' He edged forward on his chair. 'I think, after all that excitement, we should have a cup of tea.'

She jumped up. 'I'll get it.' And off she skipped to the kitchen.

He settled back with a chuckle. Redial!

*

'Oh, ye of little faith!'

'What?' Luke Preston turned to where his boss was entering the squad room from the corridor. He saw that DI Grieff was being followed by Dan Baxter, the chief of the local crime scene team.

With a nod of his head Grieff summoned Preston to follow them, and they squeezed into the DI's inadequate enclosure. Grieff and Baxter took the chairs, leaving Preston to hover above them.

Baxter sat sideways on the guest chair and placed a briefcase on his lap. Out of his whites Baxter had a gaunt, rather stiff appearance, like a stick figure drawing, in a suit. That suit, though quite neat and smart, was of an old fashioned, pale, tweed-like fabric and seemed a touch too short at wrist and ankle, heightening the "matchstalk man" look. It also gave the illusory impression that he was taller than his actual perfectly average height. When he sat the black of his socks stood out awkwardly between the beige turn-ups and tan brogues.

'Luke, here,' began Grieff, waving a hand in a grand gesture towards Preston, 'said you'd be at home in your dressing gown, watching the Coronation Street omnibus and eating hot, buttered crumpets.'

'That's not what I—' said Preston, but he was quickly interrupted.

'But here you are, slaving away for the benefit of the man who so grossly maligned you.'

It was clear that Grieff was feeling a tad brighter than he had been earlier. Possibly it was the news that they had identified the Spanish woman they were looking for. Or maybe he'd managed a successful bowel movement.

'I never actually said...' Preston started to explain, but Baxter stopped him with a dismissive shake of his head. You couldn't always tell when Grieff was trying to wind you up, but sometimes he was blatant.

184

Baxter clicked open the clasps on his briefcase and lifted the lid. 'Phone records for the mobile of one Adrian Lawson,' he said, retrieving a USB drive from the case. 'I picked them up from the tech bods on my way over. I assumed you'd be keen to see them.'

'Ah, brilliant!' said Grieff. 'I could kiss you.' He waved a finger between Preston and Baxter. 'Luke, kiss him.'

Baxter, not waiting for his reward, handed the USB to Preston, then picked out a sheaf of papers. 'All the technical stuff is on the drive, in deep and laborious detail,' he said. 'But they also took the liberty of printing off a brief summary of the more pertinent facts.' He wafted the pages. 'If I may...?'

'Please,' said Grieff. 'Go right ahead.'

'Last inward call,' Baxter pressed on, 'was from this number at 13:24.' He pointed to a list of phone numbers. The indicated item was a landline with a Haleston code. 'Registered to R. and L. Hewett, address in Clegganfield.'

'That's the vic's ex-wife and her new hubby,' Preston said. 'We know she called him to find out why he hadn't come back for his son. By that time something had happened to change his plans.'

'The call before that...' Baxter consulted his list. '...was from a J. Rafferty on a mobile.'

'That's funny,' Preston said. 'He told me he'd not been in touch with Lawson.'

'Not he,' said Baxter. 'She.'

'What?'

'J for Julie.'

'Oh yes?' asked Grieff. 'Where does that fit in with her coffee with the wife?'

'This call is at 13:19 and lasts two minutes,' said Baxter.

'Just after Donna Lawson has left her, then,' Grieff said. 'So, Julie Rafferty meets Donna Lawson, tells her all about her husband's liaison with his Spanish *chiquitita*, then immediately rings the bad boy himself.'

'But why? Preston said. 'To rub his nose in it?'

'That's a question to ask the lady herself, methinks,' Grieff said. 'Soon as we've finished here.'

'And now I've got Abba in my head,' said Baxter.

'Rather you than me,' Grieff said.

'Anything else on there?' asked Preston.

'Just a text from the wife about an hour before, informing him she's going for a coffee in town and she'll see him later.'

'No outgoing calls?

'Not all day. His GPS confirms the visit to Clegganfield where the ex-wife lives, then shows him going to the park at Blossom Hill for an hour or so. Then it's back to the ex's place.'

'That's when he drops off the kids,' Preston said.

'It's all right,' said Grieff, drily. 'I'm keeping up.'

'Then it's straight home till after the phone calls, when he makes a trip into Haleston town centre. It shows him there for thirteen minutes, then back home by 14:01. Then that's it. No more movement till he's discovered dead just after six.'

'Unless he went out but didn't take his phone with him,' said Grieff.

'Well, yes,' Baxter acknowledged.

'Does the phone tell us anything else?' Preston asked.

'He had a healthy appetite for porn,' Baxter informed them.

Grieff peered over the lid of Baxter's briefcase. 'Did you bring us any printouts of that?'

'I'm afraid not.'

'You're no fun.'

'Anything that might narrow down that four hour window?' Preston added.

'Not from the phone,' Baxter said. 'That was completely inactive after his return.'

'What about your forensic tricks and wizardry?' Grieff said. 'I'm sure you've got lots of surprises for us yet, haven't you?'

'Now we come to my own humble contribution to proceedings.' Baxter patted the contents of his case. 'Crime scene report. PM results.'

'Oh yes,' said Preston. He hadn't been present at the previous day's post mortem. Grieff had taken Annette Lee, the newbie DC along with him instead, to have her first experience of the cold room. She'd seemed a bit subdued on her return, so he hadn't wanted to probe her for her reactions. 'How was the PM?'

'Revolting,' said Grieff, with a downturned mouth. 'They had a body just lying there in the open, where anyone could see it.'

Preston ignored the sarcasm. 'Did we learn anything?'

'He's definitely dead.'

Preston sighed. It could be tricky making progress when Grieff was in one of those moods.

Grieff's face was his usual mask of sincerity. 'If he wasn't dead before, then scooping his heart out and slopping it in a metal dish would've finished him off.'

Preston leaned back against the wall with a wry grin. He knew Grieff wouldn't allow his gallows humour to interfere with their investigation. Formal briefings were always conducted with all due gravitas and with members of the public he was the height of decorum. But this was three blokes gathered around a desk. When you deal with violence and brutality on a regular basis, sometimes you need to loosen your metaphorical tie. Preston would just have to ride it out.

Baxter took pity on him. 'We have confirmation that the poker was the murder weapon.'

'Surprise, surprise,' said Grieff.

'The size of the impact injuries matches the dimensions of the point and shaft. Blood and tissue on the poker match the deceased.'

'Any fingerprints?' Grieff asked.

'I'm coming to that.'

'Take your time.'

Baxter took a breath and carried on. 'The handle and shaft had been wiped.'

'Wiped?'

'Carefully,' said Baxter. 'And there were signs of thorough and considered cleaning up throughout the house.'

'Go on,' said Grieff, all seriousness now.

'The shower had been used.'

'The shower? After the murder?'

'Yes. The perpetrator of an act like this would be heavily soiled with the victim's blood. Hands, face, clothes. They would want to get rid of that evidence. Traces of the victim's blood were found on the stair carpet, bannister rail, tiles in the bathroom and the outlet of the shower.'

'No fingerprints in any of that either,' Grieff assumed.

'No. All carefully wiped. The blood was caught in uneven surfaces – wood grain, carpet pile, tile grout – transfer stains aplenty but all wiped over and no prints left behind.'

'Our "frenzied assailant" is acting a bit inconsistently,' Preston said. 'Smash someone's brains in, then stop and have a good clean up, but afterwards run off in such a hurry that you leave the front door standing wide open.'

'What about the washing machine?' Grieff said. 'Those clothes are not going to come clean by running them under the shower.'

'I thought of that,' said Baxter, with a modest smile. 'We checked the drum and the outlet pipes, but there was no evidence that the machine had been used for a few days.'

'We should check with the wife that nothing is missing from their wardrobes,' Grieff said. 'Our man, or woman, might have changed into something from the house, rather than risk going out in their own clothes.'

Preston nodded and scribbled in his notebook. 'Choice of clothing swiped would give us an idea if we're looking for a man or a woman.'

'Unless they're a cross-dresser,' said Grieff.

'Two things are suggested by all this wiping,' Baxter

said. 'And these are just suggestions,' he stressed. 'You're the detectives, it's not my place to try to—'

'Please,' Grieff interrupted. 'Suggest away.'

'Well,' Baxter began, taking a moment to gather his thoughts. 'One place where our culprit *didn't* wipe hints at the time of the attack being earlier in that four hour window, rather than later.'

'I thought you weren't able to narrow that down,' Preston said.

'Not forensically, no,' Baxter admitted. 'Such things as body temperature can only tell us so much. After all, the heating was on in the house, but the front door had been left open, so the ambient temperature was difficult to determine throughout the period in question. The victim had lost a large amount of blood, which also has an effect on temperature.'

'But?' Grieff prompted.

'But,' Baxter said, 'there was a fingerprint on the light switch.'

'That would be the neighbour,' Preston said. 'The bloke who found the body.'

'That has been confirmed,' said Baxter.

'So...?'

Baxter closed his case and rested his hands on the lid, leaning slightly forward to ensure he had their attention. 'The switch was in the off position before the neighbour entered. There was blood on the switch, it hadn't been wiped, therefore it is safe to speculate that someone who so fastidiously wiped every surface they had come into contact with, had not in fact touched the light switch. So the light must have been off at the time of the attack. The curtains were closed, it gets dark before five PM this time of year, the streetlights don't shine directly into the room. So...?'

'It must have still been daylight when Lawson was killed,' Preston concluded for him.

'Of course, there are variables that I haven't accounted for,' Baxter said. 'The killer might have had a torch. But if

Lawson had encountered an intruder, why did he not put the light on? It's unlikely he was caught unawares, because the killer had to make it all the way across the room to the fireplace to reach the poker.' He sat back in his chair. 'But, as I say, I'm not the detective.'

'The curtains weren't closed by the killer afterwards?' Preston wondered. 'To conceal their activities as they cleaned up?'

'No,' Baxter said, confidently. 'Blood spatter rules that out. The curtains were closed during the whole attack.'

'So,' Grieff said, 'we've got the curtains closed, light switched off, twilight creeping in... We can look at the murder happening before, say, four PM?'

'Speculatively, rather than definitively,' Baxter hedged, 'I would concur.'

'Hesitation noted,' said Grieff.

'What else?' Preston asked.

Baxter blinked. 'Sorry?'

'You said two things.'

'Yes, that's right, I did. We could find no surfaces with obvious fingerprints anywhere in the house, which could not be immediately eliminated as belonging to the householders. Except, curiously, the inner handle of the front door. That had a single, clear set of prints.'

'One set?' said Preston. 'But a door handle gets touched all the time, by everybody who comes and goes. There should be dozens of sets of prints on there.'

Baxter nodded vigorously. 'Exactly! And such is the circumstance with the back door. Smudged, over-printed, completely unreadable. That's why it stood out as remarkable. It suggests, and again this is merely a suggestion, but it suggests that the handle was, indeed, wiped clean along with all the other areas.'

'Then touched again, after it had been wiped?'

'Yes. And, therefore, after the murder.'

'And the prints don't belong to Lawson or his wife?' Preston asked.

'No, nor the gentleman from across the road.'

'Do you have a match for the print?'

'We don't have an ident for the person who touched the door handle,' said Baxter. 'But we do have a match on another piece of evidence from the scene.'

'What piece of evidence?'

'The registrar's compliments slip.'

18

'Are you a copper?'

A bi-racial woman in casual clothes, fake-smoking on the steps of a police station – she could see how it might not be obvious. Jo Kershaw quickly exhaled a cloud of sweet-scented fumes, slipped her vape pen into her pocket and turned towards the source of the question. 'Sometimes,' she said. 'What's up?'

The scrawny teenager looked back at the timid woman behind him then, seeing she wasn't going to speak, he continued. 'We've lost someone.'

'You want to report a missing person?'

Alan Rafferty nodded and Margaret Harper took a step forward. 'My son,' she said, her voice breaking.

Kershaw pulled open the large glass door and waved them past her. 'You'd better come through.'

The sole Civilian Enquiry Officer on the desk this slow Sunday lunchtime was busy, dealing with a belligerent customer who appeared to be in no hurry to leave. Kershaw looked towards the seats in the waiting area, then caught the distressed sob as the woman clung to the youth's arm. Images of the pack of beers chilling in the fridge and the stack of DVDs on the floor in front of the telly flashed tantalisingly through her mind, before cruelly fading away. Any thoughts she may have entertained of escaping to enjoy her afternoon off were dwindling fast.

'Hang on.' She attracted the CEO's attention so that he could press the release button for the door, allowing her access to the inner section of the station. Coming back to the reception counter from the other side she beckoned them over, keying a password into an unmanned computer terminal.

'How long has your son been missing?' she asked.

'He didn't come home last night,' Mrs Harper said. 'I didn't know if we ought to come, with it not being twenty-four hours yet, but Alan said we should.'

'Alan is quite right,' Kershaw said, with a friendly smile and wink for him. 'All that twenty-four hours nonsense is just something they say on the telly. Is it your brother who's missing?'

'No, he's mi mate.'

Kershaw nodded and turned back to Mrs Harper. 'What's your son's name?'

'Jake,' she said. 'Jacob Harper.'

'Does Jake have a mobile, Mrs Harper?'

'It just goes straight to voicemail.'

'Let me have the number anyway, in case we need to try tracing it later.'

Mrs Harper fumbled in her handbag for her own phone, stabbing a finger at the screen to bring up the details. No one knew even their closest family members' numbers in these days of auto-dialling, Kershaw reflected, briefly trying to recollect her wife's number, and failing.

'What was Jake doing, the last time he was seen?'

'Just goin' home,' Alan said. 'We'd been out, hangin' around the streets in Merrington. I had to go in, so as far as I knew Jake was just goin' home.'

Kershaw's fingers clattered across the keyboard. 'And do you have any reason to think anything untoward might have happened to Jake?' she said, as gently as possible. 'Had he been behaving differently to usual? Had he mentioned anything that had bothered or upset him? Are there any circumstances you can think of that could shed light on what might have happened to him?'

She waited, watching the expressions of anguish and uncertainty on the faces opposite.

*

Alan took a deep breath. He had momentarily considered

193

trying to talk Mrs Harper out of coming here, to deter her from reporting Jake's disappearance at all. The moment the police began investigating what had happened, started to delve into the background of the three youths, their activities would become known. The vandalism, the car thefts, the joyriding. That old woman dropping down dead. That poor dog going under the wheels. In her distraught state she would have gone along with anything he suggested. *Wait until tonight, see if he comes home. Just give him a few more hours.* But in his gut he knew they couldn't waste any time, it was imperative that something be done sooner rather than later. After all, as he said now, in response to Kershaw's question:

'He's not the first one to go missing.'

*

Someone mentioned that modern Spanish passports have fingerprints recorded as part of the biometric data, so DI Grieff went to assign one of the DCs on the murder team the job of chasing up the fingerprints with Immigration.

Preston saw Lee come into the squad room and called her over.

'How's the farmer?'

'A bit weird but I don't have him down as our killer.' She hesitated, a frown puckering her features. Preston guessed there was a "but".

'But,' she continued, 'there's something cold about him. A bitterness. And his only alibi has four legs and a wet nose.'

'Okay,' Preston said, eager to encourage intuitive thought. 'We'll keep him in mind. Write it up, but don't put too much stress on the dog alibi bit, or the boss'll have you bringing it in for questioning.'

She nodded and smiled. All the team were familiar with the DI's ways.

'And when you're done with that,' Preston added, 'go and

have a word with that taxi driver. Find out everything he knows about the Spanish girl. We're keener than ever to get hold of her.' He told her what they had learned from Baxter. 'See if he chatted with her. Anything she said might be of value.'

'Will do.'

Grieff nodded to him from the doorway and Preston grabbed his jacket from the back of his chair. Within moments they were in Preston's Honda heading out to Merrington once again.

'How suspicious is it that this Rafferty woman didn't tell us that she'd spoken to Lawson on the day he died?' Grieff asked over the growl of the car engine, though it was clearly as much a rhetorical question as it was a prompt for discussion.

'Was there something going on between them?' Preston threw into the mix.

'Do we have reason to think there might be?' Grieff wondered. 'Apart from the fact that Lawson seems to have sniffed around anything female for miles around.'

'Someone who sounded like her rang the register office asking about how to get married again.'

'This mate of yours told you this?'

Preston nodded.

'"Sounded like?"'

'It was just a vague inquiry, so we can't definitely pin it on her. But if she was pondering a future with Lawson, she'd be as upset as Donna Lawson when she discovered he'd been messing around with this girl in Spain.'

'Having a *fiesta* during his *siesta.*'

'So she rings him up to arrange a meet.'

'Which explains why he doesn't go back to the ex-wife's place to pick up his son,' Grieff agreed. 'Perhaps he took the Rafferty woman back home with him, to try and make it up to her. He fails to convince her of his sincerity so she sets about him with the poker.'

'It's a possibility worth pursuing,' Preston said.

'Unless…' Grieff let out a deep huff of breath.

'What's up?'

'It really bugs me that we've not had a proper identification.'

'What? You still think it might not be him?' Preston said. 'That they faked it so Lawson could run away with Julie Rafferty?'

Grieff scowled at him. 'Look, I know that the forensics linked his hair and DNA, and the photo of the tattoo off Donna Lawson's Facebook matches the one on Lawson's backside, all right?'

'But?'

'Call me old fashioned but I like someone to look me in the eye and say "yes, that's him".'

'Yeah,' said Preston. 'I know what you mean.' Despite the weight of the forensic evidence there was nothing quite like a positive personal identification. Especially when most of the evidence was "mobile" and had the potential to be planted by someone with a working knowledge of crime scene practices. And in the age of *CSI Miami* who didn't have at least a basic understanding of what to expect?

'Is the wife still digging in her heels?'

'Yep, she won't budge.'

'Can we ask anyone else?'

Preston pondered the question. 'The only other person we know of who's likely to have the level of intimate knowledge to recognise Lawson with his face hidden would be the first wife.'

'Layna Hewett?'

'That's right.'

Grieff was silent for a moment. 'Have a word,' he said. 'See if she'll do it.'

'Seriously?' Considering Grieff's earlier mood Preston thought he'd better make sure this wasn't another of his jokes.

'If Donna Lawson is refusing to do it then she's forcing our hand.'

'She's away till tonight, I think,' Preston said. 'Weekend break taking the kids to Disney in Paris.'

'First thing, then.'

'Okay.'

They lapsed into silence for a few moments and Preston considered the ramifications of that course of action. Mrs Hewett might not be keen either, of course, and Mrs Lawson could kick up a fuss at the idea of the ex-wife examining the body. But if the current wife wanted to object she'd better bloody well get her arse down to the morgue and do the job herself.

'How much weight are we giving this Julie Rafferty theory,' Preston said, 'in light of finding the Spanish girl's fingerprints at the scene?'

'No stone unturned, Luke, my boy,' said Grieff. 'After all, we can't prove conclusively that the dabs were left after the murder, even though everything points that way. She's still our main priority but Rafferty is definitely hiding something.'

Preston nodded but didn't answer. He concentrated on steering between parked cars, eyeing up gaps at the kerb for any large enough to accommodate the Civic.

'What on Earth...?' Grieff leaned forward in his seat, staring through the windscreen. Ahead of them a white Ford Fiesta, bearing the unmistakeable blue and yellow patches of a police patrol car, sat awkwardly at the roadside, one wheel perched on the pavement. Two uniformed officers were speaking to a woman by a garden gate. She hugged a teenage boy to her, his face buried in her bosom, and replied heatedly to whatever was being discussed. Preston easily recognised Julie Rafferty, though he didn't remember her having the shiny purple swelling on her eye when he interviewed her the day before.

*

'You'd not long been gone,' Julie Rafferty said, peering

197

around her husband's scrawny backside as he fawned around, offering them all mugs from a brightly coloured melamine tray swishing with spilt tea. 'You and that little, skinny lass.'

Preston nodded. It seemed ages since he and DC Lee had interviewed Julie and Jeff Rafferty; hard to believe it was barely 24 hours. He paused, eyeing Jeff Rafferty pointedly. They had asked him to prepare the drinks in an effort to get Mrs Rafferty alone to conduct their questioning, but he seemed determined to hang around. With an awkward shrug and sniff he shuffled back towards the kitchen.

'Then she comes hammering on the door,' Julie continued.

'She?' asked Grieff, holding his dripping mug away from his trousers.

'Donna, who else?'

'Mrs Lawson?'

'Starts calling me all sorts of names and accusin' me of... *doing stuff* with Ade.' Julie's pinched pout showed her annoyance. 'Then she just lamps me one.' Manicured fingertips hovered near a bruised eye that makeup could do little to disguise.

'And were you?' Grieff's gaze was firm and impertinent.

'What?'

'Doing *stuff* with her husband.'

'Course not!' Julie's eyes met her husband's, where he still hovered by the kitchen door, then flicked away again.

'Do you want to make a formal complaint?' Grieff suggested. 'We can talk to her. Thoroughly investigate the incident.'

The implied threat was clear to everyone in the room, even the two uniformed constables standing awkwardly by the door, who had no knowledge of the situation. Julie Rafferty squirmed under their combined scrutiny.

'No need for that,' she said, bright red lips twitching into an insincere smile. 'She's upset, doesn't know what she's saying.'

'So what did you talk to him about on Friday afternoon?' Preston chipped in without warning.

The question took her by surprise. 'Who?'

'Adrian Lawson.'

'When?'

'Friday afternoon, as I said.'

'Adie?'

Preston nodded and waited. Grieff ran a finger around the bottom of his mug, catching the drips, and discreetly wiped it on the cushion of the armchair as he settled back into it. All eyes were on Julie Rafferty once more. Jeff Rafferty leaned forward, eyebrows raised.

'What?' she snarled at her husband. With a grin he finally retreated back into the kitchen.

'We know you rang him, Mrs Rafferty,' Preston said. 'Probably the minute Donna Lawson had left you in that café. What did you say to him?'

Julie shrugged, put her mug down on the carpet, folded her arms defensively. 'Nothin'.'

'Nothin'?' sneered Jeff Rafferty, head peering round the kitchen door. 'Just heavy breathin', worrit?'

'Shurrup, you!' she warned, but he laughed, a short, bitter laugh.

'Mr Rafferty!' Grieff barked, and Rafferty disappeared again.

'Why would you reveal his affair to his wife one minute, then ring him up the next?' Preston said.

Her face glowed red, makeup cracking on her cheeks and furrowed brow. 'I felt guilty, di'n't I? For droppin' him in it.' She picked up her mug, swilled the tea around for a second, then returned it to the floor. 'Felt sorry for him, I suppose.'

'Sorry for him?' Rafferty scoffed, his voice a disembodied whine from beyond the doorway.

She ignored him, directed her response to Preston. 'You didn't see 'er face when I told 'er. Didn't see how angry she was. She wanted to get back at him, and not just by maxing out his credit cards.'

'Did she say something to you before she left?' Preston asked. 'Something to suggest that she had more on her mind than buying shoes?'

'Not in words,' she said, folding her arms again, this time in a more assured manner. 'But she were fumin'!'

'Fuming?'

'Steam comin' out of 'er ears, smoke comin' out of 'er nostrils!'

Grieff leaned forward, placed his own mug on the floor. 'Try to resist drifting into hyperbole, Mrs Rafferty.'

'Where?'

'So you called to warn him,' Preston said.

'Yeah.'

'And to arrange to meet him?'

'Eh?'

'He went into town almost immediately after you called. Was that to meet you?'

Her arms tightened around her, hitching up her breasts. She crossed and uncrossed her legs. 'No.'

'No?'

'No,' she snapped. 'I've said.'

'You didn't see him at all that day?'

'How many times do you want me to tell yer?'

Until I believe you, Preston thought, but kept it to himself.

Grieff stood unexpectedly, making Julie flinch. 'This other business...'

'What?'

He nodded towards the uniforms. 'Your lad. His mates going missing. What's that all about?'

'I don't know, do I? I only found out about it two minutes before you arrived. We've never had those little scrotes through the door.'

'Scrotes?'

'Wrong uns, the pair of 'em.'

'Oh?'

'You know the sort,' she said. 'Steal your shoes while you're stood in 'em.'

'But you didn't mind your son hanging around with them?'

'Course I minded.' Her lip curled with contempt. 'Not much I can do about it. Can't watch him all hours.'

'Mr Rafferty?' He didn't bother to raise his voice, knowing Rafferty would be within earshot.

Rafferty skulked back into the room. His scrawny shoulders shrugged. 'First I knew about it, an' all.'

'Is he in his room?' One of the constables nodded. 'Luke, go and have a word, find out if it's anything to do with our case. I'll wait here. Best not to go mob-handed, we don't want to scare the little beggar to death.'

Preston nodded and headed for the door. 'I'll need one of you with me,' he said in the direction of the parents.

Julie gave her husband a curt nod and he reluctantly followed after Preston.

As they left the room Grieff consulted with the uniforms, found out all they knew about the missing boys. Grieff later explained to Preston that the second boy's mother was distraught; her little angel would never stay out all night without telling her. The first boy's parents were dismissive, thought it was nonsense, and that their son had just gone off somewhere and would turn up with his hand out soon enough. At least, that was the father's opinion, the mother hadn't contributed much.

Upstairs Preston tapped lightly at the entrance to Alan's room but Jeff Rafferty strode past him, shouldering open the door.

'You alreyt, lad?' he asked his son, who sat quietly on his Star Wars quilt cover, rolling a comic book between his hands.

The boy managed to nod his head and shrug his shoulders at the same time. He appeared tiny and pathetic as his father and Preston loomed over him. Preston crouched down, put his face on a level with Alan's, though he failed to hold his eye.

'What do you think has happened to your friends, Alan?'

'Dunno.' Alan's voice was barely audible, muffled as he bit his lip.

'Were they in any trouble?'

'No.'

'Where did you hang out when you were with them?'

A limp shrug. 'All over.'

'That's a lot of territory,' Preston smiled gently. 'Anywhere in particular?'

'Just round the streets,' Alan said. 'Sometimes into town.'

'Doing what?'

'Nothin'.'

'Travelling round, doing nothing?'

'Yeah.' Alan kept his head down, tearing bits of paper from his comic and dropping them on his carpet. The old-fashioned signet ring, incongruous and oversized on Alan's young, slim fingers, had shifted off-centre and Preston resisted the temptation to reach out and adjust it.

'Just the three of you, or did you meet up with others? Were you part of a gang?'

'Just us.'

'And how did you get around?'

Alan's eyes met Preston's for the first time, then quickly flicked away. 'What d'you mean?'

'Bike? Bus? This older lad, Kenny, did he have a car?'

'We always walked.' Alan glanced at his father, a note of accusation in his voice. 'I haven't got a bike.' He seemed to have latched on to a stale argument, and he watched his father flinch defensively.

'We can't afford things like that,' Rafferty spluttered.

Preston threw an ill-concealed sneer in his direction. Better things to spend his money on. Out to the pub most nights.

'Taught you how to drive though, didn't I? Set you up for

life, that will. Soon as you're working and can pay for your own car you'll be sorted.'

Preston looked from the father back to the child who huddled on the bed. 'You taught him to drive?'

'Only on private roads,' Rafferty added, hastily. 'Not in public.'

Preston stood, flexed his legs. 'If you think of anything that could help in working out what happened to your friends, let us know straight away.'

Alan nodded, eyes once again downcast.

As he led the way back down the narrow staircase Rafferty gave a rueful shake of his head. 'The set of buggers will have been up to no good, I'll bet.'

'You'll bet...' Preston stopped on the stairs as a thought struck him.

Rafferty turned, puzzled. 'Eh?'

'You said you lost money the other night, when you were in the Stag and Hounds,' Preston said. 'Betting on the boxing on the telly.'

Rafferty shrugged shiftily. 'Yeah. What about it?'

'There's no television in the Stag.'

Rafferty examined the tatty wallpaper, picking at a bit of woodchip with a thumbnail. 'My mate had it on his phone. The fight. Streaming it, like.'

'Did he?'

'Yeah.'

'That's fine,' Preston said, taking a step down. 'Just let us have your friend's name and a contact number, for confirmation.'

'Why do you need that?' Rafferty said, cheeks flushing bright red. 'I've told you what happened. Why do you need to confirm anything?'

Preston smiled, spreading his hands in a casual manner. 'Because it sounded very much like you made that up on the spot. I always like confirmation if I think someone's lying to me.'

'I'm not lying.'

'So give me the name.'

Rafferty opened his mouth, closed it, blinked a few times. 'All right, I am lying.' He took a step up the stairs, very close to the detective now, so Preston could smell the grease in his hair. 'There was a woman.'

'Who?'

'I don't know, do I?' In his exasperation he'd raised his voice, so he dropped it again, adding in a hiss, 'I gave her the money.'

'Did you meet her in the pub?'

'Outside.'

'And you didn't get her name?'

Rafferty had the good grace to look extremely uncomfortable.

Preston sighed and gestured for Rafferty to continue down the stairs, and within a few minutes the two detectives were in the Honda, heading back to Haleston.

'She's having it off with our murder victim and he's picking up tarts on the street?' Grieff shook his head and gave a huffing little half-laugh.

'I don't think it's something he's in the habit of doing,' Preston said.

'No?'

'Just the impression I got from him.' Preston carefully checked his mirrors at the junction, even though the Sunday afternoon traffic was light. 'I think it might have been some sort of payback.'

'Retribution?' Grieff stroked his chin. 'You think he knew what she was up to with Lawson?'

'Yeah,' said Preston. 'The way he kept needling her when she was talking about it earlier.'

'I spotted that,' Grieff nodded. 'Proper little wind-up merchant, our Mr Rafferty. Do you reckon he knows about the phone call and whether or not she met up with Lawson on Friday?'

'He might have guessed, but if he was at work when he said he was, then he couldn't know for sure.'

'Have we checked what time he got to work that day?'

'It was on the actions list, so it should be in the file.'

'That's something for you to look into when we get back.'

Preston glanced across at him. 'What'll you be doing?'

'I shall be experiencing my fifteen minutes of fame,' Grieff said, pulling down the passenger sun-visor and peering into the mirror. He ran his fingers through his lush, wavy hair, touching the flecks of grey above his ears, pouting at his reflection. 'I'm ready for my close-up, Mr DeMille.'

19

The text beeped in his trouser pocket as Preston pulled the Honda into one of the reserved spaces behind the station and he had to wrestle the phone free to read it.

where r u?

He checked the time on the dash clock; later than he thought. 'Bugger.'

'Problem?' Grieff asked as he fumbled with his seatbelt.

'I'm supposed to be home by now,' Preston said. 'Kerry's at mine.'

'You'd better get off, then,' Grieff said.

His boss was aware that Preston's time with his daughter was limited enough, without him standing her up.

'Don't leave the lass waiting.'

Preston glanced awkwardly at the building looming over them, visions of paperwork towers teetering dangerously on his desk tormenting him.

'Go on,' Grieff said, obviously reading his thoughts again. 'There's nothing that can't wait till the morning.'

'You sure?'

'I don't think we'll be facing chaos of *The Purge* dimensions just because Haleston's finest isn't at his post.'

Preston smiled while he tapped out a hasty response on his phone. 'I didn't think *The Purge* was the sort of film you'd be likely to have seen.'

'Heard of,' Grieff corrected. 'Not seen.'

Once his boss was safely deposited on the pavement Preston set off for home. Scorah Hill was an urban suburb of Haleston town about two miles from the centre. Tightly packed streets of terraces, mostly converted to flats, housing students and foreign nationals, and the occasional police detective. Preston's place was upstairs, halfway along a quiet side street, self-contained with its own kitchen, no garden but he could use the loft for storage. It was a far cry from the three-bed semi he had shared with Claire a few years ago, but it suited his purposes. Only one bedroom so he had to unfold the sofa-bed when Kerry stayed over. That wouldn't be an issue tonight, though, because it was school tomorrow so she'd have to be back with her mother by eight o'clock. Or thereabouts. Still plenty of time for a film on DVD and a pizza supper.

Kerry was sprawled, feet up, along the sofa, flicking through channels on the TV when he bundled into the room, full of apologies.

'I'm fine,' she shrugged. 'I've been sharing a joint with Tomasz downstairs.' She rolled her eyes towards him cheekily. 'Well chilled now.'

Preston had noticed the whiff of weed occasionally drifting up from the shared backyard, but the Polish couple who occupied the ground floor of the house were discreet and he knew they wouldn't dream of trying to ply a thirteen year old girl with class B drugs. Especially knowing what her father did for a living.

'You're not funny,' Preston said as he nudged her legs off the sofa so he could sit down.

She dug her fingers into his ribs until he couldn't help but laugh. 'What're you laughing for, then?'

'Aren't you supposed to be all sulky and moody, at your age?' He smiled at her as she raised her finely plucked eyebrow at him. 'You've got a stereotype to live up to.'

'I've got some black make-up at Mum's,' she said. 'But I can't be bothered to put it on.'

He placed an arm around her as she snuggled against him. He marvelled at how even-tempered and level-headed she seemed, being, as she was, the product of a broken home. This might be an opportune moment for a long-awaited discussion.

'Kerry,' he began, tentatively. 'You've never asked me what went wrong.'

'Wrong?' Her big, round eyes peered at him curiously.

207

'Between me and your mum. Don't you ever wonder?'

He felt the shrug beneath his arm. She looked back at the telly.

'Shit happens.'

Indeed it does, he thought, ignoring the use of the mild expletive. If an occasional curse word was the extent of her rebellious teenage streak then he was truly blessed.

And as simply as that, the discussion was over. But the thought was in his head now, so he couldn't help pondering the "shit" that had happened.

He and Claire had always strived to keep any bitterness they may have felt for one another away from Kerry's view, but it was impossible that she wouldn't have been aware of it. He had seen far too many examples of children becoming collateral damage of the war between parents.

They'd married far too young, of course. In his case it was probably a form of rebellion against his own parents, or his father, at least. Not that he had noticed. Presented with the registrars' consent form, allowing them to marry at sixteen, Preston senior had barely glanced at it before adding his scrawling signature with a shrug. If the lazy old bastard had only reacted in some way, blown a gasket, torn up the papers, taken a swipe at his unruly son's head even, then Luke's life would have very different. But instead he had tossed the form back at Luke without taking his eyes from the television screen.

Luke Preston and Claire Maxey had always fancied each other, from the first time their eyes met across a crowded classroom, but they had never really liked each other that much. When Luke had gone round to the Maxeys' house he had always spent more time in her brother Eddie's room, engaging in some form of digital combat on his PlayStation, rather than in Claire's unlit bedroom, fumbling under her top.

But they somehow convinced themselves that marriage was what they wanted. They had even enjoyed it for a while. Eventually, though, they both realised something was missing; that there was a hole in their relationship which was gradually growing into a chasm. Outsiders could see that the vital absent ingredient was love, but they sought to fill the gap with more tangible things. He joined the police. She became pregnant. Temporary solutions.

The bond between a mother and her child is a wondrous thing, a magical thing, he would never deny that. But feeling this weight against his side – his child, his offspring, idly flicking through a takeaway menu, deciding whether to go for extra mushrooms or jalapenos – filled him with a warmth and pride that no uniform or badge could ever replace.

Between ordering pizzas and selecting a DVD to watch with his daughter, Preston considered his own father's casual, dismissive attitude, and that of Jeff Rafferty towards Alan. Then he thought of Ron Hewett, surprising his family with a weekend at Disney, and Adrian Lawson, keeping Shane off school so that he could still have his weekly visit. Fathers and their children: when the bond was there it was as strong as any could be. If only Lawson had gone back for his son instead of allowing himself to be distracted, then surely he would still be alive.

*

Annette Lee nudged the front door shut with her heel, while peeling off her smart suit jacket and tugging the elasticated hairband from her ponytail. A little moan of pleasure escaped her lips as she raked her fingernails across her scalp and shook her head. She hung the jacket on the back of a dining chair in the kitchen/diner to the left and shuffled right into the living area, flopping onto the sofa and kicking off her shoes.

'Netty? That you, babe?' The voice came from the door in the corner, which led to a short corridor, off which were the bedroom and bathroom.

Lee didn't bother responding. Who else was it likely to

be? Instead she slipped off the sofa onto her knees, picking up the scattered DVD cases from the floor and arranging them back on the shelf. Collecting her shoes and jacket she padded through to the bedroom. Empty.

'You in the bathroom?' she called. It seemed to be the evening for pointless questions. There was nowhere else left for her wife to be, unless she was hiding in the wardrobe, and she hadn't done that for ages. The recollection curled her lips up in a warm smile. *Ah, the early days!*

Lee placed her shoes neatly in the bottom of the wardrobe and took out a hanger for her jacket. She slipped off her trousers and arranged them on the same hanger, then put her suit away. Once her shirt was in the wash basket she stretched out on the bed and watched the clouds swirl on the inside of her eyelids, trying not to imagine the heap of clothes she was likely to discover on the bathroom floor later, letting her tension drain from her.

Had she slept? The creak of bed springs and a slight lurch of the mattress brought her eyes open again. Jo Kershaw's gorgeous smile beamed down at her. She was sitting on the edge of the bed wrapped in a thick bath towel, water dripping from her curly, black hair.

'Hi, babe,' said Kershaw. She leaned in for a kiss.

Lee ran a finger up her warm, damp arm. 'You didn't wait for me to scrub your back.'

'I thought the boss might keep you late, with everything that's going on.'

'Nah, Grieff's in a good mood, with that telly thing later tonight.' Lee lifted her arms so she could rest her head on her hands. She saw Kershaw notice how her breasts shifted in her bra. 'Oi, my eyes are up here.'

Kershaw laughed and shook her head, flicking droplets of cold water from her hair onto Lee's bare midriff. Lee giggled and shivered.

'Speaking of putting people in a good mood,' said Kershaw, 'look, I've even brought my clothes through from the bathroom.' She pointed towards the corner where a bundle of clothes had been dumped onto the lid of the wash basket. They weren't actually *inside* the basket, but they were a hell of a lot closer than usual, so Lee smiled encouragingly.

'Hey,' Kershaw said, as a thought struck her, 'did my identifying that Spanish girl crack the case wide open?' She spread her hands in an expansive gesture. 'I hope they bear it in mind when the next round of promotions comes up.'

'I don't know about earning you a promotion but it earned me a visit to your hideous taxi driver.' Lee shuddered worse than when the cold water had hit her skin.

'Grotbags, or whatever his name was?' Kershaw pulled a face at the memory of the mountainous perv.

'Grogan.'

'That's him. Why did you need to see him?'

'Just to see if he remembered any more than he told you the other day.'

Kershaw folded her arms and made a moue of mock annoyance. 'Checking I did my job properly?'

'You were dealing with lost property,' Lee said, trying not to sound too defensive. 'Now we know she's a murder suspect.'

Kershaw winked and turned the pout into a smile. 'Did you learn anything?'

'You mean apart from the fact that he picks his nose and runs his fingernails along the seam of his jeans to clean them?'

Kershaw put a hand to her mouth, as if to prevent herself being sick. 'Yeah, apart from that.'

'Well, he claims he doesn't actually remember her, one passenger among so many.'

'Claims, Detective?' Kershaw asked, eyebrow raised. 'You suspect he may have been being duplicitous?'

'I do indeed, Constable.' Lee sat up, arms behind her, propping herself up. Kershaw's eyes flicked down at her body, subconsciously, an automatic response. Lee smiled.

211

'You saw her picture, she's quite fit.'

'Not bad.' Kershaw saw a drop of water on her wife's thigh and wiped it off with her thumb.

'You told me how he ogled you yesterday,' Lee said.

'Don't remind me.'

'And I saw how he looked at me this afternoon.'

'I'll kill him!'

'Aww, my hero!' Lee smiled, then suddenly frowned. 'But a bloke like that isn't going to forget having a sweet little thing like her in his cab.'

'She'd be straight in his wank bank,' Kershaw said, affecting a course voice to match the language.

Lee didn't laugh. 'Or worse.'

'Worse?'

'Did you notice the scratches over his eye?' Lee said, bringing a hand up to her own face in demonstration.

'Yeah, healing but recent. Some drunk bird, he said. Same night the holdall was left.'

'Do you believe him?'

'What? You think he tried it on with the Spanish lass and got an eyeful of fingernails for his efforts?'

'It would explain why he's not willing to admit remembering her.'

'I certainly wouldn't put it past him.'

'Makes you look at her in a more sympathetic light,' said Lee with a thoughtful sigh.

'But it doesn't excuse her popping round to her boyfriend's house the next day and mashing his skull with a poker.'

'Allegedly,' Lee said.

'Allegedly,' Kershaw agreed.

They smiled, staring at one another, then Lee's eyes took on a cheeky twinkle.

'Our lovely Mr Grogan certainly remembered you,' she said. 'He even licked his lips when he mentioned you.'

Kershaw stood with a shudder. 'How do you know he was talking about me?' She walked round the bed and stopped by the large mirror on the wardrobe door, running her fingers through her hair. 'He could've been talking about any stunningly attractive copper.'

'He specifically said "that black lass", and Haleston station isn't exactly over-represented, if you know what I mean.'

'Oh, I do!' She loosened the towel and let it drop to the carpet, looking herself up and down. 'Black's a bit severe, though. I'd say more "honey on toast".'

'Can you say that?' Lee rose from the bed and stood behind her, sliding her arms around her waist. 'I thought you weren't allowed to describe people of colour in food terms.' On tippy-toes she could just peep over her shoulder at their reflections.

'No, *you're* not,' Kershaw said. 'But I can.'

'Eh?'

'Well, if this was a trashy crime novel written by a middle-aged white bloke it'd be a bit dodgy.' She leant back into the snuggly embrace. 'But this is real life and I think I look good enough to eat.'

'Mmm, me too!' Lee bared her teeth at Kershaw's neck. 'Gi's a bite.'

Laughing, they tumbled back onto the bed.

*

Edward Maxey glanced at his watch again, the umpteenth time within the last few minutes. His eyes flicked to the large bay window, willing the flash of car headlights to sweep across the closed curtains and his wife to screech her little car onto the drive, jerking to a halt an inch from the garage door as was her habit. But she didn't. And wouldn't yet, not for another twenty minutes or so at least.

He smiled awkwardly at his guest, sitting across from him with legs curled up beneath her on the sofa. Alicia smiled back briefly, looking away quickly, eyes back on the television screen. Barely a word had passed between them since they had that "little talk" earlier, she clearly preferring to contain her dark, brooding thoughts inside her own head, while he seemed unable to form a coherent sentence that didn't feel either pathetically banal or offensively intrusive.

But how could he express his feelings when he couldn't even interpret them for himself? Why had he even given her his phone number in the first place? She was undeniably attractive, or had been before taking on the haunted countenance she wore now, but beyond pleasing his eye he had no ambition to please himself any further with her. Was it some form of paternal emotion he was experiencing? Certainly as he had draped his coat around her shoulders and she pressed her frail, dishevelled form against him he had felt only protective urges for her, not lustful desires. He was too damn young to be thinking of her as a daughter, surely? The "conversation" hadn't arisen between him and Nicky for a while, and it was a long time since he'd dwelt on the topic of parenthood, outside of the occasional pang when he saw Luke and Kerry together. How long could they keep saying "There's plenty of time"?

Now he had lied to his best friend and deliberately concealed a known fugitive from the police in his own home. The chance had been there for him to tell Luke where their "person of interest" was. A reasonable, responsible person would have brought Luke home with him, handed her over as gently as possible. Or put her in the car and driven her to the station, gone in with her, stayed with her for as long as they'd let him. But he hadn't done either of those things. Here she sat and, for all that she had showered several times since he brought her home yesterday, he imagined he could still see torrents of blood washing over her when he caught sight of her in the corner of his eye. Though he knew it was not the blood of a dead man he saw, it was still a disquieting illusion. He felt the ground crumbling beneath him, sucking him down further into a situation that could swallow his reputation and respectability irretrievably, and he despised himself for his selfishness. Nicky had deferred to his decision, she could see as well as he that Alicia was the victim here, suffering from layers of trauma that they could never fully understand. How could he abandon her now? They were all she had left, her only lifebelt in an ocean of despair. The way she had greeted him like a lonely puppy on his return, after he had left her alone for a few minutes earlier today, melted any inclinations he might have had for giving her up to the authorities.

That trip, though, had only unsettled him more. He had received a call from some bloke called Dan Baxter, asking him to call in to the police station to provide elimination fingerprints, if it was at all convenient. Baxter had assured him it wouldn't take long, it was purely routine, his prints wouldn't be kept on file or entered onto any database, and would be destroyed after the relevant comparisons had been made. Obviously Maxey had agreed. *Anything to help with the case.* Hah!

It was that damned compliments slip again. Two sets of prints found on it.

'Couldn't those prints belong to anybody?' Maxey had asked, accepting the cloth from Baxter and wiping the ink from his fingertips. 'Somebody else from the register office? Even someone from the firm that printed the slips?'

'Unlikely,' Baxter said, folding his arms, ready to expound on his theory. 'The batch of paper would be passed from the manufacturer to the printer in huge blocks, printed and cut by machine, packaged and passed on to your office without being touched once.'

'But what about when it's passed round the office? Everyone uses the same stock of slips.'

'True,' Baxter agreed. 'But you won't take one at a time from the store cupboard. You'll grab a hefty wad to keep in your desk drawer, am I right?'

'Well, I suppose so,' Maxey conceded.

'And even if someone else passed the pile to you before

you took it to your office, they would only be likely to touch the top and bottom sheet of the pile. Once you've given the top slip to someone, the rest of the pile is virginal. Untouched by human hand. So unless this was the very first slip you'd issued from this particular stack, it's unlikely to have been touched before you picked it up. So these prints can only be yours and those of the person you gave it to.'

Long-winded, but logical. Maxey couldn't argue with him. And now they had Alicia's fingerprints, but so what? Clinging to his belief that she was innocent Maxey shrugged off this development, but still he couldn't deny the uneasy sensation that this meeting had stirred within him. Now, as he sank wearily into the plush of his comfy chair, he pushed down the nagging doubts that tried to rise in his subconscious and let the images of the TV wash over him.

And suddenly, there she was. Right there on the television screen. Her passport photo image staring out at them from the inset over the news anchor's shoulder, her name in the caption at the bottom of the screen. They both sat there, gaping slack-jawed as the picture cut to a press conference led by a large, stocky detective inspector with the unlikely name of Grieff, asking that anyone with any information regarding the whereabouts of the young woman they were seeking in relation to their enquiries should get in touch immediately.

*

Across town, sitting in the gloom of her poky bedsit, Roz Peters crunched the remains of her cigarette into an ashtray and glared at the phone number that she had paused on her television screen.

20

Monday

Maxey hated being late.

Bruce, the car park attendant, had glanced at his watch with a curious frown as he waved him through the back gates this morning. Of the thousand or so years that Bruce had stood there, rain or shine, Maxey was aware of no instances of illness or crisis that had kept the old codger from his post. Which made it all the more frustrating to be awarded his raised eyebrow this morning, the most damning critique imaginable.

An exasperating tour of the car park, searching for a free space, added precious moments to Maxey's tardiness, and the habitual assessment of his handsome appearance in the car's gleaming bodywork became forfeit to his haste.

Maxey trotted up the rear stairs to the registrars' floor, footsteps echoing in the cold, concrete stairwell, and popped his head into the reception to gasp a hasty good morning and let them know he'd finally arrived. Roz Peters, glancing sharply across from the front counter, barely had chance to acknowledge his presence before he disappeared again, heading towards his own office. He was breathless and clammy as he kicked the door shut behind him, stripping off his jacket and draping it over the back of his chair. He even loosened his tie – an act unheard of, even in the height of the summer.

Seventeen minutes. Not much, but it was the principle of the thing. This must be the first time he'd been late since that water pipe burst a couple of years ago and they closed Main Drive while they dug up the whole road looking for the source of the leak. Traffic had become snarled up throughout the whole town, causing hold-ups for hours. Plenty of other people were made late too, and many appointments were missed or rescheduled. The bride from one of the day's weddings resorted to chasing up the office stairway, teetering precariously on tapered heels, lace hem held high up white-stockinged legs, unashamedly flashing a borrowed blue garter in her rush.

But it wasn't roadworks which delayed Maxey this morning.

By the time Nicky arrived home from her shift last night, tired and cranky, Alicia had already retreated to her room. He'd poured his wife a glass of wine and massaged her legs as she lay in a hot bath, and he felt the tension soaking away from her body. She smiled and flicked foamy water at him, enjoying the caress of his hands on her calves and thighs, and all was well with the world in that moment, so he bit his lip on the subject of the police appeal on the news, allowing her to go to bed relaxed. He knew, though, that he couldn't leave for work this morning without speaking to her, so he gently woke her and filled her in on the developments. She stared at him, groggy and bewildered, myriad expressions playing across her features.

Their subsequent discussion covered all the old ground: Alicia didn't look like a killer, didn't act like a killer. She wore the mantle of one who had suffered much through no fault of her own. Their nurturing instincts forbade handing her over to the authorities.

But...

The police were putting great efforts into finding her. They obviously had access to forensic evidence that Maxey and Nicky couldn't possibly be aware of. Guilty or innocent, keeping her hidden was hindering the police investigation. They could be harbouring a murderer, or giving a murderer extra time to cover their tracks.

Maxey proposed "throwing a sickie" and staying home with them, to protect his wife should their judgement prove mistaken. Alicia as a wild-eyed axe murderer seemed a ridiculous notion, but she was still practically a stranger. Who knew what dark thoughts might lie behind that innocent façade? Then Nicky went to rouse Alicia and found her fast asleep, huddled under her quilt on the floor, in the darkest corner of her room, and all thoughts of turning her in were forgotten.

Nicky insisted that she would be fine, so, pushing all qualms aside, Maxey had scowled at the hands on the antique mantle clock, grabbed his jacket and headed for his car. Every red light and learner driver conspired to impede his progress, as they only seem to do when you are already running late, and he'd left the detachable front panel for his CD player on the hall stand as he snatched up his keys, so he didn't even have music on the journey to sooth his savage breast.

By the time he had caught his breath and his computer had warmed up the appointment software informed him that he had barely ten minutes to snatch a quick coffee before entering the fray. As he was preparing to head to the staff room his office door opened with a brief rap of knuckles on the other side. Roz entered carrying a steaming coffee mug and brought it over to him.

'Thought you'd be gasping,' she said, positioning the mug on a notepad to protect the polished finish of his desk.

He beamed a grateful smile. 'You're a lifesaver!'

'Everything all right?' She stood with hands on hips, regarding him with concern, but something in her stance seemed less convivial than usual, not the flirty swagger he was used to.

'Yeah,' he shrugged, lifting the coffee to his lips. 'I'll be fine after I get this down me. Thanks.' He raised the mug in a toast to her solicitude before replacing it on his desk.

She waited, eyebrow raised in query.

He squirmed under her inspection. 'What?'

'What happened on Saturday?'

'Saturday?'

She huffed an impatient sigh. 'After the wedding. The

phone call, from that girl. You rushing off like a knight in shining armour.'

Saturday. Was it as recent as that? It seemed so long ago that he'd raced to the park in Merrington to rescue the distressed Alicia. Images of her running towards him, blood-drenched and bedraggled, flashed before him and he tried not to let his reaction radiate from his face.

'Nothing.' He displayed open hands in a dismissive gesture, face a mask of innocence. 'She wasn't there.'

'No?'

'Nope, not a sign.'

Her demeanour softened. She moved around to his side of the desk and perched on the edge, close enough that her knee brushed his leg, pencil skirt taut over her thighs. She looked down at him, eyes clouded with concern. 'You've not got yourself involved in something silly, have you?'

'Course not!' He held her gaze, almost daring her to contradict him.

'You can talk to me.'

'I know,' he said, finally looking away, arranging his pens on his desk, as if that were the most important thing on his mind at present.

She nodded, though her expression remained unconvinced. With a hand on his shoulder she levered herself back onto her feet, and he wondered if the pressure of her nails in his flesh was unnecessarily firm. He tried to read her face as she glanced back before disappearing from the room; apprehension mixed with annoyance?

His computer diary indicated that his first appointment had arrived, so he shook it from his mind and attempted to focus on the task in hand.

*

If the figure they'd borne out on that metal trolley still had a face at all, it couldn't have looked any more cold and dead than the expression her husband had worn when she told him she was going to the morgue to identify her former husband's body. He'd tried to forbid her to go, said they couldn't force her. Why should she have to face such a distressing burden? What a terrible way to spoil their wonderful weekend away.

But they were the police, how could she refuse? Also, beyond the initial instinctive revulsion at the thought of bodies and death, a creeping curiosity had prodded her into agreeing to the macabre request.

At least she didn't have to worry about Shane while she was off on her gruesome undertaking. The boy was in shock after they had finally broken the news to him about his father's fate on their return last night. She had wanted nothing more than to smother him in maternal affection but Ron had insisted they take him there and then, before they had even unpacked, to Layna's parents, the boy's Grandy and Marma, to spend a few days in a completely different environment with unreserved spoiling and fussing. Best for Shane, he'd said, but Layna had sensed his relief at having one less child in the house.

She'd never seen a dead body before and although if you'd asked her she would have said she had no desire to, she found herself drawn to the prospect. *Because* it was him? A deep-rooted need to be absolutely certain that he was gone, out of her life forever? Or merely nosiness taken to its grisly extreme? Whatever the true motivation, Layna Hewett had found herself staring down at the partially covered body of Adrian Lawson. A surreal and gruesome scenario. She couldn't shake the impression of being in a butcher's shop, though something didn't smell entirely fresh. And the cuts of meat on display weren't the most appetising. Even with the sheet over it she could tell that the shape of his head just wasn't *right*, somehow.

It was the same police sergeant who first told them about Adrian's death that escorted her down the cold, antiseptic corridors to this shiny, stainless steel room where the masked attendants in their white overalls and over-sized wellies waited for them.

Latex-covered fingers drew back a corner of the covering. The hair on his chest was greasy and dull, and his skin so pale! But she acknowledged the birthmark on the lower part of the right side of his chest.

The sergeant placed a gentle hand on her shoulder, turned her away from the cold, metal table, asked how she was coping. She smiled and nodded. By the time she turned her attention back to the limp form the silent attendants had turned him onto his front. It was almost comical when they whipped away another part of the sheet, exposing his pasty-white backside and the small, red devil face winking up at her from his left buttock and she bit her lip to avoid giggling aloud. She knew that design all right, even after years of aging and fading and presented on this unfamiliar grey, sagging canvas. Back in the early days of their relationship he'd taken great delight in snatching any opportunity to drop his trousers and show it off to all and sundry with the least excuse. In the pub it was a laugh but when he came to the house and repeated his behaviour, her mother had been mortified! But Adrian had that cheeky charm that could mollify even her enraged father in no time at all. The twinkle in the eye and his massive grin, a combination that couldn't be resisted. Everyone loved Adrian. Layna suspected that her parents still felt regret that she hadn't been able to keep hold of him, and had settled instead for the staid reliability of Ron Hewett. So different in every conceivable way. Adrian had been tall, broad, dashing, charismatic. Ron wasn't.

But Ron also wasn't a selfish bastard who cared only about his own gratification and pleasure. A frequent visitor to the 24-hour convenience store where she'd worked back then, Ron had seen how deeply unhappy she'd become in Adrian's shadow and reached out to her, offering comfort and understanding, catching her at a vulnerable moment. He was the antithesis of everything she had grown to resent in her relationship with Adrian, so she had fallen into his arms eagerly and allowed him to snatch her away before Adrian even noticed he was losing her.

And Ron had been her rock ever since. Mostly.

Well, everyone had their off days. The most saintly of men were allowed to be moody sometimes. Better than constant good cheer that merely masked a cold, dispassionate self-interest bordering on arrogance, daring you to feel anything but what he felt, or wanted you to feel. Being Adrian Lawson's wife had been exhausting. Being Mrs Hewett was a much more placid affair. Mostly.

Ron's coolness rarely went beyond an occasional sulk. He might go quiet on her for a while, but he never raised a hand or cursed or swore. And he was always there with an apology and consolation in the form of presents or, as with this last weekend, an unexpected trip.

And a wonderful trip it had been. Mostly.

Little Terry had taken the longest to relax, even though the whole excursion was tailor-made for him. Lots of rides, people dressed up as cartoon characters, ice cream and treats. Whatever had spooked him the other day, *that* day, when he went out with Adrian and Shane, was symptomatic of something which had been bothering him for a while. He wouldn't say what the problem was, insisted that no one was bullying him at school, couldn't put his fears into words.

She refused to entertain the dark thoughts which tried to wriggle into her mind – the boy was rarely out of her sight, they didn't use babysitters and there was no kindly uncle to sit Terry in his lap that little bit tighter than was absolutely necessary. No, nothing like that.

Ron's impatience with the four-year-old's inability to articulate the issue only made matters worse and that time the other week, when his temper had frayed to snapping point, was the first instance of Terry wetting himself. He'd roared at the boy and slammed a hand down on the table, rattling cutlery and tipping over a glass of milk, merely because he wouldn't speak up when Ron asked him a

223

question.

It was this impatience that Layna found hard to understand. Terry had always been the favourite, able to get away with so much more than his half-brother. After all, Terry was Ron's own son, not a step-child, like Shane. Shane had been the one who was merely tolerated and got to do all the fun things second. It was because Terry was the youngest, Ron had always assured him, but even at his tender age Shane could recognise favouritism. But that was then. And this change in attitude seemed to have happened around the same time that Terry had begun exhibiting this crippling timidity. So which came first, the fear or the anger? And was it coincidence or correlation?

Ron was his usual, solicitous self when Layna returned from her visit to the morgue, sat her down and brought her a nice, hot cup of tea. Put her a sugar in it, though she normally took it without. She'd need the boost of energy to combat the shock, he told her, amongst subtle questions about what she'd seen, what was it like, was it definitely him? Maybe he needed to be sure Adrian had definitely gone, too. When she suggested that maybe he should have gone with her he just shook his head and turned on the television.

*

'Three times in as many days,' said Luke Preston through a fixed smile, as he stood on the doorstep of Jeff and Julie Rafferty's cramped, mid-terrace house yet again. 'You must be sick of the sight of me, by now.' His tone left little doubt that the feeling was mutual.

Julie's shoulders slumped dramatically. 'Oh God, what have I done now?' Without the customary layers of make-up she could have been a different woman. Harder features, weary eyes. The swelling around her left eye was still livid and purple.

'Actually, it's not you, this time.' Preston stepped aside

224

and allowed Annette Lee to precede him into the house.

Julie backed down the narrow hallway to allow them room to enter. 'Have you heard something about Alan's friends?'

The question momentarily wrong-footed him. 'What?'

'The missing boys,' Lee reminded him.

'No, sorry.' He assumed a sombre mien, to assure her that the search was being treated as a serious matter. 'No news in that regard.'

'Oh, right.' She nodded and gritted her teeth. Two down, she'd obviously worked out that that only left one person they could possibly want to see. She turned and barged into the living room, to where her husband lounged in the armchair.

'Oi, arse'ole!' she hissed, giving the chair a sharp kick. 'Cops are back, looking for you.'

'Me?' Jeff Rafferty struggled to his feet from the deep, sagging cushions. 'What for?'

'Just a few follow-up questions, Mr Rafferty,' Lee said. 'Clear up some details.'

'Perhaps you could pop the kettle on, Mrs Rafferty,' Preston suggested. 'Give us a minute with your husband.'

'This isn't a friggin' café, y'know. You've had enough free drinks off us.' Julie waved a hand in her husband's face. 'I want to know what this bugger's been up too.'

'I will have to insist you give us a moment alone, I'm afraid.' There was ice behind Preston's smile. Julie grumbled under her breath, but left the room.

'No work today, Mr Rafferty?' Lee asked, her voice casual.

'Still on lates,' Rafferty said.

'Actually, we're aware of your shift pattern,' she said. 'Just as we're aware of your arrival and leaving times recently.' She tugged her notebook from her jacket pocket, keeping her eyes on his. 'Specifically, on Friday.'

He couldn't hold her gaze, eyes shifting to the door, beyond which his wife was undoubtedly standing, ear

225

pressed to the wood.

Lee flicked through the pages of the small pocket book. 'You told us you worked twelve till eight PM on Friday.' The words were a statement, but her eyebrow arched in query.

'That's when I was due.'

'Due, yes.' She settled on a page in her book and tapped her pencil against it thoughtfully. 'We've been in touch with your employers...' She left the sentence dangling.

'I was a bit late,' Rafferty mumbled shiftily. 'Car wa' playing up.'

'Is anyone able to corroborate that?'

His stared blankly back at her.

'Did you call a mechanic? Maybe a neighbour gave you a tow?'

'Sorted it meself.'

'And no one saw you with your bonnet up, elbow-deep in grease and oil?' Preston asked.

'Not that I remember.' Rafferty ran a quivering hand through his lank, thinning hair. 'I had me head down, weren't looking at who was goin' past.'

Preston stepped closer to Rafferty, toes almost touching his. 'Why didn't you mention this unexpected delay when we spoke to you the other day?'

Rafferty leaned backwards, discomfited by Preston's proximity. 'Dunno,' he shrugged. 'I was in shock. Just heard what happened to Adie. Not thinkin' straight.'

'And this mechanical fault made you almost two and a half hours late to work?' Lee chipped in.

Unsettled by the ping-ponging of questioning, Rafferty looked from one to the other of them, mouth flopping open uselessly. He shuffled backwards, heel catching the base of his chair, and fell awkwardly into the soft seat.

'Why don't we arrest the lying toe-rag?' Lee asked. By now they were back in the car, heading to the station.

Preston smiled at her eagerness. 'I'd love to, but I'm not convinced about the timeline.' He glanced across at her and saw her nod unhappily.

While he was escorting Layna Hewett to the morgue earlier, Lee had received the information from Rafferty's place of work regarding his late arrival on the day of the murder. She herself then meticulously reviewed the evidence files and plotted the movements of Lawson and both Raffertys with clockwork precision.

Preston returned his contemplation to the road ahead. 'Even if he was standing behind the door with the poker in his hand when Lawson arrived back home at just after two, he'd struggle to do the deed, clean himself up and still make it to Doncaster before half past.'

Lee sighed and slumped down in her seat. 'Yeah, I suppose.'

'But that "car playing up" business,' Preston said with a sardonic sneer, 'was clearly total bollocks.'

21

'Go straight to and from school, no detours. Stick with other kids, don't walk on your own. When you get home, stay in. Most important, don't go out after dark.'

Of course, those were merely suggestions. Official police recommendations. For his own safety. No one could be certain Alan was actually in any danger. Kenny's disappearance might be voluntary, as his father insisted, and have no connection to Jake subsequently going missing.

Yeah, right. Hell of a coincidence, though.

Stay at home all night? It gets dark by teatime. Did they really expect him to sit in his room twiddling his thumbs, or whatever he could find to twiddle? Or worse, sit downstairs with those miserable twats for hours, staring at some mindless shit on the telly? No thanks.

Sneaking out without telling anyone had seemed like a good idea at the time. Not that they were difficult to evade. His father wasn't yet home from work, and his mother was immersed in her soaps. Now, as he crept down dark, narrow streets, witches and skeletons leering at him from porches and windows on all sides, several streetlamps broken or malfunctioning, an icy chill, unrelated to the damp evening mist, shuddered through him.

He considered heading down to the cut, to where he and the others used to hang out on that stretch of the canal towpath that passed under the railway bridge. But he quickly dismissed the idea. Kenny and Jake wouldn't be there. Of course they wouldn't. A cold, damp underpass was no place to doss, not now a gloomy autumn was creeping towards a miserable winter. They'd been missing for days! And going searching by himself didn't appeal to him. The heavy shadows and thunderous roar of passing trains were barely tolerable when his mates had been there to tease him for his nervousness; they would surely be terrifying alone. Or, even worse to contemplate, he might *not* be alone. Who else might seek the shelter of the gloomy brick arch on a drizzly night? Beggars, thieves, murderers? No, the cut was out of bounds, at least until daylight.

And what was the point of investigating the gang's old haunts, anyway? Down by the canal, over on the skateboard park, at that naff youth club in the church hall: Kenny and Jake wouldn't be in any of those places. No, something had happened to them. Something *bad.* He *felt* it. More than mere common sense telling him this wasn't a coincidence; more than logic telling him that Jake wouldn't clear out when his mum had just bought a catering-size pack of mini-kievs for the freezer. His spider-sense was tingling big-time. He didn't want to think the worst, but he couldn't help it. The dark thoughts hovered constantly like cold shadows at his shoulder. After all the wrongdoings they had committed, the thefts, the vandalism, the assaults, someone had come looking for them, seeking retribution. Whoever it was had found Kenny and Jake. Taken whatever payback they thought suited the transgression. And the boys hadn't been seen since. Was he next?

Alan turned towards the lighter part of the village. The shopping precinct was only a block away. A concentration of lamp-posts around the parking bays. Shop fronts brightly lit whatever the hour; those that weren't boarded up due to the harsh economy or because some local scrotes had put a brick through their window. Mention no names.

Even there it seemed quiet, despite the occasional shopper popping into the "8 Till L8" or queuing for a kebab, chow mein or curry at "All Ways East" (who even do pizza but, let's face it, Naples *is* east of Haleston). The precinct had been another of their hang-outs, but now Kenny wasn't there, spitting at passers-by. Jake wasn't there, dancing on the bus-stop roof.

His nerves still jangled at every passing car, every barking dog. Alan was surprised how vulnerable, how exposed he felt, without the apparent protection of Kenny and Jake. Safety in numbers. Even though they had been the cause of more bruises and injury than he had ever experienced before he met them. Either through the hazardous exploits they had carried out together, or through them simply growing bored and punching him for no reason.

Now their mere absence screamed in his head. Days ago he would have been glad had they chosen never to call on him again. But he felt no relief at the lack of the heavy pound of Kenny's fist on the front door, or the squeal of the garden gate as Jake rode it like a horse. He knew that them being missing was through no choice of their own. Fear gnawed at him like a pack of hyenas worrying an abandoned carcass.

Even the happy tinkle of the bell above the door of the "8 Till L8" announcing his arrival made him flinch, and he had to take a deep breath before he ventured farther inside the shop. He didn't veer off between the aisles as was his usual practice, hiding from the mirrors and cameras adorning the corners of the ceiling, as Kenny had taught him. Instead he headed straight for the checkout. The elderly Asian woman behind the counter eyed him warily as he approached, recognising him from previous visits.

Alan placed a five pound note on the bare area between the till and the display rack sitting like a waterfall of gaudily wrapped chocolate bars. 'Here,' he said.

'What are you buying?' she asked, a little placated that at least he had brought money this time. She was more used to him sauntering in, wandering aimlessly for a few minutes before leaving without catching her eye, his Parka coat bulging slightly more than when he had entered.

'Nothing.' His face glowed a fiery red and unshed tears glistened in his eyes. 'It's for... other stuff.'

'Stuff?' She reached out a swift hand and slid the note

towards her, though her eyelids lowered in suspicion.

'Stuff I've taken.' His voice was hoarse, almost a whisper.

She didn't reply, and her muteness was its own accusation.

'I'll come back,' he said. 'Bring more. This is, like, a deposit. A down-payment.'

Silence echoed around them, eyes locked on one another. He broke the contact first, head sagging, and shuffled away.

'We do not sell redemption, young man,' she told his retreating back. 'And if we did, it would cost more than a fiver.'

*

That bitch! That fucking bitch!

Donna Lawson clenched her fist and flexed her fingers, trying to ease the ache in her knuckles. With her other hand she gingerly touched the yellowy black bruises, wondering again if maybe she had broken or dislocated something, and hoped the shiner on that cow's face was worth this pain.

She leant against the padded headboard, eyes flicking around the dim, unfamiliar space. The plain white walls, a murky grey in the darkness; the simple scenic prints dotted here and there; the heavy brown curtains keeping the world away; the small red LED in the corner of the flat-screen TV on the wall providing the only light in the room. Still no news on when she could return to her own home. She felt like a hostage – she was beginning to understand that expression they used to use in the old prison crime films, *stir crazy* – and she wondered obliquely what the Premier Inn's policy was on visitors redecorating their rooms.

Julie Rafferty had initially denied everything. But, of course, she would, with Jeff hovering around in the background, earwigging at all they said. She told him to piss off and mind his own business, and then tried to deliver a bit of home grown wisdom of her own.

'Adie didn't love you,' Julie had hissed, once her husband was safely out of hearing range. 'He'd grown tired of you. He was gonna leave you.'

'Hah!' Donna sneered, eyeing her rival up and down, lip curled in disgust. 'And go off with you? As if!'

'You don't know what he said to me, how he was with me.' Julie used the high ground of the doorstep to look down her nose at Donna.

'Of course I do!' Donna said. 'Same thing he said to every woman of shagable age in the whole bleedin' town. Same thing he said to me while he was still married to his first wife.' She pointed a finger at that smug face, and couldn't help noticing her own cracked nail varnish, the chewed skin at the cuticles. She knew her eyes were red and veined, the flesh around them puffy and grey. Her hair was matted into rats' tails and she once again wore the clothes that Julie had seen her in the day before, when she had told her about the Spanish girl and effectively shattered her life. But she held up her chin and kept the accusing finger firm and steady. Beyond the glamorously coiffed hair and carefully applied make-up the woman before her was just another trollop. One more little footnote in Adrian Lawson's extensive list of conquests. *Leave me for that?!* 'You're nothing special, you're just one of the herd. All the smooth talk, all his lies, it was just bullshit. Knicker-dropping bullshit designed to get you on your back as quick as he could. And it worked. You couldn't wait to get a proper man inside you for a change. Too bad you had to try and steal someone else's. But he'd never have gone off with you. He saw you for what you were – an easy lay. Nothing but a fucking slag!'

Julie's lips pulled back from her teeth in a grimace of pure rage and her eyes blazed. She leapt down from the step at the very moment that Donna swung up her fist and the resulting impact staggered them both. Donna clutched her hand to her chest, nursing her throbbing knuckles, and Julie tottered backwards, hand clasped to her face, her heel catching the doorstep so she tumbled onto her back on the hall carpet with a hefty thud. Donna spat at her, then turned and left her lying there, strutting down the path and swinging the squeaky gate hard so it sprang back with a hinge-rattling crash.

Donna berated herself as much for caring what her philandering husband got up to as she did for allowing herself to be drawn into a physical altercation with such a loathsome creature. He had proven himself unworthy of her devotion on many occasions. She could never have believed that trust was such a flexible element until she married Adrian Lawson. In the early days trust meant that he was hers alone, would never stray, that his commitment was absolute and unwavering. Latterly she could only trust that, when he strayed, he would at least return to her. But the rubber-band quality of her trust had been stretched to its limit by his behaviour since returning from Spain in the summer, and Julie's revelation that he'd shipped his little Hispanic whore over here, probably planning to set her up in some cosy flat in town, finally snapped it with a nasty twang.

Neither of his floozies would be able to claim him now, but nor would he be crawling back to her, tail between his legs, contrite apologies dribbling from his lying tongue.

Now she was left with his mess to clear up. Not the gruesome stains he'd left in the house, the insurance would handle that, in conjunction with the "deep clean" cleaning company that they had suggested. No, it was more mundane considerations she had to cope with. Funeral arrangements, once the coroner released his body. The car lot – she had neither the business sense nor the desire to keep a motor dealership running. His will. He had one filed away somewhere in the house, but until the police allowed her back in she didn't know what was in it, beyond a vague *you get the lot, Babe*. She had no fear that she would be comfortable once the estate was organised, having worked all that out after the first of so very many times she'd imagined him lying in his own blood and excrement. Though she wasn't proud of entertaining such grim thoughts, she even went so far as to calculate how much she could afford to pay someone to carry out the deed. She'd saved a pretty penny there!

And then there was Shane. Adrian would want some provision made for his son and, whatever her feelings towards his mother, she couldn't refuse the boy his inheritance.

Those feelings towards Layna Hewett had intensified after learning that she had viewed Adrian's body at the morgue. She shouldn't resent that fact, after all, it was her own refusal to attend that had forced the police to ask Layna, but resent it she did. It couldn't be jealousy, surely? Who could envy someone the opportunity of seeing a slowly mouldering cadaver on a steel slab? But he was her husband now, not Layna's. Once she had turned down the chance to identify him the police should have respected that choice and done without. They were just being picky. Who else could it be, for God's sake?

Definitely him, dead and gone. She was left behind to cope and carry on. Alone. For now, at least. She glanced down at her phone, finally charged again, nestled in her swollen hand. The shy young PCSO standing guard outside her house had taken pity on the grieving widow, who rested a hand on his chest and blinked away a tear, and asked the sole white-suited forensic examiner remaining inside to retrieve the errant phone charger from her bedside table. It was a harmless enough request – the bedroom wasn't considered part of the crime scene – so they had acquiesced. Seeing the device flicker back to life had felt like being thrown a lifeline. Obviously a symptom of modern society's addiction to technology but a huge relief nonetheless.

She pressed a button to revive the darkened screen,

blinking at the sudden glare, and regarded the face beaming up at her, his smile honest, trustworthy. *Worthy of trust...* Nice teeth, good head of hair, but there was something in the eyes, something *behind* the eyes, something familiar and unsettling. So she swiped left.

She considered the new face which replaced the last, pondered a moment, then swiped left again.

And again.

Again.

Left.

Left.

Left...

*

'Oh, change the friggin' record!' Jeff Rafferty had barely closed the front door behind him before she'd called him a liar yet again. 'At least let me get me coat off before you start.'

'Oh no, you don't,' Julie said, blocking his way to the stairs. 'You're not sloping off to the bog for half an hour, hoping I'll calm down.'

He peered at the swollen, discoloured face looming close to his own. 'I think that's getting worse. Are you sure she's not broken your nose?'

As Julie turned to examine her injuries in the hall mirror he slipped past her though to the living room, sank gratefully into the armchair, and looked around for the telly remote. But his peace was short-lived.

'You buggered off to work straight after the cops had finished with you earlier,' she said over his shoulder, leaning in so her voice whistled in his ear. 'Di'n't give me chance to ask you what they wanted.'

'You know what they wanted,' he sneered back at her. 'You were listening to every word. These walls are like paper.'

She didn't bother denying it. 'You don't think they

235

believed any of that crap about your car, do you?' She went to perch on the sofa, angling herself to look at him, arms folded. ''Cause I certainly didn't.'

'Believe what you like.' He leaned forward and pushed his hands down the sides of the seat cushion, gaining no more than fluff under his fingernails. 'Where've you hid the remote?'

'Never mind the chuffin' telly! What were you up to on Friday afternoon?'

He stared back at her. 'What were *you* up to?'

'Don't try and turn it back on me, it's you they were asking.'

His expression was quietly triumphant. 'Yeah, but it was you they were asking yesterday.' She didn't respond, merely shifted awkwardly on the edge of the sofa, so he offered her a prompt. 'About phoning Adie. About meeting up with him.'

'I told 'em I never met up with him.'

'You think they believed you?' he asked, his sardonic tone turning vicious as he added, ''Cause I certainly didn't!'

An abrupt realisation struck her and she leaned towards him, squinting through her swollen eye, other eye glinting with anger. 'Were you following me?' she growled. 'Spying on me?'

'Yeah,' he said. 'I were right to, an' all, wasn't I?'

'It wasn't like that,' she said. 'There were nowt going on.'

'No? Donna seemed to think there was, judging by the state of your face.'

'She's just a daft bitch.'

'I saw you digging the knife in with her, poor cow.' He shook his head in disgust. 'And I hung around long enough to see you meet up with Adie. Saw you crawlin' all over him; saw him push you away like the dirty slag you are.'

Her scowl cut into him as she sagged back on the sofa cushions. The sting of Lawson's rejection was as sore as the bruising on her face. He already knew the Spanish girl was in town, and he was furious with her for telling Donna.

'What happened?' Jeff wondered. 'Did you get your knickers so knotted up that you decided to follow him home and bop him over the head with summat heavy?'

'Don't you know?' she said. 'I thought you were watching me.'

'I only waited long enough to see you get dumped by lover-boy, then I had to get to work.' He folded his arms and raised an eyebrow. 'God knows what you did after that.'

'Yeah, well, I didn't go murderin' nobody.'

'Only got your word for that, 'aven't we?'

'You had the car,' she said. 'You'd be able to follow him easier than me.'

'Told yer, I went to work. Police've checked what time I got there, so up yours.'

'You should be a politician, the way you handle a discussion.'

He leaned forward abruptly, his voice deep with rage. 'You should be a prozzie, the way you put yourself about!'

'Keep it down, we don't want him hearing.' She jerked a thumb upwards.

'Who, God?' He gave a wry smirk at his own wit.

'No, you tit, Alan. We don't need him knowing all our business.'

Jeff dragged himself out of the soft chair. 'He's a part of the family, he should know what's going on.'

'Where you goin'?' she said, as he lumbered towards the door. 'What you doin'?'

He ignored her and went out to the hall. She heard his voice a moment later, calling Alan's name up the stairs.

'Get down 'ere, boy,' he yelled. 'Yer mum an' me've got summat to tell ya.'

Julie hurried up behind him. 'Don't you dare!'

He shrugged off her punches to his back. 'Come on, lad, we're waiting.'

'I swear to God, if you say owt, I'll...' She left the threat unfinished, opting instead for a swipe of her open hand to the back of his head.

A backwards sweep of his arm sent her stumbling and he set off up the stairs, long legs striding three steps at a time. 'Oi, I'm talking to you, you ignorant little chuff.'

Julie waited at the bottom of the stairs, fists clenched, air hissing through her teeth, but her breath caught in her throat when he reappeared on the landing alone, his face creased with concern.

'He's not here.'

'What do you mean, he's not here?' She started up the stairs towards him.

'His bedroom's empty, I've checked the bog, he's vanished!'

22

Even well into the evening the major crimes team incident room was lively as Annette Lee made her way through the bustling throng, squeezing between desks, listening to telephones chirruping away and the mumble of hunched detectives scribbling on pads or tapping on computer keyboards with receivers pinned to ears by their shoulders. As she passed Luke Preston's desk his phone joined the cacophony. She dropped her jacket on the desktop and scooped up the handset.

A soft, warm female voice spoke to her, and Lee momentarily found herself imagining the plump, red lips the words were tumbling from. 'DS Preston?' She glanced round the room to ensure she hadn't missed him when she entered. No sign of him. DI Grieff's door stood open, revealing the little cubbyhole beyond to be empty. 'I'm afraid he's not here right now, can I take a message?' She grabbed a pen and paper to make a note. 'Rosalyn Peters? And what is it about?' The woman was evasive, keeping her answers vague. 'Okay, well, I'll give him your number and ask him to call you back.' She scribbled the number alongside the name. 'Are you sure you don't want to tell me what it's about?' She realised she was speaking to a dead line. 'Oh, 'bye then.'

She put down the receiver, picked up her jacket and made her way over to her own desk. Only a few seconds later she gave a wry smile as she spied Preston and Grieff coming through the door.

'Typical timing,' she said as she rose and joined them. 'You've just missed a call. Young woman, very cagey.' She pointed out the note on his desk.

'Oh yes?' said Grieff, a wicked smile crinkling his eyes. 'I hope you're not letting your love-life interfere with your work, Luke?'

'Chance'd be a fine thing,' Preston said, glancing at the name on the paper. Indistinct memories stirred. He'd gone to meet Ed Maxey at the register office at lunchtime one day, intending to coax him out for a coffee, and was greeted at the reception by a tall, curvy beauty with green eyes and tumbling hair. That was how Ed had introduced her, wasn't it? Rosalyn Peters, known as Roz. No point speculating what she wanted, might as well just ring her back.

With his hand inches away the phone rang again. Preston answered, listened to the message from the front desk and rang off with a brusque thanks.

He turned to the others. 'Raffertys again,' he said simply.

Lee shook her head in despair. 'Now what?'

'Their lad's joined the list of the missing.'

'Shit,' said Lee. Any hopes they might still have clung to that the disappearance of his friends was mere coincidence crumbled in that moment.

'Get over there,' said Grieff, though they were both already tugging on their jackets as he uttered the order. 'Sort this out. It's all too close to our murder for my liking.'

Police constable Jo Kershaw met them at the Raffertys' squeaky gate. Preston noticed hers and Lee's hands brush briefly before they were all business again.

'The mum and dad haven't seen him all night,' Kershaw reported. 'Didn't even know he was out.'

'Bang goes their nomination for Parents of the Year,' said Preston, but his gruff laugh held no humour.

'We've driven all round, asked in the shops.' Kershaw glanced at her notebook. 'Apparently he went into the convenience store acting all weird.'

'Weird, how?' Lee asked curtly. A casual observer would think they barely knew each other.

'The woman on the counter said he gave her money for things he'd pinched from her in the past. Like he was trying to make amends.'

240

'Repentant shoplifter?' Preston speculated.

'He looked "despondent" and "distraught",' Kershaw said, waving her notebook to indicate those weren't her own observations.

'Suicidal?' Lee asked.

Kershaw shrugged. 'You're the detective, Detective.'

Lee leaned in close. 'And you look very sexy in your uniform,' she muttered, voice husky, 'but I don't need to point it out every five minutes.'

'Yes you do,' Kershaw smirked.

Preston cleared his throat, pointedly. 'What are you thinking, Annette? Some sort of elaborate suicide pact between the three of them? Topping themselves one at a time and Alan's the last to go?'

'Bit of a stretch, I know,' Lee said. 'But kids have some strange ideas, these days. Maybe the older one had some sort of Manson-like influence over the others.'

Preston contemplated that for a moment. 'Wouldn't he be the last to go then, not the first? He'd want to make sure the others didn't chicken out.'

'I did say it was a stretch.'

'Could be a gay thing,' Kershaw said. 'Some people still have trouble coping, even in these "enlightened" times.' Her tone suggested she believed the times to be anything but enlightened.

Lee nodded. 'They did spend a lot of time together.'

'It could explain the timing, as well,' Kershaw went on. 'First one does it out of shame, the others from grief.'

'Three of them, so attached they couldn't live without the others?' Preston said, unconvinced. 'I think we're grasping, here. There's something else that connects these boys. Something we haven't found yet. Whatever it is has made someone want to snatch or kill them.'

'Paedoes?' Lee said.

Kershaw shuddered.

'Targeting these kids?' Preston pulled a face. 'Bit old for that, don't you think? Especially Kenny.'

'Exactly,' said Lee. 'Old stock, used up, got rid of.'

Kershaw looked at her in horror. 'Jesus!'

Preston held up his hands. 'No point just snatching guesses out of the air. We need facts, evidence.' He turned to Kershaw. 'Any other sightings tonight?'

She checked her notes again. 'Yeah, he went to the takeaway and got chips and a can of pop. No mention of him acting weird this time. Turned left out of there as if he was heading home. We followed his expected route, found a can and greasy chip paper discarded on the pavement on that quiet stretch along Nettlehill Rise that goes up by the side of the park. Neither of them finished. It's hard to tell if they were dropped in a struggle or just thrown away when he'd had enough, but the way they were scattered around looks a bit suspicious. We've bagged them.'

'Okay, good.' Preston nodded towards the patrol car at the kerb, by which PC Cawthorne stood awkwardly. 'Have another cruise around, just in case. I know there's already about a dozen cars out there looking, but one more can't hurt. Head down by the canal, over to the park, anywhere you can think of. Let's totally exhaust the possibility that he's merely a stop-out.'

As Kershaw headed back to the car Preston and Lee headed up the path to the Raffertys' front door. No one made any quips about the frequency of their visits when Julie Rafferty, swollen eyes puffier than ever, admitted them once again. No one spoke at all until they reached the living room, where Jeff Rafferty struggled from his chair to greet them with an expectant expression and eager voice.

'Have you found him?'

Preston took a breath before answering. 'Not yet, Mr Rafferty, but we're hopeful.'

Rafferty scrubbed his hands over his face and slumped back into the chair. 'Hopeful? Huh!'

Despite their rough manners and negligent attitude the Raffertys were clearly distressed at their son's disappearance. Preston inwardly reappraised his opinion of them.

Lee put a gentle hand on Julie's arm. 'Is it okay if we have a quick look in Alan's room, Mrs Rafferty?'

'He's not there,' Rafferty said, eyes on the worn patch of carpet by his feet. 'Do ya think we've not looked?'

Lee aimed her response at his wife. 'We might find something to give us an idea of where he went.'

Julie, still silent, nodded her assent. They patiently followed her shambling progress up the stairs. The room was much as Preston recalled it from the previous evening, down to the scraps of paper torn from Alan's comic book still lying scattered on the carpet by the bed. Preston knelt to flick the confetti-like pieces with his fingertips as Lee glanced at a bookshelf containing superhero figurines, and Harry Potter and Alex Rider paperbacks.

Lee noted the creased spines of the books. 'Keen reader?'

'He's a clever lad,' Julie said, her voice barely more than a whisper. 'Used to read loads before he took up with them two.'

Preston was peering into the darkness under the bed. 'Have you got an evidence bag?' He reached a hand behind him towards Lee as he ducked his head under the bed frame.

She took a bag from her pocket and passed it to him. He reversed it and slipped his hand inside, like an oversized glove. He reached under the bed and salvaged a small, ceramic mug from the shadows, peeling the plastic sleeve back over it and sealing the top.

'What have you found?' asked Lee, as she and Julie leaned in for a better view.

Preston held up the bag. Visible through the clear material Luke Skywalker and Darth Vader faced off against one another in the image on the mug's surface.

'When would Alan have used this last, Mrs Rafferty?' he asked.

'It's his favourite beaker,' Julie said, mindlessly tangling a lock of her hair round her fingers. 'He uses it all the time.'

'Do you mind if we take it with us?'

'What do you want that for?'

'We found some items in the street,' he explained. 'If we can retrieve Alan's fingerprints and DNA from this and match them, we can better determine his footsteps this evening.'

'We may need to take some elimination prints from you and Alan's dad,' Lee said. 'In case you've touched it after the washing up – putting it in the cupboard, bringing him his drink, that sort of thing.'

'He gets his own drinks, mostly,' Julie said. 'So he'll wash it and refill it himself.'

Of course he does, Preston thought, but kept it to himself.

'All the better,' Lee said. 'That should simplify things.'

Alan didn't have a computer or mobile phone, and there were no signs of a diary or personal journal in the room. Julie and Jeff were unable to expand on Alan's activities either when he was out with his friends or even while he was above their heads in the same house. Before allowing himself to become too judgemental Preston hoped that his ex-wife was aware of their daughter's whereabouts this evening, or any other evening. He resolved to drop Kerry a casual text when they were back at the station.

'You can't keep 'em wrapped up in cotton wool,' Julie said, and shrugged helplessly.

'Much as you might want to try,' said Preston, but from the blank expressions on the Raffertys' faces he realised he was speaking entirely for himself.

*

Ron Hewett stretched and yawned and blinked his tired eyes. Early night tonight, he decided. He'd been lethargic and stiff all day. Good job he'd taken the extra day off. He thought it would be for the best, having anticipated that the after-effects of the last few days would leave him whacked out. Late night driving all the way down to Disneyland Paris, two hectic days chasing excited kids round the expanse of the theme park, trying to make sure they got on all the rides, then the long drive back. The blaring radio which acted as his only company on that return journey hadn't disturbed Layna and the boys from their coma-like slumber, nor had the cool gust of autumnal evening air surging in when he'd felt the need to crack the window to avoid nodding off too. At least Disney hadn't been as crazy-busy as if they had gone at the height of the summer, but there were still queues to contend with on the most popular rides and at the food areas.

And most of the time he'd managed to avoid letting things get to him. He'd bitten his lip when the boys had fought about who took the last seat in the front boat on Pirates of the Caribbean, letting their mother separate them. He'd clenched a fist when Terry stumbled under his feet making him drop a tray of milkshakes, but he'd hidden that fist in his pocket and merely offered the boy a few strong words to remind him to watch where he was going. Whatever the provocation he would never strike a child. After all, none of this was the boy's fault.

Hewett looked across at where his wife sat engrossed in whatever over-dramatic hogwash gushed out from the TV screen, the light flowing over her face like gentle waves on a shallow beach and glinting in her pretty eyes. She was all he'd wanted since that first time he saw her teetering on a battered kick-stool, stretching to put cans of beans on the upper shelves at the local Spar here in Clegganfield. He'd offered a steadying grip when she almost toppled off, and she'd blushed and swept a hand through her hair. Five years ago, and in all that time they had been happy and content. In all that time he'd had no reason to suspect her betrayal.

She must have felt his gaze on her, as she turned and smiled her sweet smile at him. *Like butter wouldn't melt...*

He shuffled forward in his chair. 'Cup of tea?'

'I'll get it.' She moved to stand but he waved her back.

'You watch your programme.'

'I can pause it.'

'S'alright, you carry on. I'm not really following it.' He lumbered slowly to his feet and rolled his shoulders and neck, and she winced at the cracking of joints.

'Should you take another day off?' she said, concern creasing her features. 'You still look shattered.'

'I can't afford to leave Mike on his own any longer.' He rested a hand on his wife's shoulder as he passed her chair. Despite everything his spine still tingled at the merest contact with her. 'We've got jobs piling up. Burst pipes wait for no man.'

'Are your overalls okay for the morning?' she called towards the kitchen. 'I didn't notice them in the wash basket.'

Hewett waited for the hiss of water filling the kettle to finish before answering. 'I left 'em in the van the other day.' He flicked the switch on the kettle and came back through to the living room. 'They'll be fine.'

She settled back into her place on the sofa. 'If you're sure.'

'I'm sure.' He stood behind her, fingers kneading her shoulders, and nuzzled his face into her hair, arousal slowly shifting other concerns to the back of his mind. She moaned softly and reached up to slide his hands down onto her breasts, encouraging the massaging action with a squeeze and a giggle. She tilted her head so his lips and teeth could tease her neck. He cocked a leg over the back of the sofa and rolled over beside her. They both laughed as he gently pressed her back into the cushions.

The kettle clicked off and the water gradually cooled.

A high pitched wail reached them from upstairs. Layna pulled her shirt back around her and sat up.

'Leave him.'

'I can't,' she said, easing her legs out from under her husband's warm body.

'It's just a dream.'

'A nightmare.' The screaming continued. 'He's upset.'

'I'm upset!' He slumped back and sighed emphatically.

'He's a child.' She shuffled her feet into her slippers and headed for the door. 'But you're the one who needs to grow up.'

She slipped into the darkened bedroom, hushing and soothing, sat by her son and held his hot, wet face against her chest until his heaving sobs eased.

'I've made your tea,' Ron said when she returned downstairs some time later. He avoided her eyes as he nodded to the mug on the coffee table. 'Should still be hot.'

Silently she took her previous position on the sofa and lifted the drink to her lips. Then she shook her head and thumped the mug back down on its mat, slopping liquid onto the table.

'No, not this time.'

'What do you mean?' He tugged a tissue from the box on the table and mopped at the spill. 'Look at this mess.'

'That's not the mess,' she said. 'We're the mess.' She placed her hand on his arm and turned him to face her. 'What's happened to us? We used to be a happy family.'

'Family?' he snapped. 'What does that word even mean to you?' He threw off her grip and skulked away, leaning against the wall, breathing laboured. Fingernails dug into the wallpaper as his words whistled between his teeth. 'Family was all I wanted.'

'And that's what I gave you,' she said, going to him, hands on his shoulders. 'Look around, for God's sake! Home, family, it's all here. What more do you want?'

He spun round, eyes blazing into hers. 'How can you stand there and lie over and over again?'

'I don't know what you mean.' Tears streaked her face. 'I've never lied to you.'

'No?' He pushed her aside and lurched over to the bookcase, dragging a document box file roughly from a shelf, ignoring the paperbacks that followed and tumbled to

247

the carpet. He tipped the contents of the file onto the sofa and riffled through the scattered papers and photos until he found what he was searching for. He unfolded a document and rattled it in front of her face, so close that she had to step back to focus on the words printed there.

'No?' he snapped again. 'Then explain that.'

23

Tuesday

Rain thrashed against the window pane, drawing Edward Maxey from his slumber before his bedside alarm clock had chance to chirp out its morning greeting. He reluctantly dragged himself away from his position as "big spoon" against his wife's warm back and slipped out from under the heavy quilt. He padded across the cold, gloomy bedroom to the window and pulled open one of the curtains, frowning up at the heavy black clouds crowding the still dark morning sky.

'Nice bum.'

Maxey turned and saw the whites of Nicky's bleary, tired eyes peeping over the edge of the duvet, scanning his naked form silhouetted against the window.

'I hope the neighbours appreciate the view.'

Maxey laughed and pulled the curtain back across. 'It's too dark to see anything this morning. Since the clocks went back the other day it's like waking up in the middle of the night.'

'Too dark to see this?' The green LEDs in the alarm clock cast an eerie shimmer across the soft contours of Nicky's body where she had pulled the duvet down to waist level. Maxey sensed rather than saw the teasing smile.

Nicky shuddered and pulled the covers back up round her neck. 'Bloomin' heck, it's cold.'

'Did you remember to reset the timer on the heating?' Maxey asked. ''Cause I didn't.'

'Come back in, you must be frozen.' She lifted the corner of the duvet so he could clamber back under.

He wrapped his arms around her, firm and strong. 'Give

me your heat, woman!'

'What do I get in return?' she whispered, so close her lips tickled the fine hairs on his ear. She felt a stirring against her leg. 'Good answer.'

Twenty minutes later they lay, hot and spent, covers cast aside allowing the cool morning to bring an exquisite tingle to their damp bodies.

Maxey glanced at the clock and groaned. 'Wish we could stay here all day.'

'Some of us can.' She smiled cheekily and pulled the quilt back up over herself. 'All morning, at least.' She gave him a shove to the edge of the bed. 'Go on, hit the shower, smelly.'

He chuckled and lumbered to his feet, shuffling towards the door.

'Dressing gown,' Nicky said, as Maxey was about to wander naked onto the landing. 'We're not alone, remember?'

'Oops!' He ducked back into the bedroom and retrieved his robe.

When he returned from the shower the bed was empty. He dressed with his usual finesse and went down to the kitchen, where a track-suit bedecked Nicky presented him with a steaming coffee.

'Thought you'd still be snoring your head off.'

She stopped partway through scraping butter across golden brown toast, placed the knife carefully onto the bread board and turned to face him. 'I wanted a word before you left.'

'Sounds serious.'

'It is.'

He perched on one of the high stools by the kitchen counter and sipped his coffee, waiting for her to continue.

'I've come off the pill.'

'Oh.' He placed his coffee mug on the counter, eyes wide with astonishment.

'Only just,' she added. 'It could takes weeks before I'm

ovulating again, don't worry.'

'I'm not worried,' he said. 'Just surprised. I thought, y'know, career first, plenty of time and all that.'

'Yeah, so did I.' She came and stood between his knees, arms on his shoulders, forehead resting against his. 'But all this business lately has got me thinking. How do we know we've got plenty of time? That guy...' She nodded upwards. '*Her* guy, Lawson, I bet he thought he'd got plenty of time to do everything he had planned out for his life.'

She felt his brow wrinkle and leaned back so she could look at him. Her eyes were large and clear and bright.

'I'm not being morbid,' she went on. 'I'm just looking at things from a different perspective. It feels like it's time.'

His hands were on her waist. 'If you're sure...'

'I am.'

He drew her close and kissed her, long and hard.

Finally she laughed and pushed away. 'Your toast'll get cold.'

'You expect me to eat after that little revelation?'

'Don't get giddy, I'm not pregnant yet.'

'No, but still...'

She had resumed preparing breakfast. He moved in close behind her and slid his arms around her.

'Careful, you'll get butter on your jacket.'

His hands fumbled with the zip of her tracksuit top. 'Bugger my jacket.'

'What was that?' She turned in his embrace, holding the knife between them. 'Did you say "butter my jacket"?'

He laughed and moved out of reach. She cut the toast into triangles and popped it on a plate for him.

'I'm not going to be able to concentrate all day,' he said, around a mush of chewed toast.

'Don't talk with your mouth full,' she mock chastised.

'Oh, you're going to be a great mum.'

As they basked in the warmth of their tender moment they became aware of a rapping on the front door. Maxey dropped his piece of toast onto the plate and wiped his fingers on a tea towel.

He went through and opened the front door, looking in bewilderment at their visitor.

'Luke!' he said. In the kitchen the butter knife clattered onto the tiled floor.

'Hi, mate.' Preston's smile looked forced and awkward. 'Can I come in?'

Maxey tried to remember if he had heard any movement from upstairs in the last few minutes. Hopefully Alicia wouldn't choose now to come and join them.

'Yeah, of course.' He backed into the room so that Preston could follow.

'Hi, Nicky,' said Preston, as they joined her in the kitchen.

'Coffee?' she asked, flicking the switch on the kettle.

'No thanks.' He leaned a hand casually on the counter, though he looked anything but relaxed. 'Just a flying visit. Wanted to catch you before Ed went to work.'

'Oh?' Maxey took a bite of toast, trying to appear calm, though swallowing seemed to be a chore right now.

'We've had a phone call.'

'We?' said Nicky, standing by her husband, arm round his waist. 'You mean the police?'

'That's right.' Preston took a breath. 'It's in regard to—'

'In regard to?' Maxey interrupted with a smile. 'You've got your copper voice on. That sounds serious.'

The smile wasn't reciprocated. 'It is.'

Maxey and Nicky exchanged a worried glance.

'You remember the Spanish girl we talked about the other night?'

'Erm, yeah...'

'It's been suggested that you might have had more contact with her than you admitted to.'

Maxey recalled the inscrutable looks that Roz Peters had been giving him all day yesterday. 'I don't know what you mean.'

'Come on, mate,' Preston said. 'You're squirming like a

fox in a bear trap. You look like you'd happily chew your own leg off to get out of here.'

'She didn't do it, Luke,' said Nicky.

'That's not for you to decide.' Preston shook his head in disbelief. 'She did ring you, then?'

Maxey averted his eyes. His nod was feeble.

'And did you meet her?'

Maxey's silence was an eloquent reply.

'For fuck's sake, mate! What were you thinking?'

'She's frightened. Vulnerable. I was thinking she didn't need to be hauled in to a police station in a foreign country and interrogated like a spy.'

'Well, thanks for that fair and rational criticism of my interview technique.' Preston's sarcasm had a bitter edge. 'We don't strap people to chairs and stub out cigarettes on them, y'know.'

Maxey was flustered. 'I know, sorry.'

Preston sighed through gritted teeth. 'When did she ring you?'

'Friday afternoon, after she'd been to see him, then again on Saturday morning when she'd—'

Preston cut in. 'Whoa, wait a minute. She rang you twice?'

'Yes, but...' Maxey put up a hand to mollify Preston's shocked reaction. 'She explained all that. How she didn't need the phone number. On the compliments slip. She used redial.'

'What?' Preston was baffled. 'How?'

'No one used the phone box between her calls.' Maxey smiled and shrugged, problem solved.

'But what about the first one?'

'What do you mean?'

Preston turned away from him, breathing deeply. When he turned back his fists were clenched and his voice was low and measured. 'You just said she went to see him, and *then* she rang you the first time.'

Maxey frowned as he realised he was missing

something. 'Yeah...?'

'But we found the compliments slip at the scene,' Preston said. 'So how did she know your number the first time she rang you?'

Maxey's face burned with his confusion and embarrassment. Words wouldn't come. He stammered helplessly.

'Don't apply for a detective job too soon, old mate.' Preston's tone oozed his disgust. 'Do you know where she is now?'

Maxey couldn't stop his eyes flicking upwards.

'What?!' Preston's rage finally overcame his patience. 'You have got to be fucking kidding me!'

Nicky attempted to placate him. 'Please, Luke, you've got to understand—'

'But I don't!' Preston paced around the kitchen, hands sweeping through his hair in his frustration. 'I don't understand any of this. You're actually hiding her here? Do you know how many man-hours we've put into searching for that woman?'

He strode up to Maxey, his anger-twisted face close, spittle flying along with his harsh words. 'You utter prick! Did you even think about how this would reflect on me?'

'You?' Maxey mumbled in bewilderment.

'We're supposed to be mates. I'm in charge of searching for the girl, and you've been hiding her here the whole time. Do you realise what a complete twat I'm going to look when this gets out? Fuck's sake, man!'

Plates and cutlery rattled as he slammed both fists down on the worktop. With immense effort he regained his composure.

'Nicky,' he said, his face like stone, his gaze staying far from Maxey. 'Go and fetch her down. It'll be less frightening than me charging up there.'

Finally he turned to look at the man he'd called his friend for so many years. 'You see? I do have some sensitivity.'

Nicky nodded and slipped past him, heading for the stairs. Then they all heard the thud from above.

*

She awoke to the sound of a baby's cry.

Disorientation rocked her. This wasn't her room. Where were her familiar embroidered pillows, the battered old armchair in the corner with the worn antimacassar crocheted by her grandmamma, the stern-faced Christ peering down at her from the crucifix high on the white-washed wall?

Here were only a single bed with its thin, utilitarian duvet, bare walls painted in a pastel green, and a simple chest of drawers, empty but for the few basic items loaned to her by the kind lady. A room unlived in. A spare room.

A panic fluttered in her chest. Where was the baby? Then she remembered; there was no baby. The crying she imagined she had heard resonated from inside her own head. From within her dream. Her nightmare. Images crashed behind her eyes; a vision of her impossible, unborn child, lost and abandoned in a small, rickety boat, being carried away from her on a fast-flowing river. The flimsy craft was tipping and tossing on a thrashing liquid too viscous, too dark, too red to be water.

From a thousand miles away she could feel the piercing gaze of Christ looking down on her with disdain and disappointment from his wooden cross on her bedroom wall. The cramps which occasionally still wracked her abdomen were nothing compared to the hollowness she felt when the pain subsided. She teetered on the edge of the huge chasm of her future, stretching vast and empty before her. Her father's hand, which had stroked her hair and tweaked her cheek after hanging that crucifix on her wall all those years ago and then slid happily round her mother's waist before she was lost to his touch forever, now waited clenched and judgemental a continent away.

255

How had she fallen so far? That silken-tongued man, who slid into her life, her bed, her heart, he brought her to this. That same man she had last seen spread generously around his own living room, like jam on toast, a breakfast accompaniment so favoured by English tourists visiting her father's hotel. She winced at her own grim simile. Before three nights ago the most blood she'd ever seen at one time had issued from the knee of a small boy who unsuccessfully attempted to jump down the hotel steps in his glee at a promised outing to the beach. She cleansed and bandaged the wound and handed the child back to his hysterical but appreciative mother. A bowl of soapy water tipped over the site of the incident erased all trace. How many bowls would it take to clean Adrian Lawson's carpet and walls?

Why had she returned to the house, scene of her recent shame? Was it the prospect of that dark, forbidding destiny awaiting her, alone, abandoned, lost? A couple of hours of aimless wandering had steered her feet back to the place where her heart had been so cruelly crushed. She surely couldn't imagine his stance would have changed in so short a time? But so far from home, where else could she go?

She remembered to return via the back door, to avoid the attention of neighbours – no need to antagonise him further. Her tentative tap on the glass panel of the door received no response, nor the firmer second knock. Had he gone out, maybe to meet the wife who smiled so prettily from the photo on the mantle? She tried the handle, the door wasn't locked. What could she lose by entering uninvited? She had nothing left.

His name echoed eerily back to her when she called out to him, bringing with it a sense of vacancy more striking than merely the absence of occupants. A shiver swept through her, tingling from the roots of her hair down to her toes curled in her canvas shoes. Was it the cool, autumnal afternoon seeping into her flesh, or some premonition of peril lying in wait up ahead? She almost turned and ran, but the recollection that she had nowhere to run to kept her there in that kitchen, and turned her steps towards the hallway.

The sight of the smart, trim telephone sitting on the small table near the front door brought to mind a warm smile, and an even warmer hand caressing her shoulder. She pulled the crumpled slip of paper from her pocket, smoothing it with her hand, reading the printed words "With compliments" and the handwritten phone number. She had tried to contact him earlier, adrift and afraid on the streets of a strange town, after Adrian turned her away. Maybe this time he would answer.

Before she reached the phone she had to pass the living room, where her dreams had perished just a short time ago. A strange acrid smell reached her, thick and cloying in her throat, emanating from the open doorway. She had to hold a hand over her mouth and nose to avoid gagging as she glanced inside. The room was dim, the curtains still drawn closed from when Adrian pulled them tight against the stare of neighbours, though enough daylight penetrated to allow her to see easily. But what met her eyes was not easy to see.

Swallowing down a surge of bile she staggered back to the hallway, the slip of paper sliding from limp fingers, fluttering forgotten to the carpet. She stumbled to the front door, pulling it open, but hesitated before she stepped outside. She recalled Adrian's wariness of prying eyes. She was blameless in this, but she was far from home, with no friends and no hope. Better to flee unseen, avoid any involvement in this horror. Leaving the front door ajar in her haste, she retraced her steps to the back door, heard it slam behind her as she slipped through the gate and into the alleyway beyond.

She allowed her feet to lead her, having no destination to aim for. She wasn't surprised when the park railings appeared ahead of her for the third time that day. It was the only place where she had found a moment's peace since arriving in this country the day before. How could so much have happened in less than twenty four hours?

Dusk had begun to set in, bringing with it twilight's chill. She had no belongings and only a few meagre coins in her pocket, the last remnants of the money the nice man at the register office had given her. She passed the park entrance and carried on down the road towards where a group of lights suggested a shopping precinct, maybe restaurants.

Staring in at the extensive menu through the large window of the "All Ways East" takeaway she felt her mouth watering and her stomach rumbling. Daring to enter she had to admit to the stocky man behind the counter that she had no money, playing on his compassion.

'I'm really sorry, darlin',' he'd said, with a shrug which indicated little actual sympathy. 'I'm trying to run a business here.'

Back outside she'd briefly considered asking for assistance, maybe requesting a small amount of money, from the two youths who were loitering near the road, but when she saw one of them spitting at passing cars while the other leapfrogged over the rubbish bins she hastily thought again. Shuffling into the shadows to avoid their notice she was relieved when they soon wandered off up the street, apparently to call on a third youth. She thought she heard the name Alan mentioned, but couldn't be sure.

Spying an elderly man sitting in a rickety-looking car in the farthest of the parking bays she headed over, hoping he might be more inclined towards generosity, but he started the ancient vehicle with a painful judder and rasping grumble and drove off in the direction taken by the two teens, moments before.

Amongst all her other degradations she had now been reduced to begging. She set off back up the hill towards the park entrance. A night shivering on a hard wooden bench with an empty stomach was as much as she deserved.

As darkness settled around her she felt a panic growing

inside her. Shadows were thick and heavy, and contained all manner of threats and dangers. Every sound became the squeak and screech of a rat or bat, or the creak from the shoe of a human predator. When she closed her eyes the fat taxi driver loomed over her, grubby underpants round his knees. With every breath the stench of spilled blood and expelled bowels assailed her, as if she still stood in Adrian Lawson's front room.

She hovered near the park gates, where the activity at the pub opposite, the comings and goings of people and vehicles, connected her to life, gave her a sense of being amongst others, and not quite so alone.

Then, unexpectedly and unbelievably, there was a face she knew. A memory was piqued as he swung his car into the car park, and recognition was confirmed when he climbed from the vehicle and headed for the pub door. Desperation emboldened her, so she rushed across the road, calling to him before he could disappear inside.

'Hey, you, Rafferty!' She remembered the name from the letter he had showed her, and from the marriage registration he had witnessed.

'Yeah?' He took a moment to recognise her, confusion and surprise competing for dominance on his face, before a hard, resentful expression took over. 'What're you doin' here?'

'Please,' she said, her voice beseeching. 'You are Adrian's friend. Help me, I have lost everything.'

'You've caused enough trouble as it is,' he sneered. 'Get Adrian bloody Lawson to look after you.'

'Adrian is...' *Dead! He's dead! Oh Lord of love and mercy, he's dead!* '...no good for me.'

'I could have told you that!' Rafferty shook his head. 'Why don't you go home, you daft cow?'

His blunt rebuttal, after all her travails, was the final indignity. She wailed in distress, and tears began coursing down her face.

Glancing round to ensure they weren't being observed,

he placed a firm hand on her back and propelled her across the road and into the park.

'Fucksake!' he hissed. 'You trying to get me banned from the Stag?'

She collapsed against him, her tears soaking through his shirt. She felt frail and flimsy in his arms, like a tiny, orphaned puppy needing to be nurtured.

'What do you want off of me?' he said, his tone helpless, pathetic. 'I can't do owt for you.'

'I have nothing,' she whimpered, shame choking her words. 'Can you give me money?'

He huffed a grim laugh. 'Do I look like Bill Gates?'

Her large eyes peered up at him, wet and glistening in the moonlight. She was a pretty one, he couldn't deny that, even in her present state. Old Adie always knew how to pick 'em. Adie the charmer. Adie the ladies' man. Adrian fucking Lawson, who he'd last seen that afternoon when he'd spied on his secret meeting with Rafferty's own wife, the two of them behaving in a manner which left no doubt that Julie had become yet another of the notches on Lawson's bed post.

'Yeah, I can give you money' he said, a new fire sizzling in his eyes, showing the anger and spite churning in his gut, pushing aside any pity he might feel for her. A deep sadness grew inside her when she saw it, for she knew what he would ask in return... and she knew she would give it.

He dragged her deeper into the park, making for the cover of a clump of bushes. She slumped to the ground, undergrowth rustling beneath her, and he knelt over her, wrestling with his belt.

'Get yer knickers off,' he said, hot breath turning it into a growl. His throbbing member pointed at her like an accusing finger.

Her hands shook as she fumbled with her buttons and she rested a palm against her abdomen. 'Please be gentle,' she said. 'I am with child.'

His breath caught in his throat and goosebumps crept across his exposed flesh. Looking at this fragile creature, abject and helpless before him, his whole body seemed to wilt, his ardour and inclination shrivelling along with his penis. He tidied himself away and clambered to his feet, brushing dirt from the knees of his jeans. He tugged his wallet from his back pocket.

'Go 'ome,' he said, throwing three ten pound notes onto the ground. Then he turned away and headed back to the pub.

She stared at the notes fluttering in the dirt, and scooped them up before the evening breeze could snatch them away. She could afford to go back to the takeaway, buy something hot and nourishing. She knew she should, for the baby's sake as much as her own, but her insides revolted at the mere thought of food, empty stomach heaving, retching dryly. She crawled further into the darkness of the bushes and collapsed onto the cold earth.

She had sinned, and been prepared to sin again. And that night was when the Lord had passed his heavy Judgement, and taken her child from her. Her lover was dead and her face was on the television, for all to point and blame. Her father thought so little of her he couldn't even bring himself to beat her. She had betrayed the kindness of the couple who had given her shelter, offering lies and deception in return. She felt unworthy, dirty, corrupt. Her heart was cold and heavy, her soul churned black and mournful as the thunderous clouds which hurled rain down onto the tiles above.

Voices carrying to her from downstairs told her that she had been found out. The police had arrived to claim her. The man and lady would be forced to hand her over to the authorities and her ordeal would begin anew.

A small tumbler sat on the chest of drawers, the dregs of last night's drink in the bottom. She lifted the glass and dashed it against the wall, then knelt and fumbled amongst the shards. She found one piece of broken glass, razor edge glinting in the dim morning light, and held it up for inspection. Yes, that would suit her purpose perfectly.

24

'Late two days in a row. That's not like you at all,' Superintendent Registrar Lynne Rayner said, her voice soft with concern. 'Is something wrong? Nicky mentioned the hospital...?'

Rayner had come around from behind her desk to stand near him and her hand briefly caressed his shoulder.

'It's not me,' Maxey said. 'It's a... friend. She had to be rushed in this morning.'

Maxey had popped into Rayner's office to apologise for his tardiness when he eventually made it to work, after accompanying Alicia in the ambulance and seeing her settled in a private room. Nicky had phoned ahead to let them know he would be late, so that they would be able to cover his appointments until he got there. Then she'd gone to collect him from the hospital when Luke Preston turned him out of Alicia's room and posted a uniformed constable on the door.

'Nothing too serious, I hope?' Rayner said.

Maxey considered the question, uncertain how to answer.

They had rushed upstairs at the unexpected sound through the ceiling, Preston foremost, possibly fearing his fugitive was attempting to make an escape before he could clap her in irons. Alicia was lying collapsed on the floor of the spare bedroom which had been her place of respite and solitude for the last three nights, an untidy gash across her left wrist oozing blood onto the carpet.

Preston hissed a curse and shouted for Nicky to phone for an ambulance as he knelt by the tiny injured figure. He snatched a towel from atop the chest of drawers and wrapped it around her wrist, holding it tightly in place with a firm grip. The over-sized man's t-shirt she wore as nightwear had hitched up around her waist and her flesh was pale and cool. Preston pulled the quilt from the bed and attempted, one-handed, to drape it over her. Maxey stooped and assisted him, bringing the pillow to place under her head.

Arkenbrough's quiet streets soon echoed to the scream of sirens as the ambulance tore round the twisty estate, avoiding the early morning work and school-run traffic. Alicia's eyes flickered open as the paramedics entered the room and she glanced around in fear, grasping Maxey's hand tightly, refusing to relinquish her hold even as she was stretchered down the stairs. Seeing the calming effect produced by this contact the medics had allowed Maxey to climb into the ambulance before it roared away. The flurry of activity in the A & E department at Haleston General Hospital had enforced their separation, but he had been allowed to follow when Alicia was moved to a side room to await an assessment visit from a psychiatric specialist.

But that was when Preston had put his foot down and insisted that Maxey leave. The decision as to whether Maxey would be charged with perverting the course of justice would come from a higher authority, he warned when Maxey demonstrated a reticence to vacate the room, but obstructing an officer in the performance of their duties was an offence he could deal with on the spot.

'She needs compassion and understanding,' Maxey had insisted to his grim-faced friend. 'Not handcuffs.'

'She's run away from a strict home life to follow her older lover and ended up under your roof,' Preston said. He had spoken to an officer from the Spanish police local to Alicia's home only that morning, filling in certain blanks. 'She's flitting from one father-figure to another.'

'Oh yes?' Maxey was irked by Preston's self-assurance. 'Who died and made you Sigmund Freud?' He realised the retort was puerile and illogical and was relieved that Luke declined to respond, instead stepping back into the room and closing the door.

264

'She'll be fine, they reckon,' Maxey said, and Lynne Rayner swept her shoulder-length, grey-streaked brown hair behind her ears, and her face crinkled into well-worn creases which told of a face familiar with smiling.

'If you need to take any personal time, just let me know,' she said, resting a hand on his arm. 'We'll work around you.'

'That's very kind,' Maxey returned the smile, 'but I can't do anything at present. I'm probably better off here.'

'Well, if you change your mind just let me know.' Her hand hovered again but she resisted touching him a third time, brushed some imagined lint from her jacket and turned back to retake her chair.

'Thanks, I will,' he assured her as he left the room.

In desperate need of a coffee before facing any customers, Maxey headed towards the staff room. As he opened the door he saw Roz Peters standing by the kettle, spooning coffee into a mug. Maxey considered immediately turning and leaving but steeled himself and carried on into the room.

He was gratified to see her face flush red with shame when she saw him approach. He didn't speak, taking a mug from the stack.

'Alright?' she said, completely failing to sound casual.

He made a noncommittal noise through his nose.

'Coffee?' She scooped the spoon into the jar, waiting for him to offer his mug.

'I can manage.' He reached across and took the jar from her, nudging her hand and spilling the spoonful of granules onto the worktop. His instinct was to apologise and rush for a cloth, but he bit his lip and stood his ground.

'I did it for you,' she said miserably.

'You had no business getting involved, Roz.' He couldn't bring himself to look at her. 'It has nothing to do with you.'

'She was on the news.' Roz took a step closer to him, but stopped when he visibly flinched. 'They said she killed that man.'

Now he finally turned to her, face twisted in an angry sneer. 'You saw her the other day. Tiny little thing. Did she look like a cold-blooded killer to you?'

She shrugged, defensively. 'Anybody can be a murderer. It's just down to circumstances. You don't have to be born that way, you get driven to it.'

'Is that your criminal psychology degree talking?'

'I haven't got...' she began, before recognising his sardonic tone. 'No,' she said. 'It's common sense. We've all got it in us.'

'There's only one person that girl tried to kill.' Maxey felt the excessive harshness in his voice as he spat the words out, but didn't feel inclined to hold back. 'That's herself! Damn near succeeded, too. All thanks to your interference.'

'What? How's that my fault?' Her voice quavered in distress.

'Police barging into the house scared the life out of her,' Maxey said. 'Last straw. So she tried to take her own life.'

Seeing the tears glistening in Roz's eyes Maxey instantly regretted his words but it was too late to take them back. As he finished preparing his drink and turned his back on her he contemplated Alicia's fate, and how Roz's actions had contributed to that, and a part of him felt justified in unleashing his spite and venom on her.

*

'She was never in any real danger,' Luke Preston told DI Grieff. 'The glass was brittle and snapped in her flesh before reaching anywhere near an artery. Doctor reckons she fainted from the pain. She'd gone cold and white from shock rather than blood-loss. Superficial damage, needing no more than a few stitches. They're more concerned with her mental state. She was anxious and upset, so they've sedated her and banned us from interviewing her until the morning.'

'At least now we know where she is,' said Grieff. They

266

stood in the corridor outside the media room, a large area where press and television journalists waited for them to begin the scheduled news conference. 'We'll have one positive bone to throw to that pack of mongrels.'

Preston's face burned bright red. 'I am *so* sorry about Edward Maxey, boss. I can't believe he kept her hidden from us all this time. From *me*. He still swears blind that she's innocent.'

Grieff smiled indulgently and patted his back. 'Don't fret about that right now.' Then the smile disappeared. 'We'll have a full, intensive case review once we've got someone behind bars.'

Preston released a heavy sigh and his shoulders sagged, as if he was deflating.

'Go and check the families are ready while I play warm-up man.' He nodded towards the small waiting room opposite the media room, where DC Lee sat consoling Margaret Harper, mother of the first of the boys to be reported missing, though the second to have been abducted, if their theory was correct. The criss-crossed view through the small, strengthened-glass panels in the door showed the Raffertys pacing alternately backwards and forwards, not speaking to the other people in the room, or each other.

'I still can't understand that Kenny lad's parents not wanting to get involved with this.'

'Blinkers on,' said Preston. 'They still think it's all a coincidence and that as soon as Kenny gets hungry enough he'll come crawling home.'

'Either that, or they just don't give a shit. Give me five minutes to update the hyenas about the progress with the Lawson case then bring them through.'

Grieff pressed on the door to the media room; with the first sigh of the door seals parting the room erupted with camera flashes. He ran a hand through his hair. 'How do I look?' He winked and pushed through to the hordes beyond.

267

Preston took a moment before he entered the waiting room. DC Lee and Mrs Harper looked up as the door opened, Lee's eyes soft with compassion, Jake's mother's wet with fear and anxiety. Julie and Jeff Rafferty halted their traversing of the dull, green-grey floor tiles to cast their bleary eyes in his direction.

'Is it time?' asked Mrs Harper, her voice cracking.

'Soon,' said Preston. 'Relax, there's no rush.'

Lee, sitting close beside her, placed a gentle hand over hers. 'We'll only go when you're ready.'

Preston frowned and surreptitiously glanced at his watch.

'But just remember,' Lee continued, 'we're doing this for Jake and the others. The more people who know, the better the chance of finding them.'

'We've told everybody,' said Julie. 'Facebook *and* Twitter.' She held up her phone briefly, screen towards them, then turned it back to herself. 'Hundred and twenty-four shares already.'

Margaret Harper's tiny, squeaky voice cut through the murmur of positive acknowledgements of Julie's endeavours.

'I know he wasn't an angel,' she said, and no one in the room failed to notice the past tense in the phrase. 'Far from it. But a mother sees beyond their child's faults, while other people can see nothing else.'

'I'm sure he's a lovely lad,' said Lee, and the others resisted any instinct to contradict her.

'That's all I am,' Mrs Harper continued, as if Lee hadn't spoken. 'His mum. There's nothing else to me. I've no life of my own. Just him. If his life is over, then so's mine.'

Lee felt her heart sink like a chunk of ice, cold and heavy, down into her stomach. 'We'll find him,' she heard herself saying, before she could swallow back the words. 'I promise.'

Preston stared down at the polished toes of his shoes.

*

'You need to change this.'

The man's gruffly definitive pronouncement, issued even before any introductions had been made, rankled Maxey's already fraught nerves, but he put on his best professional smile and took the proffered document from the wafting hand. He laid it on the desk in front of him and smoothed it flat with a sweep of his palms.

'What seems to be the matter with it?' he asked.

'Everything.'

Maxey sighed and tried to recharge his waning smile. 'Let's start again,' he said. 'I'm Ed Maxey, and you are...?'

'Ron Hewett,' grunted the man.

Maxey nodded and turned to the quiet woman sitting beside him.

'Layna,' she said, then added 'Hewett,' in case he wasn't able to work that out for himself. A moment later he understood why the clarification was necessary.

Maxey examined the document before him, swiftly taking in the details with an erudite eye. Birth certificate for a child named Terence Lawson, born four years ago. The mother was presumably the woman sitting across the desk from him now, though on the certificate her surname was shown as Lawson. And the father was listed as Adrian Lawson.

It seemed so bizarre, seeing that name in black and white, right there in front of him. How often in the last few days had he and Nicky avoided saying it aloud, for fear of upsetting their houseguest? Turning off the news, so that their pictures, Lawson's and Alicia's, wouldn't appear side by side with the words "victim" and "suspect" scrolling across the screen beneath them. And now, for it to be presented to him in such banal circumstances, Maxey struggled to comprehend. The vast chasm between the tragic and the domestic bridged in one surreal instant.

Was Hewett a cuckold, or was it rather he who had

269

strayed into another man's territory? Was this woman, so demure in appearance, actually playing the two men against one another?

Maxey stared at the certificate for a long moment, carefully considering his next words. How to voice his concerns without causing offence...?

Hewett helped him out. 'He's not Terry's real dad,' he said bluntly, jabbing a finger towards Lawson's name. 'You got it all wrong.'

Flicking his gaze over the certificate Maxey was relieved to find his signature was not in the column which named the registrar who completed the original registration. A colleague, not in the office today. At least he would be able to deflect a little of Hewett's irritation by standing behind an official "we" rather than having to defend his own actions.

'You must have told us that he was, Mrs Hewett,' he said, having seen that she was the sole informant of the registration. 'We couldn't have obtained the information from anywhere else. See? You signed that all the details were correct.'

She did not bother to look at the portion of the form where her signature had been transcribed, merely stared at her entwined fingers clenched in her lap, her face turning a deep red. 'I was confused.'

'About the identity of the child's father?'

'I'm the father!' snapped Hewett, leaning forward in his seat and resting a white-knuckled fist on the desk.

'We rely on being given accurate information so that we can complete registrations correctly. If a mother tells us a particular man is the father of her child, then we are obliged to take her word for it.'

'What?' Hewett was astonished. 'Don't you check? Ask for paternity tests, or something?'

'Regretfully, no.'

'Maybe you should.' Hewett sat back so forcefully that his chair slid backwards a couple of inches.

'I wish we could!' said Maxey, with vehemence. 'It would save a heck of a lot of trouble for us.' He realised he was being indiscreet but his day, which had begun on such a high note, had descended dreadfully ever since, and this encounter was not helping his sour mood. 'You can't possibly imagine,' he seethed, 'how many couples come in here, only known each other five minutes, she's already pregnant with someone else's kid—' He held up a hand to stifle Hewett's objections. 'I know this isn't you, I'm just giving an example. They're all lovey-dovey. He's promising to look after the kid like it's his own. So they come in here and tell us it *is* his own. Whether we believe them or not, we take their word for it. No choice; they've told us that's the case and we have to take it on trust. That's how it works, I'm afraid. So, we issue the birth certificate, Mum and pretend-Dad go away happy. Five minutes later they've had a massive bust-up and he wants his name taking off the certificate. Well, tough... *luck*, mate. It's not as easy as that. It's a proper rigmarole sorting out the mess caused by stupid casual lies. People don't realise that it's an offence to give false information to a registrar, even though there are signs all over the place telling them that.'

He pointed to a prominently displayed notice with thick black text on a striking yellow background. Layna Hewett stared at it, aghast.

'Am I going to be in trouble?'

Her obvious distress pricked Maxey's pumped-up indignation and his ire deflated like a popped balloon.

'I apologise for my little rant,' he said, collecting himself. 'Just a pet peeve of mine. Obviously mistakes do happen, without there being any deliberate misinformation. Let's see if we can work out what happened in your case, shall we?'

He carefully looked over the certificate once more and took a few deep breaths to give his frazzled nerves time to settle.

'He wasn't here,' Layna Hewett said. 'Adrian. He didn't come with me.'

'Were you still married to him at the time of Terence's birth?'

'Terry,' Hewett corrected. 'We call him Terry. It's after my dad. He was Terence.'

Maxey gave a little smile and nod, and the casual observer might have thought he actually gave a shit. *It's not his sodding first name that's causing all this bother. Let's just get this sorted out so we can all get on with our day.* He turned back to Layna. 'Mrs Hewett?'

'Yeah, I was.' Her face, already redder than Maxey had ever seen, somehow turned darker still. She cast a furtive glance at her husband, then looked back down at her hands. 'But we'd split up ages before. Terry couldn't have been his.'

'So why did you say he was?'

'Yeah, that's what I want to know,' Hewett chipped in, his voice harsh.

'Please let her answer, Mr Hewett,' Maxey said, doing his best to keep a level, placatory tone.

'She said I couldn't put Ron's name on it.' Layna was almost sobbing by now.

'She?' Maxey said. 'You mean the registrar you saw back then?'

'Yeah, she said 'cause I was married to Adie I had to put his name on it.'

Maxey sighed and rubbed his forehead. He could feel a headache developing behind his eyes. 'That isn't actually the case, Mrs Hewett. The registrar would have asked you if you were married to the child's natural father. The law assumes that a mother's husband is the child's father, unless you tell us otherwise. You must have said that Adrian Lawson was, indeed, the father, or the registrar wouldn't have put his name there.'

'I didn't want "father unknown".' The sniffled whisper barely carried across the desk.

'I'm sorry?' Maxey leaned forward and cocked his head to hear her.

'What do you mean, "father unknown"?' Hewett said, grasping her shoulder roughly, so she was forced to turn to him.

Maxey knew he ought to intervene but in his present mood he wanted to shake them both. 'We don't actually use the phrase "father unknown" on certificates.'

'Why would it say "father unknown"?' Hewett said.

'It wouldn't,' said Maxey, but he knew he was wasting his breath.

'You knew it was me, so why didn't you tell 'em?' Hewett went on.

As he loomed over her Layna seemed to be shrinking on her chair. 'You had to be with me to have your name on it.'

'So why didn't you tell me?' Hewett's rage was mounting. He stood and paced away from her, then turned back angrily. 'I'd have come with you if you'd said I needed to.'

'I didn't know until she said,' Layna whimpered.

'Then you should have left it and I'd have come back with you another day.'

Despite his temper Hewett's logic was undeniable. Maxey tried to find the words to calm him.

'Mr Hewett, why don't you sit—?'

'What?!' Hewett glared at his wife. She had spoken at the same time as Maxey, her soft voice buried beneath his. Hewett had caught her words, but couldn't believe them.

'I needed the benefits,' she repeated. 'If I'd waited it would have delayed getting Child Benefit.'

'Fucking benefits?' Hewett roared.

'Adie was being arsey about the divorce and I didn't want to keep begging off you.'

'Begging?' Hewett waved his arms wildly, turning one way then another, eyes wide with incredulity. 'I gave you everything you wanted. Everything I had. You never had to beg.'

'You were working all hours, I just wanted to do my bit to help.'

'You mean all this aggro, everything that's happened,

273

was over money? A poxy couple of quid?'

'We needed it.'

'Not that fucking much!'

'I thought I'd have time to sort it out.' She lifted a hand towards him, but he jerked away and leaned heavily against the wall. 'But then time went on, and it never seemed to be an issue. I thought you'd never need to know.'

'Never need to know?' Hewett spat the words at her over his shoulder. 'Never need to know that my son has another man's name?'

'He doesn't. Everybody calls him Hewett. Doctor, dentist, school. He's Hewett everywhere.'

He slowly turned back to face her. 'Except on his fucking birth certificate!'

Maxey stood and indicated Hewett's empty chair. 'Please…'

Hewett ignored him. 'It was bound to come out eventually, you stupid woman!' He lunged forward and snatched up the certificate, waving it in Layna's face. 'I thought I was doing you such a favour. Take the kids to Disney, bit of a break for you. Needed to get a passport for Terry, didn't I? 'Cause he's never been abroad before. Of course, what does the passport office ask for?'

He held up the birth certificate, in answer to his own rhetorical question.

'When I saw that bastard's name on there, right where mine should have been, I wanted to—'

The offending certificate crumpled in his hand as he raised both tightly clenched fists, his lips curled back in a furious snarl.

The unfinished sentence echoed silently around the office. Maxey and Layna stared at him. Where Layna's face was still flushed bright red with guilt and shame, Hewett's features drained of all colour, bleached white in shock. Shock at his own statements. At his own actions.

Hewett looked from one of them to the other, desperation in his staring eyes. 'I didn't, though. I wanted to, but I didn't.'

'Course not, mate,' Maxey said, feebly. 'Nobody thinks you did.'

But even as he uttered those comforting words it was clear that not a single person in the room believed them.

25

The weird snuffling and snorting sounds were the first sensations to penetrate his stupor, worming their way into his subconscious, turning dream to nightmare. Then, as the boy shook off the demons and crept warily from slumber, eyelids heavy and reluctant, light was next to encroach on his awareness, dim, fragmented, filtered through a woven fabric, like canvas or sack-cloth. Smells followed, of the dusty sack over his face, of animal dung and, cutting sharply through the other odours, the sickly sweet stench of putrescence.

Attempting to move from his recumbent position Alan Rafferty discovered he was on a hard, flat surface, tied firmly at wrists and ankles with thick rope. The itchy fabric irritated his face and an intense throbbing pounded through his skull from a tender point at his left temple, where the sack seemed to have become glued to his skin.

'Awake, are ya?' The gruff voice was very close. ''Bout time.' A sharp jabbing in Alan's ribs, as if from a stick or bony finger, startled him and made him jerk away, attempting to shuffle out of reach of the unseen assailant. An eerie floating sensation brought bile to this throat as, unexpectedly, there was nothing beneath him, but strong hands at his shoulder and the belt of his jeans dragged him back to where he had been lying.

'Stay still,' the voice commanded. 'You don't want to land 'ead first on this concrete.' The scratchy stamping of sturdy boots demonstrated the solidity of the floor onto which he almost toppled.

With a wrench of Alan's head the hood was torn away, leaving threads of hemp in the dried blood on his face. He blinked gritty eyes at the flood of light through the large, wide open doors before him. Wooden walls reached up around him, leading to a beamed ceiling above. Mud and straw littered the concrete floor, along with golden brown leaves blown in from the trees lining the yard beyond. In the corner of the barn a fenced off area, scattered with hay, housed a sheltered pen and a long trough. A smaller entrance within this enclosure led to a compound outside, but the occupants of the paddock were inside the barn, lined up against the fence, gawking at Alan between the slats with little, squinty eyes, offering encouraging grunts to their master.

Tearing his gaze away from the hypnotic stare of the pigs Alan saw he was lying on a large, wooden slab resting atop robust metal legs. The table had numerous gashes and gouges in its surface, made by a hefty, bladed instrument repeatedly chopping into it. The indentations were stained a deep rusty black and appeared moist in the stark, autumn daylight.

A grizzled, worn face peered down at him with cold, grey eyes and a chill like the approaching winter shuddered through Alan's body.

'Who are you?' he asked, wheezing, dry throat rasping.

The man's glare remained constant and he stood, statue-still, inches from the table.

'What do you want? Let me go!' Alan's pleading had no effect. 'I an't done owt to you.'

He coughed, and ran his tongue around the inside of his parched mouth. He tugged on his bonds desperately, but without result. Flitting eyes searched vainly for means of escape.

A thought crept unpleasantly into his head. 'Have you taken Jake and Kenny?'

The hard eyes flickered briefly.

'Where are they? What have you done with 'em?'

A look of grim amusement passed over the old man's face. His glance towards the pig sty was subtle, and the mud-spattered creatures responded with huffed snorts like the macabre chuckles of manic clowns, but the allusion to the other boys' fate was lost in Alan's frantic state.

'Have you hurt them?'

'Don't you bother about them,' Arthur Camm said. 'Just you worry about yourself, lad.'

'What do you mean?' Alan tried to sit up, but couldn't find the necessary leverage. 'What you gonna do to me?'

'No more'n you deserve.'

'No, please! I've never hurt nobody.'

'Huh!' Camm grunted, and shook his head.

Alan screwed closed his eyes and dropped back onto the table, images of all the idiotic games and pranks he'd allowed himself to be drawn into these past months swimming through his mind. Racing along darkened streets in stolen cars, running from shops with pockets bulging, throwing bricks at buses, climbing onto the roof of Merrington church and tearing off slates. So many stupid things.

And Betty Hoskins, as the papers had identified her, clutching at her chest as she slumped to the ground.

'Was she your wife?' Alan asked.

Camm frowned. 'What?'

'Or your mum, maybe?' Unlikely, but he was no good at judging old peoples' ages.

'What you on about?'

'It wasn't my fault.' Alan stared up with wide, puppy-dog eyes, tears forming and spilling over onto his grimy face. 'Kenny was driving that night, not me.'

Guilt and resentment fought the fear for control within Alan's pounding chest. He'd seen that old woman sliding clumsily down the wall in his dreams over and over, and awoken each morning with a heart like lead. But his anger at his companions for making him a part of their ridiculous, repugnant schemes frequently overwhelmed his finer emotions.

'I saw who were drivin',' said Camm, and the sharp stab of his eyes left no doubt who he meant. 'That's why I saved you 'til last.'

278

'No, no, you're wrong,' Alan pleaded. 'I was in the back. It was the others, they dragged me along. I didn't even want to be there.'

Camm lunged forward and grabbed the front of Alan's hooded sweatshirt in his gnarled fist, and Alan winced as he recalled the same fist had swung an iron crowbar at his head the night before. His snarl was inches from Alan's face and his bitter invective spattered spittle as he ranted.

'Don't try to bullshit me, I saw yer! Racin' about, no thought for anybody but yerself and yer larks.'

Alan felt his crotch turn hot as he lost control of his bladder.

'I didn't, I didn't,' he spluttered, drool, snot and tears dribbling from his chin. He sought the comfort of his grandad's worn old signet ring, to feel its warm metal in his fingers, the tiny scratch of the paltry jewel, the familiar amidst the horrific, but his hands were bare. He miserably accepted that this mad, old bastard must have stolen it and his heart sank a little more. 'It wasn't me,' he sobbed.

'I fuckin' saw yer!' It was almost a roar, and Alan had neither strength nor willpower remaining to argue. 'She was the only one who ever meant anything to me, and you took 'er away from me like *that*.' Crooked fingers clicked in the air.

Alan slumped back onto the table top as Camm released his grip and shuffled away towards the barn doors.

'Under me very nose,' he was mumbling, as he looked outside. 'Right there on that road.' His shoulders slumped desolately. 'I saw yer.'

Through the throbbing ache in his skull and the fear twisting his mind in turmoil a grim realisation pierced Alan's consciousness. The narrow country lanes, the speeding car, him at the wheel, Kenny and Jake urging him on, faster and faster. The shambling black shape appearing from nowhere. *Get it, get it!* The twitch of the wheel; the swerve of the car. The thump and the yelp.

'The dog?'

'Aye,' said Camm, turning back to him. 'My Bexy.'

Alan's mouth fell open in stunned disbelief. He wrestled himself up onto one elbow and stared at his captor. 'You've done all this – kidnapped me, done God knows what to Jake and Kenny – all over a fucking dog?'

Camm glared down at the limply indignant figure.

'Fucking dog?'

Alan barely saw the fist coming. His nose cracked and erupted in a geyser of blood and his head slammed back onto the wooden surface with a nauseating crack. Merciful oblivion swallowed him.

Camm crossed to a work bench along one wall of the barn, where dismantled tools and farming implements in various stages of repair awaited his attention. He found a whetstone among the chaos and studied the row of knives and cleavers hanging from hooks above the worktop, choosing his favourite.

The sibilant scrape of blade against gritted stone sent the pigs into a new frenzy of squealing.

'Hush now, lads,' said Camm, approaching the pen. 'It'll not be long.'

*

'Thanks for not saying anything to Grieff,' said Lee, as she and Preston walked along the corridor towards the incident room. Already the rumble of activity from within threatened to drown out their conversation.

'About?'

'The whole "we'll find your son, I promise" thing.'

The press conference over, Mrs Harper and the Raffertys had been bundled into squad cars to be delivered to their respective homes.

Preston's smile was friendly, if a touch patronising.

'You already know it was a bloody stupid thing to say,' he laughed. 'My rubbing your nose in it isn't going to change anything.'

'She looked so pathetic.' Lee shrugged helplessly. 'It just slipped out.'

'I would say "you can't let them get to you",' he said, opening the incident room door, 'but you already know that, too.'

He stood back to allow her to precede him into the room.

'After you, Sir Galahad,' she said, gesturing for him to go first. 'Age before beauty.'

Preston's phone started ringing before he even reached his desk. 'Give me a chance to sit down,' he grumbled, rolling his eyes at Lee.

'Preston,' he said into the receiver.

'Luke, it's Dan,' said Baxter. 'About those fingerprints.'

'Oh, hi mate.' Preston settled back into his chair. 'What've you got?'

'The drink can found on Nettlehill Rise was definitely handled by the same person who last handled the mug found in the boy's room.'

'So it's Alan Rafferty's, then.'

'Well, we have to factor in the reliability of moveable evidence,' Baxter said hesitantly. 'But it would certainly seem so.'

Preston smirked. Good old Baxter, cautious to the end. 'Thanks, Dan. We'll increase door-to-door round by the park.'

'There was another thing, which was curious,' Baxter said, catching Preston's attention before he could replace the receiver.

'Oh? What's that?'

'The fingerprints flagged up an alert on the system relating to another case.'

'Alan's fingerprints?'

'The fingerprints in question, yes.'

'What case?'

'Vehicle theft,' said Baxter. 'Specifically, the vehicle of our murder victim, Adrian Lawson.'

'What?' Preston sat up, suddenly alert. He waved

towards Lee, indicating she should join him. 'But that was linked to the spate of Taking Without Consent cases from a few weeks back, wasn't it?'

'Yes, footprints, fibres, definite comparisons with the other thefts.'

'The Raffertys and the Lawsons were friends, though,' Preston said. 'Could these prints be innocent transfers?'

'There is always that possibility, but all the contacts are in the vicinity of the driver's seat. Window, mirror, dash, steering column.'

Preston thanked Baxter and rang off. 'Well, bugger me!'

Lee was leaning in, hands on his desk, waiting for him to end the call. 'What's going on?'

'Looks like Alan and his mates were our elusive Twockers.'

'You're kidding.'

'Nope, Alan's fingerprints were in Lawson's car.'

'But the families knew each other,' Lee said, echoing Preston's earlier thoughts.

'All the easier to get hold of the keys,' said Preston. 'Lawson's car was the only one that hadn't been broken into, if I remember the files correctly. We know that Lawson was seeing Julie Rafferty on the sly. Say he comes over to visit, hangs his jacket up while he makes himself at home. Alan is either upstairs and hears them, or comes in and finds them, whatever. Out of spite he decides to go through Lawson's pockets, maybe lifts a few quid from his wallet and finds the car keys, swipes them and goes off to find his mates. Fun and games ensue.'

'Didn't Lawson realise his keys were missing?'

'He was more interested in bonking the boy's mother,' Preston shrugged. 'He couldn't remember if he'd dropped them or left them in the car by mistake.'

'Interesting theory.'

'It all fits,' said Preston.

'The little shits.'

'Doesn't help us find out where they are now, though.'

'Unless...' Lee's brow furrowed and Preston could almost see her mind working.

'What is it?' he asked.

'Remember that farmer?'

'Farmer?' Preston sifted through the cases in his mind. 'The weirdo with the dead dog?'

'Yeah, that's the one,' she said. 'We gave him a sniff for the Lawson murder, and we wrote him off partly because the timing didn't work. But also because we thought he probably saw whoever was driving the car that killed his dog, who we knew wasn't Lawson.'

'But who we now know was Alan Rafferty and friends.'

'Probably.'

'Yeah, probably.' Preston heaved a frustrated sigh. All they had were notions and suppositions. 'It's all a bit flimsy. We need to have a look round that farm. Where's Grieff? We ought to go and have a peek.'

'He snuck out to the loo, I think.'

'Shit!'

'Probably.'

Preston scowled at her. 'We can't wait, Alan's in imminent danger every second he remains missing. If this farmer's got nothing to hide he won't mind us having a snoop. If he messes us about then that'll strengthen the case for going back with a warrant. Come on.' He rose from his chair and led the way towards the door.

'Just us, or shall we take back-up?'

'Difficult to justify going in mob-handed on a hunch,' Preston said. 'We'll take one car along. Nothing like a couple of uniforms for encouraging cooperation.'

A faint vibration buzzed against his leg, informing him his mobile had received a message, the customary ping having been drowned in the office hubbub. He took out the phone and glanced at the screen. The display read:

new message from ed

'Anything important?' Lee asked.

Preston gritted his teeth and crammed the phone back

in his pocket. 'No', he said. 'Nothing important.'

26

'What was that?'

Ron Hewett halted his frantic pacing as he heard the strange electronic whooping sound and saw the mobile phone in Edward Maxey's hand, partially concealed under the desk.

'Give me that!' The paper knife, which Hewett had taken from Maxey's desk tidy moments earlier, weaved menacingly through the air as he snatched the mobile from Maxey's hand and hurled it onto the floor. 'And this!' He scooped up the desk phone and flung it down alongside the other, a strangled snarl of satisfaction rasping from his throat as the equipment shattered, fragments clattering against the skirting board.

Maxey wheeled his chair back from the desk as the knife swept the air inches from his face. He cursed his luck – the one day in years he hadn't switched his phone to silent upon arrival at work. But he had been a little pre-occupied this morning.

'Who'd you call?' Hewett growled, slamming a fist onto the desk. 'Who'd you message?'

'No one,' Maxey lied, swiftly. 'It was just a notification. Probably Facebook.'

Hewett glanced at the phone where it lay on the carpet. The screen was black, its glass surface spider-webbed with cracks.

'I told you not to mess me around,' Hewett said, turning back to Maxey, eyes blazing. 'Just sit there and be quiet or I'll...' Frustration boiled inside him and he replaced words with a wild swipe across the wall. The blade wasn't particularly sharp, but it was sturdy enough to gouge through wallpaper and plaster. Maxey held no doubts that it could effortlessly puncture flesh with enough rage behind it.

He raised his hands submissively, and remained quiet.

'Just put the knife down, love,' Layna Hewett said, her trembling voice belying her attempt to sound calm. She hadn't moved from her chair, seemed almost rooted to it.

'Shut up!' Hewett hissed at her. 'Shut up, shut up, shut up!' The knife briefly pointed in her direction, then lowered to his side. 'I need to think. Just let me think.'

'Think about what?' she said. 'Can't we just go home?'

'Don't be stupid!' snapped Hewett. 'What, go home and have a nice cup of tea? Forget anything ever happened?'

'What has happened?' she whimpered. 'What's going on?' She curled forward on her chair, sobbing into her hands.

Hewett gasped a huff of sheer exasperation and resumed his pacing.

'It wasn't my fault,' he said after a moment, words aimed at no one in particular. When he received no answer he stopped moving and turned to Maxey. 'He made me do it.'

'Yeah?' said Maxey, eyes fixed on the knife, as it twitched in Hewett's fidgeting hand.

'I only went to talk to him.' Hewett took a step towards Maxey, arms open, empty hand outstretched. 'Only wanted to tell him to keep his distance. Stay away from my family, y'know?'

'Yeah, of course,' said Maxey. 'You were looking after your own. Just being protective. I get that.'

'For months I've tried to ignore it. Let it be. Ever since I bought that bloody birth certificate.' He kicked the crumpled document across the floor. 'It said Terry was his. Years of thinking he was mine, then everything gets turned upside down by a piece of sodding paper.'

'But you said he *is* yours...?'

'Yes, I know that now.'

'But you spent months in doubt?' Maxey said, frowning. 'You didn't think to ask your wife?'

Hewett's eyes stabbed sharply at Maxey, then dropped

meekly, embarrassed.

'Not till last night. It's a legal document, I thought it must be right.'

Maxey opened his mouth to respond, but held his tongue.

'I wanted things to go on as they were,' Hewett continued. 'Didn't want to upset the status quo. But it niggled at me, all the time. Little things became big things, know what I mean?'

Maxey nodded encouragingly. *How much time had elapsed since he sent that text to Luke? One minute? Five? He desperately resisted looking at his watch. He was sure to be on his way by now.*

'I've always thought of myself as a placid sort of bloke,' Hewett was saying. He touched his wife's shoulder, seeming not to notice her flinch. 'Eh, Layna? Not easily riled up, y'know?'

She nodded up at him, her eyes wet and wide, her smile weak and crooked.

'It got to me, I have to admit. The amount of times I thought about...' His free hand balled and opened repeatedly, his jaw clenching. 'But no matter how wound up I felt I never laid a hand on you or the kids, did I?'

With the twitch of her head her whole body shook.

Hewett turned back to Maxey. 'But then the other day it was like he was taking the piss.'

'Friday?' guessed Maxey.

'Yeah.' Hewett jerked a thumb towards Layna. 'She rings me up and says he's taken the boys out for the day. Both of 'em, Terry as well as his own lad, Shane. Doing her a favour, she says. Yeah, Mister bloody Magnanimous. Never does owt for nowt. Rubbing my nose in it, is what he's doing.'

Hewett was allowing himself to become stressed again, switching the knife from hand to hand, flicking his gaze around the room, speaking rapidly.

'But when he brings them home Terry's bawling his eyes

out, bless 'im. Lawson reckons he doesn't know what upset him, but he's obviously done it on purpose.'

'Why would he do that?' Layna asked, but the glare she received in return made her regret her audacity.

'To get at me, of course!' He shook his head in despair. How could they not see it? Was everyone blind but him? Lawson had been manipulating them all for years.

'So you went to see him...?' *Keep him talking, Maxey thought. Hurry up, Luke!*

'Yeah,' Hewett said. 'Packed in work early, went round to his house. His car wasn't there, so I knew he must be out. He always makes sure he parks it where he can see it from his window. So I had to hang about, didn't I? Waiting for his majesty to deign to show his face. Then, when he does turn up, he's got some young lass with him, can't be any more'n half his age. Well, I couldn't go in while she was there, could I? So I'm forced to sit around waiting even longer.'

'Frustrating.'

'You're not kidding! I sat watching the front door, waiting for her to come out. Waiting. Waiting. No choice, had I? Just had to keep watching and waiting, waiting, waiting...'

With each repetition of the word the knife bit a chunk out of the polished surface of Maxey's gleaming desk and droplets of spittle arced through the air. He'd been cooped up in the van, eyes on the house, while Lawson was messing around in there with some young tart. Another jab of the knife and another tiny curl of wood flew across the desk. Hewett's fixed, squinting eyes followed it like the ball at a tennis match.

'I was on the verge of storming in there anyway when I saw her strolling round a corner half way down the street. She must have come out the back door. I gave it another few minutes, to give her chance to get out of sight and then, just as I was about to get out of the van, he ran from the house in a blazing hurry. He's got different clothes on, so it's obvious what they've been up to. Same old tricks. Can't change a leopard.'

He spat these mismatched aphorisms at Layna, face twisted in a sneer of disgust.

She shook her head fitfully. She had spent hours the previous evening denying any lingering romantic connection to Adrian Lawson, until no more words remained.

'He jumped into his big, flash car and drove off,' Hewett continued, the knife tip scoring a groove in the desktop like the trajectory of a car racing away. 'By this time I was well pissed off, I can tell you! It's like he knew I was there and was trying to wind me up even more.'

Hewett's breathing was erratic, veering between deep, heavy snore-like rasps and light, feathery gasps, as if fighting for air. His hair and clothes clung to his clammy skin.

Maxey glanced at the computer where his on-screen diary informed him that his next appointment was waiting to see him. Surely someone would check up on him soon? Just keep him talking a little while longer.

'So what happened?'

The knife was heavy in Hewett's hand, its blade blunt, but slim and brutal. He stared at it, his expression uncomprehending, incredulous, as if he'd never seen it before.

'That's just it,' he said, and Maxey strained to hear the sibilant whisper. 'I don't know what happened.'

*

The cars rumbled down the drive and pulled up on the yard beside the clapped out vehicle parked haphazardly near the barn. Preston and Lee climbed out of his Honda while PCs Kershaw and Cawthorne appeared from the squad car alongside.

Arthur Camm carefully pulled closed the large barn doors before prying eyes could see within, and shuffled over

289

to greet them, casually tucking his hands into the bib of his heavy, leather apron. They all noticed the dark stains splashed across the filthy smock.

'Mr Camm, is it?' asked Preston, firm but friendly.

'You know it is,' Camm said. 'They'll 'ave told you that much.' He nodded at Lee and Kershaw, who stood together, peering towards the barn.

'Not one for pleasantries, our Mr Camm,' said Kershaw.

''Appen it doesn't feel very pleasant, when you turn up wearing your nice, smart uniforms in motors with fancy paint jobs and lights on top.'

'We're not trying to intimidate you, Mr Camm,' said Preston.

'Four onto one?' He looked slowly at each of them. 'Course not.'

Lee stepped forward, turning on her patient smile. 'We're looking for some missing children, Mr Camm. I'm sure you'd like to assist us, if you can.'

'So why've you come here?'

'We'd just like to have a quick look round,' she said. 'Make sure they aren't... *hiding* in any of your outbuildings.'

'Can't be. Dog would've told me.'

At the sound of his name the silent creature lifted his head and gazed out from the shadows of his kennel, then rested his chin back on his paws when he wasn't called to heel.

Preston looked down on the recalcitrant farmer in frustration. 'All the same, we'd still like to take a peek.'

'Then you'll have brought a warrant with ya.' Camm's diminutive form was straight and strong, his stare unwavering.

'It's just an informal visit at this stage, Mr Camm.' Preston nodded to Lee and she attempted to sidestep the old man. 'If you don't mind...?'

He shifted his stance so he stayed in her path. 'And what if I do mind?'

'Then we'll get a warrant and be back in a matter of

minutes,' Preston said, hoping his persistence would show him the inevitability of the situation. He was either an obstinate old bugger or he was as guilty as hell.

''Appen that's what you'd better do, then.' The glint in his eyes seethed with malice.

Lee faced him warily. 'Could I ask you to bring your hands out where we can see them?'

'I'm quite comfy as I am, ta,' Camm said, his stony expression set solid. He made no move to take his hands from inside his apron.

For a country yokel he seemed to have a good grasp of his rights. Without the warrant they had no power of entry and nothing they said was likely to shake his resolve, but Preston hated the thought of backing off and leaving this man to continue whatever he was doing in that barn before they arrived.

'If we have to come back later there'll be a lot more of us,' Preston said. 'It could get very messy round here.' A quick glance around persuaded him what an idle threat that was.

'I expect you'll do what you have to do.'

But that glance around had brought something else into Preston's eye-line, something which took a moment to penetrate his consciousness. A tiny object catching the failing afternoon light, almost buried in the mud near the rear of Camm's battered car. He crouched and picked it up, rubbing it clean in his fingers. He recognised this thing, he'd seen it only two nights ago, sitting slightly askew on a young boy's hand.

'What's that?' asked Lee, noticing his interest. 'What have you found?'

Preston held up Alan's ring for them all to see. 'Probable cause,' he said.

'Right!' said Lee, stepping past Camm at last, eyes on the barn.

'No you don't!' Camm's voice was virtually a screech. Any semblance to the reserved, stoic individual they believed they faced vanished in that moment. His eyes were wide and manic. The knife in his hand, which had slipped swiftly from beneath the folds of the grubby apron, was keen and deadly, swinging in a determined arc high above Lee's head.

She saw the movement but knew there was no time to avoid the strike.

From his crouched position Preston was helpless to intervene.

A slender, black fist slammed into Camm's face, rattling his jaw and sending him hurtling to the ground. 'Get the fuck away from my wife!' Kershaw roared, stamping on Camm's fist and kicking the knife across the yard.

As she rolled him over and twisted his arms around so she could apply the handcuffs Preston and Lee regained their composure and raced to the barn. Heaving against the doors which Camm had moved with ease Preston reflected on the hidden strength in his slight frame, strength enough to overpower and manhandle youths a fraction of his age. He glanced back to ensure that Kershaw was able to manage him but saw she had her knee in his back and the cuffs in place.

By the time he joined Lee inside the barn she had run to the large table in the centre of the floor area. She tentatively touched the huddled shape lying amongst the blood stains, checking for signs of life. She pulled out her radio and spoke quickly into it, and upon hearing the word "ambulance" Preston let out a sigh of relief.

Cawthorne appeared in the doorway. 'Jo's got him in the car,' he said.

'Good,' said Preston. 'Now spread out. We need to see if there's any sign of the other two missing boys. Oh, and Constable, get onto the station, we need more people down here for the search.'

Cawthorne nodded and raised his radio.

Lee, who had been eyeing the butcher's slab upon which the boy was lying, strode immediately over to the sty in the corner and astonished them both by reaching over the low fence and scooping up a large slop of pig dung in both her hands. She began sifting it through her fingers like a Californian gold prospector at a muddy river bank.

'My dad was a farmer,' Lee said into the stunned silence. 'Pigs'll eat anything.'

She found a small nugget of something rough and solid, but definitely not gold, rubbed it between finger and thumb and then held it up for their inspection. 'Tooth,' she said. 'About the only thing they can't digest.'

'Shit,' groaned Cawthorne.

'We'd better get forensics down here, as well. I'll call Grieff,' said Preston. 'It'll be easier to get him on his mobile.'

He took his phone from his pocket and swiped the screen. Before he could bring up the dialler he accidentally caught his list of notifications and opened the waiting text from Edward Maxey which he had deliberately ignored earlier.

'Damn,' he said. 'Annette, can you call the chief for me? There's something I need to deal with.'

He looked with concern at the message on his display. It was a single word, obviously typed in haste, as Maxey would never be so careless with grammar or punctuation.

help

27

Ron Hewett slammed his fist into the steering wheel of his battered old red Transit van. Where was the bastard going now? Had he missed his chance? His seething anger wasn't dissipating. If anything it was growing stronger with every minute he wasn't able to vent his feelings. Should he go home, take a deep breath, have a cup of tea and let the moment pass? No, that would merely mean bottling it up for another day, and it had been festering away long enough as it was. He needed to have it out with that smug arsehole, settle it for good. Maybe Lawson had just nipped out for a pint of milk or a newspaper. He might be back any second. He could wait for a while at least, see if he returned.

Five minutes turned into ten, Hewett's raw temper fraying anew with every alteration in the digital display of the dashboard clock. The afternoon was cool and in his inactivity he was beginning to feel a chill, adding to his aggravation. After a quarter of an hour he could bear it no longer, shouldering open his door and lurching onto the road. No use hammering on the front door, the house was clearly empty. Lawson wouldn't have brought his young trollop home if his wife was in residence. The girl had appeared from the corner farther along the road and so, on an impulse, Hewett headed that way to try to find the rear exit to the house. He discovered the ginnel running behind the back gardens of the houses and worked his way along, counting the accesses until he came upon what had to be the Lawsons' garden gate. He had no real notion of what he planned to do as he pushed open the gate and crossed the closely cropped lawn. Shielding his eyes against the reflected light he peered in at the kitchen window. Neat, clean, smartly accessorised with matching kettle and toaster; three jars with "Coffee", "Sugar" and "Tea" printed on them stood in a regimental line along the worktop. No more than he would expect from Lawson's second wife.

Tempting as it was to kick open the back door and trash the place, that wasn't why he was there. So why exactly was he there? Was he being protective of his son, brought to tears by this man? But he wasn't Hewett's son, the birth certificate proved that. So was it jealousy? Layna and Adrian had been separated almost a year when Terry came along, wrangling over their divorce, even though they were both in other relationships by then. That meant that Layna must have been with him again, while she was with Hewett. Professing her loyalty and undying love for him and screwing the ex at the same time. The seething emotions roiling inside him boiled over once again and he spat bile onto the lawn, grinding it into the grass with the toe of his boot.

When Layna had told him of this morning's incident, asking for his assistance with the kids and the holiday preparations, he told her he couldn't possibly leave the job he was involved in. But then he had done precisely that, rushing the replacement of a burst pipe and not even bothering to remove his overalls in his hurry, tossing his toolbox carelessly into the back of the van so it tipped and spilled hammers and wrenches across the compartment. He'd heard them scraping and rattling loosely as he raced the van around bends and corners, chasing to this confrontation, each thump and clatter adding to his irritation.

His passionate resentment stewed in his churning gut as he stalked back and forth along the small, round slabs dotted into the lawn. How long he had been pacing he could not be sure, but he was startled from his unpleasant musing when the back door of the house opened and Adrian Lawson called to him.

'What the hell are you doing out there?'

Lawson was younger, more athletic, self-assured, but

Hewett wasn't about to back down now. 'Waiting for you.'

Lawson shrugged. 'You'd better come in, then.' With barely a glance he turned and strode back into the house in the confident belief that Hewett would follow along like a puppy.

Lawson's casual indifference disturbed Hewett's equilibrium more than ever. With no choice but to do as he was directed he marched in, leaving the door standing open behind him.

He found Lawson in the living room and the dim ambiance distracted Hewett briefly.

'Why are the curtains closed?' he said.

'Never you mind,' Lawson responded, blasé and dismissive.

Hewett gritted his teeth. 'Think you're so special, don't you?'

'What's the matter, Ron?' Lawson's teeth shone white in the dull light, that annoying grin broad and cocky. 'Layna giving you a hard time, is she?'

'Shut up, you smarmy git!' Hewett clenched his fist, wishing the familiar weight of his favourite wrench was nestled there right now. Slut or angel, he couldn't bear the sound of her name on this man's tongue. 'Don't you dare talk about her.'

'If you've come here to insult me you can bugger off right now.' Lawson waved a hand towards the door, but Hewett didn't budge.

'Just stay away from my family, Lawson.'

'I'd love to,' Lawson said through the ever-present smirk, 'but part of your family happens to be my family.'

'Ah, so you admit it!' Hewett said, vindicated by the adulterer's own words.

'I've never denied it,' said Lawson, puzzled. 'Are you drunk?'

'When did you do it, eh? Sneaking round while I was at work?'

'Do what? What are you on about?'

'Don't try changing your story now, you've already confessed.'

Hewett strutted round the room, wringing his hands. Lawson stood, arms crossed, and laughed.

'Have I? To what, exactly?'

'To being Terry's father, of course!'

That stopped Lawson's laughter. 'What? When did I say that?'

'My family is your family,' Hewett mimicked. Hands on hips he jutted out his chin and rested a foot on the hearth. The brass poker and tongs rattled against their stand as Hewett's boot nudged the base.

'I was talking about Shane, you pillock,' Lawson said.

'So now you're telling me you've not been sleeping with my wife?'

Lawson's perpetual good humour was finally strained to breaking point. 'You know what?' he said with a jeer. 'I have. We've been at it like rabbits every chance we get. In your bed. On your settee. On your kitchen table. She can't get enough of me. Yeah, Terry's mine. Don't you think he looks like me? And you'll not know this yet, but Layna's pregnant again. And guess what? That's mine as well.'

It went on, Lawson relishing his vile and vicious litany, but Hewett heard no more of it. The voice became a bass drone, washing over him, swamping his senses, impinged only by a curious clinking sound, accompanied by a gentle bumping at his ankle. He looked down and saw the poker, still swinging on its stand.

When the mental fog cleared moments later Hewett was surprised to find the poker had somehow made its way into his hand. And even more startled to discover the limp, shattered corpse at his feet, blood and brains staining the floor, walls and ceiling.

Stunned and horrified, he knew he had to get away, to escape the inconceivable insanity that had crashed down around him. Hewett dropped the poker and raced from the room, and it was only the sight of his own hand on the front door handle, horrific and gore-stained, that kept him from charging out onto the street, dripping blood like a creature from a horror film.

Rationality reasserted itself in his bewildered mind. Lawson's words, designed to incite, had done exactly that, releasing a blind fury pent up inside Hewett for far too long. But now his mind was his own again; cool, logical, practical. He peeled off his work overalls, turning them inside out and leaving him in jeans and t-shirt. The dirt on his filthy work boots disguised the blood that had splashed onto them. He went up to the bathroom and leaned over the bath, using the shower head to rinse off the worst of the blood from his hands, face and hair. He found cloths and bleach and retraced his steps, obliterating any trace of fingerprints in the blood smears he had left in his wake. He left through the open back door, using a hand inside the hem of his t-shirt to pull the door closed behind him without having to touch it.

Back in the van Hewett sat, stunned, attempting to make sense of what had happened. He was eventually prompted into action when he spied Lawson's young girlfriend returning along the street, heading back to the house. He twisted the key in the ignition with a shaky hand and the van jerked from the kerb and roared away.

*

'Hello, Haleston Register Office,' Rosalyn Peters said cheerily. 'How may I help you?'

'Hello,' began the caller, then, with a hint of recognition. 'Is that Roz?'

'Yes...?'

'Detective Sergeant Luke Preston, we spoke this morning.'

'Yes.' Roz's voice took on a rueful edge. 'I remember.'

'Apologies again for waking you. It's easy to forget that not everyone keeps the same unsocial hours that we do.'

Roz was about to reply with something dismissively forgiving but Preston continued, polite cordiality slipping away and a sense of urgency forming in his words.

'Listen, I'm trying to get hold of Ed. His mobile is off.'

'He's got someone in at the moment,' Roz said, pulling up the appointment diary on her computer screen. 'Hmm, they've been in quite a while, there are people waiting for him.'

'Try his line for me, will you?' It wasn't an order as such, but there was enough command in his tone to convince Roz to obey without question.

'That's weird,' she reported, a moment later. 'His line is dead.'

'Who does he have in his office with him?'

'Just a re-reg enquiry,' Roz said, then elucidated: 'A couple enquiring about re-registering a birth.'

'What's the couple's name?'

'Umm...' She was becoming flustered now. Feelings of guilt over calling the police in the first place, exacerbated by Maxey's reaction when he saw her earlier, and now Preston's barrage of questions, sent her thoughts tumbling. Should she even be telling him about register office patrons? They had an expectation of confidentiality in their private matters.

'Names, Roz,' Preston snapped. 'Quickly.'

'Hewett.'

The line became muffled as Preston spoke to someone at his end, but Roz thought she caught the words "ex-wife". When he came back to her his emphasis was adamant.

'Do nothing. I'm on my way. If Ed comes out of his office, ring me back straight away.' He reeled off his mobile number and Roz scribbled it down automatically, her hand on autopilot, her mind fizzing. 'Remember, *do nothing*,' he stressed.

'What's wrong?' she demanded. 'What's happened?'

'I can't say right now.'

'Does that mean you won't say, or you don't actually

know?'

The dense silence of the closed line was her only reply.

The corridor leading off behind the reception held the doors to the staff room and the registrars' offices. Maxey's was the last one, a firm, solid oak door. The walls were heavy old stone, thick and impenetrable. Secure and sound-proof. Without the phone connection there was no way of knowing what was going on within those walls. Unless…

Do nothing.

From her half-standing position the recollection of Preston's stern words pushed her back into her chair. She sucked on the end of her pen and tapped prettily painted fingernails on her desk. The coughs and shuffles of impatient customers beyond the glass screen were lost on her.

Her thoughts were in the past, almost three years ago. A gathering of the register office staff at a local hotel, a large function in celebration of Christmas, tinsel on the tables and festive evening-wear. The superintendent registrar, Lynne Rayner, had elbowed her way in to claim the seat next to Maxey and spent the evening taking every opportunity to touch his arm or hand, even brushing a crumb of mince pie from his lip at one point. He'd smiled politely, exchanged convivial conversation, but his eyes had met Roz's more than once, with a wink and raised brows. And other times, discreet as he'd tried to be, she'd felt his gaze on her low-cut dress, her deep cleavage sprinkled with seasonally coloured glitter to deliberately catch the eye. To catch *his* eye.

Many drinks consumed, and many more yet to follow, they had pressed into the throng around the bar. Forced close by the surge of bodies he had nuzzled his face into her flowing hair and rested a hand on the pleasing curve of her buttock, and she was sure that wasn't his mobile phone she felt pressed against her thigh. She playfully slapped his wrist and they laughed, then a space opened up at the bar and the moment was over.

They had never spoken of it since and, considering his state of intoxication, she wondered if he would even recall it if it cropped up in conversation. But she had never forgotten it and a warm tingling deep inside caused her breath to catch as she inexplicably summoned up the moment again now.

Taking the pen from her bright, scarlet lips she distractedly rubbed the waxy red marks from the end with her thumb, tossing it down to rattle across the computer keyboard into the shadows beneath the monitor. She shuffled forward on her chair.

Do nothing.

She sat back again and slapped a hand onto the desktop, startling an elderly man dozing in the waiting area, and bit an anxious lip.

God, she needed a cigarette!

28

Thumping the heel of his hand against his forehead, face screwed up in consternation, Hewett stood abruptly, tipping his chair back onto the floor. Maxey watched in alarm. The frantic man across the desk had only ceased his relentless pacing a moment before, while telling his fragmented tale in an increasingly disjointed dialogue, and now he was up again, turning left and right, as if lost in a winding maze.

'There's no air,' Hewett said, throat rasping. He crossed to the window, pushing at the aged sash mechanism, becoming frustrated as it resisted him.

'They don't open, mate,' said Maxey, as gently as possible. 'Nailed shut. In case we try to jump out after a stressful day.' His grin was forced and no one laughed. He glanced at Layna Hewett, a tiny thing on the other chair, curled up like an airplane passenger preparing for a devastating crash, body shaking with convulsive sobs.

Hewett thumped his fist against the glass, paper knife still clutched in his grasp, and a crack stretched across one of the panes.

'Got to get out!' Hewett lurched wildly around, hunched over, as if the walls were closer than before, the ceiling much lower. 'Out, before I'm crushed.'

'Nobody's stopping you.' Maxey pointed towards the door, just a few feet away, but Hewett peered at it as if the gap was a thousand miles, the door a dot in the distance. He seemed surprised when, in a single step, it was right in front of him, like it was beckoning, treacherously luring him closer.

'Who's out there?' he said. 'Who's waiting for me?'

'No one, I swear.' Maxey gulped back his next words. The last thing a paranoid person needs to hear is that they're being paranoid.

'My son, not his,' Hewett told the air. 'Mine.'

'That's right,' said Maxey. He reached down and scooped up the crumpled birth certificate, attempting to flatten it on the desk. 'So why don't you sit down and we'll try to sort everything out?'

But Hewett seemed to be responding to other voices than Maxey's.

'Beautiful baby boy, Dad will be so pleased. Finally produced something to be proud of. Just want a smile from Dad. I named him after you, see? One smile, one day. *Only* a plumber? What are you, then, a brain surgeon? A rocket scientist? No, a bloody office manager, pushing numbers, bossing secretaries around. Looking down your nose at tradesmen. At least I can do something with my hands instead of using them to slap and punch. That'll not happen to my son. No one touches my son.'

Hewett finally saw the document that Maxey displayed before him.

'But he's not my son.' He snatched up the certificate, screwing it up in his fist again. 'That's what this says. That's what *she* said.' He threw the balled paper at Layna and she released a shuddering squeal.

'He is,' she snivelled. 'He is!'

'He shouldn't have said what he said,' Hewett told his unseen audience. 'I only went to tell him. To say keep away from my wife. From my family. Keep away. Why did he have to say that? I didn't want to hurt him. I never went there to hurt him, honest. Just went to tell him, that's all.'

He heaved a shuddering breath and lurched back to the window. 'No air.' He pressed his face against the cool glass, leaving a clammy sweat mark and puffs of condensation from his wheezing.

Oblivious to the shiny, black Honda Civic swerving into the car park far below, screeching past the elderly attendant with inches to spare, Hewett stumbled back to the desk. The knife swished through the air, its blade now slightly curved from being jabbed against the wooden desktop, but looking no less dangerous for it. Maxey pressed back in his chair, the wheeled feet firm against the skirting.

'His head was gone,' Hewett said unexpectedly, lip curled in disgust. 'He's a mess on the carpet, and we're off to Disneyland. Two whole days of fun and frolics. All smiles. Keep smiling. It's for the kids. My son; his son. Both his? What do you mean, what's wrong? Nothing's wrong with me, I'm fine.

'What did he look like on the slab? Had they rebuilt him? Like Humpty Dumpty? Lego-head? Did he smell? Did you touch him?'

He's withdrawn, distracted.

Maxey gauged the distance between his chair and the door, around the bulky desk, assessing his chances of forcing his wobbly legs into action and darting across the space before Hewett became aware of his intentions and could react. Negligible to non-existent. And what of the wife? He daren't leave her. Hewett hadn't hurt her so far, but who knew what could happen with him in this state? It felt like hours since he'd sent out that rushed text. Had Luke seen it yet? God, what if he'd blocked him since that bust-up this morning?!

A soft, high, warbling voice brought Maxey back to the moment. Hewett was singing "It's a Small World After All", a manic smile on his face, the knife a conductor's baton in his hand. He skipped lightly for a couple of steps, then stopped, head sagging, arms slack by his side, tears rolling down his face. A low, mournful wail oozed from him.

Maxey watched as Hewett's fingers loosened on the handle of the knife. Another second, maybe two, and he'd drop the weapon and it would all be over.

Tick. Tick.

The door swung open, catching Hewett sharply in the back. Startled, he spun around, raising the knife, the force of his turn adding strength to his arm.

'Hi, Ed, is everything alri—' Roz Peters had time to say,

before a blunt, bent paper knife tore through the soft flesh of the side of her neck, then exited with a wet slurp as Hewett jerked back in shock.

A gout of blood spattered up the wall. Ron Hewett staggered away, finally allowing the knife to tumble from his bloody fingers, and collapsed into the corner, arms around his knees, shaking his head in pointless denial.

Layna Hewett screamed in horror, her overwrought brain shut down and she toppled off her chair in a clumsy swoon.

Roz Peters looked at Maxey in confusion as her legs crumpled beneath her. He scrambled over to her, scooping her up in his embrace, staring aghast at the rapidly flowing blood as it gushed from her throat and over his arm.

The phones lay in useless scattered shards around him. The Hewetts slumped senselessly on the floor. Maxey dabbed inadequate hands at the gaping wound and roared incoherently towards the open door.

'Sorry,' gasped Roz, brushing delicate fingers at the spreading stains on Maxey's suit, then her eyes flickered closed and her hand flopped heavily into his lap.

Numbly, Maxey felt a strong grip heaving him away from Roz's limp form and there, finally, was Luke, good old Luke, taking charge, bellowing orders to the smart, pony-tailed woman who'd followed him into the room.

A shock of *déjà vu* struck Maxey as he watched Preston crouching by a beautiful, blood-smeared woman lying on his floor.

Epilogue

November

The stitches had been removed now, but the dressing had been replaced. It was purely a precautionary measure to reduce any risk of infection. The restorative process was progressing splendidly, so the doctor and nurses assured her.

But that was what Alicia was most afraid of. Once the relatively minor damage to her wrist was no longer an issue, they would all have to face up to the fact that it wasn't the real reason she was still in hospital, a fortnight since she committed that most grievous of crimes against the Lord and tried to take her own life. It appeared He didn't believe she had suffered enough, after all.

The policeman was no longer outside her door, but she felt the scrutiny of the ward staff every time she stepped into the corridor to exercise her legs. The male doctor with the white coat and brown skin, with lots of letters in his name, would rush in, look at her wrist and tell her to stick out her tongue, then rush out again with a curt, formal smile and barely a word spoken. The other doctor, the woman with the round face and short, bobbed hair of a deep auburn with silver streaks, who wore a frayed cardigan with rolled up sleeves, would sit on the edge of her bed and pat her hand. Her smile was much warmer and she would ask Alicia questions in her gentle tone, about what she was thinking and how she was feeling, waiting patiently for her tears to pass, and when she left she would make reassuring promises about returning again very soon.

What happened next, once they decided Alicia no longer needed this level of care, and these limits to her liberty, and could be released back into society? Where was she to go? Her sole reason for being in this strange, unfamiliar country had been snatched brutally from her, first emotionally and then in a very real and horrific manner.

She couldn't return to the Maxeys' home. Though it had been a place of sanctuary in a time of crisis, that avenue was closed to her now. She had hoped to see more of Edward and Nicola during her recovery, but apparently he had suffered a traumatic event too and was in no state for visiting. Nicola came when she could, but was finding it a chore, with her work and tending to her husband, so her visits were understandably brief and infrequent. Alicia knew she could expect no more of them. Their relationship was wholly based on those few short days hiding under their roof, mostly in a state of shock, taciturn and withdrawn. Not the foundation of a lasting friendship.

Which only left home. If she still had a home. The bitter fires blazing in her father's eyes, when last she saw him, spoke of anger, resentment and, saddest of all, disappointment. He couldn't even bring himself to flog her with his belt. He just turned and walked away. She expected no welcome there.

Alicia resisted the urge to scratch the wound, unsure if she was feeling a genuine itch, or a deeper impulse to tear open the healing flesh and prolong this limbo of indecision, and remain pandered and cossetted by a foreign state. Or maybe to complete the atrocity, the cardinal sin she had attempted two weeks ago, and been too pitiful to accomplish.

Misery was like a physical weight upon her, and she sank back against the crisp, white pillows and felt herself become submerged in a welcome blankness.

She couldn't be certain of how long she had been asleep, only that the world had become the swirl of pinky-grey darkness that roils on the inside of closed eyelids in a lighted room. A large, black-furred wolf had been chasing her and, behind its snarling mouth, its eyes had been first

307

soft, like Adrian's, then hard and piercing, like her father's. It was the husky growl of the beast that had drawn her from slumber, and she heard that sound again now, a throaty rumble, forming her name.

'Alicia.'

She peeled open her dry eyes and feared her nightmare had followed her into the walking world. A dark-haired giant loomed above her, glaring down and shaking its head in righteous judgement.

A mouse's squeak escaped her lips. '*Papá?*'

His mouth opened but for a moment no sound emerged. When it did the single word drifted softly down to her in a tone she had not heard since before her mother died.

'*Niñita.*'

With a curiously vulnerable sob he bent and scooped her into his powerful embrace, and their tears merged on their tightly pressed cheeks.

December

Her disappointment was palpable as Donna Lawson slipped from the heat and clamour of the busy Red Lion, squeezing through the crowded smoking area, out of the gate at the side and up the ginnel back onto the street. She hurried away along Keel Road and onto Main Drive, weaving amongst the scantily-clad teens and burly bouncers, the unsteady groups singing and shouting as they tottered along, the quiet couples clinging desperately to one another to avoid being separated and lost in the crowd.

The guy had seemed quite decent at first, smiling and attentive, great hair and strong arms which she had enjoyed imagining crushing her to his manly chest. The conversation had concentrated on her, her thoughts, wishes and feelings, and she had allowed herself, briefly, to believe that perhaps not all men were the same. But Donna was accustomed enough to gin and tonic to recognise that those last couple had been doubles, despite her insistence that she intended to keep a clear head. She was grateful she'd had the foresight to scout ahead and find out the layout of the pub before choosing the venue for their rendezvous, and ensuring that there was means of escape should she need it. Now, thankful for the anonymity of the faceless multitudes around her, she sighed in relief, leaving the pub and her duplicitous date far behind.

This early in the evening the queue at the taxi rank wasn't vast, so she didn't have too long to wait, standing in her glamourous but less than comfortable heels, skirt perhaps a little short for a winter's night. Once in the relative warmth of the taxi she sat back and crossed her shapely legs, taking the weight from at least one of her aching feet.

Despite the chill Donna could see the greasy sheen of

sweat on the back of the hefty taxi driver's thick neck as she leaned forward to give him her home address. He sniffed and nodded and the taxi lurched forward.

Home. Donna doubted she would feel the cold, empty house was her home ever again. Despite a thorough clean and fresh wallpaper, the simple knowledge of what happened in that room left its own stain, invisible to the eye but indelible on her psyche. She had already begun browsing the internet for estate agents. Time for a change.

Her head lolled and she jerked awake. It seemed those drinks had had a stronger effect on her than she realised. Maybe it was more than extra gin her erstwhile suitor had been adding to them. Crossing her legs the other way her short skirt hitched high up her leg, revealing an inch or two of fine lace at the top of her stockings. Through the glass partition she saw the bulbous head of the driver craning to improve his view in the rear-view mirror and she shuffled in her seat, tugging at the skirt's hem. Had he been watching her as she dozed? It seemed all men *were* the same, after all. There was something malevolent in the squinty, piggy eyes leering back at her and she placed her small clutch bag carefully on her lap. Flicking open the catch she reached discreetly inside, rummaging past the purse, phone and keys, until her fingers curled around the cold metal cylinder crammed in amongst the other items. She gripped it tightly, willing her eyes to stay open. *Let him fucking try something!*

*

'You okay, babe?' asked Jo Kershaw.

Annette Lee stared at the television screen, seemingly unaware that her wife had turned off the set. 'Hmm?'

'Time for bed, sleepy-head.'

'Yeah,' said Lee, though she made no attempt to move from the sofa.

Kershaw swept Lee's loose hair out of her face and

gently turned her head to face her. 'Rough day?'

Lee nodded and nuzzled her face against the hand on her cheek. 'It was the plea hearing today. Bastard's going for diminished responsibility, but he knew damn well what he was doing.'

'The farmer?' Kershaw guessed. 'For killing that boy?'

'Jake Harper, yeah. And the other one, Kenny something. Not that his parents seemed bothered. Father sat there, stony-faced, like a church gargoyle. Mother seemed spaced out on drugs. The Raffertys were there, too, with Alan. They looked a bit embarrassed to still have their son.' Lee shivered. 'But Jake's mum, Margaret Harper, she looked like a ghost. Pasty white. Gone thin as a rake. Made me cry to see her.'

'We did all we could, love,' Kershaw said, pulling her into her arms.

'I told her we'd get him back,' Lee said. 'I promised.'

Kershaw held her for a long time, feeling the tears soaking into her pyjama shirt. Eventually she said, 'I know something that'll cheer you up.'

Lee sat back and gave her a sceptical look, wiping her face with the backs of her hands.

'Guess who's sat in a cell right now, nursing his sore balls?' Kershaw grinned. 'I meant to tell you earlier, but you'd got the wine open when I got home and it slipped my mind.'

'Priorities, eh?' Lee chided with a shake of her head and an indulgent smile. 'Go on then, who is it?'

'Only old Grotbags, the taxi driver.'

'Grogan?' said Lee. 'The sleazy one?'

'That's him. Up to his old tricks. And who'd he got in the back of his cab this time?'

'I don't bleedin' know!' Lee said. 'Stop making me guess things. Just tell me!'

'Donna Lawson.'

'No! The wife of the murder vic from the other month?'

'Yep!' Kershaw folded her arms, pleased with her story

and the spark it had returned to her wife's eye. 'Seems he thought she was more drunk that she actually was. He drove her out to the middle of nowhere and tried to climb on top of her. Got half a can of *Impulse* deodorant in his eyes instead. While he's crawling around half-blind she laces into him with her Manolo Blahniks. Best part is, she recorded the whole thing on her mobile phone.'

'Hah!' Lee cheered. 'Brilliant!'

'The kicking she gave him goes on a bit longer than strictly necessary, but we don't have to show the whole recording in court.' Kershaw winked. 'The jury will get the gist.'

*

They had to send someone, Maxey supposed, as he huddled close to Nicky under their shared umbrella in this typically funereal winter weather. It wouldn't be right if there wasn't at least a presence, under the circumstances. And who else would they send but the two who were actually there when it happened? He'd barely seen Luke since that tragic day. Detective Constable Lee had handled witness statements and interviews. He hadn't had chance to ask if that was official policy, because of their prior relationship, or if Luke was avoiding him. There'd been no chats on the phone, no drinks in the pub. No "later/'gators".

The thrashing rain rumbled on the umbrella, drowning the sound of the minister's monotonous drone, but Maxey wasn't listening anyway. He couldn't understand why they were here, ankle-deep in sludge, risking following the coffin into the hole on the crest of a dramatic mud-slide. Roz would have hated this. It must have been her parents' choice to go the religious route. Her opinions about church versus civil weddings were well known in the office. What was the point of making promises to a fictional character from a book? No doubt she felt the same about funerals. She'd probably had a word with whoever was up there and ordered this weather especially for today, to teach them a lesson. But wouldn't she have been surprised to find out there was somebody up there to order weather from?

The windows of the White Hare in Sproxton had quickly clouded with thick condensation as the wet funeral attendees slowly warmed up in its dim, gloomy function room, picking over the egg sandwiches, broccoli quiche and cocktail sausages. Most of the register office staff, who had turned out in force for the funeral itself, had returned to man the office, leaving only Maxey and Lynne Rayner to continue on to the wake. The superintendent registrar had got roped in to explaining to Roz's grieving parents the death registration arrangements in cases where a coroner's inquest had been adjourned for criminal proceedings.

Maxey had not yet spoken to the parents, and didn't relish the prospect of the meeting, fearing that they may blame him for not saving their daughter. And why shouldn't they? After all, he blamed himself. He should have done something to stop Hewett earlier, regardless of the risk to himself. Or alerted someone outside the room. Something. Anything.

As Nicky nibbled on a sausage roll Maxey absently pondered a tiny piece of tinsel clinging to a drawing pin near the top of the wall. Had the room already been decorated for Christmas and the trimmings hastily removed, to appease the sensitivities of the mourners, or was this the last vestige of last year's festivities, sad and neglected, unworthy of the effort of climbing up a step-ladder?

He became aware that Nicky was looking past him and turned as Luke Preston made his way towards them, manoeuvring between the tables and chairs, limp paper plate clutched in his hand. The men looked at one another, neither speaking, as the moments passed.

'How you coping?' Preston said, eventually.

Maxey shrugged. 'Y'know.'

Preston nodded, slowly. 'Nasty business.'

313

More uncomfortable seconds ticked away.

'They expect the trial to start sometime in the New Year,' Preston said. 'Could be a while, yet.'

'Yeah, your colleague said.' Maxey searched round the room with his eyes, but found no sign of DC Lee.

Preston saw the look. 'She had to get back,' he said. 'Crime doesn't take days off.'

He deposited his plate on a table nearby and brushed crumbs from his fingers.

Now his empty hands felt cumbersome and awkward, so he reached for his wallet. 'Can I get you a drink?' he offered.

Maxey gestured towards an almost full glass on the table beside him.

Preston nodded. 'Nicky?'

'Not for me,' she said. 'I'm not drinking.'

'Driving?' Preston guessed.

'Yes, but also...' Her hand hovered above her abdomen.

'What, really?'

'It's early days,' she said. 'We weren't going to tell anyone yet, but as it's you...'

'That's fantastic news.'

Hugs were required, expected, but no one felt able to make the first move.

A new silence threatened to engulf them, so Maxey took a deep breath and voiced the thought that had been bothering him for a while.

'Did you get in trouble?' he said. 'You know, because of...' He squirmed under Preston's scrutiny.

'My best mate harbouring a suspect in a murder case right under my nose?'

'Yeah, that.'

'It's on my file,' Preston said. 'I can expect it to be brought up at my next personnel review. And every one after that, for a long time to come.'

'Shit, I'm sorry, mate.'

'You would have been, if someone upstairs hadn't decided that it wasn't in the public interest to pursue a prosecution.'

Maxey shoved his hands in his pockets and stared at his muddy shoes.

Preston sighed and relented.

'Listen,' he said, 'I didn't come over here to aggravate matters. I'm a stubborn bugger at the best of times, and this hasn't been the best of times, for either of us. We've been through too much together, been mates – best mates – for far too long, to let things get screwed up like this. This isn't the time or place, but we need to have a drink, and a proper talk.' He held out a hand. 'If you'd like?

The tension, which had been gnawing at him from the moment he'd spotted Preston across the church pews at the service earlier, drained from Maxey like the rain dripping from his hair and soaking into the carpet. He had to swallow to clear the lump in his throat before he could reply.

'That would be great,' he said, and took the proffered hand.

Preston waved a thumb in the direction of the door and the hammering rain outside. 'I should get back to work. I'll be in touch, okay?'

Maxey nodded and smiled. 'Later.' The word tumbled out smoothly, warm and familiar as a pair of old slippers.

Preston's expression softened, and a smile twitched the corner of his mouth.

''Gator,' he said, and turned and walked away.